The
Strange Case *of* Doctor Jekyll & Mademoiselle Odile

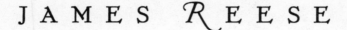

JAMES REESE

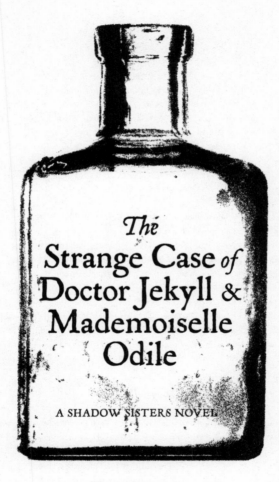

The
Strange Case *of*
Doctor Jekyll &
Mademoiselle
Odile

A SHADOW SISTERS NOVEL

Roaring Brook Press
New York

Library of Congress Cataloging-in-Publication Data
Reese, James, 1964–
    The strange case of Doctor Jekyll & Mademoiselle Odile / James Reese.
      p.   cm. — (A Shadow Sisters novel)
    Summary: In this prequel to "Dr. Jekyll and Mr. Hyde" set in Paris during the 1870s
Prussian siege, an orphaned sixteen-year-old girl whose knowledge of witchcraft includes
transformation spells meets a young medical doctor from London.
    ISBN 978-1-59643-684-8 (hardcover)
    ISBN 978-1-4299-6189-9 (e-book)
    [1. Characters in literature—Fiction.   2. Witchcraft—Fiction.   3. Shapeshifting—
Fiction.   4. Orphans—Fiction.   5. Paris (France)—History—Siege, 1870–1871—Fiction.
6. France—History—Occupation and evacuation, 1871–1873—Fiction.]
I. Title.

PZ7.R2551St 2012
[Fic]—dc22   2010053366

First edition 2012
Printed in the United States of America

1   3   5   7   9   10   8   6   4   2

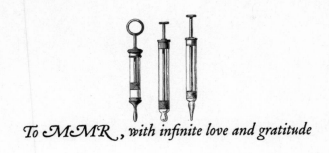

To MMR, with infinite love and gratitude

Paris, 1871

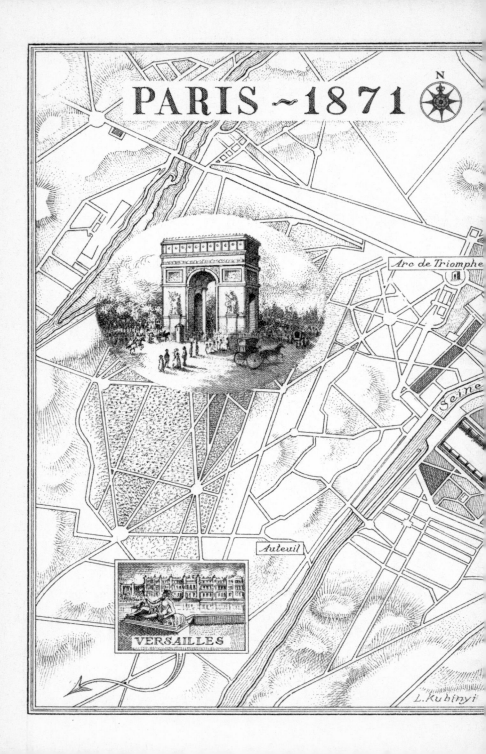

PARIS ~ 1871

N

Arc de Triomphe

Seine

Auteuil

VERSAILLES

L. Kubinyi

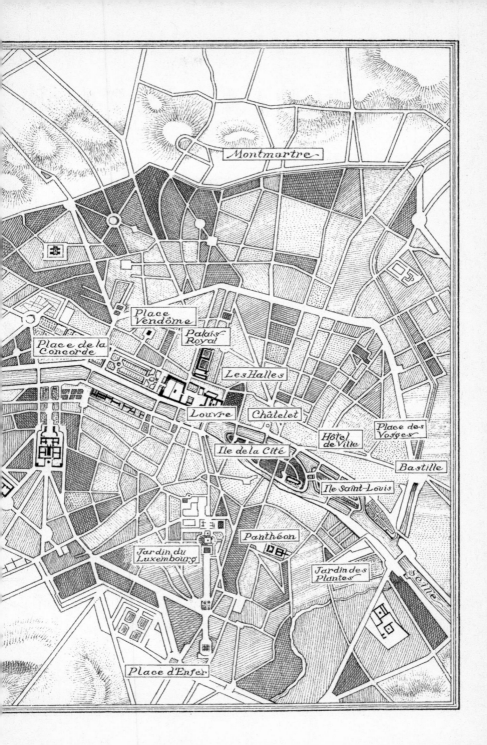

The
Strange Case *of*
Doctor Jekyll &
Mademoiselle
Odile

CHAPTER ONE

The House of Primates

T he two men mistook me for dead; but I was very much alive. And regrettably so.

No doubt I *appeared* dead. Henry would later say that his breath caught after the crash when he saw me sprawled there in the new-fallen snow, arms and legs akimbo and my skirts askew. My face and neck were sprayed with blood, droplets of blood that "glinted" (said he) in the thin, wintry light.

I'd snuck into the zoo at the Jardin des Plantes an hour earlier to conduct my . . . experiment among the primates. I'd heard on the streets that the elephants were to be slaughtered on New Year's Day. Not for sport, but rather for sustenance. For food. The elephants—Castor and Pollux by name—were much beloved, true; but the people of Paris were starving. They, no, *we* had already slaughtered all the other animals in the zoo. Now only the elephants remained. (And the chimps, of course; but they were safe for now. *Too like us*, the people opined.) It was to be a big and bloody affair, the taking-down of the elephants, with dignitaries, clergy and the like; and so I'd hoped the hubbub would let me do what I'd come to do at *la singerie*, the faraway monkey house, in peace, in private. Alas, no such luck.

Rather, I *did* conduct my experiment; but I was still staring at what I'd wrought. I was stunned, actually, too stunned for tears as I backed away from the cage wherein the chimpanzee had changed so . . . drastically. It was then I heard the approach of Henry and his manservant, Poole. Of course, I did not know them then. (And would that I'd never met them at all!)

In the late-day light, with the whole of the city silenced by the recent snowfall and stilled by the Siege—for the Prussians, having finally defeated France, having felled Napoleon III, now held Paris as choking hands hold a throat—I'd misheard the muffled speech of the men. I thought they were yet some distance off, and that I'd have time to steal away unseen.

Instead, I had just rushed around a hackberry bush—still looking back over my shoulder at the primates, as if the murdering one might bend the bars and escape, and come after me!—when I ran straight into Poole. Tall and bony Poole, who had hundreds of hammers in his jacket pockets; or so it seemed.

Whump, and down I went.

My heart was already beating wildly, owing to all I'd seen in the chimps' enclosure since I'd introduced the salts and the spell (my so-called experiment) and all hell had quite literally broken loose; but once I ran into Poole, well, the last thing I recall is the breath rushing fast from my lungs, *whoosh*. Like a bellows. Then all my other senses followed suit, abandoning me, such that I fell like a sack of grain onto the snow. And there I lay some while (apparently).

Henry knew soon enough that I was alive, quite. My pulse was strong, said he. Yet still I presented a most curious sight. For there I lay at length; and though I *am* rather tall, I must have appeared taller still, skinny as I was. (I'd been rendered down to bones by the want of food.) And I was dressed in those rags to which I'd been further reduced. Worse still: that spray of blood which colored my neck and face. Blood that had no discernible source. At least not upon my person. This Henry determined after a cursory examination (for which I was blessedly unconscious). And so: *Where had the blood come from?*

Such was the topic of conversation between the two men as I began to come round. And once my senses and reason returned, I immediately set about changing said topic. Foggy-headed though I was, still I knew I needed to sway the gentleman from the consideration of the blood and its source. A distraction was wanted. A diversion . . .

"Au secours!" I fairly screamed, sitting upright and clutching both fists to my bosom. *Help!* For Henry—who seemed to me then to be between twenty and twenty-five years of age—had laid his cold fingers along my bare neck, monitoring my pulse, and the rings (jeweled rings, I remarked) on two of his fingers were like ice. His fingers were cold, yes, but those golden rings

were worse. When he made to slip his hand further in, to gauge (I suppose) the truer state of my heart by calling upon it at home, as it were, I resisted. Loudly. *"Mon dieu! Non!"*

Suddenly I was a demure demoiselle set to scream a second time for help, not the starving streetling I'd become since arriving in Paris six months prior, several weeks shy of my sixteenth birthday.

"Mademoiselle, no," stammered Henry, drawing back. His face went pale, setting in stark relief his warm brown eyes and black facial hair: well-trimmed sideburns and a bearded triangle upon his chin. Soon he'd rouged from embarrassment, a red to match that of his full, fleshy lips. Indeed, he flushed not only upon his cheeks, but the muscled flesh of his neck reddened now as well. As did the very lobes of his ears. "You mistake my intent. I am a medical doctor and I merely meant to determine . . ." Whereupon he began to fumble both the buttons on my chemise *and* his French; but his fingers were too cold now to manage the buttons, and his skill (or lack thereof) in my native language did not serve him well. I might have pitied the man then, if I hadn't been so bent on self-preservation.

Pity? Perhaps that's not the word; but I felt . . . something for him then as he knelt beside me. If not pity, a desire to . . . to help him somehow. Why had he no hat, no gloves in this bitter cold? Indeed, in the tumult, his single concession to the cold—a red scarf—had come unwound and showed his shirt open at the neck, quite, revealing alabaster flesh and a thin trail of blackest hair tending downward.

I returned from this reverie when Henry hardened suddenly and said:

"Oh, blast it, Poole! It seems she hasn't a word of English. Do something, won't you?"

Of course, I had a few words of English all right, even back then; but what good would it do me to let *them* know that? I'd only have to answer the many questions they would ask.

The older man neared. He knelt. Then, as if *he* were the doctor, he pushed my eyelids up (none too gently) with his fingers and had himself a gander underneath. The *nerve* of him. And breathing his bitter stink right into my face all the while!

"She seems well enough to me, sir. I say, leave a few coins and let's 'ead 'ome. Best to avoid any kind of scandal with this type of . . . *fillette,* I think they call them. And may I remind you, sir, that Cheffy was planning to serve up that fine sliced spaniel with a bit of boudin, and now that we couldn't get 'old of any blood for a boudin, well, she'll be none too pleased."

Now, perhaps my English, still quite spotty on the day in question, gives me no right to quote Poole so; but his look, which sluiced with such disdain down the length of his long nose, like sewage down a drain, told me I understood his meaning all right, if not his every word. And I certainly understood *fillette*: He took me for a street whore.

The blood old Poole mentioned must surely have been elephant blood, destined for a boudin. Blood sausage. Surely that explained the presence of these two—the dandy and his

7

man—in the zoo on this day, at this hour. Were they gourmets? Epicures, bent on such . . . delicacies as elephant-blood boudin? Alas, no matter now.

"Mes rats! Mes rats!" I began to scream. *Where are my rats?* Yes: rats.

Any meat suffices in the eyes—and bellies—of the starving. Trust me. And though I'd not yet fallen to eating the creatures myself, I'd been selling rats to starving Parisians for some while. Two sous a piece. Three for the fleshier ones. I'd had a basketful on my arm when I'd crashed into Poole. I'd picked them up that morning, freshly skinned, from . . . a friend.

It was then, while rambling on about my rats, that I struck upon what seemed a surer diversionary tactic, an actual *plan*. I reasoned that if these two had braved the cold on New Year's Day to try to bribe someone into handing over a bag of elephant's blood for boudin, then surely they would be interested in actual elephant steaks.

"I know where . . ." I began, my English breaking even as I spoke it. *"Bifteck. Bifteck d'éléphant.* I know where. To get."

"Whatever is she saying, Poole? 'Beefsteak,' does she mean?"

"I think so, sir. But it's elephant steak she's on about, methinks. . . . Oh, this damned French! It slithers about the ear like a conger eel, it does. And of course there are no steaks to be 'ad just yet, sir. I'd know, as I've called in all me chits at the markets. And Rodolphe at the Café Anglais assures me that first the steaks would 'ave to be marinated a good while; and as they've only just trundled them beasts from 'ere an hour past . . ."

"*Oui, oui.* Elephant steaks. I know where you can . . . *acheter.*"
I made the universal symbol for money with my thumb, fore-,
and middle fingers. No man mistakes that.

"She claims to know where one can buy elephant steaks,"
offered Poole.

"Yes, thanks, Old Socks. *That* much I got." And turning to
me, his interest, or rather the interest of his palate very much
piqued, Henry asked, slowly, "Where? Tell me where, *mademoiselle.*"

I had him. The chimps might well have been a million
miles away.

In the course of all this confusion, I'd managed to cup some
snow in my hands. I'd used it to wipe from my face the blood,
the blood of that most unfortunate primate, the one done to
death by my . . . *miscraft,* let me call it. Now that the blood
was gone, the men—or Henry, at least—seemed to forget about
it. And still I kept clamoring for my rats, which lay scattered
here and there in the snow. My basket had rolled quite near
the primate's enclosure when I'd fallen. Now Poole was none
too pleased when his master offhandedly bade him pick it up.
And if Poole did not hate me by then, the deal was done when
next Henry said, "And round up the child's . . . wares, won't
you, Poole?"

When the servant hesitated, Henry admonished him the
more: "Really, Poole, it's the least you can do. You came 'round
that high hedge like a Prussian on patrol. Caution was in order,
man. The child's been laid out flat and—"

9

"'Child'?" muttered Poole, plucking the rats up by their stiffened tails. "If that's a child, I'm the bloody ghost of Prince Albert. And I daresay caution was called for by both parties, sir. Besides, whatever is the girl doing 'ere at this late hour anyway, before this 'owling bunch of beasts in a park closed to the public?"

Henry offered no answer; indeed, he seemed to only half consider the question. For which I was grateful, very. Yet the longer we three lingered before the primate house, the more precarious my position became.

In fact, Poole now stood near the iron rail that circled the tall cage, staring in at the simians, the maddened chimp in the front as well as his fellows cowering in a back corner of the cage. He had only to nose around a moment to discover that the primates' madness was owing to more than our collision. And I had no idea how long the chimp would hold to its changed state, seeming twice the beast it had been before I'd bewitched it so.

"The avenue Friedland," said I to the doctor, having to practically shout it over the chimps' infernal din. "*Le boucher* Deboos, in the avenue Friedland." I opened my eyes as wide as I could, and then I blinked enough to cause a breeze. *Oui*: I flirted.

"That is where the elephants are to be rendered down to meat? At a butcher's shop in the—"

"*Oui, monsieur.*" It was information enough to get the men off my scent, as it were; but I knew it to be true as well, for *mon ami* Julien was the son, the *fils* upon the butcher's sign: *Deboos et fils*. That very morning, while picking up my "wares" from him, he'd told me about the secret plans for the elephant steaks. Several were to be diverted from the main shop in the avenue Friedland to the family's outpost on the rue Tiquetonne, in Les Halles, the marketplace of Paris.

Poole dropped my basket at my side; for still I sat in the snow, no longer stunned but yet scared . . . and cold. Very. I stood up, shakily. Henry offered his arm, which I took. The sleeve of his long coat was cashmere, the cuff furred. As I stood to full height, I was heartened to see that he was taller than I by several inches.

Then, as I stood there shivering, Henry took his red scarf and looped it around my neck. I didn't refuse it. *"Merci,"* said I. I didn't know what the scarf was made of; all I knew was that it lay on my neck as soft and warm as a kiss, and was *most* welcome.

I picked up my basket. Poole had stuck the rats into it pell-mell. Their stiffened and snow-slick carcasses poked out from the bran I'd packed in the basket's bottom to absorb the last of the blood. It all made for a most horrid bouquet. I thanked Poole. He did not acknowledge my thanks, asking instead:

"Yes, whatever *is* going on 'round 'ere then? What are these beasts gibbering on about? And what's that . . . *thing* the big one is 'olding on to? Damn my eyes if it isn't one of your rats. Did the fellow squeeze through these 'ere bars and offer up 'is two sous, then?"

11

"Leave her be, Poole," said Henry, as if calling off a dog. He was brushing snow from my skirts—a gallant if somewhat too intimate act—and I feared he'd feel the beltlike band of hammered gold I wore around my waist. Had it been visible when first they'd found me, when my skirts had risen up to disclose who-knew-what-else? I flushed at the thought. Bad enough they'd seen me so indisposed, but what if they'd seen the waistlet as well, with its dangling charms, amulets, and packets of potions set among the five palm-sized books Mother had fastened to it by holes bored in their corners? It was a page in book five, *Physicae*, that had started all this, when I'd seen in my mother's cramped script—filling those pages and quite often the margins as well—a spell marked "Caution: Transformative." And so it appeared to be, judging by the actions of the chimp on which I'd cast it not a half hour past. . . . *Caution*, indeed.

Poole was speaking on and on, but I feigned ignorance of all he said, of all he asked. Then I gave Henry a look—both plaintive (*Help!*) and impatient (*Let's go!*)—and he silenced his manservant with "Her pulse is yet a piston, Poole, and she wants a spot of peace." A proper gentleman, the doctor then introduced himself. I suppose it seemed the time to do so, now that his hand was removed from my flesh and skirts, and I was finally on my feet.

"Henry Jekyll, M.D., lately of London and now trapped in your Paris, a guest of the Prussians." He sought and shook my hand, in its custom-sewn half-glove as always; when I withdrew it—a bit abruptly, no doubt—he finished with a brief bow.

You know nothing of my *Paris*, I thought of saying. And evidently, the doctor had not discerned the *Elsewhere* in my accent, as did so many disapproving Parisians. He thought I was . . . home. Hardly.

Instead, I said only, *"Je m'appelle Odile. Enchantée, m'sieur."*

"Enchanté, mademoiselle," said he in his turn. He got the French word right—intonation and all—and I confess: I felt my face flush. It had been a long while since I'd been greeted so civilly by a stranger; and never had I been greeted at all by a stranger the likes of this one, this Doctor Jekyll, "lately of London."

Of course, all of this parlor talk seemed to sicken Poole. He now turned back to a fuller consideration of the rat that rampaging chimp had in hand, and I was worried that he would conclude (rightly) that the rat had been as bloodless as the others in my basket had been once they'd been bled out, readied for sale, and so hadn't had any blood to give up in the first place. Where, then, had the blood upon my person come from?

The answer, as it were, lay dying in the far corner of the cage, buried beneath its fellows, who sought to protect it from further ravishment at the hands—and teeth—of the marauder I'd made, or *transformed*.

Just as that damnable Poole wheeled round with more questions, Henry—kind if somewhat clueless Henry—came to the rescue once again, asking:

"So can you help me secure elephant steaks, then? Truly? I'd very much like to be able to say . . ." et cetera; and so I knew he was indeed an epicure. Other words came to mind as well, if I'm to be truthful, and the man's charms seemed to flicker then like failing gaslight. Nonetheless, I determined to let his interest in the elephants be my route of escape from the present predicament and so I said with all the assurance I could muster:

"Oui, oui. Bifteck d'éléphant. . . . On y va?" Shall we go?

Whereupon old Poole let loose a hearty harrumph. "Sir," said he to the doctor, "I really must caution against your . . ." and he didn't need to finish, for his look—the arched eyebrow, bristly and white as a bottle brush; the squinting eyes, from beside which wrinkles spread like the rays of a black sun; the lips pulled tight as a miser's purse—conveyed well enough what it was he was cautioning against: *me.* And as he stood there, staring me up and down as if the mere sight pained him, his gaze managed somehow to shame me, and not for what I'd been up to—though that craftwork had been a red failure of the first order—but for what I was.

As Poole stared, my hem went even more ragged and my hands seemed even more horrid poking out from my half-gloves, gloves that left my fingers free to hand over my rats and make change while still hiding my . . . deformity. My face even *felt* ugly, and my blond hair felt unruly and about to burst the bonds of my braid. Oh, how I hated Poole then! For there he stood in summary judgment of my very self, and his judgment was that I was worthless. Worse: I saw what he supposed. He *supposed* I was offering to sell his master far more than elephant steaks. And that was something I'd sworn I'd *never* do, no matter how hungry Gréluchon and I were.

. . . Gréluchon. Yes, I had responsibility for my brother, two years my junior and already sickly. He relied on me for shelter, for food, for family, as we were the last of our lot, alone and far, very far from home. I must beg leave to put off the telling of how we fell to such a state, homeless and alone; for still it pains me to to link such words as *mother, father,* and *murder.*

Poole now lowered his voice and counseled in private tones, "Leave the girl be, 'enry, and let us go," a directive that drew a withering look from Henry. Poole backpedaled somewhat with, "Sir, Cheffy'll be a right shrew if she 'as to warm the spaniel over."

"Need I remind you, Poole, for whom Cheffy cooks? . . . For whom *you* work?"

"You needn't, sir, no. I've known me station, lo these many, *many* years."

I was doubly determined to win Henry to my side and put Poole off; for not only had he deemed me a whore, but now he set to nosing about the ape's enclosure once more. If he set in anew with his questions . . . Alas, the only answer was that I'd treated the rat with that bit of craft culled from my mother's *Physicae.* (Yes, that same craftwork she'd *cautioned* against.) And *that* was an answer I wouldn't, *couldn't* give; for it would soon lead to the even more difficult question: *Who, or rather* what, *was I?*

Understand: Among my people, the Cagots, we women are

said to have . . . the healing gift. The men are skilled with hammer and awl. They can build you a fine barrel, yes, but it's a Cagot woman you want at your bedside if you're birthing, ill, or sick unto death. And for all that healing what's our reward? The word *witch*.

Was I *a witch?* (I don't much care for the word, but so be it.) I'd come to the zoo to find out.

CHAPTER TWO
The Butcher's Boy

The answer I got that New Year's Day was affirmative; for indeed I'd worked the craft. Albeit with . . . *complications*, a word that hardly describes what happened when the larger chimp, to whom I'd fed my craft-worked rat, had transformed and tore the throat from his cage mate.

I'd stood there watching (what else *could* I do?) as the chimp's limbs grew longer, hairier, with its muscles seeming to rise up in knots. There I stood, staring, as his face took on the very signature of Satan. *I'd* done all that, and knowing as much gave me a feeling far, far short of pride. Some words spoken over an admixture of salts and herbs, and *voilà*, I had earned horrid proof of my powers: Indeed I *had* been born to the sisterhood. As I'd suspected. I was, yes, a witch. . . . *Healer* seemed hardly the word, for as surely as I'd caused the transformation of one chimp, I'd caused the brutal death of another by my miscraft. That hardly seemed to qualify as *healing*.

Ah, but now was not the time to wallow in the wonderment of my newfound . . . witchhood.

"Come," said I, taking Henry by the sleeve. "Odile will take you. Odile will show you." I stared shyly down at the ground then slowly, *slowly* raised my gaze to his.

I had him. Literally. His smile told me so. It was a shy smile, one that somehow involved those big brown eyes of his, the sole source of warmth in those snowy surrounds.

Then suddenly there came a whistle, like a kettle aboil. Ever steadier. Ever nearer.

The doctor, thinking he heard but a patrolling policeman, said, "Ah, the park is set to close. We'd best be . . ."

Poole and I knew better.

The manservant man*handled* his master into the lee of the primate house, between its bricks and a bordering bush. I hunkered behind a tree all of six inches in circumference. And scant shelter *that* would have afforded me had the shell fallen nearby. Blessedly, the Prussian mortar sailed over our heads, past the park to land somewhere on the far side of the river, in the Marais presumably, near the church of Saint-Gervais, to judge by the up-plume of smoke on view, blue against the deepening hues of night.

The primates were all the more fervid for the bomb's distant yet audible detonation. I saw that Poole was nearly eye to eye with the maddened, maniacal chimpanzee. No doubt he was near enough to see the remains of that (badly) bewitched rat it gnawed upon; but if he intended to share his observations—

full-blown suspicions by now, no doubt—with his master, another shell precluded his doing so.

Except it was not another shell.

These were fireworks. A skein of silver unfurled overhead; red dripped from its center, like blood seeping from a star. War or no, it was New Year's Day after all. Were the soldiers in the east actually answering the Prussian fire with the last of their fire*works* from the night before? So it seemed.

By that bright, colored light I saw Henry's smile as he stared up at the sky, seemingly dazed now. And I saw the last, silvery trail of the fireworks reflected in his wide eyes. As for Poole, well: "How perfectly, pointlessly French," said he.

Now, *there*, back in the corner where the others huddled, whatever was that . . . ? The other primates were parting to reveal the victim. I didn't want to see further proof of the pain I'd caused the creature. What's more: I couldn't allow Poole to see the mangled chimp, as surely he'd know it now to be the source of the blood spray I'd earlier worn. Too well I recall those barbarous acts and that iron-smelling blood spray as it came, as it landed on my lips such that I'd no choice but to taste its salty tang and . . .

I tugged rather intently upon Henry's coat sleeve. *"M'sieur, on y va?* The butcher will not stay open all night long." In my haste, I'd let slip too good an English sentence. So, in an effort to counter Henry's arched brow, I slipped my hand into his and, lest it seem somehow . . . romantic, I squeezed. Rather hard, I imagine. "Sir, *s'il vous plaît."*

19

"Poole," shouted Henry to his distracted servant, staring deep into the *singerie*. "I say, Poole! . . . I believe I will take Mademoiselle Odile up on her offer of pursuing the butcher into the avenue Friedland. What have we to lose? And won't it be worth it when I, when *we* can tell Mortimer Kransch—that prig!—that we have dined on elephant steak? He who boasted so of camel last weekend, ha!"

"Sir," said Poole to Henry, "I really *must* insist—"

"Not at all, Poole. I shall be back in the Place des Vosges before Cheffy is ready to serve the spaniel. But do, Poole, put her off an hour or two, won't you?" And with that the doctor followed my first steps from the Jardin des Plantes.

We left the park then, but not before I'd shot Poole a look both teasing and triumphant. (I couldn't help it.) In return his eyes of ice were a warning to me: *We had best not meet again.* Henry and I headed off in the opposite direction, leaving Poole, leaving the nattering chimps to mourn their murdered own. As for the murderer itself, I could only hope the effect of the spell and the salts would diminish over time; for I'd been unable to find any mention of an antidote. For my part, I'd write that very night, in the margin beside that transformative spell: *Never again.*

If only I'd honored that vow.

We headed not to the store on the avenue Friedland, no, but rather its nearer outpost in Les Halles, the infamous "belly of Paris," which was now an emaciated *quartier* of empty stalls and halls. And though the back alleys did not send up the blinding, oh-please-let-me-die-*now* stink of summertime, their wintry *parfum* was enough to embarrass me in front of a man as fine as Mister, nay *Doctor* Henry Jekyll. Now he'd know my haunts, *my* Paris (such as it was).

"*Rattus rattus* or *Rattus norvegicus?*" Henry asked while en route, nodding down to my basketed goods.

The question surprised me, for my starving customers rarely inquired into a rat's *species*, caring only that the rodents were plump of their own accord and not stuffed with sawdust, offal, or worse. These were not *delicacies* I peddled. This was supper, and the occasional supper at that, for those who hadn't the money to buy a cat. As the cat eaters hadn't money for dog. As the dog eaters hadn't money for horse. As the horse eaters hadn't . . .

Enfin, anyone with the means to secure a haunch of horse considered themselves lucky during the Siege. The doctor was evidently such a one. It would be horse meat and more for him, surely, as his money allowed him to make the most of what scant fare was available. Elephant, even.

Fortunately, Henry (though quite hearty) was still a bit too winded from following me at such a clip to speak, to ask others of the countless questions I did not want to answer. Questions about who I was, where I was from, what I'd been doing earlier at the zoo, et cetera. Questions about how I'd come to learn of the elephants' fate. No: *definitely* not questions about that, *s'il vous plaît*, as the answers would only implicate my Julien.

Julien. Where was Julien? He knew my knock—tap-tap, *rap*; tap-tap, *rap*—and usually answered right away. But there I stood at the dark back door of Deboos et fils, knocking rather insistently, and still no answer.

Where *was* he? I'd never had to wait so long; except, of course, when his father was in the shop on the rue Tiquetonne, in which case Julien might not answer at all.

Tap-tap, *rap*; tap-tap, *rap*. I even dared a breathy, "Julien! *Es-tu là?*" He'd said he'd be there all night; and in the six months of our friendship, Julien had been true to his every word.

Tap-tap, *rap*; tap-tap, *rap*.

Rien. Nothing but the occasional fireworks lighting that horrid back alley in blues, reds, and silvers so bright as to shame the weak, wintry moon; and shame me, too, standing there amid the filth beside a gentleman to whom it seemed I'd now have naught to offer but a half smile and a shrug.

Meanwhile I could discern the skittering shadows on the cobbles: *rats.* Our stock-in-trade, which we had been converting to cash since the start of the Siege and the steady disappearance of food. Indeed, the food for sale now in Les Halles didn't even merit the word; but oh how different things had been but a few months prior, before the Siege.

＊

Gréluchon and I had first come into Paris via the marketplace of Les Halles.

It was an early morning in August. We'd been lucky to escape

22

our Cagot homeland on the very day of our parents' murder; for such was Mother's witchly renown and the distrust it had given rise to that she was, yes, murdered, as was my father when he rose to her defense.

Gréluchon and I had been out exploring some neighboring caves, as was our wont. Fortunately or not, I cannot say, but as we made our way homeward that day we came to that same crossroads where our parents lay dying. (We must have missed the ambush by mere minutes.) Thusly did we see things no child should ever see, and thusly did I hear my mother's last words to me, which were "Take us with you." Or so I thought she said, adding, "Away." *Take us away with you.* In truth, her speech was but a bloodied rasping. (I can only imagine, now, all she wanted to say; for she'd long alluded to a secret that would be mine in time.) To me, to my then-innocent ears, her words, her order, made perfect sense. I *would* take them with us. I would see to a proper burial. But where, and how? How were two children going to transport the bloodied, broken bodies of their parents? And what had she meant by "Away"?

The answer to that last question seemed plain when I ran back to our home, hopeful (I suppose) of summoning help along the way. I can recall crying out for help, and hearing naught but the buzzing heat, the cicadas, coming in reply. There was no one. Then I found that our cave had been ransacked. Was this the work of the murderers as well? And whyever would anyone seek to turn our home inside out? Money? We had none. Secrets? There were none there that I knew of, not yet.

I heard again that last word I would ever hear from my mother's lips: *Away*; and I knew that I, that we—Gréluchon and I—were to run. (I must have already realized, stunned though I was, that my parents were dying, would indeed die.) And so, as if by instinct, I went into my mother's secret cupboard—secret, thankfully, to all but her family—and from it withdrew in a rush all that was there, vials, potions, powders, and what little money she'd managed to save. All this I tied into a white, black-striped shawl she'd favored, and then, only then, did I return to the crossroads alone to find the most horrid tableau, one that will haunt me all my days.

They were gone, dead, and Gréluchon lay crying with his head in our mother's lap and his tiny hand tucked into our father's. As for me, well, I hardly had time to understand, let alone mourn and see to that proper burial of our parents they so richly deserved; for, coming up the road opposite, I saw a band of armed men. Spying me, they now started to run. Toward us. *At us!*

A screaming Gréluchon rose and started to run at the men; but somehow I managed to restrain him, reason him into obeying me, and together we turned, running away—*Away!* as told—and never once did we dare turn back.

And I was lucky to have first smuggled away my mother's band of books and charms, taking the key from around her broken neck and, with fumbling fingers, unlocking that waistlet which I've worn from that day to this. Locked, and with the key worn on a chain around my neck, as it had always been around my mother's.

Alas, we'd been days, no *weeks* on the road up from our caveland home in the far southwest, near the Spanish border, and at times I'd feared Grel would not survive the journey. It was on one such occasion—he looked so terribly weak—that a rare stroke of good fortune befell us.

We were close to the city—its walls were finally in sight—when we came upon a caravan of sorts. Here were farmers and marketers making their way into Paris pulling carts, driving drays laden with produce. Here was food, here was transportation, here was salvation if only I could secure it for us. Thankfully, I did not have to beg. (I *hate* to beg.) A slovenly yet self-confident woman atop one of the larger wagons saw us standing at the side of the road. She—Mère Poulet, or La Poulette, so known owing to her tendency to busily cluck about the stalls of Les Halles, dropping gossip as hens drop eggs—took pity upon us, and next I knew we were both in the back of her wagon, dozing among the sun-warmed melons and lettuces.

I woke a short while later thinking, quite improbably, that there was *un tremblement de terre*, an earthquake; for my rude bed was shifting beneath me as the wagon was unloaded, as the melons were rolled off and the bushels of lettuce handed down. Poor Grel would have slept through an actual earthquake, so weary, so worn was he. Workers off-loaded the still-sleeping boy as if he were meat to be sold by the pound.

We were in Paris finally, at Les Halles; and no matter her measure of pity, La Poulette had her wares to set up and sell.

As these were the pre-Siege days of plenty, a busy La

Poulette had larded us down with foodstuffs snatched from here and there and sent us on our way with "*À bientôt et bonne chance.*" *Good-bye and good luck.* She'd work to do, yes. The mothers, maids, and restaurateurs were already bustling about, barking orders at her. The streets and halls were like a spilled cornucopia. Everywhere tables were bowed beneath the weight of their wares, and it would all be gone before the sun was high in the sky. But there was one problem: We had nowhere to go. No one awaited us. In fact, no one even seemed able to *see* us amid this citified madness.

Paris? What had I been thinking?

There I stood, legs and heart atremble, longing for the country and the cavelands we'd left behind, when a boy of roughly my own age approached me.

"Are you looking for work?"

Was I? What little money I had—taken from the clog at the back of my mother's closet, where she'd hoarded what she could—would not last long. That much I knew. Still, no answer came.

"In Les Halles," continued the boy, "you are either selling or buying. If you're not doing one or the other, you're going to draw some trouble down on yourself." Still I said nothing. His French was fast. City French. Parisian French. "Come," said he, finally. "Follow me."

And I did, dragging Gréluchon behind me. For still I trusted in people. And happily that boy—Julien—did not betray me. Instead, he'd become a friend.

Rather more than a friend, in fact; for Deboos et fils became the closest thing we had to a home. Not the store proper, of course, but rather the alley behind it. We'd venture into the store only if Julien's father was elsewhere and his mother's mood was good; and Madame Deboos's mood was good . . . generally. And it seemed she liked me well enough—until, that is, the day Julien slipped with a knife and I . . .

Well, you'd expect a butcher's wife to be accustomed to the sight of blood; but *that* day, seeing her son cut so, Madame Deboos started screaming and scurrying about the shop like one of the headless chickens we'd sometimes see set out onto the streets as a prank. She was useless. Indeed, a swooning Julien, blood spurting from the heel of his left hand, was only worsening his wound by trying to calm his mother. As this was doing neither of them any good at all, I stepped in; and though I set Julien to rights, his mother would never forgive me. Better her son bleed to death, I suppose, than that the blood flow be stanched by one such as me. Then again, I admit it: I could have effected the healing with a bit more . . . subtlety.

Instead, I sat Madame down and hushed her as best I could. (My brusque tone would *not* be fondly recalled, when all was said and done.) Then I turned to Julien, sitting him down on the stool beside his mother's; and with a few fast turns of a tourniquet—the fabric torn from my skirts—I slowed his bleeding somewhat. Still, there was some healing to do, and so I did it.

To an attendant Gréluchon, I said, with a nod toward the market street beyond, "Greens. *Leafy* greens. I don't suppose you'll

27

find any moonflower hereabouts, but the tops of some carrots ought to do." These he found fast; so it wasn't long before we four stood in a huddle in the back room of Deboos et fils and I set to work upon the wound, packing Julian's hand in carrot tops and dirt from off the rue Montorgueil, which I lathered up a bit with some spit. (And you should have seen Madame Deboos when I let that spittle fly! She blanched, such that I wished I'd already found a good reviving spell somewhere in Mother's *Medicum*, for it seemed certain I'd need one.) . . . Well, what more can I say than that I worked some craft and willed the wound to heal. *Willed* it, yes.

In truth, I stopped short of a full healing. Somewhere in the books I'd seen a spell that could (supposedly) seal split flesh. I thought I just might, *might* be about to concoct a descarifying something or other with a bit of ground purple loosestrife seed. Alas, Julien would have to wait for all that; for suddenly I had his mother to contend with.

"What . . . what . . . what have you *done?*" Madame Deboos was sputtering, her words coming like water from an ill-primed pump. Her eyes were wide, and she'd thrown her arms over Julien from behind, as if to secure him, as if to stop me from flying off to a Sabbath with her beloved boy seated aback my broom.

"I stopped the bleeding, is what I've done;" said I, adding, after a most pregnant pause, ". . . and that's a *good* thing, *madame.*"

And indeed it was a good thing, even if it marked me as

otherworldly (to put it politely) in the eyes of Madame De-boos. As for Julien, well, he was grateful, very. And when he asked me, the next day, how, how, *how* . . . ?

Well, by then I'd spent a sleepless night wondering what to do, and by morning I'd decided to tell Julien *all and everything*. Which I did. As we sat in the shadows of Saint-Eustache, its clock striking the hours of ten, eleven, and finally noon.

He took in my every word; and for the sum of them all—*all* my truths—he paid with a look of purest sympathy. It was the sweetest deal I'd struck in all my days.

And ever after, Julien would meet my appearance at the back door of Deboos et fils—and anywhere else, for that matter—with a wide and wondrous smile, one that did to me what a bit of mandrake once had when I'd found it among my mother's medicaments and had dared a nibble: It caused my heart to *tick, tick, tick* like an overwound clock. Ah *oui*, that sweet smile of his. It was a constant, an everyday gift of the highest order.

Until, of course, New Year's Day. That evening, well, Julien was unsmiling, and none too happy to find me at the back door of the butchery with an English gentleman in tow. *None* too happy.

⁂

Tap-tap, *rap*; tap-tap . . .

The door opened.

"Julien! You're here!" It was as though I'd not seen him in a lifetime.

"Uh . . . *oui*. Where else would I be?" He was tying on a fresh (or at least fresh*er*) apron. Julien did this every time I came to the shop, as if to hide from me—or maybe from himself—the bloody work he'd been about a moment earlier.

I don't know what I said, no doubt excitedly; but I well recall the response it drew:

"Shh! You'll bring my mother out here." And like an actress hearing her cue, Madame Deboos called back from the storefront:

"*Julien, mon chéri? Tout va bien?*"

"*Oui, Maman.* Everything's fine."

"Keep stirring, Julien. Papa wants that elephant blood nice and thick, eh?"

Oh dear. I hoped Doctor Jekyll, standing off in the shadows, hadn't heard *that*. It wouldn't do to have him coming back here in a few days' time—or ever!—in search of that elephant-blood boudin he so coveted.

"*Oui, Maman.*" And just as Julien gave me that smile of his, we heard the bell on the shop's door. Soon Madame Deboos was addressing a customer in the insincere, silly-sounding tones of a shopkeeper needful of a sale. We had a few minutes, little more.

"Back so soon? Your basket was full at sunrise, *non*? Have you already sold . . ." Julien's voice fell to a whisper and he stopped himself: He wouldn't dare utter the word *rat* in the shop's precincts. "You had a basketful this morning, and usually it takes—"

"Who's that?" His smile and words fell away fast as Julien spied Doctor Jekyll, who now showed himself.

Henry cleared his throat. He was hopeful of being introduced

30

now, though a man of lesser means would simply have spoken up. For his part, Julien was startled at first, then angry: He'd never have expected me to bring anyone—save Gréluchon—to the back door of the butcher's shop, and yes, he was *very* displeased that I'd done so.

"He's an English . . . friend. He knows about the—"

"*Un ami,*" Julien echoed, reaching out to take up the tasseled end of the doctor's red scarf. (I'd forgotten I wore it still.) For a moment it seemed he might yank it from around my neck. But that would have been very . . . *un*-Julien of him; and instead he simply let it fall, shot me a murderous look, and made to step back inside the shop. By the light emanating from the back room, I saw that his face, his perfectly pale and opalescent complexion, was flushed, and his pursed lips were barely holding back the flood of words I feared.

"Julien, wait!" And I added, of course, "I can explain." But could I? No. Not with the doctor standing at my side. There'd be no, *I snuck into the zoo earlier today and tried that spell I told you about on the chimps and . . . and . . .* No. Instead, I said again, "I can explain." And angling myself so only Julien could see my face, I set about the most pathetic pantomime, eyes wide, eyebrows bouncing, in an effort to communicate, *Trust me, please.*

But Julien just looked at me as though I were having a fit. "What's *wrong* with you?" he said. He could have meant the question any number of ways, and no doubt did. *Why was I screwing up my face so? Why had I brought a bourgeois to the back door of the shop—the rats' door—when I knew full well what his*

31

father would do if he discovered us, discovered our little scheme? And right he would have been: These were lean times, to say the least, and Monsieur Deboos had seen his business fall away to next to nothing. If word got out that we were dealing rats out the back door, his business would go bust and never recover, not post-Siege, not ever. He'd be through. And so Julien and I had been discretion itself since first we'd started our little, loathsome trade in vermin; and now here I was, seeming the very soul of *in*discretion.

I slipped my foot between the door and its jamb, so Julien would not slam it shut, and I said, gesturing to Henry, *"Voilà, monsieur . . ."*

Henry bounded forward with his hand extended as if he'd just been introduced at court. "Henry Jekyll, Doctor Henry Jekyll, lately of London and . . ." And there he stood, his arm extended and his hand very much unshaken.

This wasn't good. *Not at all.* Oh, but I ask you: Who would seek to shake the hand of a butcher's boy disturbed at his work? Henry Jekyll, that's who.

Now if only Julien would shake the doctor's hand, then maybe . . . Oh but then I saw that the situation was even worse than I'd thought:

Julien's hands, both of them, were bloody and beginning to drip.

Julien was self-conscious of his hands, horribly so. (I could sympathize.) In Julien's eyes, his hands marked him, marked him as something he was and did not wish to be. It was his father who had him butchering, and it was his father who'd decreed that Julien would someday take over Deboos et fils, raising his own *fils*, his own son, to labor in the bloody back room as Julien now did. This was not what he wanted. At all. And to Julien, his hands were horrid, meat-smelling, blood-stained . . . *reminders* that he scrubbed when he could and hid when he had to.

As for the rest of Julien, well . . . When first he'd approached us that August day, my heart might have fluttered if it hadn't already been beating so fast, far too fast for fluttering. (I had other things on my mind then. Survival, for one.) But it wasn't long before I'd noticed that the boy—my age or older; seventeen, maybe eighteen—had a bearing, a physical bearing, to match his demeanor. I mean to say, he was, *is* beautiful. Inside as well as out.

Julien stands a bit taller than I, but otherwise he is my opposite in every way: thick black hair to my wispy blond; a Parisian pallor countering my southern, sun-done darkness; and while my eyes are a limpid blue, Julien's verge on violet, with lashes so delightfully long they cannot hold a curl but rather fall as fringe. (I had only ever seen such lashes on the giraffes at the zoo. Before they were slaughtered.) He is well-muscled, too, from his heavy work: His neck, shoulders, chest, and arms fairly ripple as he works, hauling, hammering, hacking bone from joint. But yes, it is a job he disdains. No, he *hates* it. It shames him, and that saddens me; for yes, I suppose I'd loved him from the moment my gratitude evolved into something more. That is to say, I'd loved him from the hour I'd met him. And loved him all the more as he took all my secrets—all my strangeness—in stride.

But here he was now, growing ever angrier with me.

"Odile," said he, looking back into the store from habit, fearful habit, "you know what my father would say, would *do*, if he knew . . ."

The doctor, having seen Julien's hands, came nearer now to say, "Here, let me have a look. That must've been quite the cut . . ."

"It is not *his* blood, sir," I said, rather curtly; and I daresay I might have rolled my eyes at having to school the doctor so.

Having peered into the back room and sized up the situation, I was able to then retake to my plan and explain (*plus ou moins*):

I told Doctor Jekyll—and my English was improving proportionately with my predicament—that Julien's father had secured the better portion of the same elephants' blood that he'd coveted so, and that the firm would be offering elephant-blood boudin. ("So *that's* who got it. Interesting." Doctor Jekyll was jealous, and Poole would no doubt be getting an earful later on.) What I *didn't* say was that Julien's father had charged him with the blood, and evidently had commanded him to stir it over a low flame till it thickened. To stir it by hand, *with* his hand as per the family's secret (and disgusting) recipe. And if Julien hesitated in hearing the order, his father would have threatened the boy, bodily or otherwise. Such that there Julien now stood, his shaming hands dripping blood, elephant blood, onto the white tiles at his feet, his fingernails looking like inlaid rubies.

There both men stood, in fact, staring at me expectantly. . . . My plan? Ah *oui*, my plan.

Luckily, Julien's father was indeed at his larger store upon the avenue Friedland, where he and his lieutenants would now be dealing with the elephants in ways I did not care to consider. But from Julien I'd learned that very morning, when picking up my . . . wares-for-sale, that several of the prized steaks were to be expedited to the Tiquetonne store, yes, there to be picked up by the maids of the Marquise de Nullepart. And so it was that while I was hurrying Henry into Les Halles, I was also hatching the plan that now I had to effectuate, somehow.

"Julien, Doctor Jekyll here is *very* much interested in . . . today's meats," said I.

"How nice for him," countered Julien. "But the marquise will be sending her maids 'round any minute for . . ." and he let his hurried French fall away. *Whatever was I up to?* was what he wanted to ask. I saw the question on his face.

"Ah yes," said I, showily, "the marquise. Wasn't it she who sent her kitchen maids 'round a few nights past for mule?"

"No," said Julien, with lessening patience. "Don't you remember? I told you, Odile, I waited all night but the maids never came and . . ."

He quieted. He tipped his dimpled chin, just so. He was on

35

to it. *Finalement!* I wanted him to give the marquise's maids the mule, and sell the elephant steaks to Doctor Jekyll.

He nodded. "I'll . . . I'll be right back." Julien disappeared into the shop (after a last, lingering glare at Henry). There I stood in the doctor's company for what seemed an eternity.

Finally, Julien reappeared, pulling tight the door behind him, and holding two packages, each as long as his forearm, wrapped in shiny white paper. He looked at me and shrugged— *I hope you're right about this*, were his unspoken words—before actually saying:

"*Voilà, monsieur*: Castor," as he handed over one package, "and Pollux," as he handed over the other. In exchange, Doctor Jekyll handed Julien money enough to make a new life. Or nearly so. It was easily twice what we had saved from selling six months' worth of rats. And so our larger plan might come to pass sooner than we'd hoped: *Escape*. Julien's escape from his father, and my escape from the streets. Julien was smiling now—rather absently; or rather, *not* at Doctor Jekyll—and I knew his thoughts were a match to mine.

I took my leave at once, though I longed to stay to celebrate with Julien. *Another time*, we said to each other, wordlessly. For his mother was milling about. And there was the mule to prep for the imminent arrival of the marquise's maids. More: I did not want Doctor Jekyll to read too much into my relationship with Deboos *fils*. I could not have said why, precisely.

And so yes, I took my leave, hesitating only slightly when the doctor insisted that he see me home. It was an offer I declined with firmness; for home was a corner of the catacombs, entered via a sewer grate near the Place d'Enfer. And when I made to hand back his scarf, Henry said it was a gift, adding, shyly, "Perhaps . . . ?" But I must have begun to shake my head, *No*, stopping him from saying anything more; for I knew that a "perhaps" from a man like Doctor Henry Jekyll could in no way preface any part of *my* future. Of that I was certain.

I slept well that night. Rather, as well as I ever slept in the catacombs, the cold, drear, dank catacombs, one eye ever open and watching lest Gréluchon take a sudden turn for the worse. But I must confess: I was surprised upon waking to find that I'd tucked Henry Jekyll's red scarf within my thin pillow. *Merely to plump it*, I'd have said then.

❦

My plan misfired, as it were, and the shrapnel hit us all.

It seems the marquise had guests that night who'd lately dined on mule and knew it either by taste or texture, such that Monsieur Deboos was called shamefully to task and threatened with ruin, even, by Monsieur le Marquis himself. So, too, was Julien shamed and threatened in turn. More than threatened:

His father went at him with the broad side of a rubber mallet, breaking everything about the boy save his bones. Julien's subsequent lies—that he'd made an honest mistake in switching the steaks, the meats being unfamiliar; that he hadn't known the man who'd come to the back door in search of the elephant, and to whom he'd thought he'd sold the mule; et cetera—*alors*, his dissembling had enabled him to keep Doctor Jekyll's money; but the beating the boy took would scar, scar horribly, even if only on the inside.

Worse still: Julien came to blame *me*. He would not speak to me. I cannot fault him for that, neither for blaming me nor for denying me at his door the day I returned. *Denying* me? It was rather worse than that: He forbade me to return to the store. And while I tried to reason with him (and oh, the tears I shed!), his mother appeared at his side to threaten me. *Threaten* me! Had Julien (rightly) laid the blame for the mix-up on me? Regardless, Madame Deboos was now certain of her long-held suspicions: I *had* come into the world to both ruin her husband and steal her son.

Now I was not only heartbroken but hungry as well, and with no rats to sell. In a word: *desperate*.

So it was that I found myself wandering the Marais some days later with a fast-failing Gréluchon in tow, seeking out the English doctor whose scarf I still wore and whose door I'd have sworn I'd never darken.

CHAPTER THREE

The House on the Square

Since meeting Julien that first day we'd arrived in Paris, I'd often given thanks to whatever gods hadn't abandoned us. *Merci, merci, merci*, I'd mutter, half prayerful, half playful.

Julien was fast to offer me work (albeit in the rat-selling business); and work meant money, which meant food. (This, of course, was back when there'd still been a bit of food to buy.) And though he'd not been able to offer us shelter—he risked enough smuggling us bits from the shop—Julien did arrange for me to meet Timon of Athens.

La Nouvelle Athènes, that is. New Athens, the neighborhood near the new Opéra where Timon and his toughs ruled. And it was Timon who provided us with that corner of the catacombs near the Place d'Enfer that we would call home for far too long. For four sous *extra* per month, he'd also offered us "protection," whatever that meant. (I'd been happy enough to never find out, though still I paid.)

In truth, I'd have preferred life in the light; but that was costly. And for his part, Gréluchon quickly took to the catacombs. They reminded him of home, where we'd lived in the cavelands outside Pau, as close to that city as its citizens would allow us. I was sure the subterranean life was not good for Grel's health; but I let him insist and there we'd stayed despite my brother's overprotective bent: More than once he tried to take on Timon and his thugs over slights, real or perceived, he thought I'd suffered at their hands. Insults and sexual innuendo, mostly, which I bore without a second thought. The harder part, by far, was getting my brave little brother to back down from conflicts that might well have gotten him stabbed or shot.

As the war went worse and worse for France, I had kept close to Julien. By early September, when we lost the Battle of Sedan and the emperor fell, well, it is fair to say I knew no one else. Paris intimidated me, mightily; and even more so as the city changed under the Siege, as the now-victorious Prussians decided not to strike at a stubborn Paris and take her by force, as they had the rest of France, but rather to starve her into submission from their stolen seat at Versailles. And of course the Parisians—among whom Gréluchon had quickly come to number himself—swore they'd never submit, never collude with the conquering Prussians as our non-Parisian brethren beyond the city walls had done. Yes, now it would be Paris versus Prussia *and* the provincials beyond the walls; but within those walls things quickly worsened.

Soon all communications were cut off, save for the carrier

pigeons (which had to contend with the falcons imported by the Prussians). The few people who dared leave the city did so in the dead of night by hot-air balloon, hoping for a safe landing somewhere, *any*where. And nothing came into the city either. Least of all food. Soon we were starving while (so it was rumored) heaps of produce were left to rot on the far side of the city gates. So it was that by New Year's Day we'd slaughtered all but the elephants, leaving only a few mangy lions and those damnable apes.

It was all I could do to survive, then, to keep Gréluchon alive and by my side; and so I did not concern myself with spells and such those first days in Paris. Still I wore my mother's books locked around my waist, for both safekeeping and comfort. And I healed Julien's cut, yes, but otherwise I told myself I'd return to the books in time.

So I had; and now look what I'd done.

Enfin, it's true: I knew no one but Julien; and so when he denied me, I had nowhere else to go but to Doctor Jekyll, who'd shown me kindness in an unkind time.

What was it I sought? I say again: survival, mine and my brother's. *And nothing more.* Rather, that's what I told myself then.

Prior to the wintry day in question, when I went in search of the doctor, I'd never been in the Place des Vosges, that fancy square tucked in the Marais. My "sort"—as Poole would have put it—ventured into such places only in search of unlocked doors or opened windows and, *whoosh*, a quick five-finger discount. Silver, cutlery, foodstuffs, something, *any*thing that could be sold.

It was early, not quite noon, when we entered the square. The sun shone down, pinkening the identical townhomes bordering its large park. The effect was magical as the sun hit the roseate stone with which they'd all been built. The tiles of the roofs seemed hewn from sapphire. We walked past home after home after home, all down the lengths of the four arcaded streets comprising the square, as I tried to summon courage enough to knock upon the doctor's door. Finally, we sat in that park, its trees still skeletally bare against the bright blue sky. I watched the Jekyll residence, hopeful I might catch the doctor coming or going, and thereby avoid the unpleasant Mr. Poole.

The day's first shells began to burst in the far west of the city. "Ah," said Gréluchon, who followed the war in ways I did not, who always knew where war things stood. "Those'll be from Vanves, or maybe Issy." I looked at the boy, his ear still cocked to the west.

"How*ever* do you know these things?" True: I was forced to leave him alone while I worked; and despite my strict orders that Grel stay away from the city walls, I suspected he prowled them like a cat, gathering news before it even became news.

"We live in a world at war," said he, flatly, matter-of-factly. "How do you *not* know such things?"

Perhaps he had a point. *Alors*, I'd deal with Gréluchon's zeal for the war later on. Now I decided it was high time to hurry us both across the square and to the doctor's door.

I'd heard Doctor Jekyll refer to the Place des Vosges in speaking to Poole that day in the zoo, and I'd only had to ask around to locate him more precisely. He was renting a mansion in the southwest corner of the square. I'd finally found it a few days earlier. I'd even approached near enough to read the gold plate newly set beside the bell: *Henry Jekyll, Jr., M.D., D.C.L., L.L.D., F.R.S.* A strange alphabet of success, it seemed to me.

But how best to approach now? There was, yes, the slight matter of the detestable Poole, who no doubt still detested me in his turn.

Oh, but in truth, I wanted a word with Poole. *Needed* one.

I'd hurried Doctor Jekyll from the zoo, but a suspicious Poole might well have lingered longer. Or snuck back, as I had, though I'd learned precisely *rien* in the process. Nothing. For the transformed chimp had either *un*transformed or been removed from the precincts altogether. I couldn't tell, and the *gardien des singes* had had less than nothing to say about the situation. *Bref:* On the off chance that Poole had any answers, any information at all, about what had eventuated among the chimps, I wanted to know, *needed* to know; for if I did not master that particular spell, how could I use it to strengthen, indeed *to save* Gréluchon? For my brother had grown so sickly of late, so weak. Always shivering from cold and who-knew-what-else, and now nearly blind in his left eye. I'd pored over Mother's books searching for something that might suit, something curative of what seemed to ail him; but all I'd found was that "Fortitude" spell, marked with words of caution. . . . *Caution?* Indeed. Tell that to the changeling chimp and its murdered cage mate. But still . . .

Yes: Truth be told, I went in search of Henry Jekyll and his manservant, both.

Little did I know what I'd find.

⁂

We were turned away from the kitchen door. Twice. (I hadn't even thought to present myself at the front door.)

The first time, the older Frenchwoman who answered the door in an apron (Cheffy, I presumed) said she needed no scullions and had already doled out the day's charity; and, *slam!* The second time a teenaged maid-of-all-work answered, though she made it seem a mere coincidence that we stood there: She was far more intent on pouring milk into an array of saucers set beside the door than listening to us. Finally she stood, stepped clear of the several cats that had come from the shadows, looked me squarely in the eye, and said, simply, *"Non."* Then she, too, tried to shut the door dismissively, but I pulled Gréluchon into sight and said again we'd come in search of the doctor, Doctor Henry Jekyll.

She looked my brother over, eyeing the piratical patch he'd taken to wearing of late, saying that the sharp wintry sunlight hurt his eye. In fact, I'd sewn the patch for him, cutting the fabric for it from the white shawl lined with black stripes. It had been my mother's, yes, and though it pained me to cut

44

the fabric, Grel was appreciative (albeit sad). What pity the maid possessed now prompted her to say (in fast French) that *patients*—and she emphasized the word, still doubting us—were received at the front door; whereupon she slammed the back one so as to set to rattling its several small panes.

If I'd been nervous at the back door, well, I know not the word for what I felt as we moved to the front.

Still, I knocked; and knocked again.

And who should finally answer but the same little snit who'd just snubbed us? I saw now that she was close to my age, quite tidily proud of her appearance—I'd not have opted for "pretty," though she did fill out the frills and flounces of her uniform well enough, I supposed—and so arrogant you'd have thought her the mistress of the house. *"Oui?"* said she, as if she'd never seen us before.

"I . . . rather, *we* are here to see Doctor Jekyll, if you please."

"Do you have an appointment?" There was something triumphant in the smile that spread now beneath her button nose, her blue eyes, and the high, tight black bun sitting atop her head like a finial.

I said nothing; and she'd already begun to close a second door upon us when Gréluchon piped up:

"Yes. We do."

"Ah, *oui*? . . . For what time?" There was that smile again, the kind that begs a slap.

"Now." Gréluchon got the better of the girl with that—he even managed to wink at her with his good eye—and grudgingly she let the huge black door fall back upon its hinges. *We could pass*, was implied. Further implied: *Wait right there while I get someone even meaner than myself to deal with you.*

Poole, probably. Or perhaps there was a Mrs. Jekyll who ruled this golden roost?

Golden, indeed. From the foyer I could see the sunlight dancing upon crystal and silver in the cabinets of the dining room on my right, and gilt and enamel throughout the salon to my left. Straight ahead there rose a stairwell so grand it must surely lead to Saint Peter himself. But no: down it now came the decidedly less saintly Poole.

He stopped mid-stair . . . and stared. A bushy white eyebrow arched, and he held his mouth as if to spit something venomous.

"Rat seller," said he. "Fancy finding *you* 'ere."

The maid seemed pleased to find us unwelcome; but the smile fell from her pretty but pinched face when Poole dismissed her with a wave, as if deeming her unworthy of words. I must say, I heartened somewhat at seeing her dismissed so summarily.

"*M'sieur*," said I, with a nod. "I come to call upon the doctor."

"Do you now?" Poole proceeded to the bottom stair, stopped, and then quickly approached Gréluchon and me. He stood too near—toweringly, intimidatingly near—but I held my ground.

He echoed me now: "'To call upon the doctor'? Hmm." He spoke in his best, most butlery tones.

"Yes," I countered. "I . . . I'd like to see Doctor Jekyll."

"You've said as much, yes. But I regret to inform you, *mademoiselle*"—and clearly it pained him to apply the word to one such as myself—"that the master is indisposed at present." He paused. He leaned nearer still, so near I could see the brown pickets of his lower teeth as he added, "That means: *No.*"

Our standoff ended when there came an ear-splitting whistle. At first I thought it was a shell about to land on the doctor's very doorstep; but as I turned to grab my little brother and seek cover somewhere I saw that it was Grel who'd somehow made the noise by tucking a thumb and forefinger into his mouth. And as Poole stood before my brother trembling with anger—rabid-seeming, in fact, with spittle bubbling upon his baggy lower lip—Gréluchon puffed himself up again, with the very last of his reserves, and readied to loose a second such siren upon the household. But just then:

"I say, Poole: What's the trouble down there?"

A slippered and berobed Henry Jekyll stood atop the stairs, his hair disheveled, his cheeks unshaven. I looked away and no doubt blushed: He seemed so . . . revealed. I found myself fingering the red scarf, teasing its tassels with my fingertips.

As Poole turned to disclose us, the doctor squinted downward; for the light was at our backs, bursting in through the transom. He recognized us nonetheless, or me at least; and—practically skipping down the stairs now—exclaimed, "Mademoiselle Odile! Welcome."

"Tea for our guests, Poole, if you please," said the doctor a moment later, trying to tamp down his sleep-tousled hair.

But there Poole stood, sneering. Still as a statue.

"No, sir," I demurred. "Please, don't bother . . ." I meant not a word of it, of course. For not only did I very much want Poole *to bother*, to do the doctor's bidding, but I, *we* were famished. It had been days since we'd had anything but the thinnest of gruels, stewed of who-knew-what.

"But I insist," said Henry. And turning to Poole, he commanded, "At once, Poole!"

The manservant slunk away like a kicked cur. I could all but hear his growing hatred.

"Come in, please," said Doctor Jekyll, gesturing to the salon. He tightened the belt on his black silk robe. "You'll pardon my appearance, but I was sleeping-in this morning; or rather, sleeping as late as those damnable shells allow." The doctor was begging our pardon of *his* appearance? Our rags had shamed me when, once again, Poole had looked us up and down at the door; but we'd no choice but to wear all we owned, both for warmth and to spare its being "borrowed" by our neighbors in the catacombs. The young doctor—so very young to be so . . . *achieved*—had noticed his scarf around my neck, looking rather worse for wear, I'm sure.

Our host now pulled a gold-tasseled cord that hung beside draperies sewn of scarlet damask. (Of course, I did not know damask from dimity then. Oh, but that would be among the *least* I'd learn in the Jekyll mansion.) I thought he meant to let some sunshine into the room, but instead a bell rang in the offing; and when that same surly maid reappeared, this time bearing a broad smile for her employer, he had her lay a fire. She might have been an automaton, or a trained orangutan, for all the attention the master paid her; meanwhile, he seemed to hang upon *my* every word. How strange. I almost felt bad for the maid as she set about her dirtying work. Almost.

"So," said the doctor, seated upon a deep divan and gesturing us into two chairs opposite. I had to tell Grel to sit, for he stood looking around the room, slack-jawed. "I hadn't dared hope to see you again, mademoiselle; though I am very grateful for the opportunity to thank you for the steaks you helped me procure."

"They were good?" I asked, hopefully, eager to deepen any debt the doctor might feel. (And hoping he'd not heard about the dust-up with the marquis and Monsieur Deboos.)

"Well, no, in fact. But that's rather more the elephants' fault than yours, I should think." It was a joke, but I realized it too late to laugh. "Rather tough. Still and all, one's able to say one's dined on elephant; and silly as it is, that *is* the point of such games as we play."

I played no such games; but still I mustered an agreeable smile. Or so I thought. (Gréluchon would later insist it was more of a smirk, but so be it. He'd further insist that the maid had been *very* pretty, whereupon I chose to ignore both his comments.) Regardless, the doctor shrugged. Was he embarrassed? Did he know such "games" were silly, or worse? I hoped so.

"And who is your companion, Odile?"

"Oh," said I, stupidly. *"Mon petit frère."*

"Gréluchon Ricau," said that name's owner, shooting to his feet—somewhat unsteadily, I noticed—and standing with his chest puffed, as if anticipating a medal to be pinned upon it. *"Enchanté, m'sieur."* Then he shot me a glance before amending his words. *"M'sieur le docteur,* I mean."

"Please, be seated," said our smiling host. "You are most welcome here, Gréluchon." He swiveled his glance toward me. "Your sister did me a favor of late. And I'm afraid I remain in her debt for damages done to her by my manservant that day—"

"It was nothing, sir," I interrupted; for Gréluchon knew next to nothing of my expedition to the zoo and my experiment upon the chimps. And I preferred that he not know more. Not yet. I didn't want to raise his hopes regarding the spell; for, as things stood presently, I'd *never* have tried it on him. No: Much more experimenting would have to happen first. *Much* more.

Grel looked at me for an explanation. But blessedly I was spared having to speak, to explain, by the reappearance of Poole.

Here he came across the marble of the foyer and the parquet of the parlor so slowly as to seem inanimate. Finally, he set his silver tray noisily down upon the table between Doctor Jekyll and ourselves and then passed the master his breakfast of tea, toasts, and a hard-boiled egg, sitting upright in its porcelain cup. He handed over a strange utensil, a scissory thing, which—before I saw the doctor put it to purpose on the egg— seemed a tool for torture, well-suited to snipping the fingertips from a street snitch.

Then Poole set two cups of tea on the table between Gré-luchon and me. Cups of tepid water, really, over which a single teabag had been waved. And there was a cracker, adrift upon its blue plate. One cracker. Looking like a raft lost at sea. Grel looked at me, fairly desperate, and smiled when I motioned that the cracker was his, all his. *"Merci,"* he mumbled, tucking into the tea and cracker as if it were manna from heaven. This was not lost upon the doctor, who stilled the shuffling-away Poole with a purposeful clearing of the throat, followed fast by:

"Have Cheffy round up a breakfast for the boy, Poole. A *suitable* breakfast, if you please. And for you, Odile . . . ?"

I assented with silence, partly to perturb Poole and partly—no: largely—from hunger.

"Two breakfasts then, Poole. Two eggs each. Bacon, jam . . . the lot of it, man."

Poole took the order in without turning, nodding at no one and then moving back toward the kitchen under his own, now considerable steam. I raised a gloved hand to my mouth; for, as my smile could not be helped, it ought at least to be hidden. For propriety's sake, I supposed.

We three then sat before the fire. The conversation was scanty, at first, Doctor Jekyll realizing that some of his fancier English was lost on me while all of it, nearly all, was lost on my brother. As for his French, well, he resorted to so many all-purpose words—everything was *une chose* or *un truc*: a mere "thing"—that his speech carried no purpose at all. But some-how we made do; and I so admired the doctor for his attempt to speak French that I disclosed more of the English I'd earlier hidden. Thusly, we got reacquainted, if you will, while Gréluchon attacked his breakfast of true tea, toasts, two eggs, bacon, and a bowl of beef broth. To do so more efficiently, he made to take off his half-gloves—twins to mine—until I, with a cough, forestalled the act: *No. Leave them on.*

"*Désolé,*" said he. *Sorry.* He returned to his breakfast, holding his spoon as if he were digging in the dirt. Alas. And we didn't have another word from him until, with shells bursting ever nearer the Marais, he stopped, looked up, and opined, with an all-knowing nod, "Issy. *Définitivement* Issy."

I tried to shush him—earning for my pains the poked-out tip of his tongue—but the doctor had heard him; and so, with a sly, appreciative smile, he asked:

"You're following the war? . . . The Siege?"

But Grel was already back at his breakfast, his face half-obscured by the bowl of broth he'd raised to it, slurpingly so.

As for me, I devoured my breakfast as daintily as my hunger allowed; which was, I daresay, not so daintily. Meanwhile, Doctor Jekyll spoke on—mostly in English—sparing me having to ask any questions at all. What I understood was:

He'd come from London some months before the war's end and the start of the Siege, fed up with certain (rather cryptically recounted) events in his native city, events centered around a group of *peers* (his look upon pronouncing the word told me he did not regard them as such, not truly) in the Royal Society. A society of what, of whom, I'd no idea; but I rightly assumed said peers to be fellow doctors, scientists, and such. And somehow I knew, too, that the doctor hinted at a question of . . . tarnished reputation. His own.

"But Paris . . ." I prodded, "surely you knew of the war and—"

"Ah, *oui, oui*. But I'd never witnessed a war and . . ."

Ooh la la, thought I. *And you've* still *not witnessed a war. Not here in your mansion, with your cupboards full.* And how dare he come here for amusement while famine fell like a drape over Paris? Was he simply being foolish, or was he actually a fool—a man of too much means, a man too rich to have any sense? And indeed, even as he'd spoken those last words, the doctor seemed to know they were foolish, that he'd been foolish in coming to the City of Light when those lights had been so dimmed by recent events. And so I asked why he'd not left when he'd been able to. An Englishman of means might have left the city freely up until just a few weeks prior.

The doctor gave no answer; but I fancied I found one in his look, which was rather forlorn: He had nothing and no one to return to. Already I'd sensed, somehow, that his was a womanless home. A home devoid of family. Doctor Jekyll was alone, and lonely. His eager conversation only confirmed it. And I was happily stopped from further consideration of the doctor's solitude by his quite pointed question:

"And you? What brings you and your brother to—"

"He is sick, my brother," said I. Of course, saying that my brother was sick was stating the obvious, especially to a man of medicine.

We both turned now to stare at Gréluchon, still bent over his breakfast. I did not need to point out the hollows of his cheeks nor the dark half-moon risen beneath his patchless eye. Nor the pallor of his skin. Nor the skeletal hang of his clothes . . . But then I saw that Doctor Jekyll was taking us *both* in. And how I regretted, now, not hiding our hands differently—that is, we each wore our common half-gloves, which were identical in being tailored to our hands, to our common . . . characteristic.

You see, our people have common traits. The flyaway blond hair, the blue eyes, yes; but it is also common among our kind to be born with the three middle fingers of one or both hands fused—webbed, if you will—to the height of the first knuckle. For Grel and me, it's both hands. It is not a horrid sight, but still we preferred to hide this with half-gloves sewn to conceal so bizarre a birthright.

I was certain Doctor Jekyll was about to inquire about our common gloves, but instead he said, "Your eye . . ." continuing only when Gréluchon looked at him over the rim of the soup bowl ". . . what is wrong with your eye, son?"

Gréluchon looked at me; and I in turn looked to the doctor, saying, "I do not know, sir . . . but I fear for his sight."

Only then did I learn of Doctor Jekyll's specialty—ophthalmology (though, in truth, the doctor's truer interests ranged amid "the mystic and the transcendental," as he would put it, or "unscientific balderdash," according to the aforementioned peers, for eventually I'd have their account of late events in London as well). *Quelle chance!* That he'd been a doctor

54

seemed lucky enough, but here he was a doctor of the eye. Maybe there was a god somewhere after all. Or maybe it was just our parents, somewhere *Above*. Or witches' work, something I'd somehow brought about myself. Who knew?

Doctor Jekyll was all seriousness now, crossing the salon to stand before Gréluchon, whose eyebrows arched as he sat back in his chair. "It's all right," I said in fast French. "He wants to examine your eye."

This the doctor did; but deeming the light in the salon deficient, he said, or rather commanded, "Come. Follow me. My consultation room is upstairs."

I stood, first arranging my spent breakfast plates; but then the doctor looked at me, truly puzzled. "You may leave those," said he, "for the maid." And I realized that I had never, in all my life, left a post-meal plate untended to. It felt odd, rude; but then I thought of the maid and wished we'd had a hundred plates to leave her.

As for Gréluchon, he too stood, albeit as unsteadily as a foal upon the field of its birth, struggling to its feet for the first time. And up those grand stairs we three went, Doctor Jekyll in the lead, I following, and Gréluchon behind, one gloved hand on the banister and the other tucked tightly into mine.

⁓

The news was not good. At all.

We had followed Doctor Jekyll up, up, up into the mansion, down carpeted hallways—hallways large enough to support rather pointless-seeming furniture: tables, tiny chairs with their backs pressed fearfully against the papered walls—and past rooms that were downright cavernous. *All this for one man?*

Gréluchon let go a *"Mon dieu!"* as we passed a metallic man standing to full height: a suit of armor, complete with a sword that seemed ready to fall. Worried though he surely was, Grel suddenly went stiff-limbed, mimicking an armored man's gait. I stilled him with a look—iron in its way—before Doctor Jekyll saw any of the charade.

On the third of four floors, we finally reached the doctor's cabinet, his small examining room. Through a second, half-opened door, I saw what was surely the doctor's bedchamber. The pinched-faced, pale and (*oui*) pretty maid was there now, making up a four-posted bed hung with heavy napery. From this door I turned away, something inside me deeming it improper that I should see where the doctor slept—this despite the fact that he'd seen me, *examined* me even, while I lay unconscious in the snow. I found myself standing instead before the third and last doorway on this floor, which disclosed the doctor's laboratory.

Well, I thought of Mother immediately. She'd kept a small cave nearer our larger one where she'd worked her craft. She'd had apparatuses similar to those I now saw: glass containers of every shape, their snouts snaking this way and that, here disgorging into a metal vial, there into a test tube suspended over a low flame; multicolored racks of who-knew-what medicine, each substance labeled in a neat hand; and books, books galore, both professionally printed and empty, the latter lying opened, waiting for the doctor's own pen to record his discoveries.

I must have stood there in the hallway, staring; for I did not return to the present, to Gréluchon's predicament, until the sunlight in the laboratory slowly, strangely, began to recede as the doctor, stepping in front of me, reached to shut the door. "Excuse me, Odile," said he, turning a key to lock said door. He kept quite close then, and he smelled good: soapy, and still somewhat . . . sweet, from last night's sleep. "If you please . . ." said he, gesturing toward the lesser cabinet sitting beside the laboratory. That fantastical laboratory.

Doctor Jekyll wheeled a stool up beside Gréluchon, sat down, and, after what seemed a most cursory examination, announced to me—as though the boy himself were not present—that he, Gréluchon, was due to lose his sight and perhaps the eye itself, "Unless something be done."

"What 'something,' sir?" This from Gréluchon, who'd understood the doctor's prognosis all too well.

"I make no promises, son, for it may well be too late for treatment"—here my heart sank: If only I'd brought the boy around earlier, if only I'd . . .—"but there's a rather rare protocol I can attempt."

The doctor saw that he'd lost Gréluchon now with a bit too much English ("protocol," in particular), and saw, too, that I was lost (in self-recrimination and a host of other emotions). "Where do you live?" he asked. I said nothing. I was elsewhere. "Odile, where do you live?"

It was a simple question for the asker, less so the answerer. I sat there staring, saying nothing; struck dumb by guilt, by . . . Finally it was Grel who piped up with:

"We live in the cata—"

"Nowhere," I interrupted. "We live nowhere, sir." A nonsensical answer, but an answer nonetheless.

Suddenly the doctor shouted, startling us both. "Cézette!" I sat with my brother's hand in mine as the doctor turned toward the closed door and barked the word a second time. I could see a shadow on the door's far side, upon the floor.

"Cézette, open the door and show yourself at once."

The cabinet door came creakingly open, till there stood before us, chin tucked to her chest, the maid. A striped cat wound itself around her ankles, looking no less abashed than the girl as she put forth a worried, warbled, "Sir?"

"Cézette, I have told you before: My consults in this house may be rare, but they *must* be conducted in the strictest confidence. If I catch you bent to another keyhole, it shall be you and your cooking auntie who'll be living on the streets along with those cats of yours. Is that understood?"

The girl nodded that it most certainly was, and I took note that she had enough English to understand the threat.

"Good. Now go make up two rooms upstairs and tell Poole we'll be two more at table. . . . And I want no bones about it from anyone. Understood? And keep those damnable creatures outside!"

The girl scooped up the cat and backed from the cabinet door, daring to shoot me a sneering glance as she did so.

"Servants . . ." said the doctor, apropos of nothing, once the girl was gone.

"Sir, you are too kind. I'm afraid I, *we* cannot . . ."

"Nonsense, Odile. If your brother returns to the damp and chill of the catacombs"—so: He *had* heard the word—"well, that is a most *un*healthful place for one in his quite compromised condition. Here, I will see to his health as best I can; though I say again, Odile . . ." and, turning now to look at Gréluchon, he let his words trail away. No, this was *not* good news.

"All the same, sir . . ."

"Odile, may I be frank?"

What does one say to that? I just sat there staring, no doubt flushing, till finally he spoke on:

"I feel indebted to you, Odile."

"But, sir, they were merely steaks."

The doctor looked down at his slippers, as did I, noticing the monogrammed *HJ* upon their plush tops. "Odile, we are a small community here these days, small and rather tight." I rightly supposed he referred to the rich, the *foreign* rich. "I have heard of . . . events involving the marquise and the butcher, Deboos."

A sudden inhalation bespoke my surprise. "Sir, how . . . ?"

"Please, Odile. . . . Some days ago I returned to Deboos et fils—"

You didn't! was what I wanted to say. But instead: silence.

"—and I saw the boy. . . . Will you tell me his name?"

"Julien. Julien Deboos."

"I meant to thank him for his . . . discretion; for my name has not been brought up in the—how shall I say it?—*le scandale.*

59

The elephants, the mule, the marquis . . ." I knew full-well what he referred to. "And, well, I was horrified to find the boy bruised so."

Tears had welled in my eyes, but I knew it only when they began to fall. The doctor handed me a kerchief from his robe pocket, one that was whiter than any linen I'd seen in six months and redolent, too, of rose water.

"Did his father do that to him?"

I nodded.

"Damn the man!" And the doctor slammed his fist down upon a small table, sending his stethoscope snaking off for cover. All the while, Gréluchon sat there mystified, much lost. "Well, now I wonder if I did the right thing?"

"Sir?"

"I told Madame Deboos that I would be switching all my business to Deboos et fils, owing to my displeasure with my present butcher. Amends, I meant only to make some sort of amends. Perhaps things are going better for the boy now?"

"I . . . I cannot say, sir. I do not know."

He understood. "Well, if it eases your mind, Odile, I saw only bruises and no broken bones. He will mend. Bodily, at least . . . Though I know, believe me, that the inner damage a father can do is often worse than the outer. Why, in fact, my very own father . . . *Ach*, never mind all that."

Henry had stopped himself, as if at the edge of an abyss. Now he waved the memory away, as if it were a sudden stink, and added, rather as an aside, "Damn him and be done with it!

That's what I said then, and it's what I say now." What had he meant to reference? Had events with the aforementioned Royal Society devolved to something . . . scandalous? I could only wonder, though it seemed safe to assume the Jekylls, father and son, were, at present, estranged.

Henry spoke on. "What a brute of a father, lording it over so good a boy! He *is* a good boy, Odile, isn't he? Or rather more of a man, I suppose."

"The best, sir," said I, my quavering voice betraying me now as my tears had a moment earlier. "The very best."

"Well," said the doctor, standing. The consult was over; and so, too, was all talk of Julien. "Your rooms will soon be ready. Go back to the cata—go back to your . . . to the . . . If you have things to gather up, I say, go do so; and come back here as soon as you're able. We'll dine at seven of the clock, as I'll want to see this fine gent"—and he squeezed Gréluchon's shoulder now, rather innocently causing the boy to flinch—"I'll want to see you, young sir, in this very room at nine, precisely, for the first application of a salve that will . . ." Again, his words fell away. He was not hopeful, not hopeful at all.

But I was—hopeful and thankful, both. We'd have a night—at the time I thought we'd stay but one night—of fine food and solid shelter. We'd be spared the worry of bombs collapsing our corner of the catacombs, spared the dank chill that bothered our bones so, spared the innumerable spiders and the stink of sewage seeping down the walls. We'd be able to sleep with both eyes shut, as it were. When was the last time

I'd had *that* luxury? . . . And Julien need never know I was under the roof of my *"ami."* Which presumed, of course, that he'd have even cared where I was, or who I was with.

I might have refused the doctor's invitation, or at least tried harder to refuse it, had it not been for the factors above, primary among which was the saving of my brother's sight. All that, yes; but also there was that glimpse I'd gained of Doctor Jekyll's laboratory. It was ten times what Mother's den had been, and look what witchery *she'd* accomplished in that rudimentary space. And so it was I set to wondering: What might *I* accomplish if I had such a spot as the doctor's laboratory in which to hone my craft?

It was a question to which I'd soon get a most regrettable answer.

CHAPTER FOUR
Domestic Derangements

I'd accepted Henry's offer of shelter (along with food and, above all, the care of my brother) intending, truly, to stay but one night, two at the most, *but no more*. Now February had come and nearly gone, and here we still were.

And, *mon dieu*, what a strange household we made.

We were six, in sum: Doctor Jekyll, Poole, Cheffy, Cézette, Gréluchon, and myself.

The two men of the mansion suffered well enough the woman who controlled the kitchen; for food, of course, *very much* mattered to Doctor Jekyll. Cheffy, in turn, seemed content in steering clear of Poole as best she could; and as for the doctor, well, it seemed to me she begrudged him both his money and his means.

Of course, it stood to reason that Cheffy and Cézette would be in league with each other, sharing both blood and background as they did. That said, Cheffy did not seem overly fond of the girl, and vice versa: The innate antipathy between the two sometimes flared up like an ill-trimmed wick. As for Grel and I? Cheffy seemed to notice us anew at each meal, at once both bothered and resigned, as if we were but a fever that would one day break; and until then, well, we had to be . . . endured. And fed. Nothing more. Cézette? She treated us as if we'd come as claimants of a kind, to take what was rightfully hers.

Understand: Cézette, rather predictably, had eyes for the handsome master. Doctor Jekyll, in his turn, seemed to consider the girl but a mere appendage of her aunt: a sort of satellite somehow capable (barely) of dusting, polishing, serving at table, and bed-making, with an added and most bothersome habit of always, somehow, being underfoot. Indeed, it was as though the girl thought that if only the master would *see* her, he'd drop to a knee and propose an immediate marriage; and so she willfully put herself in his way. And very much resented my coming onto the field of play, as it were. Poole, for his part, treated Cézette as if she were but another of those bothersome cats—mere shadow cats, really, starving as they were—to which she smuggled saucers of ever-scarcer milk. I often had the impression that he'd have kicked her, too, if he could have.

Of course, there was Grel, me, and the doctor, who was on our side (quite) and even insisted that we call him Henry (which we didn't, not at first). So, yes: *me + Grel + Doctor Jekyll*, or Henry. It seemed a balanced equation. For a time.

＊

I'd soon enough overheard Cézette voicing her displeasure at our continuing presence, complaining to Poole in her merely adequate English. "But I am made to *serve* her, sir! It isn't right! She should at least be made to remove those horrid gloves of hers and help serve at table—that's what *I* say." Such was the gist of it all. And to this Poole harrumphed his assent before adding, offhandedly yet *most* ominously:

"But beware the girl if ever she offers to salt your meat."

Cézette was of course as puzzled by this comment as I was chilled. *What had Poole seen at the* singerie? *What had he learned in the days since?* Oh, how I tried then to will, *to will* Cézette to ask him further questions; but no . . . Her will was her own, then, and as hard as her head. Instead, she returned to her previous point; but her cause was a lost one.

Poole had already waged (and lost) a war that would have seen my brother and I put to work, me in the kitchen and he in the scullery, replacing the day-laboring boys Cheffy pulled in off the streets to scrub and scour. Yes, Poole had carried his suit to Henry, only to have the latter deny him and demand, once again, that we be treated as his guests. "My guests and nothing less!" were his exact words; for I, too, had acquired the habit of "conversing" via keyholes and such. (Mere survival, it was.) Indeed, I'd been party to the whole conversation and even heard a heated Henry Jekyll add, "And they will *not* be asked to work for their keep, Poole. Is that understood?"

In fact, I was treated as rather more than a guest by Doctor Jekyll, and the hours he and I passed together, in study, earned

me no points among his staff. For we'd immediately established a tutoring routine, swapping French for English, English
for French. I'd never imagined I had anything to offer such a
man except, well, what *other* men so often hinted at wanting;
but Henry was polite and prized not only my knowledge of my
language but my ability (so he deemed it) to teach it as well.

"You really are a most remarkable tutor, Odile," said he one
day when I'd opined that, in practice, he'd have little need of
the imperfect tense and so ought not to bother mastering it.
"And I am a student of knowledge, so I know whereof I speak."
His smile was as warm as his eyes, and when he went on to com-
pliment me on my learning as well as my teaching, I blushed
to find myself sitting taller, straighter, in the leather chair that
had become, from habit, "mine."

Thusly did I earn Doctor Jekyll's treatment of my brother,
and much else besides; but still I had no *purpose* beside this
fireside pedagogy. And I very much wanted to work.

Rather, if I'm to be truthful, there was one job I wanted in
particular; and I wanted it for reasons all my own.

᭐

I went to the doctor one day in his laboratory, where he sat
hunched over a microscope with an open notebook at his side.

"Sir," said I, "your kindnesses to my brother and I—"

But the doctor could be rather . . . direct at times, especially
while at work, and he cut me off with "I fear I shall be unable
to save your brother's sight, Odile. Perhaps not even the eye itself. I should hardly refer to that failure as a kindness."

This news was not unexpected, yet still it stung.

Though Doctor Jekyll had been treating Gréluchon for some time already, my brother's eye had gone from bad to worse, such that now it was as perfectly pale and opalescent as a full moon and steadily seeped milky tears. He swore he could still see through the eye, Grel did; but I—observing him carefully, and seeing bruises bloom here and there as testimony to his increased clumsiness—I knew better. Mere weeks, days perhaps, and the boy would have but one working eye. Worse: The doctor continually hinted at the eye needing to be excised. *Removed.* Lest the disease spread.

This was the worry of my every waking moment. To hell with Poole's implied threats and what he may or may not know about events at the *singerie*; . . . to hell with Cézette's pettiness, her machinations and maneuvering; . . . to hell with the Siege, even, though things were worsening by the day and word in the street—carried back to the mansion by Grel, who steadily refused my suggestion that he stay in the mansion, that he rest— was that something needed to be done. Rather, something *would* be done. And soon. And that "something" was likely to be civil war.

Alas, these were not the concerns I brought to the doctor that day. No: It was a favor I sought. An appointment of sorts. And, summoning the courage, I pursued it pointedly, in that well-practiced English I borrowed from some servant's-tale novel I'd lately read, saying:

"Sir, I shall forever be grateful for all you've given us, truly;

but I fear the debt shall be overwhelming unless I begin to repay it now. But to do that I must earn my keep here, *non?* It's . . . it's a job I mean, sir."

"Ah," said he, and without so much as batting an eye he reached for his billfold.

"No! It's not money I seek, sir." Though, in fact, I had none. At all.

"It's not a handout, you realize, Odile. In fact, I must apologize: I have been remiss in not offering to pay you for . . . *Attends!*" *Wait!* And now he raised a finger as if he might find his French on the nonexistent breeze. "To pay you for *mes leçons de français.*"

"Our lessons are an exchange, sir." This wasn't going well. "I've not made myself understood, I'm afraid. You see . . . I have an idea."

"An idea?" Only now did he straighten where he sat, pulling up from his microscope. He looked at me squarely, waiting for his own eyes to focus. "So, too, have I had an idea, Odile. One I've been meaning to share with you."

"Sir?"

"Our language lessons have gone on swimmingly, wouldn't you say?"

"I would, sir, yes." Indeed, our present conversation was proof enough that those hours fireside had been time well spent (even though the doctor's newfound familiarity with French was yet another reason for Cheffy and Cézette to disdain and despise me the more, for now they couldn't talk about him as freely as before). In fact, I looked forward to those sessions, very much.

It made no matter whether I was the tutored or the tutee, as still it was fun, and often our foibles and faux-pas led us to laughter.

"What say you we broaden our focus a bit? . . . Our 'focus,' I say." Doctor Jekyll was rather fond of (bad) ocular humor: an occupational hazard, I suppose. Off that topic, he was quite the wit and very well read, too; indeed, I'd come to envy him his education.

"Sir?"

"Science," said he. "I am speaking of science. . . . Don't think I haven't noticed the way you *eye* my laboratory, Odile." I blushed at this, surely—the truth of it, not the joke. "I shall very much like to see you enjoy *this*"—he gestured, broadly, to the laboratory in toto—"as well as my books. Consider the latter yours to peruse at your pleasure; but, as for the former"—here he made the same gesture: the laboratory—"it'd be best to explore it under my eye." *Wink, wink.* "For a laboratory can be a dangerous place. *Most* dangerous."

"That would be wonderful!"

For weeks now I'd been mad, positively *mad*, to get into the laboratory, to see what I might make of the legacy left me by my mother; but doing so under the doctor's eye, as it were? That would be complicated. I'd love to be taught by him, yes; but it wasn't his science I'd want to pursue, not primarily. No: It was, well, witches' work I wanted to do.

Indeed, I still wore Mother's books on that waistlet, hiding them from all the household. I even slept with the waistlet on, until the discomfort made sleep impossible. Then I began slipping the hoop off after Gréluchon had gone to bed, placing it under my pillow or mattress.

And as for accessing the doctor's books, I confess I'd already begun to do so, prior to his giving me permission; hence my fast-improving English. Even as we spoke, I had a volume of Galen stashed beneath my bed, for I was interested in all the Roman physician had written on the topic of aconite (*Aconitum napellus*) and its many uses. For who knew? Perhaps knowledge of a lesser poison would someday prove . . . *utile*.

His offer accepted, Doctor Jekyll then returned to the careful consideration of whatever was on his slide—he *really* didn't care to be disturbed at his work, and Cézette would periodically catch hell for doing just that—and so I turned toward the door, thinking I'd best save my request for another day, a day when the doctor was less distracted; but then:

"Odile?"

"Sir?"

"Your idea, Odile. What is it?" Still he sat there, his eye fixed to the microscope.

My idea. Well, I'd been considering it some while—best to take greater care with my *ideas*, I reminded myself, primates and elephants all too fresh in my memory—but still I stalled, now that the moment to speak was upon me. But then I cut straight to it, for Henry (I knew) appreciated precision in all things. "I can be of some use to the household, sir. I know the streets."

"Pardon me, Odile," said he, looking at me now, "but I take some measure of pride—pleasure, even—in thinking I've spared you a life upon the streets." There was such a forlorn look upon his face then: I thought I'd hurt him, somehow.

"You have, sir, yes; for which me and my brother both . . ."

"But . . . ?"

"But I know those streets, sir, better than Cézette, better than Cheffy, even. . . . I can procure what they cannot."

The doctor nodded: *Aha*. I had him. And far be it for Henry Jekyll to doubt my skills as a procuress. If I'd gotten him elephant, what else might I . . . ? "What do you propose?"

"Let me do the marketing, sir. The more . . . *delicate* parts of the marketing. I've had word, sir"—and I did not add that I'd received this "word" from my own little brother, who still took the pulse of the streets like no other, despite his sickly state— "that there are certain delicacies on offer for those who know where to look: ducks, deer, even yak, sir, at five francs the pound. A fortune, certainly; but I know well your taste for—"

"For yak? Hardly." Henry was smiling now. "But I see your broader point, Odile. . . . Do it," said he then, plain as a pikestaff. "I shall inform Poole." I'd not considered this. Now the household staff would hate me even more! No matter: *I needed a reason to see Julien*. I missed him terribly. I ached, actually *ached* over how we'd left things. And if I came shopping, with money to spend, he'd *have* to open his door to me. Such was my oh-so-sly reasoning in appealing to the doctor thusly.

Doctor Jekyll had returned to his work, but now he called

out to me as I set my hand upon the faceted glass of the door-knob. "Odile?"

"Sir?"

"Take care out there, won't you? Things have worsened of late, and simple shopping is no doubt a cutthroat endeavor."

"I shall, sir. Take care, I mean."

"Good. . . . And, Odile?" He'd returned to the consideration of his slide.

"Sir?" said I yet again, feeling the fool.

"Do be sure to give my regards to young Monsieur Deboos." And I saw a half-smile form upon the doctor's profile. At least, it seemed a half-smile—sad, wry, or otherwise, I could not have said.

"Sir," said I, bowing and blushing as I backed out the laboratory door.

The tables in Les Halles were empty, yet still they were bowed as if by the phantom weight of all the wares they'd once held. True: It was late—the moonish face of the clock of Saint-Eustache moved unto midnight—but there'd been little or no commerce earlier in the day. In fact, there'd been little or no commerce for months now. But I'd been by Deboos et fils on occasion, though I'd not dared to go in or knock upon the back door, worried Julien would deny me once more; so I knew the family was still in business.

Weeks passed before I returned to that alley door on the final day of February.

It was late, yes. And dark. And cold.

Tap-tap, *rap*; tap-tap, *rap*.

I hoped Julien would be alone in the back room of the shop, as typically he was, cleaning up, hosing down the bloodied tiles, the end of one day's business blurring into the beginning of another.

Tap-tap, *rap*; tap-tap . . .

Is it possible I felt his approach before I knew it, before I saw a shadow move beneath the door? It surely felt that way. I felt it in the hammering of my heart, the sinking of my stomach. Then again: My senses were confused. How else to explain that I'd have sworn, *sworn* I wasn't crying, only to feel the proof, the warm *fact* of a tear fast appear on my cheek? I wiped it away just as the door opened, slowly.

"Julien," said I in a rush, before I could even see him, "please . . . just listen."

There he stood. (He didn't shut the door: *progress*.) His black hair had grown to curl at the nape of his neck, and those wondrous curls brought home to me the hard fact: I'd not seen the boy in some while. Far too long. I wanted to say that I'd missed him, but I didn't dare expose myself so, not yet.

He leaned against the door's jamb, a relaxed pose that told me, yes, we were alone.

"*Oui?*" said he. There was no warmth in the word, none at all; mere curiosity. And as he spoke it, he cocked his head, just so, till he was lit by both the moon (which shone upon his beautifully white cheek) and the flickering light from within the shop (which caught one of his blue, nay violet eyes, polishing it to a high sheen).

"Please, don't shut the door."

He held his pose.

I continued: "Last time I came, well, I didn't dare knock; but I'd brought you something . . . for the bruises."

"An apology?"

"No," I answered, dumbly. "A salve. Made from the last of Mother's mugwort."

"Sounds tempting."

"It would have helped the bruises heal, but I didn't dare leave it in case your father or mother—"

"They healed. The bruises, I mean."

"And for the pain. I mixed in a bit of *sangre de drago* that would have helped the pain."

"I didn't want any of your . . . your witchery," said Julien. "And I wanted the pain. To remind me."

"Of what?"

His back went ramrod straight. His eyes flared and his voice rose. "To never listen to you again! To never do your bidding— like a damned dog!—just because you tell me to."

"I . . . I am sorry, Julien." The words seemed so inadequate. *I* seemed so inadequate.

Julien let loose weeks' worth of invective now, and it was best to just let it flow from him, like poison from a wound. "And then that . . . that *gentleman* of yours comes 'round—"

"He is not 'mine,' " I interrupted, before shushing myself.

"—he comes 'round to announce that he'll be switching from Rochat to Deboos et fils from now on. Well, let me tell you, I had half a mind to tell him where to take his business, half a mind to tell my father that here was the chap who'd been the cause of it all and—"

I raised a hand to still him. "*I* was the cause of it all, Julien, not Henry."

"*Eh bien*, it's Henry now, is it?" He nodded knowingly. I hated that. But I saw him swallow too, hard; and indeed, it seemed now that a welling tear gave his eye an added sheen. No doubt it may sound cruel, but these things heartened me; for these were not signs of anger, no. These were signs of something more, though I didn't dare deem it . . . love.

Finally, Julien let me explain my half-failed plan. He did not invite me into the shop. He just stood there in the doorway, breathing a steam that might as well have been coming from his ears. (It was cold, yes, but for once I'd had foresight enough and I'd *not* worn the red scarf, Doctor Jekyll's scarf.) But Julien calmed as I spoke, beginning the tale, truthfully, with, "I was desperate."

I did not add, as well I might have, *And I am even more desperate now.* For if Julien denied me again, well . . . In who else could I confide? And who else could I trust? . . . *Enfin*, I suppose I was very much in love.

I told him how Gréluchon's impending blindness had driven me to scour my mother's books for a spell, something, *anything*, to help spare his sight. (I'd known Julien but three months before I'd shown him the books. Something I thought I'd never,

ever do with a man, and a non-Cagot to boot!) I told him how, thinking I'd found just such a spell, I'd mixed "this and that" with certain salts so-marked by my mother, not even bothering to distill it down in a solvent of any sort, and, stupidly, stupidly, *stupidly* tried it on a chimpanzee at the zoo. And I told him all that ensued.

"A chimpanzee?" he asked, incredulous. "Whatever made you . . . ? Never mind. You say they saw you? Casting the spell?" He'd come back to me now, or almost. *Alors*, at least he was listening to me. I saw the tension fall from his shoulders, his arms, even his face—the furrow was gone from his brow, and the set of his lips loosened. Oh, those lips of his . . .

"No, not exactly. Doctor Jekyll and his butler—or whatever the hell he is—surprised me just after the worst of it, when the chimpanzee had already . . . changed. Oh, but Julien, I don't know when—or even *if*—that chimp changed back! I snuck back afterwards, but I couldn't tell if any of the chimpanzees was the same one I'd transformed or if—"

"Transformed?"

"Oh, it was a horror, Julien." And so it had been, what with the creature gnawing at the salted rat till its eyes reddened, and gnawing the more as its teeth grew—grew!—along with the nails of its hands and feet. And hairier, too. Somehow the beast grew hairier, its muscles twitching beneath its fur and skin and seeming to grow . . . no, *actually* growing, writhing like snakes in a sack. Till finally it attacked and tore into the innocent primate trapped in the cage beside it.

"And you think you caused this?" asked Julien.

I paused. I swallowed hard. Was it the cold or the truth that caused me to shiver so? "No. I *know* I did. I strengthened that chimpanzee. I made it . . . monstrous."

Julien did not judge me. He just tried to absorb more of my strange truths, as ever he had.

"Come in," he said, finally. "Come in. It's cold out here." Happily, oh so happily I stepped into the shop, and then into Julien's warming arms. I set my head in the crook of his neck. And, surprising myself, I cried. I cried like I'd not cried since the day my parents had died. No: I cried like I'd not cried since the day he'd first denied me.

Julien understood why I'd done what I did. He even offered to share the blame, saying, "I should have remembered we'd sent out mule the week before. I should have sent the marquise some camel . . . or some zebra from the freezer. Stupid of me."

"No," I said. "Thank you, Julien, but all the blame is mine."

Already he was on to a more important matter: "But what about Gréluchon? Is this doctor . . . this Doctor Jekyll, is he treating him?"

"He is, yes; but I can tell it isn't working."

"Is he . . . blind?"

"Soon," said I. "Unless . . ."

Julien knew my mind so well. "You're not considering . . . Why, Odile, would you think that a spell that made one chimp rip another to shreds would spare your brother his eyesight?" And it did seem absurd, now that he'd put it *that* way.

"Because . . ." I began, nevertheless ". . . because I have no other option! The spell is marked 'Fortitude' in my mother's books . . ."

"Don't forget the 'Caution' part, eh?"

"And . . . and maybe if I dilute the salts next time in . . . something, or cut the dosage. It *did* strengthen the chimp, Julien, as well as a mouse I then tried it on at—"

"A *mouse*?"

I nodded, and forbore mentioning the horror I'd felt at seeing that creature's eyes redden, feeling and hearing its tiny bones juddering beneath its fur. I left out, too, how it had nipped at my fingertip before it had disappeared behind the baseboard at double speed. Yes: That was all the proof I had of the potion's efficacy—a murdering chimp and a sped-up mouse—and still I was ready to try it on my beloved brother.

"That's one hell of a chance you're thinking of taking, Odile."

"But do I sit by instead while my brother goes blind? My mother would have tried—"

He set his hand on my shoulder. "*Chérie*, you are not your mother. . . . Not yet, anyway."

"I know that all too well, *merci bien*," said I, rather too quickly. I even shook Julien's hand off my shoulder; but a moment later I took it—he *let* me take his hand: progress indeed—and I set it back where it had been. I even thought to kiss his fingers first but I must have telegraphed my intent, for he stalled me in the act, shaking his head and all but saying, *No.* Or perhaps, *Not yet.* And when next he actually spoke, I heartened to hear him say:

"Well, you do have a . . . talent. And he *is* your only family . . . for now." Julien looked down, embarrassed; and I, too, turned away, lest he see my quiet smile or the tears that welled anew at those last words he'd let slip, which I took for, what? Forgiveness? Plans for our future? All but a marriage proposal?

Alas, *oui.* Julien would come to agree with me: *I had no choice but to try.* To experiment some more, and then try. I owed it to my brother. And I owed it to my mother, who'd bequeathed to me who-knew-what spells, who-knew-what healing powers.

Julien locked up the shop that night and accompanied me home along a winding route, past the Hôtel de Ville and then detouring down along the banks of the Seine. No shells fell. No gunfire fouled the night. Mostly, we were silent as well; but it was in that silence that I heard, or rather *hoped* I heard, Julien's promise: *I am here, and I will help.*

But he did not *say* the words. In fact, as we stood in the Place des Vosges, in the park across from the doctor's mansion, he said nothing at all. He'd not watch me walk through Doctor Jekyll's door, no. Neither would he kiss me. Not even on the cheek, though I leaned in for it, quite. And so I could only watch him walk wordlessly away—hands stuffed deep in his pockets, shoulders hunched against the cold—and wonder when, if ever, things would be the way they'd been before the New Year had rolled so ignominiously in.

"Grel," said I, whispering, "meet me down in the doctor's laboratory tomorrow at first light. Please." I'd slipped into his room before retiring that very night, only to find him staring at the window, at the stars beyond.

In response, all I got was an arched brow above his patch-free eye. Perhaps the "please" had thrown him off, as it was hardly my habit when addressing my baby brother.

"Where?" He'd heard my every word, and knew well the room; but Gréluchon had no idea that I'd been using the laboratory in the small hours of the morning for some weeks past— *preparing*, might I say?—while the rest of the household slept. Or so I hoped; for, time and again, I'd thought I'd heard rustling in the doctor's adjoining room. *Insomnia*, thought I, letting the matter go at that.

I held up the sticklike key the doctor had given me and said:

"Yes, the laboratory. Tomorrow. At dawn. And *don't* let Cézette hear you." Whereupon I ducked out of my brother's room, slipped past the meddlesome maid's, and retired for the night into my own. Not to sleep, no; rather, to read—for the umpteenth time—that spell written in the fifth and last of my mother's books before slipping down into the laboratory to prepare. And as I read, oh how I wished, *wished* more words would appear upon the page. Words of reassurance, of promise. Or at the very least: an antidote, yes, just in case I did something I'd want, *need* to undo . . . But I found nothing more, least of all an antidote.

As directed, Gréluchon rose at dawn. I'd not slept at all, busy as I'd been distilling the salts—it seemed any solution would do, and the few other ingredients specified in *Physicae* were easily had as well—and rendering them down to a bluish brew. I'd not dose him with pure salts, as I had the monkey, no. And so I'd arranged the brew in vials, each with a few milliliters more than the last; for danger inhered in the dosage. *That* much was written in *Physicae.* I'd been hours calibrating it, just so. But when Grel came to the laboratory door at dawn, he was dressed for a day on the streets.

"What are you up to now?" I whispered. "Headed out? At this hour?"

I pulled him into the laboratory, where—if he even spied the brew abubble—he said only, "It's today." He was not excited; resigned, rather. Sad. "I thought that's why you wanted to meet so early."

I was confused. "*What's* today?"

He clarified things, saying, as if I were Queen of the Idiots: "The Prussians are coming into the city today, Odile. As part of the . . . *peace.*"

I stared at him. Rather vapidly, I suppose; it's true.

"Where the hell have you been?" he added, a bit brusquely for my tastes. "I've told you a hundred times—"

"Hush!" I said; though I really wanted to answer his question and say, *Here. I've been here all night, you little so-and-so. Trying to figure out a way to save your sorry little—* But no. I just shrugged, and my brother informed me further:

"Everyone's talking about it. They're going to march right through . . . no, they're being *allowed* to march right through the Arc de Triomphe, those damned sons of . . ." and he concluded with a few *gros mots*, words I was surprised he knew, words *I* didn't even know.

"And so?" I asked. "What of it?"

In truth, I was already feeling relief at the thought of putting off the experiment a while longer. And only then did I realize how scared I truly was; for I recalled the redness of that chimpanzee's eyes, and too well I recalled the way it had . . . *Oui*, a few more experiments in the field, as it were, would be time well spent. "I cannot miss it," said Gréluchon then, categorically. Of course, he meant that he *would not* miss it.

"All right," said I. "I suppose it'll hold." I referred to the brew—in truth, I'd no idea what would happen to it, now that it had been brewed. And as I supposed, further, that I would simply make more, I decided to dispose of it down the drain, giving no thought at all, *none*, to those creatures that doubtless came to roam the city's sewers. Neither did it dawn on me that the source of the salts might be . . . finite; for I then assumed that, in time, the books would surrender all Mother's secrets and the supply of salts would be *in*finite. It would require but a bit of *this* added to *that*, the lot of it then mixed with *the other thing* and *"Voilà!"* (My naïveté knew no bounds.)

Alors, my mind had wandered in the course of all that supposing; for a pesky Gréluchon summoned me back to the present with:

"Hell-*o*? . . . Odile? I really have to go now. . . . What'll 'hold'? What are you talking about?"

"Never mind," said I, adding, as though it had always been my intent to accompany him, "Let's go."

"Really?" How happy he was now to know I'd not stop him, that in fact I'd go with him.

"Really," said I. "Give me a minute."

I knew he'd not be dissuaded. I might have said (truthfully) that he looked weak, pale, and that the thinnest of cauls could be seen descending over his other eye, his *good* eye, but it would have all been in vain. Still he'd have gone out onto the streets to see, nay *to seethe* at the Prussians as they paraded. And so it was I did the only thing I could think of: I turned low the flames beneath the smoking vials of brew and I snuck upstairs to dress for a winter's day, quickly coming back down to accompany my half-blind brother onto the streets of a soon-to-be-shamed Paris.

Hatred of the victors coursed through the city as surely as the river Seine. Worse still: The hatred simmered beneath resignation, beneath shame. We could not fight back. We hadn't the will or the way, for we'd been starved of our strength and stripped of our weapons. This was the "peace" we'd agreed to? Watching as the city—and we, its citizenry—were methodically shamed?

As we walked from the Marais, up to the Place de la Concorde and down the Champs Elysées to that triumphal arch commemorating a glory that was no longer ours, we saw that black blindfolds had been tied over certain statues to spare them (symbolically, at least) having to watch the city give itself over to the Prussians. Alas. The greatest of nations are sometimes shamed. Today it would be our turn. Of course, Grel was rather less cavalier than I. In fact, real tears now fell to chap his cold cheeks.

Elsewhere, women wept openly and men milled about on street corners. And all the while the drums of the Prussians grew ever louder. Finally, a gray line of high-stepping soldiers could be seen. Here they came.

Gréluchon turned the collar of his coat up. He was shivering, and not solely from the cold; but when I sat my arm over his heaving shoulders, he shrugged it off. He threw back those bony shoulders, stood tall. Had this warring somehow made him a man? I supposed it had, in a way. And he was resolute: He'd bear witness to this shaming.

They came and went, the Prussians. What more can be said? By nightfall the "occupiers" had left the city as they'd come. The simple, shaming show was over. Now they'd return to their encampment at Versailles. There they'd continue to shame us on paper rather than in person, with treaties and bills of reparations we'd be generations paying.

We went silently home. But in the long days since, I've often wondered if I should have encouraged Gréluchon to speak and spill all the shame and spite he felt that day. For I can only wonder if all that pent-up poison didn't play its role in his own . . . transformation, and all that so fatefully followed.

We'd had to stop time and again as we returned to the doctor's mansion in the faraway Marais from that parade of Prussian soldiers, for Gréluchon weakened with every step. Some strange illness had hold of his body; but it was no secret what had broken his spirit. With every passing day, every passing week, he worsened, till finally it came to seem as though he were the literal embodiment of the war, or rather the shame felt in its aftermath owing to that supposed peace.

Doctor Jekyll despaired; his treatments had helped little, if at all. And I despaired the more, for the treatment I was readying . . . well, was it really *ready*? Efficacious and safe? Would it ever be? Oh, but the boy was nearly blind now, and suffering so. He ran a steady fever; and when feverish he spoke of how he'd have fought for France against the Prussians, and how he'd now fight for Paris against the traitorous French, if only . . .

If only.

Finally, I could not stand his suffering, his steady dissolution, one moment more.

March the sixteenth, it was, at midnight, when I helped Gréluchon downstairs and into the doctor's laboratory, thinking that all the household slept. And there I sat him down and explained what the doctor had lately told me about his present state, about the imminent loss of not only his sight but his diseased eye as well. (I said nothing about the disease's likely spread.) I told him I had an idea. I even told him, *warned* him of what had happened (more or less) at the *singerie*. He wasn't dissuaded. And when I revealed Mother's books, locked on the ring around my waist, Gréluchon brightened for the first time in a very long while and said, simply, "Do it, Odile. . . . Please, *please*."

And so I stupidly did.

CHAPTER FIVE
Transformation

Having seen what I've now seen, having done what I've now done, I no longer doubt my nature: I am not a healer, *I am a witch*; and surely not the first of that sisterhood to effect terrible things at the aptly named Witching Hour.

Alas, as midnight tolled, I sat in Doctor Jekyll's laboratory beside my brother.

The door was locked. We were alone. I'd lit as few lamps as possible, raising only enough light by which to work. Still, the laboratory was deeply shadowed, so too Gréluchon's face. He sat on the far side of the doctor's high table, formerly put to unpleasant purpose in a surgeon's suite someplace. It showed stains I did not care to contemplate, and had sluiceways down either side to allow for the run-off of blood; a crank beneath the table allowed it to be tilted so that the gore would have run down the gullies and into two holes at the table's end, set there as if to catch billiard balls and not things . . . *bodily* in nature.

Between my brother and I there rose the monstrous-seeming thing I'd built: A Hydra of sorts, a multilimbed, twisted glass-scape of alembics, ampoules, tubing, and other such whatnot I'd once again used to render the salts down to a brew. *Six* brews of varying strength, rather.

I ought to have been suspicious, I suppose, of the freedoms Henry had afforded me regarding his laboratory and everything in it. He'd made it known that the room was mine as much as his. I thought I was merely favored by the doctor, might even have flattered myself and used the word *friendship*; and so I did not think it strange that no one in the household save I—not even Poole—had a key to those heretofore very private prem-ises. What a fool I was.

Henry had shown me every inch of the laboratory, too. He gave me the key to a drawer in which more keys were kept, keys to open every drawer, cupboard, and cabinet; further, he explained to me the contents of each. I learned the names of every ingredient in the many hundreds of test tubes standing at attention in their metal racks, each label bearing both the Latin and popular name in a carefully crafted hand.

Of course, to know the names was for naught unless I knew the substances' properties, and so Henry taught me these as well or showed me where to find this information, in which of the many leather-bound volumes that were arranged on the shelves via a quite idiosyncratic system at which I was soon expert: Each volume had been placed according to the import of its contents, further cross-referenced by (first) language and (second) author's last name. The only books off-limits to me were the many identical black-bound volumes that ranged down the length of a shelf in a glass-fronted cupboard set above the doctor's desk; these—Doctor Jekyll's personal notebooks—sat behind doors, doors that were locked with a key the doctor carried on his person. He had long ago acquired the habit of secrecy owing to the strange, even scandalous nature of some of his research into what he described—once and once only—as "the mystical, the transcendental."

In addition to teaching me about the contents of his laboratory—from those hundreds of chemicals to the apparatuses he used to combine and *re*combine them all—Doctor Jekyll took me with him as he made the rounds of the city's many chemists. There, with a combination of insistence and cash, he procured all he needed; and if a chemist could not provide what it was the doctor wanted, he simply wrote to the four corners of the world till a package arrived at the Place des Vosges. Of course, during the Siege this was rather hard to do—it would have taken *quite* the carrier pigeon to carry him his antimony, loose mercury, thallium—but no matter: The doctor seemed far more interested in teaching me at present, and so helped me procure any and every thing I thought requisite to my own work, various botanicals mostly, herbs, plants, and sundry seeds.

And with all that Doctor Jekyll gave me, I grew overconfident. Yes: Overconfidence was among the first of my many faults, followed quickly by a curiosity just like that which killed the proverbial cat.

᭜

There sat Gréluchon now, looking at once hopeful and forlorn, staring at me with his one good eye through the maze of glass this-'n'-thats in which I'd brewed the salts. I'd committed those pages of my mother's *Physicae* bearing the spell to memory. And let me here add that I supposed, then, that Doctor Jekyll knew nothing of my mother's books. Leastways, I never consulted them in his presence. And on those occasions when we shared the laboratory, I owned up to no specific *goal*, per se. "Experimenting, sir," is all I would say, this despite the doctor's increasingly frequent questioning. He wanted to know what I was working on, for he rightly supposed that I was indeed working on something . . . special. Still, "Experimenting, sir," is all I would answer, though that would suffice for but a short while before the questions came anew. Yes, the doctor was quite curious himself; and, it seemed, never very far away.

Once, when alone in the laboratory, I combined two substances that ought never to be combined—as any first-year chemist and certainly any witch worth her salt (indeed!) would have known—and Doctor Jekyll had suddenly appeared at the laboratory door, entering to help douse the steaming, stinking result of my miscraft. Another time I slunk down to the laboratory in silence for one of my midnight sessions only to find an array of utensils exactly, *exactly* suited to my present purpose,

90

a distillation of the salts that I'd had to stop trying to effect the night before for want of those very tools. Coincidence? I convinced myself so.

"What the heck is *that*?" asked Gréluchon now from the table's far side. I'd told him to keep to his seat, for I did not want him at my shoulder as I worked. It would not do to let him see the work effected firsthand. Too dangerous. And so I put him off with a reminder of something he knew to be true: The Cagot craft passes mother-to-daughter. Therefore this was "woman's work." That succeeded in dousing his interest somewhat. But wasn't he entitled to witness its being worked, especially when the craftwork was intended for his own benefit? Right or wrong, yes or no, I cannot say; but in the light of all that soon would transpire, I am relieved that I held as tightly to the Cagot craft, its substance and secrets, as I did that night.

"Tell me!" Gréluchon struggled to keep his voice to a whisper, for neither of us wanted to wake the night-quiet house, and Doctor Jekyll slept but one wall away. "What *is* it? What have you there? . . . Tell me, Odile!" My brother could be so very fourteen at times.

Gréluchon moved this way and that, trying to see better, to see more of the test tubes that stood arrayed before me and into which I was then dropping those final ingredients that would (so I hoped!) render the transformative, the *healing* salts.

"Patience, you!" And as I measured, oh so carefully, bits of this, bits of that, all according to Mother's book, I added, "And. Don't. Be. Such. A. Brat." But when I heard the tall clock out on the landing chime twice, I realized time had escaped me and Grel had in fact been quite patient.

Yes, I'd taken great care to calibrate the contents of each tube, to brew the six drafts to differing degrees of efficacy. Now there they were, the numbers on their labels running—left to right—ONE through SIX. And in English—a habit already, and one in accordance with the laboratory "rules" as laid down by Doctor Jekyll—I'd added MOU to the label of ONE and CHI to the sixth, meaning MOUse and CHImp. It wouldn't do, *at all*, for me to confuse that concoction with which I'd later sped up the mouse in my attic rooms with that which had worked so disastrously upon the chimp at the zoo.

Why I even brewed that CHI quantity again—that brew which I'd used to douse the rat before sprinkling it with pure salts—I've no idea. Overconfidence? Perhaps, yes; though I must allow that sheer stupidity played its part as well. How else to explain putting such a strong-making, transformative draft within literal reach of a half-blind, dying boy who fancied himself a soldierly type? Which I did, all too literally tempting both my brother *and* fate.

There stood the six tubes, themselves looking like soldiers in their ranks. Different from soldiers, though, in that each was "uniformed" in a different color. The MOU brew was a grayish blue, scentless and nearly smokeless; and these characteristics—the depth of blue, the stink and the smoke—increased right-ward, till finally the CHI tube took on a purplish hue, and stank and smoked horribly. Indeed, the stink traveled on the smoke, and soon the laboratory was filled with both. I bade my brother open a window, which he did, and we watched as the wisps of sulfurous smoke wafted out over a wintry Paris. Yet still the tubes smoked on, as though the interaction within them would go on forever.

Across the table, across that glass divide of beakers, burners, tubing, and whatnot, Gréluchon was growing ever more impatient. And lest I forget what we were about, what our purpose was, he flipped up his black-striped eye patch. Seeing that ruined orb, now and again magnified by the glass through which he stared as I worked, as I *tried* to work, well, it had its effect.

This was not science, not even craftwork in the abstract, no. I was working to spare my brother his sight, his eye and likely his very life. (Doctor Jekyll had never said as much, but I'd sensed that he thought Gréluchon might indeed lose his life not long after losing his eyes, plural. *Degenerative* was the dark word he used, and he'd been vague as to where said degeneration would stop.) And so I said sooner than I ought to have, "Come here"; and I gave him the healing draft.

Again, that's all I'd meant for it to be: *healing*. I'd intended to strengthen Gréluchon *just enough* to restore his sight and the health of his eye, and to forestall the creep, that degenerative *creep* of whatever corrosive disease was coursing through his veins and had already begun to work upon his good eye. The brew I'd give him would be that of the MOU and I'd up the dosage, moving rightward along the rack, slowly, *slowly*, from the lighter to the darker blue brew.

And at first all went well.

Gréluchon did as I told him, for his trust in me was complete, as well it would have been. Was I not his older, supposedly more sage sister? Had I not looked out for him all the days of his life, exclusively so since the death of our parents? More: Hadn't I powers, talents akin to those of our mother? Yes, yes, and supposedly so; but how I wish his trust had been somehow *less*, for then I mightn't have moved as fast as I did, mightn't have had to watch as he . . .

Transformed.

There he sat, come round to my side of the surgical table. I'd pulled a stool up beside my chair, and I'd trained a lamp to shine on Gréluchon's face, for I *needed* to witness the salts at work if I were to effect a fix of his health.

I poured from the grayest of the tubes into a wineglass snuck up from the dining-room cupboard. Poole would have something to say about *that* if he discovered it missing—and he had indeed taken to regularly counting the crystal, the silver, and even the painted porcelain plates since our arrival, usually right under our noses—but I could not be certain that any vessel found in the laboratory itself would be *un*corrupted by some other ingredient. And as this dosing was a delicate business indeed, I couldn't run those risks.

Gréluchon took the glass from me and, before drinking, winked with his good eye. He then trained that eye on the brew itself, swirling it around the glass as we'd seen Doctor Jekyll do while sitting fireside, about to enjoy some fine wine or port. I couldn't help but smile, and so too did Gréluchon, knowing he was less than believable playing the role of dandy. Then he sniffed the brew and drew back from it in disgust.

"What the hell *is* this, Odile? *Blech!* It smells like you poured cat pee into it."

"I . . . I don't know what it is," I said, more truthfully than not; "but it works. Trust me and take it! *Drink.* And besides, when was the last time you sniffed cat pee?" Of course, I was not nearly as sure of myself as I sounded. I had simply developed the habit of telling my younger brother what to do. And as was his habit (usually), he obeyed: He drank.

At first: Nothing.

Nothing I could see, rather, though I sat hunched over Grel, the lamp shining directly into that eye which sat now in its socket like a perfect, pearlescent orb, the pupil totally occluded. The light pained him—he asked if he might flip the eye patch down—but I insisted he sit there, perfectly still; and I did the same, staring into his eye. Nose to nose we were, waiting. And waiting.

Nothing.

The questions that came to me were many: Had I underdosed him? Misremembered the recipe (though the word *recipe* seems better suited to biscuits than sulfurous brews)? Or had I somehow adulterated this batch, too? Had the hellebore leaves I'd used—*Helleborus foetidus*—been too far gone? They had seemed a bit shriveled, a bit turned-up at the edges, true. Had the seeds of the henbane (*Hyoscyamus niger*) dried beyond efficacy? Or maybe crystal wasn't a suitable conductor, or maybe there'd been some residual liquor in the glass that had . . . On and on. My brain was abuzz. Nothing seemed too preposterous an explanation; for, after all, were we not already deep in the realm of the *in*explicable?

"Well," I asked of Gréluchon, "anything? Anything at all?"

"That light, it hurts when you—"

"Not the light! The light always hurts your eye. The . . . *potion*. Do you feel any effects from it? At all?"

He shook his head.

"Are you absolutely sure?" I had the slightest suspicion there was something he wasn't saying. I don't say he was *lying*, not really; rather, he was no doubt fearful I'd stop the experiment. I asked again, and again he shook his head. *Nothing.*

And as I saw no effects either, I took tube number two from the rack. Pouring a quarter of its contents—fully *a quarter*, fool that I was!—into that same glass, I handed it back to my brother. "Drink," I said, and needlessly so.

Gréluchon had already lifted the glass to his lips. It was still smoking and—to judge by his sudden squint—still stinking, too; yet he downed it all at once. And the waiting, the watching recommenced. I even opened my own notebook and took up a pen, thinking I'd follow Doctor Jekyll's example and *record it all*. But there was nothing to write but . . . "Nothing," and that's all those pages would ever bear. *Nothing.*

Still the laboratory window was open, and I ascribed my shivering to the resultant chill; but in point of fact I'd begun to worry, quite. What if I couldn't help my brother? I felt such an enormous responsibility to do so, knowing, *believing* that my mother would have been able to forestall his blindness. Worse: What if I had to progress further, unto the third test tube, thusly coming closer to that sixth, marked CHI?

I tried desperately to recall how quickly the chimpanzee had changed. Had it been immediate, the moment it had first begun to gnaw upon the salted rat? Or had it been more gradual? And though I recalled the transformation in all its horrid particulars—fair to say I'd been haunted by what I'd witnessed—I could not recall the timing of it all. How quickly had the chimp's eyes reddened? What had begun to grow first, his hair or fingernails? When was it I remarked that snaky movement of his muscles? *Enfin*, how fast had been the beast's transformation from chimp to monster? I could not say.

"Anything yet?" I asked. "Anything . . . unusual?"

"I am tired, hungry, and cold," said Gréluchon. "And there's nothing unusual in that. So: No, nothing."

"Nothing . . . ?"

"Nothing! . . . *Zut*, Odile! What do you want me to say? Do this! Give me more or let's be done with it!" It was unlike Gréluchon to let his temper flare as it did then, and I fancied I saw an uncommon wildness in his good eye as he did so. *Fancied*, I say, though now I suppose it was a fact: He'd already begun to change, though neither of us knew it.

"Okay, okay," said I, assuaging him so. "Here . . ." And I handed him half—*half!*—the contents of the third vial. And

I was determined, *determined* to go no further. Or so I thought; though now I must ask myself again: *Why then had I brewed a fourth, fifth, and even a sixth vial?* Yes, I found myself handing over a very blue glassful of number three to my brother when he demanded I do so. *Demanded,* I say; which action I should have seen as a sure sign that my brother, my beloved little brother, had begun to change. Indeed, mere math should have told me as much; for Gréluchon had now consumed—in quantity and quality alike—a potion likely half as strong as that which had changed the chimpanzee so.

It was then I heard the most horrid sound I'd ever heard.

I'd turned away from Gréluchon for a moment so as to raise the light in the lamp, for it seemed, *seemed* I could discern once again the pupil of his bad eye moving in tandem with its good twin as my brother looked from me to the test tubes, back and forth, rather skittishly.

Turning back toward Grel, who'd risen from the stool and stood quite close to me now, I could see that pupil, yes. For the caul that had grown to cover Gréluchon's eye was dissolving, and the milky tears the eye had long seeped were nowhere to be seen. And just when I might have felt a measure of joy, a *great* measure of joy and even pride at having effected this healing, I heard the sound, that most specific sound. A sound I'd unfortunately heard once before. When standing before the *singerie.*

At first I thought (. . . hoped . . . prayed) that the sound was coming from outside, for it seemed a sound of nature. On the contrary, it is a most *un*natural sound that mocks nature, mimics it, sounding so like:

A wave dragging stones from the shore out to sea.

Ice beginning to break.

A boulder beginning to roll, slipping grindingly from its stony perch in advance of an avalanche.

I'd heard the same before the *singerie*, yes. When the chimp first began to change. And now, as then, I was slow to realize what it was I heard:

Bones. Bones breaking only to reset themselves, the salted body *re*ordering itself. Changing. In a word: *transforming*.

I saw the transformation in Gréluchon's smile as I turned back to him where he stood, so near now that I had to look up into his face from where I sat. The pupils were both clear now, true, but the irises were no longer blue. They were black. Yet what struck me even more—for it frightened me—was the nature of his smile, more aptly deemed a sneer, maybe even a snarl. Yes, a snarl; for it came from a mouth now featuring teeth suddenly quite canine in aspect. Gréluchon's actual canines *had* lengthened, surely; and he seemed to take a savage delight in baring them when next he asked, "What next, witch?"

My brother knew how I hated that epithet, *witch*; but he only smiled the more when I communicated as much with my most withering older-sister stare. Here was *the* look—as best I could summon it under these strangest of circumstances—that had previously stilled my little brother, caused him to stop whatever sister-bothering business he'd been about; but now it seemed only to embolden him the more, for he asked again:

"What next, witch?" And with the jut of his chin—his every feature now seemed more prominent than before—he gestured to the fourth vial.

"No," said I, though he'd made no direct request. *"No."*

He looked past me to the three remaining vials—of a blue deepening unto purple, all still stinking and smoking—and said, "Oh yes, sister. Oh, *yesss*." He drew out the word horribly, hissingly. And as he set his new self in motion, making to push past me for the vials, I heard the *pop, pop, pop* of his bones being put to purpose, realigning themselves beneath, betwixt, and between muscles of a newfound size and strength. I could *see* this happening, could see the muscles writhing beneath the skin but moving not as muscles in motion ought to move, but rather like . . . like newborn pups slithering free of the sac in which they're born, that caul of another sort. Yes, here was birth-like motion; but still, somehow, the sound of it all—that grinding, grating, God-awful sound of bones in motion—was more horrid than the sight.

As he reached toward the vials, I saw his forearm—hirsute now, whereas my brother had been hairless as a babe—shoot from the frayed cuff of a sleeve that had formerly hung from his hand but now was too short. And as I maneuvered myself between my brother and the brew, that forearm was quite near my ear, such that the sound made by his elbow as it . . . *broke*, yes, broke and reset itself, was like that of a hammer striking

100

off a steel spike. It echoed in my ear, and the sound gave me gooseflesh.

And then as he, or rather *it*, sought to take those vials in hand, I saw a fist forming and re-forming as the myriad bones within it blew, *blew* like kernels of popping corn. I caught the scent of blood, too, and saw that the nails of the hand had somehow lengthened and rounded, splitting, bloodying the cuticles. They were convex now, set like claws at the ends of ten fingers quite graspingly intent on their target: the next and bluer vial of brew.

I now stood, the better to set myself between the beast—my beloved brother, Gréluchon, was nearly gone—and the brewed salts. I said nothing. What was there to say? What words could have dissuaded that boy, that beast . . . *whatever* he'd become? None. This I knew. And lest I doubted that he, that *it* would brook no interference from me, it raised its new hand as if to slap me, but then backhandedly brushed me away from the table instead. Doing so, it said, in guttural tones that had *not* belonged to my brother, "Go! Go from here before . . ." It was then, I believe, in that very moment, that I saw, deep in the beast's now sighted but black-irised eyes, the very last of my brother.

And rather than be beaten back, again, as I knew I'd be, I stepped aside.

Whoever, *whatever* it was had risen to bedevil my brother had, yes, struck me to the floor when I had more pointedly, more purposefully put myself between him and the remaining vials. *He'd have them.* That much he made perfectly clear.

I felt no real pain, though he'd caught me with a claw, and it is perhaps more correct to say he *shoved* me to the floor. Regardless, from that position I tried again to defend the brew. I grabbed Gréluchon's leg; and his knee gave, or rather transformed with a hollow *pop*, which rang in my ear like the report from a pistol. I all but climbed that leg, trying to pull myself to my feet, the better to see what he was about, the better to somehow stop him. I could not let him progress through three vials more, no. But each time I tried to rise, he shoved me back. He did so casually, as though he were a hungry child and I were but a wasp buzzing around his jam sandwich; but in so doing he caught my neck with one of his . . . claws, and he cut me. I must have then cried out his name; for, from my vantage point upon the laboratory floor, I watched as he turned to stare down at me over his hunched shoulder. The look was horrific. Steam came from between the lips he now licked—he'd bolted back more of the brew!—and as our eyes met, I saw that his eyes were changing still. At first I thought he was crying, and so I heartened somewhat, thinking that now I might reason with him; but his eyes were reddened not by tears of remorse, indeed not by tears of any type. Rather, his eyes had reddened, were reddening still, as the chimpanzee's had. How I wished then that he might settle that eye patch back into place, sparing me at least half of his ruby-eyed stare.

I fell upon the floor, thinking all hope was lost. Yet in the moment before I began to fear for my own safety—and *fear* I most certainly would—I clung to a last scintilla of hope: If perhaps I could impede his progression through the remaining vials unto (and including) the sixth, then mightn't the transformation be incomplete, mightn't I preserve something of my brother's presence within the . . . *thing*?

I scurried back, crablike, from the base of the surgical table. If I tried to stand while near Gréluchon, doubtless he'd bat me back again; but if I were to stand beyond his now considerable reach, then perhaps I could see what he was about. As it was, I could only surmise, from the crash and crunch of glass, that he was making mayhem upon the laboratory table.

I stood, but to no avail. Spying my lengthening shadow upon the far wall, Gréluchon turned and hissed, verily hissed like a cat caught in a corner; and lest I even *consider* approaching him, he showed me the back of a hand, now grown broad and quite hairy. "Ssstay," he hissed, seeming to struggle for control of his tongue.

I backed away from my brother, staring at him all the while, and stopped in a darkened corner of the laboratory only when I came up against the wall. Had it not been for that wall, I might have backed from him forever, for I dared not turn from what I then witnessed. I could not.

So it was that I watched as Gréluchon gave himself over wholly to the brew; but he did not progress fourth, unto fifth, unto sixth, no. He passed from the third, which I'd so foolishly handed over, straight to the sixth.

Dark though it was, with the laboratory lit by but that one lamp and with that pale, wintry moonlight seeping in, I can say with certainty what it was I witnessed then, even though the very memory sickens me.

Having downed all, *all* the purple, stinking and steaming contents of the sixth vial, Gréluchon turned to me where I sat, having now slid down that wall to cry in the deeply shadowed corner. He could see me clearly, despite the near-dark. I could tell. And he could hear me too, though I tried to stifle my sobs, fearing that they would draw the whole household to the laboratory door. Surely Doctor Jekyll, at least, had heard the ruckus on this, the far side of his bedroom wall. I sat there wishing he *had* heard it all, wishing he would apply his key and come into the locked laboratory to . . . *save me.* For I feared that I might soon need saving, yes, and I would not care from what quarter it came.

My crying seemed to anger Gréluchon. I wonder if he hadn't caught the stink of my fear on the air, as they say animals can. He looked as though he were onto a scent, yes; but then he suddenly began to twitch, and to twist his neck this way and that. It was then I heard another of those popping sounds and reasoned—if *reason* it be—that his body must simply be accommodating its growing spine. Its *mis*growing spine, I should say; for I saw now that his back was misshapen, hunched somewhat.

He came near me now where I sat, and I could do nothing but curl myself into a tighter and tighter ball, bringing my knees closer to my chest. And though I wanted to look away from the creature as it came on, I could not. Instead, I stared. Thusly can I describe its loping gait, and that odd twitching about the neck and shoulders, as if still it sought to situate its head atop a shifting spine. The clothes my brother had been wearing had ceded to the body's new shape: The sleeves, as said, had all but split to accommodate the sudden musculature and an extreme length of arm; indeed, the cuffs were a good six inches above the wrist, yet the pants fit as they had, save for a lessening of the slack about the thighs and buttocks. And he'd kicked off his worn boots, which could no longer accommodate his foot, grown so. He was barefoot, and his feet were akin to his hands in appearance: *animal-like.*

"Grel!" I cried now, appealing to the last vestiges of my brother buried within the beast; but nothing. He simply came nearer, staring at me as if I, too, were a relic of a former life, a memory all but lost. "It's me," said I, ridiculously—for how could he not know as much?—"It's Odile. Your . . . your sister." But nothing familiar, no recognition rose within the red of his eyes. I might have been a stranger to him; or worse: an enemy.

He knelt now, and I cried all the more at catching from the creature's skin the scent of that soap I had lately shared with Gréluchon. I saw, too, that the features of the face were still my brother's at base, albeit greatly changed somehow. *How*, precisely, I find I cannot say. But, yes, there was that mole above his upper lip, a lip that was as chapped now as it had been some hours before. *Quelle bizarrerie!* What in all the wide world could account for what I was witnessing? And however had I effected as much with but a handful of those salts—dissolved in a simple solution and paired with some herbs and the briefest of spells—bequeathed to me by my mother?

"Grel," I ventured a final time when his face was but a foot from mine. "Gréluchon, it's me."

"I know who you are," said he, finally, with a wry smile. If I had hope then, it soon blew away on the fetid breath accompanying his speech. It was as though that stink had risen from Hell itself. "Give it to me."

"Give you what?" I said, turning from his sulfurous speech. "I'll give you *nothing*!"

Now *I'd* changed! What was it about the creature that caused me to spurn it? I daresay I hated him suddenly, and instinctively so, whereas a moment earlier I'd been . . . sympathetic, perhaps. I'd have thought it would be an apology I'd find upon my tongue when finally I dared to speak; but no, far from it. It was scorn I gave voice to, responding to the reeking command that I turn over . . . *what*, precisely?

I could only assume he referred to the remaining brew; and if it was *that* he wanted, why not simply take it? I could not stop him, and he knew as much. But no: He referred to something else, and this I discovered in a most unpleasant manner.

He stood now, and opened his palm to me. Though he was backlit by the lamp that still burned upon the table—and which, luckily, he had not knocked over, for then we might all have gone up in chemically fired flames—I saw him silhouetted by the pale moonlight. And what a strange silhouette it was, twisted and strong as steel bent to some unnameable purpose.

Now he set his horrid hand upon my person. It was hot and sweaty upon my neck; for he wanted that makeshift necklace of twine I wore with its two keys: the first to the laboratory door, the second to the waistlet I wore. I do not know which key he sought, if not both; for I all but barked:

"Never!" He'd have to take my life before he took those keys. Rather, he could have the laboratory key—what cared I for the laboratory now?—but the waistlet containing all my mother's witchery? *"Never!"*

At my barking the word a second time, he snatched the eye patch off his forehead. He held it in his fist, where, had it been friable—a clod of dirt, a chunk of coal, even—he'd have ground it down to dust. Then he backed away and made for the laboratory door.

I rose. I ran after him, worrying that if he left the Jekyll mansion—as surely he would—well, once he was out in the larger world he'd be lost, a danger to himself and others. Indeed, it was the larger world I ought to have worried for.

I ran and reached him at the locked laboratory door. I beat his hunched back with my fists, saying, *screaming* that he could not leave the laboratory, let alone the house, that we would work together to find an antidote, even saying that the spell would pass and that he'd soon return to himself. Of course, I had no idea if this were true. I had no idea what effect the salts would have upon *a human being.*

"Stop! Please," I cried. All to no avail.

Indeed, he needed no key to leave: He simply tore, *tore* the glass knob from the door and tossed it to the floor as though it were but a trinket, a child's toy. The lock gave and he opened the door so forcefully—and seeming to surprise himself somewhat in the process: Clearly, he did not yet know his own strength—that the wood of the door cracked as it blew back against the wall.

Neither did he know his newfound speed. I watched from the landing as Gréluchon took the stairs two at a time, leaping down, down and out of the doctor's house in a blur. I knew I stood no chance of following him, none at all. And if I would not be able *to follow*, I would have *to find*. And soon. Oh, but how? Alas, hearing the front door slam with such force that a pane in the fanlight above it fell, crashing upon the foyer floor, I could contain myself no longer, for:

Gréluchon was gone.

I sobbed, and soon found myself sobbing in the arms of Doctor Henry Jekyll. He was shivering himself, standing there in naught but a nightshirt. "There, there," said he; and when I struggled to somehow explain—my breath ragged, my words as confused as my thoughts—Doctor Jekyll said simply, "No need to explain, Odile . . . no need at all."

<hr/>

The ruckus had roused the whole household. Cheffy and Cézette were rudely sent back to bed by Poole, who'd been first to join the doctor and I on the landing, where now we

108

three stood. I was inconsolable, but still Henry tried to stanch both my tears and my nonsensical speech. Whatever must I have been muttering? I cannot imagine. For I was trying to dissemble (*oui*: lie) while somehow making sense for myself of all I'd lately seen.

When I made to move into the laboratory, ostensibly to clean up the mess within but really to ensure that I'd left no traces of whatever hellish craftwork I'd done, Doctor Jekyll stopped me. Indeed, he suddenly launched himself in front of the laboratory door. "No, no," said he, "this can all wait till the morrow."

"But, sir, I'm afraid we made a fearful mess and really, I must—"

"Not at all," said he. "I will go inside only to ensure that there's nothing dangerous within. Douse the lamp, cap certain chemicals, et cetera." He smiled a false smile. "While Poole here will . . . will . . . see you to your rest, I suppose." And here the doctor gave his manservant a most helpless look.

"Come," said a bemused Poole—he all but shrugged—and before I knew it I was being led toward the stairs and up.

"No," said I, stopping on the second stair. "No, please." In truth, I didn't know what I was saying *no* to. I knew only that I did not want to mount those stairs to the row of attic rooms where I'd be very much alone, with Gréluchon gone, and where a sneaking Cézette would be waiting for me with countless questions. Mostly, though, I did not want to be alone, not then.

"Yes, yes," seconded the doctor. "I understand." He then

nodded to his own bedchamber, adjoining the laboratory. Oh, but it seemed he'd misunderstood, mightily. Surely he didn't mean for me to . . . didn't think that I'd . . .

And then he added, his voice rather shaky, rather high, "Poole, see to Odile's comfort, won't you, please? Meanwhile, I'll . . . I'll . . ." Whatever had gotten into Henry? He looked down the stairs, as if after Gréluchon. He looked at the broken laboratory door. His nerves were quite frayed, nearly as frayed as mine.

I let myself be led into the doctor's bedroom, something propriety would have forbidden under normal circumstances; but circumstances such as these were far from normal, indeed about as far as I could conjure. I'd deal with the household consequences (which would be many) another day. As for right now, well . . . I'd made a beast of my beloved brother, after all, and now he roamed the wintry streets barefoot and hell-bent on who-knew-what mischief (though *mischief* seemed hardly the word for what I imagined he might get up to while under the influence of the salts).

I'd seen the doctor's room before, glimpsed it from the landing through a half-opened door, but I was taken aback now by its size. It was large, quite. There was a reading chair of black leather and brass tacking beside the hearth, a tall ward-robe, a desk nestled in an alcove beneath a window that gave onto the park three stories below, and a bed: a large four-poster bed that was, I noticed, most improbably made. Still? At this hour? Had the doctor not slept at all? Odd, as he was not of nocturnal habits and typically rose at dawn. But then I saw a pile of books beside the black leather chair, one of them open and overturned atop the seat itself, and reasoned that the doctor, dressed for sleep, had been reading beside the fireplace on the far side of that wall adjoining the laboratory. Doubtless he'd dozed off and had been fast asleep there in his chair; otherwise, how to explain the fact that he'd not come to the laboratory door at the first sounds of struggle? Curious, that. Poole quickly drew the coverlet down in a manner long perfected by practice, so that the blue monogrammed *HJ* sat center-all, and wordlessly readied the bed for me, mumbling all the while. When Doctor Jekyll came into the room some moments later, I said, "Oh no, really I must head up to—"

"Nonsense, Odile," said the doctor, half smiling. He seemed to have composed himself somewhat in the interim, though still his cheeks were flushed and he would not meet my eyes. "The room, the bed is yours . . . and yours alone, of course. You'll be more comfortable here, I wager." As who wouldn't be? It was quite true, my upstairs cot being no match for his ebony four-poster. "Poole will turn down a bed for me in one of the second-floor rooms, won't you, Poole?"

The manservant grunted. Would I never cease creating more *work* for the man?

"Now hop up there on the edge of the bed," said Doctor Jekyll, "and let me have a look at your neck."

My neck? Whatever did he mean?

Ah, yes: the damage unwittingly done—*Oh please*, thought I, *let it have been unwittingly done*—by Gréluchon when he'd back-handedly slapped me away from the surgical table. That inch-long cut on my neck, on the right side some two or three inches beneath the line of my jaw.

"Oh, really," said I, "it's nothing. I just—"

"You'll 'just' let the doctor have a look at it, lass," said Poole. "That's *just* what you'll do. Now 'op up on the bed like—"

It was the doctor's turn to interrupt. "Poole, won't you be so kind as to find Mademoiselle Ricau some sleeping clothes, a robe or some such . . ." *Mademoiselle Ricau?* Here was a first. How very strange Henry was behaving.

"Wherever I am to find such whatnot as *that*?" Poole was nothing if not blunt.

Said the doctor, "If I knew where such things were, Poole, I've have applied the verb *to get*, not *to find*." And then, rather more forcefully: "From Cézette, man! See what spare fripper-ies the girl has tucked away upstairs."

I heard Poole stomping up to the attic rooms, and—wearied, worn, worried as I was—still I can recall a slight measure of plea-sure at imagining Cézette being made to turn over her best nightgown to me.

"Sir, really, it's nothing." But now the doctor stood quite close, holding a candle so near my neck I feared he meant to cauterize the wound. "Sir, really!"

"You'll be going nowhere right now," said he. "You'll rest, right here. Doctor's orders." He was at once quite determined in saying so and yet distracted as well, seeming *drawn* to my wound. "Fascinating," said he, more to himself than to me. No diagnosis, this. "As if . . . as if from a steely hook, it is, so clean a cut."

"I . . . I don't even remember how I cut myself," said I, feeling my eyes flit away from his, fly about the room like birds. Like lies.

Doctor Jekyll looked up at me and twisted the corner of his lips. Not a smile, but rather something . . . *knowing.* And so I said nothing else. I sat silently by as he dressed the wound, trying somehow to still a pulse that was racing not only from the events of late hours but also from the doctor's near-indecent . . . proximity. Blessedly, an icy Poole soon returned to toss a lacy confection onto the foot of the bed.

"'Ere," said he, adding, "and she was none too 'appy about it, neither, might I say. 'Twas like taking a ball o' twine from a kitten."

"So show her the streets, then," said the doctor, so coldly I was shocked. "See how happy she'll be about *that.*" But then he seemed to remember it was me he was working upon, and amended his words so: "I mean to say you'll make amends to Cézette, won't you, Poole?"

Silence.

"*Won't* you, Poole?"

"I will if you say so, sir, yes. . . . It's me job to do *as I'm told.*"

"Good . . . Now hold this candle, steady, Poole. Just . . . there." And the doctor returned to his work, which now involved the application of some cold, numbing salve to my neck and the threading of a bent and overlong needle with some wiry, waxy black thread.

"It's quite a cut, Odile," said the doctor. "I'm afraid a bandage won't suffice, not at all. One or two stitches and you'll be right as rain."

What could I say? Such was the prognosis; such was the prescription; and such would be the procedure. After all, wasn't I lucky he hadn't already had Poole show *me* the streets? For the laboratory was a shambles, and my brother and I . . .

The doctor was some while setting the first of the stitches into my skin, and I saw it was because his hands still shook terribly. "Poole," he commanded, "my bag. Bring me my bag."

Poole set the doctor's black satchel on the end of the bed, and from it the doctor drew a bottle of blue pills. "Here," said he, handing me two, "these will calm you some." He bade Poole hand me a glass of water. Meanwhile, the doctor himself returned to his portable pharmacopoeia and none too subtly swallowed four pills of another sort, all but snorting as he washed them back with a snifter of brandy rather more politely provided him by Poole. A few moments more—moments in which Doctor Jekyll washed the wound, bathing my neck first in water and then some sanitizing tincture—and the doctor returned to his work, which I forbore as best I could, hoping Poole didn't slip (accidently on purpose), hit the doctor's elbow, and send the needle *through* my neck. Oh, but truthfully, no bodily pain could then have matched the pain I felt within.

Sutured and changed, I was to rest. Doctor Jekyll himself

tucked me into the plush bed, as though I were a child, while Poole stoked the fire. Again, I tried to explain, to apologize, but the doctor would have none of it.

"And by the way . . ." said Poole then from the shadows to which he'd retired, startling me ". . . whatever were you two up to in there? And what's become of that runty brother of yours? 'E's run off now, 'as 'e?"

"Poole," said Henry, coldly, "wait for me on the landing. And do *not* go into the laboratory. Is that clear?"

"It's as clear as your English typically is, sir, yes. But come now: Let me start setting the place to rights, long as I'm awake. I 'ave other things to do with me morning and—"

"I'll see to the laboratory myself. Is that *clear*, Poole?"

"Sir" was the servant's sole word of response; and then he left us.

Already the posts of Henry's bed were bending like black reeds in some ill-borne wind, and the lamp in his hand bore fire in the form of . . . bunnies? No, birds. No . . . Alas. The drugs were finding their full effect, and sleep was not far off. Sleep and forgetfulness; and so, I thought, *Let it come.* I closed my eyes and tucked my cheek into the cloudlike pillow, as pleasurable as . . . as the loss of all thought would soon be.

I had started to sink into sleep when all of a sudden I heard Doctor Jekyll and Poole conversing beyond the half-closed door, on the landing, in tones *most* urgent. Poole went stompingly downstairs, but the doctor . . .

What if he went into the laboratory now—as of course he

115

would—and saw not only the shambles Gréluchon and I had made of the place but also the remnants of the miscraft I'd conjured? What if he saw and took an interest in those racked tubes of blue brew still standing there? Vials four and five?

I bolted upright in bed.

My head was aswim, and my vision was none too clear owing to those blue pills I'd swallowed. Sleep was coming on, and fast. Indeed, now it seemed to me that the far wall—that wall separating the doctor's bedchamber from his laboratory— was winking at me, *winking*. For though a fire had been laid in the hearth there, only one sconce sitting atop and beside the mantel held a lit candle, now burned rather low. It all formed a face of fire which was, yes, winking.

The unlit sconce had had its hurricane glass lifted from it and set atop the mantel, it bore no candle now, and unless I was very much mistaken, its brass base was somewhat . . . askew. I focused the more. Yes, the circular brass base of the sconce was most certainly askew, like a picture gone cockeyed on its nail.

At first, having struggled to rise from the bed, groggy as I was, and gain my balance, I headed toward the bedchamber door. I'd return to the laboratory, summon what senses remained to me and somehow . . . lie, falsely explain what it was had disordered the room so. But then, halfway to the door, I stopped. *Could it be that . . . ?*

My blood went cold, but the thought that then came chilled me to rights, too. And so I went instead to the sconce and, yes, slowly, oh so slowly twisted it aside on its single pivot to reveal the peephole behind it. "No!" I breathed aloud.

No need to explain, Odile, he'd said. *No need at all.*

Indeed not: He'd seen it all as it happened! He'd been spying on us all the while!

I went up on tiptoe, set my eye to the peephole, and beheld, there, on the far side of the wall, standing at the laboratory table, Doctor Jekyll. He was tugging at his hair with his right hand—seemingly trying to pull his own panicky, disordered thoughts into place—while with the left he held test tubes four and five, deeply blue and full, and smoking still.

No! How foolish I'd been to leave them behind! Oh, but how dare Henry have betrayed me so? Spying like this. And for how long? How many nights had he watched me work? No wonder he'd taken such care to set me up just there, atop that table so perfectly set within his spying line of sight.

I had to do something, and fast. But what?

My mind was racing, but the doctor's own potion, or pills, was impeding ordered thought. I fell woozily back from the wall. I wiped away tears, and when I swallowed those that returned to my throat, my stitches pulled and brought even more tears. I returned to tiptoe, slid aside the sconce, and reset my eye to the peephole, oh but now . . . no one, nothing. *Where had he gone?* Surely he was still . . .

I blinked the more, and waited till the man might show himself or make himself heard; and while waiting for what seemed an eternity, I noticed that those tubes of brew numbered four

117

and five—which, in combination, would of course be stronger even than the sixth—were most definitely gone from the rack where they'd stood, *gone*. I may have cursed him aloud then, I cannot recall. Certainly I'd wanted to! But as I stood there willing, *wishing* the vials back into that now empty rack, I felt a breeze blow through the peephole, causing me to fall back slightly and blink, and when once again my vision was aright, I reset my eye to the hole and saw . . . nothing. *Blink, blink.* Again: nothing; but now it was a *different* nothing. Darkness, as though a wisp of storm cloud had come to occlude a moon. Then the cloud somehow cleared and the pupiled moon blinked. Here now was an eye set mere inches from mine.

We cannot have stood there, eye to eye, toe to toe but for the intervening wall, for three seconds before I fell back, fell back and down. Onto the floor.

It was then that I fainted, fell dead away.

CHAPTER SIX
Tending the Lie

I woke in Doctor Jekyll's bed, not knowing where I was, not remembering what had happened. Not at first.

"Comfy?" There stood Cézette, staring down at me where I lay. My shoulder was yet sore where she'd poked me into wakefulness. I suppose she'd come into the bedchamber as she did every morning, following Poole—whose job it was to wake and dress the doctor—to bring the doctor his breakfast and right the room, make the bed and whatnot. Of course, she was none too pleased to find me in the doctor's stead; and then suddenly it all began to come back to me and I . . .

Slowly I turned to see that the pillow beside mine was, blessedly, plump: No one had slept beside me . . . *with* me.

"How . . . ?" I began; but Cézette had already moved from the bedside to the window, where she now pulled back the heavy drape, not deigning to spare me the screech of rings on rod as, no doubt, she did the doctor. A thin wintry light filled the room. So too did those noises that the rags stuffed round the window's edge were meant to muffle: The day's bombardment had begun, and shells were landing none too distant from the doctor's door.

With a raised hand, I shielded myself from the sun. "How did I . . . ?" and I got no further before Cézette said, with a harrumph:

"You're asking *me*? *Alors*, all I know is that I was asked . . . no, I was *told* to come see if you were in need of anything." A pause. "Well?"

"No," I said, "thank you." And Cézette could not have made it to the door faster if the bedchamber had been afire. "Wait!"

She turned at the door, turned and stared expectantly from beneath her furrowed brow. . . . What now? Did I need anything? *Oui*, an explanation of how I'd ended up in Doctor Jekyll's bed, for one, as all I could recall was being eye-to-eye with him at that horrid peephole before fainting to the floor. And while she was at it, perhaps Cézette could tell me what had happened to my brother, my beautiful brother, and how long the spying had been going on, and and and . . .

But then I let my eye rove to where that golden sconce had swung back into place—were those new screws set into the now-immobile sconce?—and, as her eye followed mine without purpose, failing to alight upon the sconce, I understood that Cézette knew nothing of the spying. So it was I moved on to another of my countless questions:

"How . . . ?" was all I managed. I must have been fingering the frills and furbelows of the nightgown I wore, for Cézette understood and explained, thusly:

"*Oui*, that's mine. And you're welcome." The starch fell out of her stare, her shoulders too, and she took two steps nearer the bed. "All I know is it was two, maybe three in the morning when Poole"—pausing first to peer over her shoulder, she then wrinkled her nose as she repeated the name—"*Poole* started pounding on my door. I'd finally returned to sleep, thank you very much, and here he was rousing me to come down and settle you into bed . . . into this bed, *the master's* bed. He said you'd fainted."

"So it was you who undressed me and—"

"And who else might it've been, *mon amie*?" She gave me a knowing look, a not nice and all-too-knowing look. She needn't have worried: We were *not* friends, and I knew it as well as she. "He's not yet hired you your own lady's maid, has he?" Another harrumph, this one accompanied by a big puff of cheek and an eye roll. "Although I wouldn't be the least bit surprised, as he's provided you with everything else." She looked over her shoulder now, toward the door. "And you might as well tell me everything," said she, swiveling her gaze back to me, "as *he* . . . as *I* find out everything in time."

Whatever did *that* mean? Who was the "he" she was referring to? Doctor Jekyll? No: Poole, more likely. Regardless, I had more pressing concerns just then.

I slipped a hand under the bedclothes, to feel for . . .

"Yes," said Cézette, "what *is* that thing you wear? . . . Weird, if you ask me."

I certainly *hadn't* asked her, and wouldn't; but if weird was all she thought it was, I'd consider myself lucky. For I'd been wearing both the key to the waistlet and the waistlet itself the night prior, and if Doctor Jekyll had discovered as much and been so inclined, he might well have . . .

"It's . . . it's a sort of charm bracelet, is all. It was my mother's."

Motherless and now *aunt*less Cézette understood. She said nothing more. She might even have smiled sympathetically. *Somewhat* sympathetically. But lest I took her for a sister of sorts, she added, mysteriously, *"Merci bien.* You've spared me having to ask the armored man." She leaned nearer where I lay and, popping her eyebrows in a manner best suited to spooking a child, added: "There are no secrets here, Odile . . . for the armored man knows all." And then, pleased with her performance, she stood upright, smoothed her apron, and said:

"So then, I take it you can see to your own needs . . . such as they are."

"I can," said I, wondering what in the world she'd meant: *The armored man?* To whom was she referring? It seemed not the time to ask. "Thank you. And I shall return your . . ." but Cézette was already out the door. Once on the landing, I saw her stop before the open laboratory door and say, "She'll be here presently, sir."

I heard no response from within. Cézette went off unhappily, in a huff: Would the doctor *always* ignore her?

Thusly did I learn that Doctor Jekyll was present in his preferred workspace, waiting for me.

※

There'd be no slipping past the laboratory and up the stairs. Nor would I be bolting past the door, down the stairs, and out of the Jekyll manse as my brother had. Of that I'd lately become certain; for, though my mind was yet fogged from whatever soporific I'd been given—not to mention that roiling sea of emotions within me—I'd quickly realized that I could not run.

Where would I go in a city edging nearer civil war? How would I survive if I returned to the streets, now even more dangerous than they'd been before? How would I eat, and where would I sleep? Alas, my reasons were legion, and, yes, my having grown accustomed to comfort may have played its part, this I admit; but mostly what I wondered as I lay there waking in the doctor's bed was this: If I left Jekyll's home, how would Gréluchon know where to look for me? For still I believed he'd look for me, still I believed that my brother would come back to me. He had to! For how would *I* find him? *How?*

No, I'd not run. I'd stay. For now. Until such time as I'd be able *to follow, to find* Gréluchon if he did not return. And if lying was the cost of my survival, I'd find a way to pay.

So it was that I cooperated in the tending of the lie, the *living* of the lie, as it began to take shape the moment I rose from bed, dressed in what I'd been wearing the night before, and went to the laboratory door, the *new* laboratory door; for already the broken one had been replaced. And having seen the now-secured sconce, its newly set screws preventing its being swung on its pivot of old to reveal the peephole, I suspected some degree of denial from Doctor Jekyll as well. And so it was . . .

"Odile!" said he, turning toward me where I stood in the laboratory doorway. "Good morning!" He sat upon the very stool that my brother had sat upon hours earlier. He stared at me, perhaps waiting to take my lead. *If I lied, then he'd lie as well.* I let him wait. For my part, I stood staring not at Doctor Jekyll but at a laboratory showing no signs of the previous night's debacle. "Or should I say good afternoon?" asked the doctor now, words accompanied by an obviously rehearsed resorting to his pocket watch. "Hmm. Nearly noon. How did you sleep?"

"Soundly," said I; and well he knew it, for hadn't he sent me off into such a sleep so as to prowl the laboratory alone? And hadn't I slept through the installation of a new laboratory door and the sly work on the sconce as well? Not to mention the day's early shelling.

"Good, good," said he now. "Quite the night, that was. Eh?"

I nodded, said nothing more; and that was it: Thenceforth it would be as though *nothing had happened.*

Yes, of course, Gréluchon was gone; and though this was known by all, it was not spoken of. *Nothing* was spoken of, nor would it be. Starting then.

The look upon the doctor's face did give me pause as I stood in the doorway, so . . . unaffected did he seem by all he'd witnessed through the wall. Here he was, seeming so very *normal.* Soon I could see the effort this took, however; and no doubt maintaining this mask of normalcy required an effort equal to that he'd expended in setting right the nearly ruined laboratory. Had Poole played his part in that? I thought not, judging by the purplish half-moons that hung beneath the doctor's eyes: He'd not slept a wink. Yes, I stood there as if dumbstruck, wondering where all the detritus had been taken: the shattered glass, the broken apparatus, and, most of all, those fourth and fifth vials, which I'd left standing in that very same rack that now I saw had been returned to its place in the cabinet and . . .

Ah! Sly devil. He'd hung a framed periodic table over the laboratory side of the peephole. And so there went any last thought, any lingering hope, that the previous night had been but the worst of dreams. So too did my fast-forming plan of returning later to the laboratory to look for those distilled salts disappear—and I *had* seen the doctor with them in hand, had I not?—for the door's new hardware, its new lock, caught my eye as the weak wintry sunlight found and brightened its brass.

"Good morning," said I, finally, forbearing to add my usual "sir." He was no longer a *sir* to me, nor would he be *Henry*. He was no longer worthy of such signs of respect, of familiarity. I'd come to this conclusion neither by head nor by heart; rather, I knew it in my body, in my very bones. Indeed, the man repulsed me now, whereas before . . . *Enfin*, let him keep his scarlet scarves, his fancy food served upon his painted porcelain plates . . .

But then again: Had I not already decided I'd need to linger some while longer under his roof? I had. And so it'd be best not to let my disdain show. Best to . . . to take up the lie he was proffering and tend it in my turn.

"It *is* rather late, isn't it?" said I, feigning a yawn. "I'm sorry if I . . . if we made a mess." Quite the understatement, that; but I could think of nothing else to say.

"Not at all," said Henry. Then, silence. This was worse, far worse than . . . *awkward*. "You must be famished," said he, finally, and that was as near as he'd come to addressing the extraordinariness of that night. "Shall I ring up some luncheon?"

"No," said I, rather too emphatically; for even as he spoke Henry was reaching for the long cord that would set a bell to tinkling in the kitchen. The last thing I wanted then was the return of Cézette, or worse: Poole. It was difficult enough dealing with Doctor Jekyll. "I am not hungry. I'd like to . . . I'd like to return to my room, if I may."

Henry stood there with his hand still upon the cord, and he nodded. We shared a long stare, and for a moment it seemed he might speak—say something, *any*thing, of the strangeness he'd seen, or rather espied. But no: He simply smiled—rather sadly, it seemed to me: Was that *apology* playing at the edges of his smile?—and nodded his assent a second time. Whereupon I turned from the door, crossed the landing, and took to the stairs. I was climbing with increasing speed when Henry called out:

"Odile?"

Hearing his voice, I turned to see him standing in the laboratory doorway, staring up at me.

"Oui?" What I'd wanted to say was *Leave me be, liar!*

"He will come back, Odile. . . . We must hold to the hope that he will come back."

Hope? Oh, I had hope, all right; but doubtless it was of a different species than the doctor's. *I* hoped Gréluchon would survive out on the streets and then return, once again to be my brother, while Doctor Jekyll, for his part, cannot have hoped for more than a second shot at so strange a . . . *specimen.* Indeed, how thrilled the doctor must have been to discover such . . . *science*—if I may call it that—beneath his very roof. What plans might he already have for that pilfered potion? For no mere description of what he'd seen would suffice, no, no. Proof was needed, *required* by the Royal Society, surely. And said proof depended upon my brother's return; or, at minimum, upon my cooperation, my agreeing to do *again* what Henry had witnessed. Thusly did I wonder: Had I a measure of power over Henry? Perhaps so, for none but I could give him what he wanted, needed, *would have.* Of course, it was not long before I came to understand both the limits of that supposed power and the very real danger occasioned by the doctor's desire. The danger to *me.*

Alas, I said nothing in response to Henry's having mentioned Gréluchon and the hope *we* must hold to. I simply turned and took the stairs up to my attic room, leaving the doctor at my back, standing there in the laboratory doorway and holding to his infernal hopes.

Once upstairs, I fell to my knees and, scrabbling half under my cot, pried loose the floorboard that served as my secret spot. I unlocked the waistlet and slid it inside. And with that a dam gave way within, such that I fell crying onto the cot; and there I stayed for some while, intent upon my tears and longing for a shell to come whistling in from the surrounding hills and take my heart for its target. Until:

I understood what Cézette had said. *Of course!*

In such a household, each member tended their own secrets and lies. I had my loose floorboards, did I not? Poole? He had his suit of armor.

I waited, and waited some more; and in the small hours of the night I snuck down to the second-floor landing and confirmed the suspicion.

It was hollow, of course, that suit of armor I'd first seen on my maiden visit to the mansion (and had all but ignored since).

My heart pounding—*Was I being watched? Was this a trap, set by Cézette only to be sprung by Poole?*—I carefully, as quietly as I could, tapped the suit here, there, and everywhere till finally, low on the left leg, I found where it was most decidedly *not* hollow. *Did I dare?* I did: I bent that leg at the knee—and blessedly, Poole kept that particular joint well-oiled—lifted a hinged flap, felt within, and, *yes*, withdrew a black cardboard cylinder. I recognized it at once: The doctor's well-aged Scotch—which he enjoyed in private and which Poole no doubt sipped on the sly—came in those cylinders.

My hands were trembling so badly I feared I might drop the cylinder, light though it was, containing naught but . . . paper. I'd removed its top to disclose, yes, papers of sundry sort secreted within. *Secreted*, indeed.

I scurried upstairs; and I daresay there was never a mouse more content at having run its maze and found its cheese. Oh, but then I slipped the furled contents from the cylinder, flattened them on my floor, and started to read; and soon that maze seemed more a mousetrap.

There was correspondence sent from a London address, from one Gabriel John Utterson, Esquire, pertaining to the last will and testament of . . . Well, at first, with a fright, I thought it pertained to the death of Doctor Jekyll—*Whatever could Poole be plotting?*—but soon I realized the death, the *imminent* death in question was that of Henry's father. Did Henry even know about all this? About his estranged father's illness and these plans for the disposition of an estate whose monies reached into the millions? Or was Poole parceling out this knowledge as it suited his own nefarious purposes? Rather the latter, I reasoned.

There were articles from all the London papers recounting Doctor Jekyll's fall (from a rather great height, it seemed) owing to his quite particular research . . . none of which pertained to matters of the eye, might I add. Indeed, it seemed the doctor harbored a downright Frankensteinian interest in "postmortem animation," as one paper put it. Another referred to his research in the "transcendental" as "an affront to all the *solid* sciences and practitioners thereof." What, exactly, did the doctor hope to "transcend"? Alas, on the day Doctor Henry Jekyll had finally sought to impress his own, less than "solid" science upon the Royal Society, well, yes, he'd fallen far and fast unto ruin. A scandal, indeed. No wonder he sought the salts so: They were indeed *proof* of all he'd proposed and presented (so ignominiously) regarding the . . . *mutability* of man.

Were these articles and letters—seething letters, threatening letters from both Doctor Jekyll's peers and persons representing this or that capital-s Society, some of whom alluded to "legal actions already undertaken"—a form of insurance for Poole? Blackmail? Presumably so; for I also found sheets upon which Poole (stupidly) had practiced *both* Jekyll signatures, senior and junior. Further:

There were deeds to London lands and property *in Poole's name*, along with correspondence bearing on same from lawyers other than the Jekylls' Mister Utterson.

There were deposit books from sundry banks wherein (no doubt) Poole had squirreled away all he'd been able to pilfer from the house funds during his decades of service.

There were even documents—receipts, mostly, for amounts paid out—that seemed to speak of Cheffy's having been beholden to Poole and all but indentured to Doctor Jekyll.

And there were letters on pink paper that still held their perfume, addressed to Doctor Jekyll and beginning, typically, with such supplicating words as "If you pity me . . ." "If you can but recall the feelings we once shared . . ." et cetera. These letters from a long-ago lover I didn't care to read. Not at length anyway. And I could only wonder if the doctor himself had even read them . . . or had Poole "disposed" of such matters himself?

All this and more—insurance, certainly; blackmail, probably— but I could no longer linger on the lot of it once I made a far more significant discovery. This was a letter addressing my own precarious position regarding Poole, which I copied as quickly as I could, in as steady a hand as the situation allowed; and thusly can I include the horrid thing here, in its entirety:

Sir,

I write at the request of one Monsieur Jean-François Duval, presently in the employ of the Zoological House of the Jardin des Plantes. As the good monsieur wishes to follow up on your recent converse of 2 January, yet hasn't the English to do so, and what with you being a foreigner with no use for French, I write at his behest. Please know that M. Duval is at my elbow as I translate and transcribe his words, and his alone. THUS:

My good fellow, I write in the hope and trust that you will forgive me my ill manners of some days past. Understand that I was yet beside myself, which is to say upset, at the bloody scene I'd come upon in the primate house the day before. Understand, further, sir, that those

131

beasts are dear to me, to a one; and that seeing such Horrors of late in that Happiest of Habitats led me to tears I'm yet hard-put to suppress. Tears and questions, too. As many questions, sir, as you posed during your recent visit.

As I told you on these very premises, sir, there was nothing, *nothing* in his history to explain to my satisfaction the murderous rage that overcame my Tito on New Year's Day (as passed). My Tito, yes; for them chimps have long been brothers to me, their keeper. As you saw for your own self, sir, me and the missus lead a nice life in the keeper's cottage. (Which life, by the way, has been made more nice of late by your gift of Irish tea and them sweetmeats so very hard to come by these days; and so remiss I'd be, not to mention subject to the Wrath of my woman, should I fail to thank you here, sir, for both those comestibles and your cash, which latter is always welcome.) All that said, sir, neither your kindnesses nor passing time allow me to answer your recent query (recv'd: 9 January) with any news that is new. I can only repeat what I told you the day of your visit, and so I say again:

Tito was a good chimpanzee, sir; and never once did I see him exhibit behavior that hinted of his being capable of the *murder by mauling* of his cage-mate, Champagne (that was), himself of a Spirit that earned him that bright, bubbly name. Sadly, both of these former friends have now gone to their rest; for there was nothing for it but to bury what remained of Champagne and to put Tito down, by bullet, when this horrible year was but two days old. Me, who used to feed Tito by hand, sir, I could not even approach him; and when finally he took hold of little Shaza, well, as I say, there was nothing for it but to put the chimp down.

That's all, sir. Other than to report—because you ask—that the remaining chimps are yet shy and still not their old selves. It is as if they've seen a right ghost. Ghost or not, I cannot say. But what they saw with their very own eyes, poor creatures, on New Year's Day, well, it *wasn't* Tito, of that I'm certain. He was "off" some-how, sir, like good wine that's run to vinegar; though the How & Why of it I fear we will never know.

As you ask, too, after any Evidence that may have been turned up, I add here that there has been none. Other than that residual powder, that silver salt, of which (I believe) you have some grains in your possession; which is good, sir, as the rains have washed what remained of it away since your last visit. You ask after Witnesses, too, and so I say: There have been none. No one but Tito and the Good Lord know what passed that day in the *singerie* and (forgive me, sir) neither of them is talking.

Yours,
J.-F. Duval
Gardien des Singes

P.S. The missus tells me to add that you, sir, are welcome in our humble cottage anytime.

P.P.S. One more thing, sir, which I'd have forgotten but for the missus's reminding me just now. A girl did come around asking questions, just as you said she might. Not two hours after your own visit, in fact. No more than sixteen, she was, and fitting your description hand-to-glove. A most deucedly curious creature, if you'll pardon my saying so. But as you requested, sir, I told her nothing. Nothing at all. Such that she went off in quite the huff, and I've not seen her since.

At least now I knew why the guardian had kept so stonily silent when I'd gone back to the zoo. Poole had beaten me back there. *Zut!* I thought to tear the letter to shreds, but no: If need be, Poole would simply bribe Monsieur Duval into writing another. And if ever I needed to access again his . . . *treacherous trove*, well, best to keep the secret of its existence to myself. For now. But oh, that damnable man!

Not only had he been nosing around the *singerie*, as supposed, he'd somehow managed to take a sampling of the salts! Off the bars? Off the floor of the *singerie* itself? No matter, that. What mattered was this:

If ever the connection was made between events at the zoo and our work in the laboratory, by either Poole or Doctor Jekyll, alone or in tandem, then my failed witchery would be discovered and I'd be the worse for it, by far. Who knew what Doctor Jekyll would do? Would he be encouraged, even more driven to discover my secrets? Perhaps lying and spying was the least of it; and if so, what next? As for the bribing, blackmailing Poole, well, if he put any more pieces of the puzzle into place, he'd have a completed picture, one with which he could betray me *publicly*, taking it to the Paris police, just as he was no doubt preparing a case against me that he'd present *privately* to Doctor Jekyll, as it suited him. He'd stop at nothing if he truly believed I stood between Henry and his inheritance, between Poole himself and access to the Jekyll millions. *Bref*: Who knew what might come of all this dark knowledge compiled by Poole? I knew only that it boded ill for me.

Enfin, I replaced all those incriminating papers in the cylinder, precisely as I'd found them, crept downstairs, and returned the tube via the armored knee (which bent more creakily this time, so loudly it seemed certain to rouse the whole house!). I then retook to my room, where I worried away what remained of the night.

Chapter Seven
Civil Wars

Though my heart was yet hammering and I'd a headache from all, *all* I'd found in the armored man and read by the light of a first, a second, and finally a third dying candle, somehow I fell asleep. It was some while later—I did not know the hour, but I saw that the sun hadn't risen very high—when I heard a scratching at my door. Not a knock, but a scratching. As from a claw.

"Grel? Is it you?" I was up in a trice, flipping back the flimsiest of locks.

It was not he, of course; rather, it was Cézette, who stood now proffering a banded roll of bills. Perhaps she had knocked, and I'd not heard her. Regardless, I saw now the preferred kitchen pet at her ankle, the striped she-cat, Tigre, still scratching at my door, scratching till I nudged her back with my foot, sending her, mewling, to twist herself around Cézette's dainty ankles.

I dared not say a word about my discovery of the night prior; and, blessedly, Cézette must have thought me too daft or distracted by my courting of Doctor Jekyll to have made much of her hint regarding the suit of armor. So, instead:

"What is this?" And my curiosity was genuine; for Cézette had grabbed my hand and set the bills within, folding my fingers into a fist. It was as if she could not trust herself with the money a moment longer, and indeed I wondered how much of it, if any, was already missing. "What am I supposed to do with . . . ?" With Doctor Jekyll's money; for surely it was that.

"The *master*," said Cézette with undue emphasis, "says you are to take to the streets when you're well enough and procure whatever you can . . . whatever you *want*. He said he's heard tell of mutton somewhere. . . . Brabant's, I think it was," she added with a shrug, and I saw she'd considered not passing on the master's tip, thusly sabotaging my mission.

"Thank you," said I. Then I gestured to where her nightdress hung over the back of my chair, behind me. "I'll launder that and—"

"I'd rather you didn't," said she, looking down at my half-gloved hands, all too pointedly. "I'd rather you not handle it at all." She held out her hand now. "May I?"

"Fine," said I. "*Fine.*" I took the nightdress off the chair, and as soon as I stood within reach, she snatched it away. Then she was gone, gone before I could slam the door upon her button nose.

❦

He was cagey, Doctor Jekyll; and right he'd been, too, in assuming that I'd take his money, his *order of mutton*, and speed to Julien, enlisting the butcher's boy in the search for my brother. That is precisely what came to pass, albeit a bit . . . slowly. For I needed time *alone* and out of that house; too, I needed time to think before seeing Julien.

Once again, I had fast resolved to tell Julien *all and everything* (. . . excepting, perhaps, the part about my having spent the night in the plush, silken surrounds of Henry Jekyll's bed); yet in my head I heard, and *re*heard, a most improbable script. How very strange it all seemed when wedded to words!

Rehearsing my speech—and indeed I hoped to tell the night's tale straight through, without hesitation or tears, and keeping mention of Doctor Jekyll to a minimum—I wandered the backstreets. The occasional shell burst far to the north, and rifle fire rang to the east; but still I took care to steer clear of any stray soldiers I saw. And all the while I looked for Gréluchon in every shadowed recess, around every bend.

Having cut through the gardens of the Hôtel de Sully, tucked into the corner of the Place des Vosges, very near Doctor Jekyll's rented mansion, I came out onto the rue Saint-Antoine, passing rather too quickly from the quiet of its courtyard to the mayhem of marketry. The few still-open shops had laid out their wares streetside on carpets they could quickly roll and secrete away if the war came closer. Of course, other shopkeepers dared not flaunt their wares so, but rather displayed their delicacies—such as they were—behind thick windows. One shop, on the rue Saint-Paul, had piled in its window, pyramidally, several tins of foie gras wrapped in blue ribbon, *silk* ribbon. It seemed a most insolent show. Proof to the poor that, yes, the rich were yet provisioned.

I felt Doctor Jekyll's money in my apron pocket, pressing upon my body as though it were a bandage. More than once I thought about tucking it into the palm of someone seemingly in need—and that meant anyone, really; but I did not do it. Instead, I continued on my slow, wandering way toward Deboos et fils.

I crossed the Seine, then the Ile Saint-Louis, and I walked toward the Sorbonne. (*Not* toward Les Halles. Not yet.) Up near the Pantheon the streets were bald, all but bare; and though some pavers had been put to purpose in the building of barricades, others, I supposed, had been pried up for no purpose at all, mere vandalism. And those vandals would soon be ready to revolt. The time was nearing. I'd heard as much from Gréluchon back before he'd . . . alas, such *anger* there'd been then in his voice, his feeble, boyish voice.

I descended the rue Soufflot, putting the great dome of the Pantheon at my back. All about me, the buildings bore the scars of war, as if it were a pox: bare spots, here and there, where a shell had had its effect; elsewhere the bombs had had an even greater effect, such that balconies hung crookedly across buildings, seeming like black sutures sewn into the stone as mine had been sewn into my skin.

Finally I began doubling back toward the river, toward the

right bank beyond and Les Halles, walking through the shattered glass on the sidewalks as though it were puddled water.

Nearer Les Halles, nearer Julien, there were carts in the streets; but it was not as it had been in the early days of our arrival, when La Poulette had ruled this marketing roost. Now a few of those food carts of old still bore provisions, yes—gray, multi-eyed potatoes; or turnips selling for an extortionary eight sous per pound; or pies whose meat was of dubious origin— but other carts now trundled the dead to a fast and too often anonymous burial. Upon one such cart I saw not a dead but a dying man, staring skyward. It seemed as though he sought shapes among the clouds; but then the cart's back wheel took a rut and the man's head turned, such that now he seemed to be staring at me, *at me*, and I could see where shrapnel had all but halved his head.

Oh, Julien. *Where was he?* Blessedly, I found him fast, for he answered my secret knock. He stepped out into the alley with a *shh*, lest his parents hear us, and seemed none too surprised when I fell, crying, into his arms. And his next shush was of an entirely different sort, speaking not of secrecy but of succor. Of comfort. Of love.

～

Of course, as soon as I saw him I'd abandoned my script. And a quarter-hour later—it was a quarter-hour of heaving sobs and half-nonsense, but never mind that—suffice to say that soon I'd told Julien all that had happened. And once again he was true to that tacit vow: *I am here. I will help.*

He'd taken me to a café at the corner of the rues Tique-tonne and Montorgueil. He'd ordered me a tall glass of some-thing; and though whatever it was burned its way through me, such that I thought myself about to breathe fire, it did calm me. . . . Calm. Everyone seemed so impossibly *calm*, either seated at the tiny tables or passing before us, going about what business there was to go about. At the curb, the proprietor's young son knelt before a window box into which he was set-ting the season's first geraniums, which later would hang upon the café, seeming like bursts of blood. Were they all in denial of the *death* there'd been, of the death to come? Or were they simply focused on survival? The answer, I know now, was both; for sometimes the denial of death is requisite to survival.

And it was at that café that Julien—sensible, sweet Julien—listened to all I said, telling me in his turn what I ought to have known myself.

"Odile," said he, "answer me this: What would an angry boy like Gréluchon do if suddenly he found himself unaccountably strong?"

The answer was plain: *He'd fight!* Gréluchon, in his present state, would throw in with the rebels who'd lately been spurred into action by that Prussian parade. Of course he would! He had long wanted to fight the Prussians, and now he'd want to fight the traitorous French forces headquartered at Versailles. He'd been all but blind and too weak to take up arms for the war and first Siege; oh, but now, *un*blinded and newly . . . brut-ish, well, he'd play his part in the second. And no doubt he'd be *most* welcome among those rebel forces now massing on the highest hill of Montmartre, stockpiling arms, readying (it was said) to somehow strike back against Versailles, against the government that had surrendered so easily to the Prussians, brokering such a pathetic "peace" and then training its guns against those Parisians who'd wanted no part of it.

I was recalled from my reasoning when Julien slapped his palm upon the tabletop, rattling our glasses. "Of course!" said he.

"What is it, Julien? *What?*"

He was staring off into the middle distance, squinting even, as if trying to focus on a vision, a memory. "It was him! It *must* have been him."

"You've . . . *seen* him? You've seen Gréluchon?" I clamped both hands on to Julien's arm, hard. "Tell me!"

"I . . . I can't be sure, of course," said he, "but after your description, after realizing that *of course* Grel would join the battle if finally able to fight, I remembered . . ."

"What, Julien? Speak!"

"Just yesterday, it was. Yesterday morning. I'd gone out into the alley to leave a bag of garbage for the carters and . . . and someone stepped from the shadows, startling me."

"It was Gréluchon? Do you think it was really—"

"I didn't think so at the time, no. Of course not."

And this made sense: Gréluchon was hardly recognizable now, not even to one who knew him as well as Julien did.

Again he slapped the table. "But now that I think about it,

and if he's changed as much as you say . . . *Mais oui!* He was wearing the red trousers of a guardsman, Odile! I see it now!"

"Did he approach you, say anything? Did you—"

"No, no. I . . ." Julien stopped, but it seemed I heard his unspoken words: He'd recoiled from the creature, as anyone would. "I'm sorry, Odile. It's just that . . ."

"I understand, Julien," said I, newly saddened by my own admission. "I understand perfectly." And I did. "But what happened. Tell me!"

"He must have come looking for food, which makes perfect sense. Where else would he go? To whom else would he turn, right?" I nodded in agreement, for it did seem sensible that Grel would return to Deboos et fils, where first we'd found food, where first we'd found a friend in Paris. "But when I . . . when I waved him away . . . I'm sorry, Odile, but I waved him away!" Julien's violet eyes were glistening now. "I . . . I waved him away like I'd wave away a stray dog begging for scraps."

I said again, "I understand, Julien. I do." Oh, but it was all I could do to contain my own tears now. Had I lost my only lead on the whereabouts of my brother? No, I had not; for:

Julien stood suddenly, staring down at me where I sat grasping my now-empty glass with a trembling hand, and said, "Come. Let's find him." And when he held out his own hand, saying with increased urgency, *"Come!"* . . . well, I stood up so quickly I overturned my chair. Some stared, but what did I care?

And so hand in hand we headed north, toward Montmartre.

Our progress through the streets was slow—barricades were

being built here and there, and we sought to avoid bands of soldiers from both sides—but still we made it up into Montmartre safely and with the sun still high in the sky.

And once we arrived atop the butte, that hill atop which Montmartre sits, staring down over the city of Paris, I knew that peace was indeed long past. My personal peace (such as it was) may have ended that night in Doctor Jekyll's laboratory, but the city's peace was long over as well. It was as though war hung upon the very air, a horrid, heavy scent. I remembered it all too well from the first days of the Siege, some months earlier.

Civil war was brewing, and battle lines were (literally) being drawn. The newly federated forces—those disparate bands of National Guardsmen who'd joined forces in defense of the city—were carting their cannons, amassing their sundry weapons of warfare. Les Fédérés were readying for war, civil war, against the regular forces headquartered at Versailles.

Alas, *that* war had not yet begun in earnest. No Parisian blood had yet been spilled in the streets by other Parisians; but before it devolved to that—brother against brother, waging a war within our own walls—I had best find my own brother.

Those few people who stopped for us in the streets knew nothing of the boy I described. Even those less bent on self-preservation and willing to help us in our search were unable to do so. Some shrugged, while others excused themselves, sadly, and seemed close to shedding tears to match my own. One woman, clutching a brick of bread from which I saw straw filler protruding, like whiskers on a kitten, observed that Montmartre had become crowded with unsavory "types," the imminent war having drawn young men as dung does flies. Her own boys had been away from home for days, said she, but had lately come home newly caparisoned in guardsman's garb and in the company of other boy soldiers never before seen in the *quartier*. It was the coming of all these strangers, said the woman, looking us over, head to toe, that had been the worst of it . . . "so far." And then she was off, though she did manage to toss back a *"Bon courage,"* as one would toss a bone to a dog.

Finally it was Julien, listening to me describing Grel for the umpteenth time, who brought the harshest of realities home.

"Odile, that boy you're describing, he . . . *That* Grel doesn't exist any longer. I mean, you are describing your brother *as he was*, and as he was when healthy, before events in that . . . that *Jekyll's* laboratory." How Julien hated to even say the name Jekyll! "You're describing a boy of long, long ago, not . . ." And he kindly let his sentence trail away.

Of course, Julien was right: I was looking for a person who existed only in my mind, in my heart and in my memories, and *that* person was nowhere to be found upon the streets of the city. The tow-headed boy who'd been at my side all his life, my baby brother. . . . Yet having realized my error, I found I hadn't the words to describe Gréluchon *as he was*, presently.

Nonetheless, I tried a few times more. I even approached a group of boys who were milling about with menace, too young to enlist but old enough to contribute to the coming troubles, but the lot of them looked at me as though I were crazed. Which perhaps I was.

Again, it was Julien who called me back to reason. "We came up here assuming Grel has thrown in with the rebels. We came up here in search of a *guardsman*, did we not?"

I nodded.

"So then, let's see if we're right. . . . *Allez*, to the source!" It was a sort of comic rallying cry, I suppose, meant to bolster my spirits.

The next time we came across some uniformed guardsmen, we approached them (having first observed them from a distance and adjudged them sober, or at least sober enough). In truth, it was Julien who approached them while I hung back in the shadows.

I watched as Julien puffed his chest with false pride and asked (as he'd said he would) where a willing recruit could go to sign up to protect Paris from . . . well, let me simply say he'd acquired quite the vocabulary among the merchants of Les Halles.

"Follow me," said Julien then, the named place being but one block distant. And so it was that soon I stood outside a low-slung, barrackslike building as Julien prepared to go inside to enlist in the National Guard. Except, of course, he had no intention of *actually* enlisting.

We both stood outside the building a short while and watched the line of raggedy men waiting to go inside, to enlist in the Guard. By our calculations, that line moved at the rate of one newly enlisted guardsman every three minutes. Julien calculated further, and thusly did he determine that he'd need nine—"*Non!* Ten. Make it ten minutes before you barge in, Odile."—ten minutes then, after which I was to act a role we'd no time to rehearse. Ten minutes, reasoned Julien, ought to be time enough for him to approach and peruse the register before having to set down his own name (fictive though it would be).

And so, precisely ten minutes passed before I made my debut.

"There you are, you *rat*!" I fairly bellowed it, such that all eyes were upon me now. I'd blown into the barracks like the most ill of wifely winds, shrewish to the extreme, having first peered in the one window to see that Julien was indeed approaching the register. Such was my agreed-upon cue.

"I've looked all over for you, you . . . *bâtard*!" Julien had taught me other *gros mots*, but they fell from my head and I resorted to that stand-by. "Now I know you're in here somewhere." I squinted at the assembled soldiers, playing blind-as-a-bat, or nearly so. "Do you think you can go off soldiering, willy-nilly, as you please, leaving me at home with two *petits* and"—and here I clutched at a fast-deflating ball we'd found in the streets, and which I'd stuffed up under my blouse—"and a third about to drop? Answer me!"

Ooh la la, sang the soldiers in chorus, one adding, "Whoever you are, my friend, you'd best answer the lady. And fast."

"You need balls for the Guard, *mon vieux*," said another would-be soldier to no one in particular, "and it seems someone else has hold of yours." There was laughter now as I barreled blindly from man to man.

Julien didn't look up from the register, and so for a while the milling men didn't know whom I addressed. I was careful to give no clues, at first; for it was only under cover of my sightless charade—groping my way around the room, bumping into things—that Julien could scan the names in the book to see if Gréluchon had indeed enlisted. And it was all proceeding as planned; which meant that I'd home in on Julien only when he gave me the agreed-upon sign (a wink, we'd determined, rather unimaginatively).

Alas, no wink. It seemed Julien would hover over that register another hour! And so I was left to carry on like *une folle*. A crazy woman. As the assembled turned to one another, trying to determine who it was that this harpy harped upon, and all shrugged their *Not me, Not me*, I had no choice but to delve deeper into my character (as it were) and cause an even greater commotion.

Indeed, what followed should have earned me a lasting fame upon the stage, or at least a chorine's role at the Comédie Française.

Tears. I turned them on like I didn't know I could. (My many tears of late had all been true.) And I proceeded to spit forth such curses as to curl the hair, for now Julien's tutoring all came back to me.

All present were enjoying the spectacle, the spectacle that was *me*. I even thought I saw Julien swallow back a smile as he hunched over the ledger.

Now I began to truly stalk the soldiers like a lean and most determined lioness, one by one, squinting up into their faces. "You? Nah! . . . Where is he? I know you're in here, Esteban?" . . . *Esteban?* Wherever had *that* come from? Decidedly *un*-Parisian, it was a name from nearer home, from nearer Spain.

And all the while I kept sneaking looks at Julien, waiting for that wink. When finally it came—*finally!*—I let loose a great, "Aha!" and pounced upon him, saying to all and sundry, "You don't want him anyway. He drinks like a fish and lies like a rug!" Exclaiming so, I nearly delivered myself of a third *petit*, then and there, but blessedly I caught the ball before it dropped; though I did play that unexpected turn for all it was worth, acting as though the ball-baby *had* dropped, and delivery was imminent. Which, of course, achieved the desired effect: The guardsmen-in-charge hurried us all too happily from the barracks so that our baby might be born . . . *elsewhere*, anywhere but there upon the barracks floor.

In the hubbub, I did not forgo the opportunity to twist Julien's ear. *Really* twist it. For he *had* been smiling, I was sure of it now; and I was sure, too, that he'd left me to play the shrew longer than was strictly necessary.

I didn't let go of his ear till I'd dragged him from the barracks, pen still in his hand. Actually, I didn't let go of his ear till I'd dragged him down the street and around the corner, *then* I released him, or rather *it*. His pinkened ear looked like a slice of dried pear that had been run through a wringer. "Well?" I asked.

Despite his pain, he couldn't help but smile fully now. "Yes, yes, I got it; but . . ."

"But what?"

He paused, rubbing his ear and hopping foot to foot against the pain. "But, really, Odile . . . *Esteban?*"

I'd not laughed in so very long. It felt good. It was my turn to shrug, and so I did so while birthing forth the ball, which rolled lopsidedly away, coming to rest against a basket from which a bemused kitten popped up like the proverbial weasel. Which, of course, only redoubled our laughter.

"I've no idea where that came from," I said, hardly able to stand up straight. For his part, Julien was doubled over despite the (temporary) damage I'd done to his ear. When I could, I kissed that pathetic appendage in apology, and was ashamed to feel it so horribly hot beneath my lips. Had I done that, *truly?* Alas, for whatever reason—guilt, love, or something less—let me say that I'd never felt for a man the way I felt for Julien then, at that all too short-lived moment in a backstreet of Montmartre.

And it was short-lived indeed.

"We were right," said Julien in due course. "He has signed up with the Guard."

And suddenly it seemed like nothing would ever be funny again.

"He signed up early yesterday morning," said Julien, "to judge by the line in the day's register. His was the first name; but . . ."

"But *what?*"

"Well . . ."

"What is it?" I was fairly wild, though now I cannot say if that was owing to relief, great relief that Grel yet had the presence of mind to actually sign himself up with the Guard, or fear that the little brother of my memories had enlisted as a soldier on the very eve of war.

"It's nothing . . . perhaps," said Julien; "but come. Let's sit." And so we settled at a café, at an unsteady, teetering table, ordering two coffees. "No," amended Julien, calling back the server, "make that wine. *Deux verres de vin rouge*."

How well he knew me. Though I was *most* impatient to hear what it was he had to say, he knew to distract me for a moment, lest I overreact. And indeed I'd come off the boil a bit by the time our wine arrived and I asked again, "What is it, Julien? Tell me."

"Gréluchon is right-handed, is he not?"

I nodded.

"Odd." Julien threw back his wine at once and ordered two more. "Drink up," he said to me before going on: "What's odd is . . . Well, it was Gréluchon's name I saw, of that I'm certain; but the signature was strange. He'd used a back-slanting, left-handed script. And the address he gave . . ."

"He gave an address?" I was excited. I hadn't realized a new recruit would have to give an address, though of course now it stood to reason. "What address?"

Julien told me, reading what he'd hastily written upon a torn-away corner of the register itself, copying directly from Gréluchon's entry.

It was the same address we'd sometimes used while staying

in the catacombs, an aboveground address; and for the privilege of accessing it—as, indeed, we never had: *What need had we of an address?*—we'd had to shell out two sous extra to Timon of Athens. Hearing the address, well . . .

"Why are you crying, Odile? We're that much closer to finding Gréluchon. Now we know where he's staying and—"

I held up my hand, stopping Julien's speech. And I simply shook my head, *Please, say no more.*

I was overwhelmed by this news. Not of the address, no. It was rather more than that.

Enfin, owing to all I'd witnessed in the laboratory, I'd begun to wonder if perhaps I had lost Gréluchon to the salts entirely, that my brother had been wholly supplanted by a . . . a *beast*, a being for which I had no better name. And I'd wondered if his mind would devolve as his body had? If so, would he even remember me if, *when* I saw him again?

But now that I knew he'd signed up for the Guard by using our shared address of old, well, his mind, his memory, must be intact. So too must all our shared memories remain just that: *Shared.* It was this that gave me hope, a hope that overwhelmed me as I sat at that café table beside Julien, my hand trembling such that I could not take up my second glass of wine, badly though I wanted it. Alas, I had not lost my brother, the last of my blood, changed though he may be; and now all that remained was to find him. Somehow.

As for his sudden left-handedness, I took it for nothing more than further proof of his *otherness*. Best to simply focus on finding him. But finding Gréluchon would be no easy feat in Paris at the best of times, and this certainly wasn't that.

Before I knew it, I was able to lift my glass, for Julien had stilled my hand in his as he sat beside me, so supportively silent; and the wine went down well.

I gathered myself, eventually; but my (relative) calm was short-lived.

"What if Grel *has* gone back to Timon up in Nouvelle Athènes? That world is warlike in peacetime, never mind now. And what if Grel . . . ?"

I couldn't finish my sentence, so worried was I that Grel, in his present state—whatever *that* was—might try to exact revenge for those untold slights and insults we'd suffered at the hands of Timon of Athens when we'd rented from him our corner of the catacombs. Gréluchon was nothing if not a holder of grudges.

"You can only worry about so much, Chérie," said Julien when I'd voiced this latest concern. He ordered us another round of wine and began to ask about food. He said I wasn't ready to head back onto the streets just yet; and, impatient though I was, I supposed he was right. "Worry about the things you can control."

"But I really think we should head over that way and see . . ." I let my words trail away, for I was happy enough to not have Julien balk at the "we." And I was certainly in no hurry to reenter that world—Timon's world, the catacombs—from which I'd tried so hard to extricate us, Grel and myself.

"Let's think about this, Odile. Is it really a good idea to seek out this Timon now?" He nodded upward, skyward, referencing the twilit hour. And though Julien knew far less of that literal underworld than I did (lucky him), right he was in assuming that Timon's realm would just be coming alive. Indeed, twilight was when all the undead denizens of the catacombs rose to do who-knew-what kind of misdeeds. "Won't we be better off finding Timon—and hopefully Gréluchon, too—at first light?"

Julien was right. We stayed put, ordering two bowls of broth—which was all that was available and which I cannot, *cannot* refer to rightly as soup, its having been but water in which some chicken bones had been bathed, and in which a lone onion now bobbed—and some more wine. (Wine is all that was never in short supply during the sieges. Wine and coffee, which made for an even more jittery citizenry.) When I asked the server if he had any bread to go along with the broth, he simply sighed and looked at Julien, who (irritatingly) apologized on my behalf. "Bread . . ." said the server as he turned on one worn heel and walked away, saying, "*Non*. Not for months."

Of course, they were right. *Bread?* Had I actually asked for bread? Oh, I felt so horribly . . . *foreign* then, as if I'd just fallen into Paris from one of those hot-air balloons or something. Or worse: As if I'd been living out the Siege in a millionaire's rented mansion in the Marais, with food aplenty.

It was as though Julien read my mind just then.

"And how *is* the good doctor these days?" asked he, eyeing the bandage on my neck.

"Not good," said I. "Not good at all."

"Unwell, do you mean?" He checked his hopes somewhat before adding: "Ill?"

Unwell? Was Doctor Jekyll unwell at present? I could only wonder. Much depended, I supposed, on what he'd done with the potion he'd pilfered from the laboratory, vials four and five. "His health is fine," is what I decided to say, ". . . as far as I know. I was referring instead to the state of his—"

"Conscience?"

I nodded, though in truth I wondered about the state of his soul as well. If he'd indulged, if he'd salted himself, or *over-*salted himself, well . . . But, as Julien had counseled, I'd do best to worry about what little I could control.

"Oui," said I, "his conscience." And oh, how I wish I'd stopped there, but instead I added, under my breath, "And Lord knows the man has enough to be sorry for." I'd only in-tended to reference the "bad things" I'd already told Julien about; but he interpreted my words differently, and he nearly overturned our table as he stood, stood as though a randy Henry Jekyll had just come into the café calling out my name.

"No, no, Julien," said I, trying to calm him, "it's nothing like that, nothing like that at all." Surely I blushed at realizing what he'd thought but it was my trust the doctor had abused, not my honor, not my . . . *person.*

"What is it you're referring to then, Odile?" Still he stood, staring down at me. The flesh of his cheeks had now reddened to match that of his mangled ear.

"Julien," said I, extending my hand to touch his, "please sit."

He did. Whereupon I promised to tell him *all*, tell him what it was I'd left out of my earlier recounting. I told Julien about the spying again, yes; but now I told him how finding that peep-hole leading into the laboratory had made me feel filthy, as if I had indeed been violated. This proved a most unfortunate choice of words, and Julien once again grew angry.

"How then can you even *consider* going back there . . . *back to him*?" And indeed I had mentioned, rather offhandedly, what I took to be the day's obvious course: I would return to the Jekyll mansion that very evening.

Now, granted, these plans may well have seemed nonsensical to Julien, and indeed to anyone else who might have heard my reasoning, but to me the plan was simply that: *reasonable.*

I'd tend the lie alongside Doctor Jekyll until Gréluchon could be found and somehow . . . fixed. For still I held to the notion of an antidote, and where else was I to experiment, to brew one in wartime but in the doctor's laboratory? Moreover, I shuddered to think what might become of Gréluchon if he returned to the manse in search of me and, finding me gone, fell into the clutches of Doctor Jekyll. Too easily I imagined the doctor absconding with the boy, securing his much-vaunted redemption by returning to London, to the Royal Society, with both the brew and a "specimen" in tow. And those vials: How would I ever recover the contents of those vials if I didn't . . . ?

Bref, how would I ever undo the damage I'd done if I simply removed myself from the Marais mansion? And if I *did* remove myself, well, not even I was naïve enough to think that Doctor Henry Jekyll would not apply all his many and considerable means to finding me.

Julien, as I say, was having none of it, and I feared that at any minute he'd up and leave me sitting alone in that dingy café. But he stayed, and that limpid broth in our bowls seemed to shudder from the tension between us. Luckily, it was just then that two louts standing at the bar began to banter, back and forth, and quite loudly. The elder and drunker of the two men was in the Guard (so said his cap), and the younger was a new recruit, or soon would be if the other man had his say. And have his say he did, so loudly we hurried with our soup, agreeing, tacitly, that it'd be better to be back on the streets than here, subjected to this bullying blowhard.

But just then I heard the elder man say that, aye, times were tough and so on, but he might, *might* know where the other could lay his head provided he promised to first sign himself into the Guard, of course. "The zoo," said he. "Ain't no more animals"— and here he patted his stomach, grotesquely so—"and so I hear some of the newer boys have bribed their way into the cages and such. It ain't posh, but there'll be a roof betwixt you and the rain now, eh?"

I stiffened. Julien, sensing this, asked, "What? What is it, Odile?"

"The zoo," I whispered, nodding slyly back to the guardsmen. "Did you hear that?"

He had, yes, of course; but only now did he make the connection I had.

We were up in an instant. Our coins were yet spinning on the table as we bolted from the café; for it seemed then to make perfect sense:

The zoo. Of course Gréluchon would seek shelter at the zoo; for, if he had sense enough to search out food behind the butchery and to sign himself into the Guard using Timon's address, then it stood to reason that he'd want to go to the zoo to learn what he could of his, *our* . . . sibling, might I say? For Grel had once heard me allude to the "mystery" of the chimpanzees when talking to Julien, and though I'd downplayed the talk, tried to tell him he'd misheard me, well . . . Alas, long gone were the days when I could simply spell a word and thusly leave my bothersome little brother flummoxed. Indeed when he, Grel, had questioned me, I'd only succeeded in piquing his interest the more; such that now he, too, along with Poole, would want to learn *all and everything* about that salted simian whose fate must surely, somehow, mirror his own.

❦

Well, yes, it had stood to reason at first; but by the time we'd gotten to the zoo, the notion stood none too steadily at all. Doubtless Gréluchon would be newly interested in that chimpanzee's fate, but how would he learn it at the zoo proper? By asking the zookeeper? No chance: Monsieur Duval was in Poole's pocket. And so, who? How? By observing the lone and mangy lion he'd have found there, the last of the animals, who'd

lately been starved into a delirium that made him too dangerous to move, to even approach, let alone seek to slaughter? No.
And of course all the chimps were long gone from the grounds.

We found ourselves back at the zoo anyway, having tra-
versed the city north to south. And being there . . . well, it
chilled me somehow. Literally. I felt a most unaccountable,
spine-length chill as we passed the now-empty *singerie*; empty,
yes, save for a few tatterdemalion types we found secreted
there, would-be soldiers, none of whom could tell us one word
about Gréluchon (despite their taking the last of Julien's coins
with hints that, yes, they could tell us something, if only they
had a few sous to stave off the night chill by buying a bottle of
this or that). *Bâtards.* I was none too happy with those men
and wanted to tell them so, perhaps even hunt up some morning glory seeds to slip into their drink and *really* send them on
their way; but Julien once again assuaged me, led me from
danger. And too, he held me close, against that unaccountable
chill.

And how did I repay him? By blurting out that, alas and
alack, and *again*, I'd no recourse now but to return to the Place
des Vosges and . . .

Boom! The boy went off like a bomb. And at the very same
time that chill I could not shake redoubled, and I began to
shiver. Then, I thought it was owing to Julien's anger, which
was extreme, or the new-fallen night.

Yes, Julien blew: "You cannot *possibly* intend to spend even
one more night under that man's roof! Odile, it's . . . it's . . ."

"It's what I intend to do, is what it is," said I, in as steely a voice as I could muster. Why couldn't Julien understand? I *had* to return there, I simply had to.

"It's a choice, 'is what it is,' Odile," said he, snidely, tossing my own words back at me. "You have to choose: Me or him." And then he backed away from me, slowly, palms up in a pose of surrender, before turning and beating a most hasty retreat from the zoo. I was able to follow him, none too easily, till finally he reached the outer fence of the Jardin des Plantes; and, breaching it as we had earlier, he then took to the quai and made his way home—or at least *away*, away from me—alongside the Seine, no less turbulent than the river itself.

"Julien!" I called to him, again and again; but he did not even turn. And soon I stood no hope of catching up to him. Well, yes, I could have run; but I'd be *damned* before I'd run after a boy, even a boy like Julien.

So I simply stood there, shivering, as the moon rose high enough to cast its reflection on the river. "Fine!" said I, petulantly and to no one in particular, before crossing the river at the Pont de Sully, headed back to the Marais and a certain mansion therein. Was I thus making my choice? Perhaps; and though I *preferred* to think I was simply putting off doing so, I was much mistaken:

I'd chosen, indeed; and fatefully so.

༚

Need I say that I did not exactly hurry my way "homeward"? Not at first. But then there came that chill, again and again. It was as if I'd donned a cloak of ice, and neither Julien's mood nor the night's temperature was to blame. Spring had been on the air all day, and so it was that night. How then to account for this most wintry chill? Solitude, I thought at first; but then I began to sense, most distinctly, that it could not be owing to solitude; for I came to doubt, *very* much doubt that I was alone.

In fact, I knew it: *I was being followed.*

I'd not gone a half-block up the boulevard, headed toward the Bastille, before turning to stare into the shadows through which I'd passed. But . . . nothing and no one.

The corner from which I'd come was gaslit, and into that light I now called out, "Julien?" For I was certain . . . no, now I *hoped* the boy had thought better of his too brusque departure and had come back to accompany me home. As well he should have. But no. Nothing . . . no one.

It was silent save for the breeze blowing through the rickety branches of the linden trees lining the boulevard; and behind me, farther behind me with every step, I could hear, no, could *sense* the strength of the rushing river. Otherwise, I heard nothing at all. Nothing and no one.

Up ahead now I could see the lights of the Bastille and the several streets spoking off of it. One of those would be the rue Saint-Antoine. I'd take it until I could turn up the rue des Tournelles, whence to the Place des Vosges and . . . home (such as it was). But there, at the nexus of the Bastille itself, I could see soldiers lounging about on barricades, no doubt drunk, their blood lusting for war and who-knew-what-else. Best to avoid the soldiers, although I did linger within sight of them just long enough to see that Gréluchon was not among them. And then, crazy though it seemed, even to me, I called out, "Grel? . . . Gréluchon, is that you?"

Nothing and no one.

I sped through the shadows onto the rue Saint-Antoine, blessedly unseen by the soldiers, and soon took to the rue des Tournelles. Now I was practically running—propriety be damned!—though I was in no hurry to reach my destination. Simply, I wanted to be rid of the dark, and the shadows and the chill it all occasioned. The breeze dried my tears, and no new ones fell; for that inexplicable chill, well, it had brought me past tears of fear to something else entirely.

Finally I rounded off the rue des Tournelles, such that the Place des Vosges was now mere lamplit steps away. Oh, but where now was the relief I'd thought I'd feel in gaining such familiar ground? In fact, I was yet far from the doctor's door; for there I stood diagonally across the square from it, damning myself for ever having judged that perfidious place preferable to the streets! Yet I dared not take the most direct route, through the deeply shadowed park, and so I took instead to those vaulted galleries, the covered sidewalks that squared the Place. The galleries were dark now, too, with only the occasional mansion leaving its gaslight to burn back the night.

Let it be said I strode with purpose, nonetheless, toward the Jekyll mansion, my ears pricked, varying my step lest someone, the shadowed someone behind me, seek to secrete their footfall in the sounds of mine.

I let go a sigh, as it seemed all the breath I could summon, while at the same time I began to brace myself for whatever I might find on the far side of the doctor's door; for such was my relief to stop, stand perfectly still in the silence, and hear nothing and no one, to hear that I was not being followed after all.

As indeed I was not, no. For in fact my pursuer had somehow gotten ahead of me, and when finally he burst forth before me I was stilled, utterly stilled by surprise and a fear for which I haven't the words.

My blood went cold and stopped in its course. And my scream—and surely I must have *tried* to scream—was stifled by the cold, clawlike clamp of his hand, his horribly hirsute hand, the touch of which came with an accompanying "Shush," uttered so close to my face that his warm breath stung my wide-open eyes, staring now into his.

And nonsensical though it will seem, I here avow that I knew him at once yet knew him not at all.

CHAPTER EIGHT
Masters of the House

I t was Doctor Jekyll standing before me now in the shadowed arcade.

Or was it?

What I mean to say is this: It was no one *but* Doctor Jekyll—
not Gréluchon, not Julien, not some soldier or stranger seeking
to accost me in the streets—yet it was not the Doctor Jekyll I
knew. He was suddenly . . . *other*. And it was in realizing this
that my fear ceded to wonder and I knew:

The salts.

It made perfect sense. Doctor Henry Jekyll, once and finally
in possession of the salts—the stolen vials four and five—would
not have waited long before putting them to purpose; but upon
himself? That rather surprised me, despite my earlier suspicions. But there stood the proof before me.

It was as though he'd donned a disguise; yet, as with anyone

one knows well, I knew him by his eyes. The very same eyes into which I'd sometimes dared to stare during our many discussions, our many conversations, our language lessons. Yes, those were indeed the doctor's brown eyes; yet behind them, now, there shone the darkest of lights, indeed a seeming absence of light. And it was from deep within that horrid void that this other had risen to transform Jekyll so, to make manifest that same brutishness I'd seen in Gréluchon.

He stood as tall as the doctor had, or rather he would have had it not been for the brutish stoop he now adopted. He bent at the waist as if shouldering an unseen burden. It was this that gave him an apish appearance, for it made his arms seem preternaturally long. Indeed, once he'd unhanded me—an act sped, surely, by the application of my ten nails to his hairy forearm—his arms went slack and I saw that his knuckles fell nearly to the level of his knees.

And the clothes he wore were definitely not drawn from the doctor's wardrobe. Rags, these were. Or rather, he'd made rags of them through rough usage. His cuffs were shoved up over those forearms of his, seemingly composed of corded rope; and the hem of his slacks trailed through the dirt of the streets.

Could the salts alone have effected such changes in Doctor Jekyll? Perhaps I'd not had the time or presence of mind to see the salts affect Gréluchon similarly. Perhaps my brother had left the laboratory before the salts had had their full effect. Surely I had an idea of the internal changes wrought by the salts, but could they actually change the outer person so perceptibly, making them appear a different person altogether? Or did they just seem so, owing to the *internal* changes?

I had no answers yet my questions were many; and I say again that wonder quickly overcame my fear, such that there I stood, this other's hands only lately fallen from my throat, staring into his lightless eyes, when I heard myself ask:

"How . . . ?"

I was my mother's apprentice, after all, *still*. There were things I wanted, *needed* to know more . . . precisely; oh, but where to begin?

"Who *are* you?"

At this the other laughed, loudly. He sounded rather like a braying mule; no: a hyena. He cared not a whit if he were heard now, though moments earlier he'd sought to stifle my scream with those suffocating hands of his, the taste of which—the salt of his sweat, the tang of turned earth—was still on my lips. And the sound was so impolite, so non-Jekyll, if you will, that I was surprised, stunned even, to hear a response in what seemed the doctor's voice:

"You know full well who we are," said he, that odd plural *we* lost upon me at first, for his words had trailed off in a snarl of sorts that made my blood run cold. And as the words echoed away from me, down the brick-and-stone gallery where we stood, it seemed his words took on a different tone, one with added heft, added depth, as if his now-barreled chest were hollow (as perhaps it was, for he would soon prove that it housed no *human* heart).

"What do you want?" Of course, I knew the answer: *the salts*. Or rather, the secrets behind the Cagot salts. Yet when his precise response came, it would decide both our fates; for what he then said was:

"More . . . We want more."

"More what?" I asked, infusing the words with all the insolence I could muster; but he would have none of that, and fairly leaped, *leaped* nearer me to say, to sneer into my face:

"Enough, witch!" He seemed a coiled cobra now, swaying mere inches from my face and readying to strike. "More of the salts. We want more of the salts and—"

"I don't *have* any more of the salts. And you've evidently stolen the last of what I've already brewed. You had no right to—"

"Liar!"

And before I knew what had happened, I'd fallen back against the brick pillar; for he'd shoved me, hard, with the heel of his hand. I felt the air rush from my lungs. Tears sprang to my eyes, tears which I quickly wiped away.

"It's *you* who are the liar," I countered. "It is you, *sir*," I continued, rendering that *sir* quite ironic, "who has spied and stolen, who has betrayed both my friendship and my trust."

"That was Jekyll did that," said he, "not me." His words came accompanied by the slyest of smiles.

Had he transformed or . . . or somehow split into two selves? I could not know, not yet. Oh, but how very strange it felt to both address Doctor Jekyll—for was this not the doctor before me, or at least some strange twin, some odd manifestation of himself?—and yet speak of him as though he were absent, as this other did; but I adopted the habit fast, and asked:

"Why? Why did . . . *he* do what he did?"

I knew the answer: *Redemption*, in a word, redemption from his earlier *Ruin*. And so my question was really more of a test, a sounding act. I wanted to know if Doctor Jekyll and this other shared the same memories, the same emotions. I supposed they did, and proof positive came when the other launched into a tirade very different in tone from anything I'd ever heard from Doctor Jekyll, yet on a most familiar topic: The "imbeciles" of the Royal Society, those same scoffing scientists whom Doctor Jekyll constantly derided, yet never with anything approaching this vehemence. Indeed, in speaking of those scientists who'd ridiculed Doctor Jekyll's research, who'd laughed him from London, the other used the bluest vocabulary I'd ever heard; but the gist of it all was this:

The two selves of Doctor Henry Jekyll—and now they seemed more and more like two distinct entities: tenants, if you will, sharing the closest of quarters—both selves sought the salts, yes. And if earlier Doctor Jekyll had sought them for redemption, now the other wanted them as well but for very different reasons. *To live. To exist.* For Doctor Henry Jekyll was reveling in the freedoms afforded him by this other, secondary self. He confessed as much, going on about how he could now see to his own "perfidious pleasures" while yet his Parisian reputation sat in shelter, of how he could, seemingly at will, "spring headlong into the sea of liberty"; and so on. Need I say that this was all quite eerie, quite discomfiting to hear?

Finally he spoke of having found me, of having then followed me and Julien—whom he referred to only as "the boy"—to the zoo. How, exactly, he had found me I did not care to know; for the other spoke unapologetically, even proudly, of having *tracked* me. It was predator versus prey, and it made my skin crawl. When he spoke of having spied upon Julien and me at the *singerie*—had it been *that* occasioning the chill I'd felt?—well, that was altogether too much. Embarrassed and mad in equal measures, I simply walked away, saying I was headed home.

It was an odd and unfortunate choice of words.

"Home?" He loosed that horrid laugh again, and appeared, suddenly *appeared* before me as he had earlier even though I'd walked a good five paces past him and hadn't heard him move at all. "The 'home' to which you refer is Doctor Jekyll's. He'll say when, or *if*, you'll be returning to it."

"I'm cold," said I, standing my ground in the gallery, "cold, tired, hungry, and very much in need of sleep. Could you kindly relay as much to the doctor and ask him if I may pass, homeward?"

My sarcasm seemed to confuse the other, who then cocked his ear as if to hear an inner voice. He had taken me literally! It was disconcerting to see, and even more disconcerting *to hear* the other relay, in a third-person pronouncement, and with some disdain, "The doctor says he has a plan."

Bref: If I sought a return to the mansion, so too did the

other; and he needed me to achieve it. They both needed me, in fact, as Doctor Jekyll, in his present state, could not have walked into his own home.

"What if Poole knows me, even so?" asked the doctor with a gesture meant to take in his . . . selves.

Understand: While I had recognized Jekyll, hidden though he was by the other, *within* the other, his appearance would surely have puzzled (to put it mildly) anyone else. The other told me, in fact, that sundry men of Jekyll's acquaintance, lately met, had not known him *at all*, had greeted him as a stranger. Oh, but what would Cheffy or Cézette have to say if they saw this hideous *other* come into the doctor's household? And while it seemed probable that Poole, of all people, having been so long in Jekyll's service, would be the one to recognize *the man within the man* if anyone did . . . *alors*, it was all too risky.

"Doesn't matter what that slattern of an ash-girl might think," said he, "assuming she thinks at all." This was Cézette, of course, to whom he so rudely referred. "And her cooking auntie has finally run off, showing sense enough to leave the fool girl behind. *Ha!* Good riddance, too, I say! Her damn sauces were all the same anyway! But as for Poole, *ach!*"

Poole, indeed. Ever the problem; first mine, and now the doctor's, which I'd have found rich, comical even, in other circumstances. For if Poole did not recognize the hidden Jekyll, he'd bar the door to the other; and if he *did* recognize Jekyll, why, then the questions would be many, and all unanswerable. So it was that—absurdly!—*I* was to make way for them, the dual being. Doctor Jekyll was *un*transforming, if you will; but I did not know that then, for I'd never seen the *un*state occasioned by the salts wearing off. Yes, I was to help them home. How, precisely? It remained to be seen.

"Hours past," said he, said *it*, "when I found you so *intimately* in the arms of your butcher boy—"

"I was *not* being intimate with anyone, *sir*! I was chilled, and Julien—"

"Ha! You lie!"

I began to speak heatedly in my defense, my skin once again acrawl at realizing that I'd been stalked, hunted by the other, whom I'd never have addressed as *sir* had I not then sought to appeal to whatever decency of the doctor's lay dormant within; for yes, it seemed now that the other was in ascendance (for want of a better word). But he knew no decency, none. Not only had he accused me of having been "intimate" with Julien—which I was *not* guilty of, if guilt be the word, though I will admit that if Julien had offered comfort of that sort I would have been sorely tempted to accept—not only did the other accuse me of said improprieties, he now accused me of *lying* about it. And to preclude my lying further, he'd interrupted my self-defense with a slap.

Yes: He'd slapped me into a stunned silence.

It was then I grew newly fearful; for what mightn't this second, lesser self of Doctor Jekyll's do if he were bold enough to strike me so? No matter the doctor's many faults—the lot of which I'd only lately discovered—he was not a brute.

And so I stood listening to the other, seething still, tasting blood in my mouth and wanting to strike him in retaliation but . . . I didn't. I couldn't. I could do nothing but submit and listen, wishing all the while that I'd not been born my mother's daughter, that I'd not come to Paris, that I'd never, *never* cracked those infernal books.

"Do not waste my time with lies, girl," said the other before continuing. "I trailed you for hours, *mademoiselle*." He seemed now to be mocking the doctor's manners. Or had that been Jekyll who'd spoken? Oh, the confusion! I had to weigh the being's every word to determine the speaker. The other's voice was weightier than Jekyll's, yes, his sentiments harsher by far; but his emotions were Henry's, albeit exaggerated. It was odd, *very* odd!

The sun had begun to rise, rendering the top of the trees in the park first gray then green, and depriving the shadows in which we stood of their depth. Here was dawn, the dawn of a day as dark as any I'd yet known.

"Oh, it was all too easy," bragged the beast, "tracking you two." *Tracking*. Indeed, it seemed then that he sniffed the very air before leaning nearer my neck to take in my own scent. "I was near you, quite near your so-innocent self, while you and your butcher boy visited that *singerie*, behaving little better than those monkeys of your late acquaintance, the ones you—"

"They were chimpanzees," said I, my cheek still stinging, "not monkeys." It mattered little; rather, I did not want to know what, if anything, Jekyll may have learned of my earlier miscraft.

No, I did not want to hear those truths spoken by the other. And so it is that, to this day, I cannot say if the other was close enough to hear me confiding in Julien again that night at the *singerie*, each of us scouring the shadows in hope of finding Gréluchon there, or if the knowledge had, in fact, come from Poole. The latter, I presume; but in fact the question would pale in significance against others that were soon to present themselves.

"Chimps, monkeys, men, it's of no matter to me. All that is the doctor's concern. I simply wanted to find you and your bestial brother."

"Gréluchon? Have you seen Gréluchon?"

"I have indeed," said he, pleasant as you please, whereupon he rooted around in a pocket before making me a present of Gréluchon's eye patch of old. "My, my, however did I forget to give you this?" And he flung it at my feet.

"Where did you . . . ?" I retrieved the eye patch from the pavement. "Did Gréluchon give this to you?"

"Questions, questions! Oh, so many questions." He stood there, smiling, looking like a cur about to bite. "What say you *I* ask a few, eh?"

Suddenly he stepped nearer and dared to lay a hand upon my hip, feeling for the waistlet and the books. "Where are they, those books of your witch mother's with their—"

He did not finish the sentence, for now it was my turn to silence *him* with a slap. This I did with all, *all* my might, saying, "Do *not* touch me again. Ever."

He merely laughed and came at me again, too quickly, too determinedly for me to resist. He felt me about the hips and waist, and seethed to see that I was not then in possession of Mother's books.

"Where are they? Tell us."

"And if I were to tell you? What then? Would you tell me all you've learned of Gréluchon? Would you—?"

"Tell us. Tell *me*!"

I tucked the eye patch into a pocket. I'd learn nothing more from him in his present state. In truth, I was stalling now, trying to hide my great relief that Mother's books had not been discovered where I'd secreted them under that floorboard beneath my cot. It was then, too, that I came to understand that though the two beings shared common memories, common emotions, the other was yet mentally *less* than his host, as it were, the slyer, sneakier Doctor Jekyll. *He* would have known to keep me guessing as to the whereabouts of the books, whether they'd been found or not. Not the other, who was . . . direct as a dog digging for a bone, and whose only recourse, when thwarted, was menace. And so it seemed I might manipulate the other, given the opportunity; whereas with Doctor Jekyll, sly and spying Henry Jekyll, it was he who'd made a marionette of me!

And damn him for pulling those strings, again and again.

"And who should I say you are? What name should I give?"

I'd given in, agreed to play my role in whatever ruse would

allow Doctor Jekyll ingress to and egress from his own house, no matter what self was in evidence at the time. That Jekyll's lesser self was yet unnamed was problematic; for it had been proposed (rather strenuously so) that I accompany the other across the square and into the doctor's mansion. As said, I assented. First, it was made all too clear that I'd no other choice. But second, the other had offered *proof* of having met Gréluchon, had he not? Proof in the form of the eye patch. Too, I was not yet inclined to disbelieve his every word. I was yet doubtful the plan would work, however, for I could *see* Jekyll; but perhaps that was owing to something innate in me, some witchly . . . *something*. Others, friends of Doctor Jekyll's, had not recognized his transformed self; and so perhaps the plan *would* work. Of course, I hoped so; for if it did not, my predicament would worsen alongside the doctor's. For if ever Poole was in charge of that household, well . . .

"It's my house, *dammit* all, and I want the run of it no matter who . . . no matter what . . ."

"Fine," said I. "*Fine*. I understand what I'm to do, and I'll do it." And indeed it would be best if our plan worked and Doctor Jekyll *and* his other had access to the mansion as and when needed; but to gain that, now, well . . . "We will have to introduce him . . . you . . . *whomever* into the household as a stranger, and hope Poole's none the wiser. But to do that, we'll need a name."

Silence. The strange cocking of first this ear then that as the selves conferred in silence. Odd, that. *Very* odd and unnerving.

175

I stood by, waiting, watching that strangest of conversations and wondering if the eyes I saw beetling out from beneath a too-prominent brow were the other's, or were they Henry's, hidden within . . . And then it hit me:

"Hyde. I shall introduce a Mister Henry Hyde, if that suits"; and then I could not stop myself from adding, cynically, ". . . lately come from London."

"Not Henry," said the other. "Edward. Have it be Edward."

I nodded. "A Mister Edward Hyde, lately come from London and . . ."

The other, this Mister Hyde, took me hard by the arm. Evidently that self, too, recalled the words with which Henry had introduced himself to me some months prior, and did not appreciate the manner in which I used them at present, so said the blossoming bruise on my forearm, which I wrenched free of Hyde's hold. And indeed I *had* intended to tease the doctor with those words, words uttered by him back when his word had worth. We stood near the house now. Anyone looking out a streetside window would have seen a strange couple standing there beneath a rising sun, yet no one, no one could have guessed how *truly* strange said couple was.

"Wait," said Hyde in his gravelly tones. "Who am I?"

I stared. A loaded question if ever there was one. If *he* didn't have an answer, there was no one else but I who might; but I had no answer, none at all, until Mister Hyde clarified the question.

"A history," said he. "Something plausible, a *reason* Henry would have Edward in his home." And so it was decided that I would present Edward Hyde as an old family acquaintance of Jekyll's, yes, lately come from London. "Make him a cousin," said the other. "Poole knows of a lower branch of Jekyll relations, yet he's never met a one of them."

We furthered the ruse: I was to hint that Hyde was somehow involved in the fracas in France, that he was a spy who'd snuck into the city from Versailles to report upon the rebel activity in the east, in Belleville and surrounds.

"No! Do not specify a side. 'A spy' . . . then say nothing more."

"And what about you?" I found myself needing to specify now, though indeed I sensed the slow, steady return of Henry Jekyll: "What about Henry? Where should I say Henry is?"

A pause. More cocked ears, more tacit converse. "Say that Doctor Jekyll shall be along shortly. That he has been delayed." And he took my arm again; but this time he did it gently while adding in milder, Henry-ish tones, "And tell Poole that I am not to be badgered, not to be waited up for, and that I shall be wanting my peace and quiet in the morning given . . . given events of late."

By "events of late" I knew he referred to the fact that he'd been carousing the streets and their sundry dens of iniquity that night (when not *tracking* me and mine). He was spent from all the "secret sinning" (as he'd come to call it), spent yet exhilarated by the freedoms afforded him by a secondary, lesser self. Doubtless Henry was thinking of this "sinning" when he said, musingly, the menace gone now from his voice, "If Poole knew what I've been up to this evening . . . Lord alive, I'd catch bloody hell!" I almost, *almost* felt sorry for him then, reduced as he was to boyhood by the looming prospect of a confrontation with Poole.

Our identities (such as they were) now set, we crossed the street, homeward bound.

His gait was changeable: In the short distance that we walked down the arcade, onto and across the street to the mansion, the being beside me walked two different ways. The loping, apish amble of Mister Hyde, and the more upright, manly mien of Doctor Jekyll. The . . . *creature* was confused in its every sense.

Oh, but it was definitely Mister Hyde who said to me, "Go now!" And he all but shoved me past the front door, with its gold-plated plaque—he even seemed to sneer at the Jekyll name presented there alongside all its attendant initials, all its alphabetical success—and pushed through the servants' door, leading me down alongside the house and into the back courtyard. And right he was to do so: I would never have dared to introduce a man like Mister Hyde into the Jekyll household via the front door, via the foyer and parlors. No: Hyde was most decidedly a servants'-door type.

Down the dark, dingy alley we went, and I remember thinking it strange that Mister Hyde was leading the way, for I very much doubted that Doctor Jekyll had ever entered his own home via the servants' alley and kitchen door. I wondered what he must be thinking, deep down within his Hyde. Oh, but then I had wonders, questions of my own with which to contend; for whatever was that tub doing sitting in the center of the courtyard?

A wash basin, it was, dented and bent and filled now to the brim with water. A makeshift lid, a plank of sorts, sat askew, disclosing not clothes within, no, but rather . . .

"Come now," said Hyde, reaching for my arm, "that's of no never mind now."

I evaded his grasp and stood staring at the tub, staring until I saw what it was within and . . . and barely succeeded in stifling a cry. Horrors!

Sunlight had begun to seep into the courtyard, reflected down, window to window, from on high, and the gas lamp beside the kitchen door was still lit, and . . . Alas, there was light enough for me to see the matted fur moving on the water's surface. I even recognized the palettes and patterns of the shadow cats I'd grown accustomed to over the months, including Cheffy's preferred Tigre. How had the cats met such a fate as this?

For yes, the tub was chockablock with cats, *drowned* cats.

Who could have done such a deed, dropping the cats into the water and then covering the tub till they were drowned? I saw the rocks that the culprit had piled atop the plank, fallen now beside the tub, for there was no longer any danger of the cats' scrambling free. Two, three, perhaps four cats, all bobbed lifelessly on the black water. I saw Tigre's striped fur waving in the water.

And then, as if in response to my unasked questions—*Who? Why?*—I heard bolts slide back on the far side of the kitchen door. Poole. The man revealed himself, and while he stood staring down at Mister Hyde—how well I knew that so-disdainful stare!—I saw that his shirtsleeves were yet rolled high, disclosing his bandaged forearms.

At least the cats had not died without a fight.

Poole was staring at me now, having not even deigned to address a question to my companion—whom he seemed to know not at all, *not at all*: remarkable, this—staring at me and seemingly daring me to speak. For my part, I could not help but pleasure in the blood I saw seeping through those mismade, mummylike bandages: Clearly, Poole had had to see to his own wounds.

I soon gathered myself sufficiently to offer a "Morning, *Monsieur* Poole."

"Well, well," said he, hands to hips, "look what . . . no, look *who* the cats 'ave dragged 'ome." It seemed a most inappropriate turn of phrase; that is until I realized Poole was proud of his late handiwork. "What do you want, girl? *Speak.* I 'aven't all day, as the master's due any moment and . . ."

Amazing, this. The master, as it were, stood before him as he spoke those very words. Such was, such *is* the change that comes over a salted man.

"I've come back to—" I tried to respond.

"I can *see* that, foolish girl. You dared to come back 'ere after the mess you made of the master's laboratory? You've more cheek than I knew, you do. Why, I've 'alf a mind—"

"Yes, well, that being so," said I, drawing a snigger from Mister Hyde standing at my side, "still I *have* come back, Poole, and I carry orders from . . . from Doctor Jekyll himself."

"Orders, eh? For me *to follow*, I suppose?"

There he stood in the doorway, backlit and seeming quite, *quite* big; He'd bar the door to both of us bodily if need be. (Though I could feel Hyde thrumming at my side like an idling motor, waiting for the slightest excuse to thrash the old servant.) But I drew strength (oddly) from the sight of the drowned cats and stepped forward.

"Doctor Jekyll is . . . delayed; but I've been instructed to tell you, Poole, that this . . . er, gentleman, this gentleman is to have the run of his house until the doctor's return."

Poole's eyebrows went up, arching like arrowheads, while his dark eyes fell to take in Hyde from tip to toe. He was . . . unimpressed, shall I say; but still he gave no sign of recognition, though I worried a bit when he lingered on the eyes. If he'd recognize Jekyll, who seemed now to be in total abeyance, it'd be by the eyes; but he showed now the black irises of Edward Hyde, not the brown ones of Henry Jekyll.

"That so?" said the manservant.

"Yes, it is," I countered. And then, most improbably, it fell to me to introduce Doctor Henry Jekyll to the man who knew him better than any other alive. "This is a . . . friend of the doctor's, name of Hyde, Mister Henry—"

A half-cough, half-growl from the being beside me brought me up fast, and I knew my mistakes.

"A *cousin*," I corrected, half-bowing to the beast beside me, "excuse me. A cousin named Edward, yes, of course. *Edward* Hyde, lately come from London and . . ."

Before I could drop any hints, pursuant to our plan, Mister Hyde had shouldered past Poole, pushing the older man back against the kitchen door. No easy feat, that; and there Poole stood, wholly nonplussed. "Sir! This is *most* unacceptable. I . . . I . . . I . . ."

And then, wheeling on me, Poole found his words: "Where does 'e think 'e's going anyway, that . . . that . . . ?" So it went with Mister Hyde: People—even Poole!—would react to his . . . *nonspecific deformity*, let me say, and then their words, their thoughts, would trail away, as if the *revulsion* they felt could not be suffered a moment more.

Of course, Mister Hyde knew his way to the laboratory, which I rightly assumed to be his destination; for the house was his, was it not? It seemed to me he ought to have dissembled somewhat, to secure the ruse; but no matter.

I had best push past Poole myself, before his questions could come; and this I tried to do. But of course, the manservant slid before me. He stood quite near now, puffed up and presenting himself like the door to a vault. He made a crucial mistake, however:

He dared to take hold of my arm, exposing his own forearm in the process; and need I say that I did not hesitate, not in the least, to sink five fingers into his bloodied bandages.

I could have stood there an eternity watching him wince;

but alas I said only, "You have your orders, Poole, and believe me when I say they come directly from the doctor himself."

I wrested myself free of Poole and pushed past him, moving farther into the kitchen. My path was clear, but I could not resist turning to ask, with a nod to the courtyard beyond, "Whatever could a cat do to deserve such a death as that?"

I did not expect a response, yet one came:

"That, too, was done upon the doctor's orders, *missy*." But where previously Poole would have reveled in the act, the control and meanness of it, he seemed now to go (dare I say it?) a bit rheumy, a bit misty about the eyes. That, more than anything else, told me that things in the Jekyll mansion had most decidedly changed since the doctor had gotten hold of the salts and wasted no time in starting his experiments.

Poole seemed to be speaking to no one in particular now; certainly not me. "They went plum wild, they did, all of a sudden. Couldn't be controlled. Cheffy's own Tigre attacked her and . . ." Poole's words trailed away, for he'd caught himself on the verge of confiding in me and drew himself up short; but his eyes trailed from mine, too, and I followed them to Cheffy's long worktable, which I'd never, *ever* seen in such disarray. And seeing it, I knew, too, the source of the kitchen's off, *very* off odor: The guts from half-filleted fish lay strewn atop the table, and bloodied rags were piled on the workbench. Whatever had happened with the salted, ensavaged cats had happened fast. And as for Cheffy, well, it was little wonder that she'd left the house in such a hurry, doubtlessly running fast and far. After all, were those not the corpses of her beloved cats bobbing in a tub outside the kitchen door?

Once I'd quit the kitchen and taken to the stairwell leading up to the laboratory, well, I all but fell upon Cézette. There she sat in the half-light, shivering. Her eyes were wide, and so it was that I knew what had just transpired.

"Who . . . ?" she began, raising a tremulous finger in the direction of the laboratory. "Who . . . was . . . *that*?"

I would not have been surprised to hear that Cézette had been knocked down by a fast-passing Hyde—for Doctor Jekyll, to the extent that he thought of Cézette at all, considered her a sort of household . . . pest—but I did not pursue the point with the girl. I did, however, consider taking to the stair beside her and soliciting her account of what had passed within the mansion of late. All this change in less than two days' time? But I had more pressing matters in the laboratory, for whatever would Doctor Jekyll get up to in there under the influence of Mister Hyde . . . or vice versa?

So I stepped lightly past Cézette, offering what kindness I could—and dare I say that a little kindness went a long way just then—laying my hand atop her tensed shoulder and saying, "You'd best go to your room, Cézette."

She stared up at me and I saw that her pretty face had been rendered blank and bloodless by her encounter with Mister Hyde. As she did not move, I prompted her further with an ill-considered, "And lock your door." This had her standing in a trice and then tearing up the stairs as if the flounces of her silly uniform were afire.

True: There'd been a day, not long past, when I'd have de-lighted (I admit it) to have seen Cézette in such a state, to have scared her so myself; but not now, and never again. I pitied the girl her confusion, and wondered how frightened Cheffy must have been to have fled the house so fast. What a calamity the drowning of the cats must have been, and what *sounds* it must have made! And who'd been crueler: the doctor, ordering the deed, or Poole, seeing it done?

I breathed deeply and set my steps toward the laboratory door, wondering who it was I'd find on its far side.

CHAPTER NINE
The Fortress of Identity

The laboratory door was ajar; but as soon I pushed it wide and stepped into the space, the door slammed shut behind me. I heard several bolts thrown. (There'd not been bolts before, just the single key.)

Clearly, they'd been waiting for me.

Aside from the bolts on the door, the laboratory was much as I'd last seen it. In fact, overly so: It was too neat, too orderly; and this only served to further my suspicions. Surely Poole, let alone Cézette, was now denied access to the premises; and so this orderliness must be the doctor's doing. And he would order a space so precisely only to hide something. I knew him that well at least. My eye fell upon the worktable, and the stand thereon. And . . . nothing. No vials.

He had them still, of course, and doubtless had hidden what remained of the brew.

Pathetic, really, that Doctor Jekyll would continue to deny the fact when the evidence was plain. He'd wasted no time in experimenting with the stolen salts, had he not, first corrupting the cats and then (the fool!) himself.

"Where are they?"

"Where are what?" He'd moved from behind the laboratory door and stood far across the room now, gazing down into the street. He seemed . . . distracted, discomfited. The light rose behind him, obscuring him, and though his stance was somewhat stooped, I could not tell for certain which self I dealt with at present; and so I tested him.

"You know full well what I'm referring to, Henry."

He turned, slowly; and after a long stare, said, "Henry isn't here at present." He seemed as confused as I.

"Oh, but I think he is," I ventured, risking Hyde's wrath; though, in point of fact, that was precisely what I meant to do. "Tell me, *Jekyll*, where are the stolen vials?"

He rose to his full height now, turned, and came fast to the laboratory table that separated us. With a slap of his palm upon the hardwood, one so fierce as to set the glassware to rattling, he said again, "Henry isn't here! I . . . I don't know *where* he is!"

I held my ground and I held his gaze, though it took all my strength to stare deep into the eyes of Edward Hyde; for, yes, the eyes were yet Hyde's though the transformation had begun. And I believe the doctor welcomed it, though surely Mister Hyde did not. Horrid as it was to watch, I could only be relieved. I'd gain no ground with Edward Hyde, that much was clear. If I had hopes yet of . . . of *resolution*, they rested with Henry Jekyll.

And so I waited, and I watched the doctor's slow ascendance.

It began with the brow, or at least that's what I noticed first. It seemed somehow to recede, to slip back from Hyde's apish brow to Jekyll's high and dignified one. I suppose this may have owed something to his stance; for Doctor Jekyll always stood upright, of course, while Mister Hyde was bowed, nearly hunchbacked. But if changes to the brow were perhaps illusory, well, those to the hands were decidedly not.

We stared at his hands together, he and I; for Doctor Jekyll, and perhaps even Mister Hyde, was as intrigued as I by this first *un*transformation. His fingers were splayed atop the table, and as they went from the hairy, knotted digits of Hyde to the smooth hands of Jekyll the thinker, the spoiled inheritor, Jekyll the man who'd known not a day of manual labor all his life long, well, I must admit it: I found myself sympathizing— incredible but true—with Edward Hyde, for the transformation quite visibly hurt him.

As Doctor Jekyll came on—again, I could gauge the balance of his being by the black irises devolving to brown—still there was a trace of Mister Hyde about his face, a grimacing trace. It was like looking at two men simultaneously, each sporting a mask of the other, a watery, changeable mask.

With each pop of a knuckle—the audibility of it all is the transformation's most disturbing characteristic—Mister Hyde flinched. He seemed to want to withdraw his hand from sight, from the table, as if it were blows from a hammer he was enduring; but he held the hand there, as transfixed as I by the transformation. If the Doctor Jekyll *of old* had been present, and the transforming being someone else, he'd have been scribbling furiously in his notebook.

Once the hands were no longer Hyde's, Jekyll withdrew them from the table. Rather, the doctor could not keep his hands there, could not steady them, for he was then wracked by pains of another sort as (it seemed!) his spine straightened, his legs lengthened, and his chest went from convex to concave.

So it was that the being before me was returning to its natural, or rather its original state: Doctor Henry Jekyll, "lately of London . . ."

Ironic, that: Had he waited but an hour or so longer outside, on the streets, Doctor Jekyll would have been able to walk into his own house as he always had. He'd not have needed my escort, nor the ruse about Edward Hyde. Of course, neither of us knew that then, for neither of us had yet seen a salted being return to his original self. (And would that I'd never seen it a second time . . . or *successive* times.)

Seeing this, the *un*salting, horrid though it was, gave me hope. Perhaps, then, the salts would run their course with Gréluchon as well, and when I found him on the morrow (as I fully believed I would) he'd be . . . *reasonable*, as he'd not been when he'd run from the laboratory. Oh, but what would that mean for his health, his blindness? Would that blight have returned as well?

Doctor Jekyll was a long while ascending, regaining full and complete possession of himself, or rather *his selves*. This fact I learned, most eerily, when again I asked him—and I thought it was Jekyll and Jekyll alone with whom I dealt now—for the salts, only to hear:

"He doesn't have any salts."

Was this Jekyll speaking of Hyde, or Hyde speaking of Jekyll? Or the one speaking *for* the other? I was confused! Indeed, we *all* were; for the voice I heard seemed an odd amalgam of the two voices, Jekyll's *and* Hyde's. "Well," said I, "I believe that he . . . rather, that *you* do indeed have—"

Hyde (it was Hyde!) let loose his hyena-like laugh. Most odd, this, coming as it did from a body that more and more resembled Henry Jekyll. "Are you calling the good doctor a liar, then? My, my."

I would follow his lead. *What else was I to do?*

"I am, indeed," said I. "For I have learned that the doctor is *not* good, in fact. He is a spy and a liar, and no friend of mine."

He began to twitch. He cocked first this ear then that toward the ceiling: First Jekyll listened to Hyde, then Hyde to Jekyll; and all the while I heard not a word, for none was spoken aloud. Then, finally, the warring selves split in a most surprising way, surprising even to them: They *shared* the ascendancy now.

First it was Hyde who said, "He'll not be happy with you, girl, to hear himself spoken of in that way. I warn you."

And then, most oddly, I heard the less hearty, more heart-felt tones of Henry Jekyll rejoin with *"I am sorry, Odile."*

"And . . . and he'll take *action* against such insolence. I swear it!"

"What you say is true, Odile, and I apologize. It's just that I . . . I . . ."

The lips moved with each utterance, so there was nothing ventriloquial about the speech; still the effect was most bizarre. And this effect was added to by the changing, the flashing of the eyes within a face that was, now, yes, decidedly that of Henry Jekyll: black to brown, brown to black, in accord with the speech of each.

"I was wrong." Here was Jekyll struggling for purchase, for control of his disparate selves. *"I was wrong to have spied, to have lied."*

"Wrong? What's that: 'wrong'? All I know is that he'll do it again. I'll see to it."

"I won't!"

"Indeed he will!"

"I . . . I . . ."

"You will do it again," said I now, speaking to Henry. "It was you who spied and lied without Hyde's help. How can I believe you won't do worse, now that you've gotten ahold of the salts and have . . . *him* to contend with?"

"Right you are, girl," said Hyde, triumphantly. "Right you are."

"Yes," said Henry. *"I . . . I am afraid you are right. I haven't control now and—"*

I held up my hand to silence him, to silence Jekyll. "You had no self-control then, when you were simply . . . yourself, without Hyde. And if you persist in lying about the salts—you have them! you must!—then how am I to believe a word you say? How am I to trust you when you cannot even trust . . . *yourselves*?"

Henry hung low his head. A Hyde-like snigger escaped his mouth.

I spoke on: "You've no business experimenting with that brew, Henry, none!"

Doctor Jekyll said nothing, but when he looked up at me his eyes had gone murky and black.

"Maybe not," said he; "but it was *your* business, Odile, your dickering here in this laboratory and your concoction that found me. That *freed* me! Can you really expect, now, that we'll stop in our pursuit of the salts? Henry, whose reputation rides on them, and me, whose very *existence* does. No, no, let me assure you, Odile, Henry *will* indulge again. Why, he's become an instant addict!" Hyde thought this quite rich. "And may I commend you, witchling, or whatever you are? For those salts, or rather the resultant brew, well, that's some *heady* stuff. It makes absinthe seem suitable for children, it does. And after the time we've had out on the town? Ha! Suffice to say that Henry here will remain . . . oh, how shall I say it? *Disinclined* to part with any salts, any residual brew he may or may not have." Which speech he closed with that hyena's laugh, so strong, so loud that it brought Poole to rap at the laboratory door.

"Sir? Is that you? Sir, are you all right in there? . . . Henry? . . . Hal, answer me!"

"Indeed we . . . indeed I am, Poole, yes." Here was the voice all the household would know as the master's. "All's well. I shall ring if you're needed, man; otherwise, leave us be, *please.*"

Silence. Poole's presence could be felt as he backed away from the door to which his ear, no doubt, had been pressed. I wondered what the manservant had heard, yes; but my greater worry by far regarded the man he served.

In point of fact, Poole's coming, his sudden knocking upon the laboratory door, would, in retrospect, seem to have united the two selves of his master. Henceforth, they spoke as one. To be precise, I found before me now one being composed of a Jekyll whose edges, let me say, were yet unfiled and a Hyde more given to reason, more inclined to heed the unwritten rules of converse. I watched his eyes, and as long as they remained a deep and watery brown, nearly but not quite black, I knew I dealt with both Jekyll and Hyde *at once,* albeit in the guise of Jekyll; and that was as I wanted it, for only then might we *three* make any progress toward, yes, resolution. Just what shape that resolution would take, well . . .

Once Poole's shadow was gone from beneath the door, once his tread could be heard upon the staircase, headed downward, his master moved to the laboratory's wall, the one shared by his bedroom. He swung that framed periodic table aside to disclose the peephole, and whispered, "This was his idea."

"Poole's?"

"Precisely. He hasn't trusted you since that very first day at the zoo."

He had good reason not to, is what I thought but did not say.

"Tell us why," said he, returning to his customary chair at the laboratory table; and so I found myself telling him—telling them—about events as they'd passed at the *singerie*.

Why? Well, his was a trained scientific mind, after all, and I was *open*—to put it mildly—to whatever help he could offer regarding the salts; or, more to the point, Gréluchon. And I suppose, too, that I intended it to be heard as a cautionary tale. Alas, I'm afraid it was heard as something else entirely: *Proof*, perhaps. For I was disheartened to hear that all their questions were of a scientific sort, related to the process, and how to replicate it; and underlying all their questions was that one word: *More*.

Of course, I had precious few answers.

This displeased them, but Jekyll continued to wheedle, while Hyde forwent his ranting. And it was this balance that somehow encouraged me to speak on, rendering my would-be cautionary tale a pure confession. And soon confession ceded to cooperation.

Yes: I would cooperate. All in the hopes of finding some resolution to this strangest, *strangest* of situations.

After all, hadn't Mister Hyde intimated that he'd had news of Gréluchon? He'd handed me back that eye patch I'd sewn for him, so long ago, which (evidently) he'd recovered from the boy himself, now that he'd no need of it. And what else could I do besides cooperate with Doctor Jekyll if I'd any hope of recovering the stolen salts and deciding, myself, on their disposition? I supposed I might make more, if ever I had peace and privacy enough, yes; but still that first batch would be in Jekyll's (Hyde's) possession. Not good; not good *at all*. Moreover: I'd doubtless need them both, Jekyll *and* Hyde, if I were ever to find Gréluchon in a city on the very brink of civil war, if I were ever to understand what it was I'd wrought. For yes, I'd done this, *all this*. And so, I supposed, I bore some responsibility for the being, for the *beings*, plural, before me.

Cooperation, yes. . . . It seemed like a good idea at the time.

I knew what Doctor Jekyll wanted to know, and—*cooperating*, putting all thoughts of Gréluchon and Julien as *out of mind* as best I could—I told him.

Mister Hyde, for his part, cared less about the *how* and more about the *now*, as in: *More! Now!* Thusly did he recede, and happily so.

Henry had wanted the salts, too, of course; but *that* he'd already achieved by spying, by lying, by stealing . . . facts that I tried my best to set aside just then. What he wanted now, perhaps even more than a fresh store of salts themselves, was the *secret* of the salts, knowledge of how to make more. "Odile, do you know what this discovery might mean?" he'd ask, again and again. Indeed I did: It *might* mean that the knowledge, the secret of the salts, would redeem Doctor Jekyll with the Royal Society. Assuming, that is, that capital-R Redemption was still foremost on his agenda, ahead of being able to transform into Hyde *at will*, for this uncontrollable transformation, this unbidden back-and-forth, was, well . . . *problematic*, to put it mildly. An antidote was what was wanted. An antidote, indeed.

Alas, yes, I opened myself to questioning that morning; and this I communicated to my interlocutor—ever more Doctor Jekyll with each passing minute—via raised brows as he sat across the table from me. *Well? Now's your chance.*

The sun had risen, yet the laboratory was still deeply shadowed. So, too, was my companion, sitting with his back to the windows and listening intently, too intently. I adjusted myself so as to be able to see his eyes.

I heard the doctor's first question before he could voice it, practically; for he'd asked it of me a hundred times: *Wherever were we from?*

In the past I'd dissembled, though I'd never lied. I'd said "the south." Of course, Doctor Jekyll now wanted nothing more than for me to spread a map upon the table and locate our village precisely. That I would not do, *ever*; for he had both the mania and the means to go there and turn the village inside out in search of salt-related secrets.

Hewing to that spirit of cooperation which (stupidly) had settled over me, I knew I had to offer more than I ever had before, but before I could speak, I had to first fight back tears.

My thoughts had turned to my mother. . . . And please please *please* might those books of hers still lie secreted beneath the floorboards above, beneath my cot. I was fairly sure they were still there, for had not Mister Hyde felt me for them, bodily, out in the arcaded square? *That* memory I suppressed alongside those of my mother. Only then was I able to speak on without fear of tears.

"Where are we from, you ask?"

"Yes," said Doctor Jekyll, "I'd very much like to know." Here was proper, parlor-bred Henry Jekyll; but I reminded myself that Edward Hyde was yet present, like a simmering cauldron off which one need only lift the lid to free a most fetid odor. I'd take care to keep that lid secure.

"The south," said I, yet again.

"Yes, yes, I know," said Jekyll. "Can you not locate the place more *precisely*?"

I said I could not, said that Gréluchon had been the navigator in our journey to Paris. This last was true, in fact; but I did know a bit more than that. "The far southwest," I then said, "in the cavelands around Pau." And before he could press, I said, peremptorily, "We fled after the death of our parents . . . the *murder* of our parents."

"I, too, lost my mother at an impressionable age, Odile. I understand—"

"You speak as if you *misplaced* your mother." If that was cruel, I didn't care. "*My* mother was murdered for being a witch."

That word, *witch*, caught him, as of course it would; but his well-bred habits had been deeply engrained, and he said, "I am sorry to—"

"Murdered, yes; and so, too, was our father murdered, killed for coming to her rescue against . . ." I found I could not continue; but then anger spurred me on: *"He"*—and perhaps I put an undue emphasis on the word so as to make my point plain—*"he* was an honorable man."

Doctor Jekyll heard my meaning and turned his head away. The shame was short-lived, and the doctor fast rejoined with the expected:

"A witch, did you say?"

"A witch, yes." And there I let the matter lie.

He was silent awhile, then: "A *witch?*"

"Yes," said I, again. And briefly I wondered if the salts hadn't split the man in thirds, the last part being parrot.

The doctor would return to the word soon enough, but for now he pressed on. "And so you and your brother were left alone, orphaned."

"Well, yes; but you knew as much, Henry, did you not? You *knew* we were alone in the world."

That accusing dart met its mark; but the doctor's heart had perhaps been hardened by the advent of Mister Hyde, and so he simply asked, again, as I'd known he would, "Your mother . . . Was she really a . . . ? Are *you* really a . . . ?"

"I suppose she was, and I suppose I am." As I didn't want to consider the question of witchery further, I spoke on, offering what seemed, and what perhaps *is*, the more salient fact regarding my mother and me. "We come from a people of the southwest called the Cagot. And we Cagot women are reputed to have . . . powers."

"Powers," parroted he. It was looking as though I'd have to lead this conversation. "What sort of powers?"

"Well," said I, truthfully, "you of all people ought to know."

Doctor Jekyll stared at me now as if I were about to hop up onto the sill, shape-shift myself, and fly off in bird form to rendezvous with the devil. "Healing powers," I continued, cocking my head toward the laboratory wall adjoining his bedchamber. "Healing powers such as those you witnessed from your little . . . hidey-hole."

Hidey-hole? Alas, the words may have belied the menace I'd spoken them with, but oh well. Henry heard the accusation nonetheless; and where Henry Jekyll of old would have proffered an apology, this Henry, this new and Hyded Henry, simply returned to his line of questioning even more intently than before:

"But how, Odile? *How* did you heal him?"

It was my turn to dissemble now, as *I don't know, really,* seemed hardly the response to keep my questioner cooperative, as I'd want him to be just that when *I* started asking the questions, as soon I would. "You wish to know?"

The answer, *Yes!,* was so plain that Jekyll did not deign to voice it, not at first; but soon it was clear my prevaricating, my putting-off of what (little) I knew, had brought him to the very brink of . . . *transforming,* whether he wanted to or not; such that when he finally spoke, his voice had a bit more of the baritone, a bit more Hyde about it.

"Yes, yes, Odile, we very much want to know." Jekyll caught himself then, and his voice, when next he spoke, had retaken to Jekyll's higher register. Too, his fists went slack. And amending the betraying pronoun, he said, "I mean to say that I, *I* very much wish to know how you effected those changes in your brother, those very salutary changes to his eyes, to his sight. Odile, you must understand the medical implications of that."

"And you, *Doctor*, must understand that I do not suppose, not for a moment, that you prize the 'medical implications' of the salts over the . . . *fellowship*, let me say, that you have found in Mister Hyde."

"No . . . well . . . I . . ."

"Precisely," said I, sparing his having to stumble to the end of yet another lie; but then, quite suddenly, Doctor Jekyll leaped up from his seat so as to lean over the table toward me, *at* me, with self-pitying tears seeping from his eyes. When he spoke, well, it was most decidedly Doctor Jekyll, albeit more animated than I'd ever seen him and, though somewhat Hyde-like in his intensity, nonetheless he was practically *mewling*. Dare I say I'd soon come to long for a bit more Hyde behind his words?

"All my life," said he, so near I could feel his words upon my face, "I have lived in fear of what others have thought of me, *expected* of me. . . . Fear of my father. Fear of my fellows.

And, yes, fear of finding my truer self, imprisoned in the fortress of identity."

The fortress of identity? Rather highfalutin, that.

I was suddenly quite tired. I wanted to sleep and dream of Julien, gather my strength, and then retake to the streets to find him and fix things—how, I'd no idea—and set off again in search of Gréluchon. I was tired, yes; but surprised, too, at how deeply I'd come to disdain the doctor I'd all but worshipped (it's true) not long ago. Still, I thought it best to listen to him with interest—*feigned* interest—and without comment, though a part of me very badly wanted to say that I'd thought the only fortresses Henry Jekyll had ever known were mansions bought or let with his father's money. But, no: I said nothing. I sat back, stifled a yawn, and folded my arms atop my chest, readying to take in Henry's speech; and a speech it seemed, well-rehearsed and meant to win me to his cause, meant to secure my *total* and unquestioning cooperation, as he sang the praises of . . . *duality*, I'll call it. And it was all I could do to forbear, to keep my silence as Henry Jekyll spoke then in roundabout praise, *praise* of the other, of Mister Hyde.

"All my life," said he, "I have been a . . . a secret sinner. Until now. Until our Mister Hyde—"

"He is hardly 'ours.' Hardly."

"Hyde has freed me. Your salts have freed me, Odile! And I *very* much like my newfound freedom."

Just what "freedom" he was referring to, well . . . Only a

fool would have failed to surmise what he, what *they* had lately gotten up to among the gamblers, whores, dandies, and no-gooders who were, I knew, as active as bees from a broken hive now, with Paris on the precipice of war. Still and all, I asked: "What, pray tell, is 'secret sinning'?"

"No matter, that," said Doctor Jekyll. I'd not have credited him with the ability to still be embarrassed, yet embarrassed he seemed. "What matters, Odile, is how . . . ? Whence comes this . . . this too-literally *terrific* recipe that renders a man so free, so . . ."

He was too excited at the prospect of my answer to even finish his question. He leaped up again and started to pace before the tall windows of the laboratory. I saw him in silhouette, turning his head toward me at every other step, watching me, seemingly *willing* me to speak. I felt very much a bird in the company of a cat; and if this bird did not start to sing, and soon, the cat would surely pounce.

But oughtn't I to use his heightened, too-curious state against him? Indeed, why should I answer his questions without securing answers in my turn?

"Tell me," said I. "How does it feel? Why are both your . . . *selves* so intent on having more of the salts?"

He stopped pacing and stared at me, loathingly; but he understood what it was I was proposing: *A trade.* And by my ensuing silence, I let it be known that the next offering had best be his. He owed me that much at least. And so it was he said, "Freedom, in a word.

"As Hyde," he continued, crossing the room, back and forth, like a lion in its cage, "well, Hyde has infinitely more courage than I. He is unafraid to be the self I suppress for society's benefit."

Et voilà! Finally he'd gone to the heart of the matter.

"Imagine it, Odile! I hadn't yet indulged, as desired, in the brewed salts . . . had only experimented upon—"

"The cats," said I.

"Yes," said he, with but the slightest trace of remorse. "But then I went last night to the Café Anglais, where I have dined a hundred times in the stiffest company."

Of course, Doctor Jekyll had just confessed to being in possession of the pilfered salts; but I let that go unremarked upon. For now. I said instead, "And . . . ?"

"And imagine the joy, the most *illicit* joy, of walking into the café as Doctor Henry Jekyll—hellos and huzzahs all around, harrumph, harrumph and all that—and then ceding my place, as it were, to that self we've since named Hyde. All I had to do was remove from my vest pocket the silver flask into which I'd poured . . ." His words trailed away.

"Into which you'd poured the pilfered contents of vials four and five."

Suddenly his eyes blackened and Hyde-speak rumbled up from deep within him, thunderingly so, to say, "Shut up, girl, and let him speak!"

The doctor soon regained ascendancy and spoke on in rather more measured tones. "Which I stole, yes," said he, "and which

I lied about stealing, yes. I am sorry, Odile. It's just that I, that we—"

"Enough," said I, for truly I'd never before heard how . . . *simpering* Henry Jekyll could be. I hadn't the patience for it at present. "Go on," I prodded. "You were at the Café Anglais, on the verge of self-salting."

Henry seemed relieved that I'd not made him belabor his apology. He spoke on at a clip now. "Well, I paid my bill, made my good-byes, and snuck into the cloak room—"

"How very dignified," said I; but he continued without comment.

"—and I drank. I drank! And sure enough, the very cloak of self soon fell from my shoulders and . . ."

Mon dieu, had the man always been such a melancholic bore, given to such sappy turns of phrase? *The very cloak of self*? Indeed.

"And returning to the dining room, well . . . People who knew me well—my fellow clubbers, the odd diner, even Jean-Charles, the maître d'—were looking upon me as a total stranger! I ingratiated myself, saying I was a guest of the just-departed Doctor Jekyll, making the man's excuses for him; but then, under the guise of gossip, I proceeded to tell them everything that I, that Jekyll, thought of them all! Something I'd never have dared do as *mere* Henry Jekyll."

"Mere and *sane* Henry Jekyll," said I. "Surely you are finished in society now, if your club friends know you to be allied with that Mister Hyde."

"And so be it! Nothing can counter the thrill, the *freedom* I felt as Hyde called each one to account for his hypocrisy. I told one gentleman what I knew of his wife from several messieurs of our mutual acquaintance. I even accused Rodolphe, the chef and owner, who is constantly crying poor, of what everyone was whispering: That what he was serving us—at six francs the slice!—was not mutton but rather dog, and *street* dog at that!"

Indeed, that must have been quite the luncheon. *"Doctor Jekyll and Mister Hyde? Party of two?"* Would that I'd been there to witness it. Surely society was abuzz about it still, despite more pressing concerns as, in a word, *war*.

Through with his tale-telling, Doctor Jekyll now looked at me, expectantly, implying that his off-color tales of mere misanthropy had earned him access to my secrets. *Trade and trade alike*, was what was implied. He even settled himself at the table and opened his notebook, inked his pen and proceeded to stare at me; expectantly, yes. Quite ready, he was, to transcribe my every secret.

Said I, "I come of a very secretive people."

"And it's no wonder," said he, dipping the dried tip of his pen, "as it's quite a secret they keep." He looked up. He dared *smile* at me, even.

Had I then told Henry Jekyll to sit up and beg for a biscuit, he'd have done it. *He was mine*, in other words; and, as Mister Hyde was in abeyance, as best I could tell, I determined to take advantage of the fact.

"First," said I, "tell me all you know of Gréluchon."

Mister Hyde had spoken of having seen my brother, of having had news of him; and whatever Hyde knew, Jekyll knew, too.

"*Hyde* lied," said a disingenuous Doctor Jekyll.

As it turned out, they knew nothing more of Gréluchon than Julien and I had learned in Montmartre, for Mister Hyde had been following us along the same cold trail after that high-society show he'd put on at the Café Anglais. *Wherever had he gotten the eye patch, then?* It'd be some while before I learned the answer to that question. I felt the fabric of the patch in my pocket and . . . and though I could have easily, *so* easily wept, I somehow mastered myself.

"I am sorry, Odile, but I have so little control over . . . *him*."

"Rubbish!" I'd not be manipulated a moment longer; and so it was I stood—and I can only wonder now how I dared do this—and said to Doctor Jekyll, who yet hung upon my every word, "I am sorry. I am tired and must sleep, and I've had enough of your lies." And with that, I turned and walked toward the laboratory door, hoping against hope that I'd not riled the doctor and . . .

Yet I had; and it was Mister Hyde, *not* Doctor Jekyll, who made it to the door before I did, who now barred my way.

"Lies? *Lies.* Do you think lies will be the worst of it, girl? Then just you wait. We'll have your secrets soon enough, no matter the means."

"Are you . . . threatening me?"

"Yesss," said he, and the sibilance came accompanied by spit, spit that alit upon my face.

Scared though I was of this sudden-coming Hyde—and make no mistake: *I was scared*—I reasoned, with great effort, that he'd not hurt me. For any knowledge they hoped to gain depended on my imparting it, and I could hardly do that if . . . dead. Still and all . . .

"You tremble, witchling," said Edward Hyde, his black eyes mere inches from mine, "and so I fear you mistake my threat. It is not *you* I mean to threaten, no. It is your beloved brother."

"Gréluchon? What do you mean? He . . . Doctor Jekyll . . . just admitted that you know nothing of—"

"Oh, fear not: I will find him. I can track any prey, and Jekyll will contribute whatever means necessary. Bribery, after all, is the order of the day during wartime." He moved his face nearer mine, though I'd not have thought that possible. We were now nose-to-nose, horribly so, close enough . . . *to kiss.* "And when I find him, if still he be salted and strong owing to that overdosage, we will yet win him to our ways and train *all* our selves upon you, Sister. You'll be no match for us. No, no; you will *happily* surrender your secrets in the end. And if he has returned to his weakened, runtish state, well then . . ."

"What? What then?" For of course I hoped he *had* become my brother again.

"We shall hide him, and ransom him for your secrets."

"And if I . . . if I refuse . . . ?"

"In that case," seethed Hyde, "I shall petition my pettier

self for permission to kill him; and he, Henry, will grant it, for . . ." and here he paused to great effect, and loosed his laugh upon me ". . . believe me when I say it is always the mildest of men who are most drawn to murder."

I was pressed flat against the laboratory door now, and—*damn him!*—I'd begun to cry. I thought to call out to Cézette, perhaps even to Poole; but just as I was about to do so, the monster backed away from me. I now had just enough room to turn, to turn and task my shaking hands with those thrown bolts and the doorknob itself. As I did so, I heard that horrid grinding—bone on bone, *self on self*, that transformative sound akin to shoreside stones being ground beneath a breaking wave—and I turned back to see that . . .

Doctor Jekyll was trying to rise, trying to fend off Mister Hyde.

Henry then spoke, saying, weakly, *"Forgive me, Odile! He is too strong for me and—"*

"Shut up!" Here again was Hyde; and beneath his bellowed command it seemed I could hear the doctor's apology sputter to its non-end. I then saw the strangest of sights: Mister Hyde, with a hairy, horrid hand, wiped backhandedly at tears that had sprung not to his eyes, but to those of Henry Jekyll.

I quit the laboratory and took the stairs up to my room two at a time.

Behind me I heard Mister Hyde say, "Midday, my dear. You have till midday to decide: Share your secrets or suffer the consequences."

As soon as I returned to my room, I fell to my knees and yes, *yes*, thankfully my mother's books were where I'd secreted them.

I rose from my knees, jammed my one chair beneath the doorknob—it was the sole defense available to me—and having first found my hand mirror and my tweezers, the tips of which I heated over candle flame, I picked those stitches from my neck, for I'd be damned if Doctor Jekyll would ever touch me again. Only then did I fall crying upon my cot.

In time I took up paper and pen: I would explain *all and everything* to Julien. Oh, but the weirdness of it could not be contained in words! Regardless, I wrote. I apologized, and I pled for both his forgiveness and help. *What was I to do?*

I must have cried myself into a dreamless sleep, and blessedly so. My wakeful visions of Gréluchon and of the beast belowstairs had been bad enough.

I was woken by the rattling door. Someone was working the knob on the far side, quite insistently so. Hurriedly, I folded my letter to Julien, smoothing it first—for the tears had dried upon the pages, wrinkling them and rendering the writing as senseless as the sentiments it held: a mishmash of *sorrow, apologies, pleas*—and I slid the pages into an envelope.

"Go away! Leave me!" I knew not how long I'd slept, knew only that I'd not slept long enough. I took up my pen again and hurriedly addressed the envelope to Julien: *Deboos et fils, rue Tiquetonne.*

Whoever, *what*ever it was on the far side of the door seemed about to break it down now. I took in my surrounds—a lamp nearly devoid of oil, a flimsy blue curtain through which mid-day light was seeping—looking for a weapon of sorts. I found none.

"Odile! Open up, please." It was a whispering Cézette, whose voice I'd never have thought I could be so happy to hear.

"Are you alone?"

"Yes, yes, of course. Open the door, Odile!"

She was crying, and I knew I had no choice but to trust her; though with no difficulty at all I imagined Mister Hyde stand-ing behind the girl, manipulating her like a marionette.

But no: Having slipped my letter to Julien into the pocket of my shift, I opened the door to Cézette alone, and she all but fell into my arms. I shut the door and reset the chair in its place. "What is it, Cézette? Has he . . . ?" And I dared not fin-ish the question, for hadn't I left Mister Hyde in a rampaging state? What if he'd . . . ?

"It's terrible," said Cézette, her beauty buried now beneath a weight of worry. "Terrible!"

"What is terrible, Cézette? Speak!"

"It's begun," said she.

"*What* has begun?" I had her by the shoulders now, and just as I was about to shake it out of her she set her forefinger to her quivering lip, shut her eyes, and said, "Shh. *Listen!*"

It was then I heard the steady shots and shelling, far away upon the hills of Montmartre.

My eyes refound Cézette's just as her bloodless lips puckered in a vain attempt to voice the word, *war*.

And indeed, the bloodiest of ends had begun that day in the post-dawn hours, just as I'd sat in the laboratory waging a war of my own.

CHAPTER TEN

Martyrs' Mount

My long months in Paris had been . . . unpleasant, and now things had segued to strange, very, *very* strange; but I'd not seen a dead body in some while, and so what I saw that morning in Montmartre disturbed me, deeply. It put me in mind of my mother and father. And it seemed yet another example of a life lesson I'd long tried to deny: There is nothing one man will not do to another.

. . . *Alors*, Cézette had come to my attic room in hysterics. Once I calmed her sufficiently, she said she'd heard from Doctor Jekyll's bread woman in the rue de Turenne that war had broken out that very day at dawn. Now I knew that Les Fédérés, having lately grown even more distrustful of the regular army at Versailles, thinking they were in collusion with the conquering Prussians, had moved the cannons purchased during the first siege from depots in the west of the city to Montmartre.

The baker's wife was reporting that last night the president had ordered the regulars to march up onto Montmartre by first light to *re*requisition the cannons.

And indeed, from the attic rooms high atop the Marais mansion, we could hear the resounding proof of all this ourselves: the report of the occasional cannon and the steadier *rat-tat-tat* of lesser arms.

I wondered why this news would have upset the girl so. After all, such an engagement had long been expected. What's more: There were few places in the city as safe and well-provisioned as Doctor Jekyll's home. Despite the master's disdain for the girl, I imagined it'd be easy enough for her to stay in his employ, especially now that Cheffy had run off; for the doctor would want his meals, and, war or no, Poole would refuse to enter the woman's world of the kitchen to prepare them.

Cézette, however, did not see things as I did; and I had to give some quarter to her view. Now that her aunt had "run off," leaving her very much in the lurch, with neither money nor news of her whereabouts, Cézette considered herself very vulnerable indeed. She no longer had the more *valuable* woman's weight behind her. And I supposed she had a point: *In extremis*, as now we were, perhaps neither Doctor Jekyll nor Poole would hesitate to give the girl the boot and make do as best they could; and as for Mister Hyde, well . . .

Still, I had problems of my own, did I not?

I had to get up to Montmartre before the warring worsened,

before Gréluchon could come to real harm . . . Or *cause* real harm.

"Cézette," I said, taking the girl by the shoulders so suddenly, so fiercely, that she stopped her sobbing (thankfully). "I need your help."

"You . . . you need *my* help? Why do you think I came up here, Odile? I need *your* help. If *you* don't help me—"

"Perhaps . . ." I reasoned, "perhaps we can help each other." And I meant it, for hadn't Cézette helped me (albeit inadvertently) by leading me to the armored man and his secrets?

Cézette was suspicious, and how could I blame her? We'd not exactly been the best of friends since my arrival chez Jekyll. Still, to the girl's credit, she knew her options to be few, and so she said, "How? Tell me how."

How? How, indeed?

But then it came to me.

"Where is he?" I asked.

"Who?"

As simple a question as it was, I found I could not answer it, not truthfully, not to Cézette; and so I rephrased it. "Who is in the laboratory?"

I was certain the two selves would have been in there all night, swapping ascendancy, Jekyll bent over the brew, analyzing it, scribbling away at his suppositions, Hyde hurrying him on while keeping an ear cocked toward the hall beyond the laboratory, lest I wake and try to slip from the house.

"I . . . I'm not sure," said Cézette. "I did not see either the master or that . . . that *horrid* acquaintance of his leave in the night. And the doctor—at least I think it was he—rang down for a cold meal of meats a few hours past. As far as I know, Odile, they're both in there still."

Good. That was good.

"Cézette, can you scream?"

She looked at me strangely, and no wonder: It was an odd question indeed; but as it was no more odd than the goings-on in the manse of late she soon answered, in all honesty, saying, "*Not* screaming has been the greater effort of late, Odile. Indeed, I should very much like to scream."

"No, no! Not now." I had to slip my hand over her mouth, and did so just in time. She'd sucked in enough air to fill a sail and was about to scream *then and there*. "Save your scream, Cézette. What I, what *we* need you to do is this . . ." and I explained my hurriedly formed, haphazard plan, conceived with all the hope I could muster. Either it would work or else . . .

As I did not care to consider the *or else*, I hurried Cézette to her place, which was downstairs in the kitchen. And then I waited, and waited some more before taking to mine.

Zut, the girl could scream!

The sound came to me, *through* me, as I sat in a crouch atop the stair landing, staring down through shadows and the slatted banister to the laboratory door.

Nothing. The door did not open.

I'd told Cézette to scream until she'd gotten the doctor's

215

attention, not just Poole's, and so she screamed again. This was even louder than the first and had something eerily . . . genuine about it, such that I hoped she hadn't fallen into Poole's cruel clutches.

It worked: I heard the bolts thrown and now the laboratory door was wrenched open. Out he came, seeming, just then, rather more Jekyll than Hyde. "Poole! Poole, what is that racket?" he shouted down the stairwell. I was still as stone. If he turned his head he would see me, mere feet away, crouched there in the dark at the top of the stairs.

And then, bless her, Cézette let go with another bloodcurdler. "Scream," I'd said, "until you draw the doctor downstairs."

"What then?" she'd countered.

I had to think about that one for a moment. "Have the finest breakfast you can muster all laid out and ready. Remind them that now that Cheffy's run off you're their last link to food." And it was true: Once the Jekyll larder was run through, who would hunt the streets, cash in hand, if not Cézette? Needless to say, my offer *to market* no longer stood, Poole hadn't enough French for it, and as for the doctor fending for himself? Hardly. Food would be Cézette's salvation. Such was our wager.

"Well and good," reasoned Cézette; "but how do I explain the screaming?"

"Tell them . . . tell them . . . Tell them you've seen the cats!"

"The cats are dead as doornails, Odile!" She began to sniffle, tears welling. "Did you not *see* what that horrible Poole did to them? He drowned them all! He . . . He—"

"Yes, yes, I know. I mean, tell them you've seen the *ghosts* of the cats."

She stared at me. "What? *What?* Do you think they'll retain me once I've proven myself freed of all my senses? I'm certain they'd be able to find a *non*-crazy woman to cook for them, even with war broken out. . . . Come now, Odile."

"You can explain yourself. Scream until Doctor Jekyll comes into the kitchen, Jekyll and Poole *both*, and then apologize, say that you'd have sworn, *sworn* that you'd seen the cats themselves out in the courtyard. Allude to your aunt's having left you. Allude to . . . I don't know what! Then say your hands are shaking too badly to bring the doctor's breakfast to him, but be sure he *sees* the breakfast, Cézette. Have you something, *anything* to make it more tempting than usual?" Cézette had nodded, said she knew where Cheffy had secreted a bit of cured ham, hiding it for herself.

Now Doctor Jekyll, uttering Hyde-like curses, hurried down to the kitchen to see what the matter was, for still Cézette was screaming to (it must be said) *great* effect. My own ears were ringing. And, as hoped, he'd walked away from the laboratory door in a huff, shutting but not locking it; for, of course, I didn't yet have a key to the new door.

The very second he was out of sight, I sprang from my crouch, slipped down the stairs—holding tightly to the waist-let, which I once again wore, for it does sometimes clack about so, with its pendant charms and whatnot!—and slid into the laboratory. Yes, there it was: A single vial of the brewed salts.

In his experimenting, Doctor Jekyll must have already gone through half the stolen salts, or rather the brew made therefrom; and there, in its stand, was all that remained of the Cagot salts, *my* salts, deeply blue and steaming still.

I corked the vial and, well . . . To say I snuck downstairs, past the commotion in the kitchen, to and *out* the front door is an understatement. *I flew!*

And only on the streets far, far from the Place des Vosges did I spare a thought for Cézette. I was grateful, very; for not only had she *screamed* me free, as it were, she'd also agreed to post my letter to Julien. It was a long shot indeed: *If* the post continued to be picked up now, *if* the letter somehow found its way to the rue Tiquetonne, *if* it cleared the clutches of first his father and then his mother, *if* . . . If ever Julien got my letter, it would be a miracle.

Alas, I let all such thoughts pass for now; for I'd a war to witness, and a would-be soldier to save.

It was quite cold, and my breath came in clouds as I ran northward, toward Montmartre, and then finally my lungs tightened. I could run no more, no matter how I wished to. Thusly did it take me some time to cross the city, south to north, for I knew I had best take great care en route.

I did not want to give Mister Hyde a straight trail to follow. (And certainly not a trail leading straight to the rue Tiquetonne.) And so I serpentined, here, there, and back again. It was on the boulevard Beaumarchais that I thought I saw Julien, yes, disappearing around a corner. *Could it be?* Impossible. I called out after him, ran after him, even; but whoever it was I'd seen was gone. And it was naught but *a hope* I'd seen, surely. So it was I tried, *tried* not to give my supposed sighting of Julien a second thought.

Finally I found myself following the flow of the river to the Louvre. It was there that I heard someone say that the regular army was in retreat to Versailles, that indeed the National Guard had held Montmartre and, more important, the ordnance—the two-hundred-odd cannons—that they had stashed up there, high on the highest hill of the city proper.

I would later learn that the regulars had arrived on the mount well before dawn, as directed, and taken the gun park without a problem; but someone had failed to command horses, enough *harnessed* horses to wheel the cannons away. And so, while the regulars—cold, hungry, many of them back amid their own people for the first time in some while—waited for the horses, they began to fraternize with the Montmartrois and even the ragtag Fédérés. Civil enough, in the truest sense. Now just how it devolved from that to what happened next, well, I'm not sure I'll ever understand that.

Yet it did. It devolved terribly; and by that time I'd made my way uphill to the site of it all, my fist holding to the tightly corked vial in my pocket. I did not know if I might need some small dose of the salts; for of course I'd no idea what state Gréluchon would be in when I found him, as I was certain, *certain* I would. Was he *changeable*, as Doctor Jekyll was, with one (or more!) selves swapping ascendancy, or had he changed *wholly*, having downed all the strongest brew?

Alors, by the time I reached the very heights of Montmartre, whipped by an icy wind, first blood was about to be shed. Word had spread quickly, of course, that early morning, and as I ran uphill, I heard all about me cries of "Treason!" and "They've come to take our cannon!" Citizenry equipped with the crudest of weapons were headed up to the heights despite the bitter cold, and coming downhill I saw many regular troops, deserting.

I followed the flow of people through the tiny, winding *ruelles* ringing the mount itself. Someone in the crowd had a drum that they beat incessantly, till it came to seem the quickened pulse of the people. Here women pulled tight their shutters; there they threw them wide, tossing down makeshift weaponry and shouting encouragement to the mob, now shoving a uniformed man along at its front.

Never could I have imagined events as they were soon to unfold.

While moving as one with the mob, I only half-watched what was happening, for I was more focused on finding Gréluchon, certain he'd be there, somewhere; but I did not see him. I took to calling out his name, crying it. Still, nothing but the occasional sympathetic stare.

Somehow I made it to the very middle of the mob, carried as a boat is by the current. I cared not a whit what dangers I might be exposing myself to, for now I could see the surrounded soldier and . . .

It was not Gréluchon.

It was, in fact, General Lecomte, leader of the failed, *horseless* mission. I heartened when it seemed cooler heads would prevail, albeit briefly; for I heard it rumored that the general, for his own safety, was to be led to an impromptu prison along with General Clément Thomas, who'd foolishly, fatefully, walked uphill from the city center to see what was happening. That was *not* to happen, however; for just then a cry rose up, a lone voice commanding the remaining regulars to load and fix bayonets.

Whether the command came from one or both of the generals, I cannot say; but they were held responsible for it.

And as for the regulars, well, not a single rifle was readied with its bayonet. It seemed that now *all* the rifles were being held upside down, in fact; for the remaining regulars—now vastly outnumbered—took care to raise high the butt end of their rifles, lest they too be set upon by the people.

Cries of bloodlust went up in reply to that failed command regarding the rifles, and soon prison was forgone, the idea forgotten. Instead, the generals were delivered to those who'd gathered behind a rather nondescript house, in a garden replete with climbers and trellises, and . . . and I remember thinking, incongruously, that the garden would be so beautiful in a few months' time, come June, when its roses would bloom, but alas . . .

Someone—and history will never know who, I suppose— fired upon the generals, shooting first General Thomas and then General Lecomte, both in the back; after which anyone with a weapon seemed to take their turn. It was horrid, and endlessly so; for the men were felled by forty, *fifty* bullets, easily. I could not get away, but neither could I *turn* away from what I was near enough to witness, for I'd made my way into that very garden—where the noise of . . . *execution* was deafening now—in the hopes of finding leadership there, someone, *anyone* who might have word of Gréluchon. Or perhaps I'd even find Gréluchon himself; for, loath though I was to admit it, the beast he'd become was likely to be found at the heart of such a mob as this. But, no: He was not there; and as for leadership, well, every mob is a hydra, a many-headed thing, and I saw no sign of a soldier in charge.

Soon I was carried from the garden involuntarily, by the murderous mob itself. Oh, but now that the generals had been murdered—and this was, of course, a declaration of war, civil war—alas, the mob moved from murder to mutilation.

The broken bodies were then cast into the street like offal, and there I watched, admittedly unable to turn away, yes, as a brigade of beggarly women raised high their skirts and . . . and pissed upon the medaled uniforms of the murdered men. The urine rose as steam, infernal steam off the bodies, and it was seeing that, *smelling* it, that caused my stomach and soul, both, to cave.

For when last I'd seen broken bodies in the street, they'd been those of my mother and father. Was I soon to find my brother's as well?

I fought my way to the mob's edge, then back into that Golgotha, that garden of execution. It was there that I vomited so violently that I had to cling to a thorny trellis for support, heedless of the hurt to my hands, heedless even of the blood that would well when finally I pulled back. Thorns came away in the fabric of my gloves, and soon my blood began to seep through.

Was I living some horrid dream? There seemed no other explanation for what it was I'd witnessed (and still I could hear the harpies on the far side of that garden wall, and it sounded like they were pecking at the corpses as crows would). It was all real, *too* real; and I was recalled to that fact by a voice, a voice quite deep and stern, telling me, no, *commanding* me to stand.

"Get up, Odile."

I turned where I sat, fallen to my haunches in the gravel of the garden. The thin wintry sun was behind his head—a Satan-sent halo—and so, though squinting, turning this way and that, still I could not see his face. Too, there were tears with which to contend; many tears.

"Get up," said he, again; but this time he proffered a hand to help me stand.

I took his hand. The hurt thus occasioned—for his hand was strong, and he squeezed my bloodied hand hard, pushing the thorns deeper—roused me to reason. And, heartsick, I reasoned rightly that I knew but one man with a hand as strong as that:

Hyde.

It was Hyde. I was sure of it.

I stood. That tocsin was still being beat in some distant street. I remember thinking it was a sort of anti-music, music for murderers. And then the sun must have slid behind a cloud, for it no longer occluded my view and I saw who it was had so rudely commanded me to stand.

It was not Mister Hyde, but rather my brother. "Gréluchon!"

Finally, I'd found him! Rather, he'd found me; but never mind. I hugged him, oh how I hugged him . . . but it was as though I'd thrown myself on stone, on statuary.

My brother's arms lay limply at his sides till finally he raised them, raised them to push me away.

"What are you doing here, Odile?"

It was more a rebuke than a question. I know that now. Then, however, I was busy taking in the boy, *the man*; for, yes, he'd most definitely changed and . . . No, he'd *transformed* entirely; and my realizing the difference between variance, or change as I'd seen it exhibited with Doctor Jekyll and Mister Hyde, and *this*, total, salt-induced transformation, came with an accompanying *thud*, as if my very heart had fallen from its place. *What had I done to my brother?*

At first, I tried to tell myself that he'd pushed me away out of pride. Grel had always borne a pride in direct disproportion to his size. How often had my father lost even the slightest, silliest of competitions with his son at the last minute, throwing fate Gréluchon's way lest the boy brood about it all day long?

But pride seemed not to be at issue now, for there was no one in the garden but us, no one to see the soldier indulged so by his worrying sister.

And a soldier he was! Had it not been a uniform of war, his (admittedly ragtag) guardsman's garb, I might have taken a moment's pride in his appearance, I'd have lamented the fact that my mother—who'd always worried so about her son's size and state of health—was not there to see him now; for he was . . . robust, strong.

More than strong, in fact. *Salted*. And thinking back to the transformation, well, I dare say I half-expected an apology, but no.

"You don't belong here," said he. "You must go."

Even his voice was bolder now, baritoned.

"You don't belong here either," I countered; whereupon Grel, my Gréluchon, turned hard on his heel and made to walk from the garden.

"Stop! *Wait!*"

He did not break his stride, did not even slow in approaching the garden gate.

I ran to him. I grabbed hold of his arm and felt a musculature that, simply, had never been his, and that he never could have acquired on his own in the days, mere days since I'd seen him last, in the laboratory. The thin red fabric of his guardsman's trousers seemed about to burst at the thigh, and so too did the fabric of his brownish blouse strain at the buttons. He wore no jacket. He was a specimen of health and strength, albeit brutishly so.

Alors, how else had my brother changed? I needed to know.

Reason, I told myself. *Reason*. I knew I had but precious little time, and I think I knew, too, that Gréluchon was already gone from me for good *unless the effect of the salts wore off.* Oh, but could what I, what *we* had done with our strange, so very strange bequest—the Cagot salts—ever be *reasoned* away?

I breathed deeply. I stoppered my tears, my sad thoughts of yesteryear. I gave no thought to good-bye but rather tried to meet my brother anew, as a stranger, a stranger in possession of secrets I very much needed to know.

The first was, of course, this: *Had he transformed irreversibly?* Jekyll clearly had not. Jekyll struggled with his Hyde, who seemingly rose in relation to his moods, his mania. But unlike Doctor Jekyll, Gréluchon had drunk *all* the strongest brew in that sixth vial.

"Gréluchon," said I, "look at me."

He turned and stared down at me—*down at me*, whereas he'd looked up to me, both literally and figuratively, all his young life—with his now jet black eyes, the very eyes of Hyde, it seemed. I looked into those eyes, long and hard; but alas, I might have stared into a well with equal effect.

"What has happened to you? What . . . what have you done?"

Nothing.

"Grel," I said, "do you remember Mother?"

"Of course I do."

"And what about the time we were lost while birding in the uplands and—"

"I remember everything, Odile," said he, coldly. "Yet now I choose to forget."

"Why? *Why?*"

"This is war, Odile! I haven't the time to dicker about days past. I must go."

I knew better than to try and restrain him physically; indeed, I dared not even touch him again, lest he throw me off once more.

"You do know how this happened, don't you?"

"I know," said he, "about as much as you know, I suppose." If he bore any residual humanity within, he might have shown it then; but instead he said only, "Mother. Her books."

"Yes, Mother. And me. And those books."

"Mother is dead, Odile. And I am not. Thanks to you, thanks to those books, I am *very* much alive."

"And this is the thanks I get?"

He laughed, but it was a sound I'd never heard from my brother before. It was . . . *bestial*. "Thanks for what, Odile? You simply did what it is in your nature to do: You *healed* me. What's done is done, and now it is my turn to act in accord with *my* nature."

That he did not ask after more of the salts told me that he, unlike Jekyll, did not waver in his transformation. He was wholly another now, cold, brutish, bestial, yes, and . . . and my brother, regardless. He'd always be my little brother.

"But how do you know it is natural, what you've become? Perhaps it is *un*natural and needs to be undone . . . Somehow."

"Leave it be, Sister. And leave *me* be as well."

Another guardsman came to the garden gate just then, saying, "Captain, there you are." *Captain?* I will not call it pride I felt then, for it was ruined forthwith and fast when the lesser soldier, smiling, followed up with, "What should we do with the generals' bodies, Captain?"

Gréluchon held my gaze, purposely so, as he asked the soldier, "Are they dead?"

"Yes, sir," said the soldier, some years older than Gréluchon yet trembling, *visibly* trembling before him.

Still Gréluchon held my gaze, but it was the subordinate soldier he addressed in saying, "Kill them. Again."

"Sir?" queried the soldier, stunned; but Gréluchon pushed past him without another word. The soldier followed him fast, drawn like metal to a magnet.

The garden gate slammed shut and Gréluchon was gone. Worse still, I found I was afraid to follow him. *Afraid.*

I fell to my knees, alone now in the garden, and cried into my bloodied hands.

⁂

I sat there some while. It seemed a safer place than the streets beyond, despite the bloodied bullets now lodged in the wall against which I leaned: It was the proverbial *scene of the crime*, yes, but the criminals had not yet returned; and so in the meantime I might hide and . . .

228

Hyde!

I had felt a sudden shiver, as if a snake—cold and clammy—had slithered up my shift, along my spine. And then, at the very thought of the man, the monster, I felt that shiver cede to . . . resignation. Utter and complete resignation; for:

He'd found me.

There he stood now, smug, leaning upon the garden gate, the *sole* gate leading from the high-walled garden. Of course, I knew there was no point in running. And was *that* not the height of irony, that there would be no hiding from Mister Hyde, not now, not ever?

I was not surprised to see him; indeed, to be honest, I must now ask myself if I wasn't waiting to be found; for what else was left to me now that I'd been denied by Julien, denied by Gréluchon . . . what else was left to me but the fateful unfolding of my relationship with Doctor Jekyll and Mister Hyde?

And so I stood and went to him, all but surrendering; but then:

"There is a way, you know," said he.

Whatever did he mean? A way for what?

Alas, I simply stared, and said nothing. Mister Hyde spoke on:

"Impressive," he mused, somehow menacingly. "Your brother is . . . impressive. And Doctor Jekyll will be most keen on hearing that *his* transformation is seemingly complete, and likely permanent. Interesting . . . But let us take up that thread later; for now, I say again: There *is* a way to win your brother back." He then cast those hard black eyes of his down at the

pocket in which I held the last of the brewed salts, uncon-
sciously, in a bloodied fist so tight I might have cracked the
glass of the vial; that vial which he surely knew I had on my
person and which yet he did not demand, or take, as I expected
he would.

I'd seen Doctor Jekyll smile, but never in the guise of Mister
Hyde. It was discomfiting, the more so as his smile came accompanied by the most smug of suggestions. Said he, with a
shrug of his shoulders, as if the words he'd utter were simplicity
itself:

"If you can't beat them, Odile—and you cannot—well then,
you might as well join them."

Join who? Whoever did he mean? The rebels? He and my
transformed brother?

Simply, I hadn't the strength to inquire. It seemed that the
answer to every question I'd asked of late had only brought me
lower; now silence seemed the wiser course.

I pushed past a laughing Hyde, following the trail of the
generals' blood from the garden, from the gravel onto the pavers
of the street beyond. None too distant, I saw the field of fought-
for cannon. There they stood, facing west, as cumbersome and
dumb as cattle. And then I simply walked down from the mount,
as if I could *simply* walk away from war . . . and from all the
wrong I had wrought.

Mister Hyde did not follow me. He did not have to, and we
both knew it: He could track me at will. That much he'd proven.

And in many ways, that knowledge was worse than if I'd turned to find him in the shadows behind me.

Where was I going? I knew, but I would not have admitted as much to myself, not then.

What was I thinking? Nothing; for Hyde's words, his strange suggestion, his riddle, resounded in my mind, crowding out all thought, all *rational* thought.

CHAPTER ELEVEN
Strategic Surrender

I wandered the streets like a ghost, a ghoul, stunned into senselessness at having met my *un*brother, at having been tracked yet again by Mister Hyde . . . *enfin*, by all the other bloody and bizarre events in Montmartre.

War changes those who witness it, and though it seems it should change the whole world as well . . . alas, here was life progressing *as usual* in the center of the city. A handful of men who'd no doubt have been known by name to Doctor Jekyll—whom perhaps Mister Hyde had cussed out at the Café Anglais, even—came out onto the sidewalk before Les Frères Provençaux, murmuring of how the fare had fallen even further in quality. "Horse, was that?" asked one. "Hardly," opined another, adding, "One can only wonder what it is one eats . . . and simply order more sauce Toussenel!" Their words then dissolved in peals of laughter. Laughter! It seemed to me the most incongruous sound I'd ever heard, backed as it was by the sound of gunfire high on the hills to the north. Elsewhere, cafés were yet crowded; and people were actually queuing up outside the theater of the Palais Royale.

It all seemed a charade.

I understand now that many Parisians did not know of the severity of the situation, and those who did know, well, they doubted it was really a war and assumed the . . . *skirmish* would quickly run its course. I knew better, and it was all I could do to not scream "War!" the way one would scream "Fire!" to save one's fellows in a burning building. Instead I simply wandered on, wondering—and *not* for the first time, mind you—about the strange ways of man. Oh but to say I wandered is a bit disingenuous: I had a destination, and soon I achieved it:

The very same street, indeed the very same *spot*, where I'd stood upon first setting foot in Paris. In Les Halles; for, yes, I'd come in search of Julien.

Deboos et fils was shuttered, and seemed permanently so. However would I find Julien now? Undo with words or deeds the foolish choice I'd made? Win him back to my side? Via undeliverable letters? Hardly. And I *needed* Julien beside me.

I sank to the street, drew my knees to my chest, and shivered, shivered in time with my tears.

It was cold, and night was coming on fast. The streets of Les Halles, typically quiet at so late an hour, were now all but empty. No doubt word of war had spread to all and sundry, and they'd have known that the streets of the workers' *quartiers* would be unsafe come nightfall. Storefronts were shuttering even as I watched, and I could not discern that sound from the distant report of gunfire; both sounds cracked through the cold night air, both sounds left me skittish, shivering all the more.

I cannot say how long I sat on that street corner, staring through tears at the swirling patterns of the white pavers set into the street until darkness precluded my doing so. I rose and resumed my wandering, soon finding myself before that clock of Saint-Eustache beneath which I'd confided in Julien. It seemed a literal lifetime ago. And now it was as though I were willing time to return to the day, to the precise time and place of my arrival in Paris, as if then I might start anew, relive the last months of my life and *do things differently*.

Ironic: If I had somehow been able to relive those months, I'd never have gone to the Jekyll mansion in the first place, yet that was exactly where I decided to go.

If only Julien knew that after recent events I *again* returned to that mansion in the Marais . . .

Oh, but understand: If formerly I might have starved on the streets, now it seemed likely I'd be shot *before* I could starve. And where else was I to weather winter *and* a war? The cold catacombs, where Timon was sure to be charging exorbitantly? Hardly. And to whom was I to appeal for help? Julien himself was gone, perhaps for good. And Gréluchon, well, he too was gone, gone from me.

I was scared, I admit it; and my options were . . . none. None, save one:

I had the brewed salts and I wore the waistlet; and so it was I knew I'd be welcome—if *welcome* be the word—at the door of Henry Jekyll.

⁂

"Odile!"

Cézette was as happy and relieved to see me as I was to see her. Odd, that: My first Parisian enemy was now my only friend.

I'd snuck down the alley and waited in a shadowed corner of the courtyard for her to appear, alone, in the kitchen; which presumed, of course, that they'd not fired the girl owing to those ghost cats she claimed to have seen.

It was Poole I was wary of and wanted to avoid at all costs. Doctor Jekyll? Mister Hyde? I paid them no mind; for a light coming on in the doctor's bedroom, followed fast by the parting of drapes, the peering down into the darkened courtyard, told me that Doctor Jekyll, in an animal-like, Hyde-ish way, had sensed my return and knew I was near.

The swirling wind in the courtyard had nearly frozen me through by the time I saw, no *heard* Cézette. She *was* still in the doctor's employ!

Had I somehow dozed while upright, braced by the stony corner of the courtyard? I can only say that I heard a crash in the kitchen and it roused me at once.

There stood Cézette on the far side, on the *warm* side of a window of wavering panes. She had just set, or rather *slammed* a silver tea service down upon the kitchen table. The teacup that she cracked in so doing, well, I watched her toss it into the

235

trash while the look on her pitiable, pinched face seemed to say to the master, to his manservant, to the maniac who'd lately taken over the mansion, *So there!*

I presented myself at the door, not daring to knock lest it draw the omnipresent Poole; and finally, with a start, Cézette saw me.

"Odile, come in here!" She had the good sense to whisper, despite her excitement. "Are you well? I was so worried." Then she actually drew me to her, hugged me; and I did not resist. Indeed, it was all I could do to not cry, *again*.

Soon it was clear that Cézette had already accustomed herself as best she could to kitchen work: In seeming imitation of Cheffy, she set water to boil for tea and replated what was left of the doctor's evening meal for me. Simultaneously, or so it seemed, she relieved me of the sodden shawl I wore, Mother's shawl of old. She set it to dry on a rack before the fire and, half-turning, as if afraid to face me full-on, I saw that firelight catch her welling tears.

"Odile, oh Odile . . . can you forgive me? I should have given it to you, not . . . *him*."

Whatever was she talking about? Who was "he," and what had she given him? But she could say no more, not then. In truth, there was no need; for slowly she turned back toward the shawl and, in an instant, I knew all and everything.

"I found it while sweeping the sidewalk the morning after . . . after that night in the laboratory, when . . ." Her confession fell away, but I heard it nonetheless:

Gréluchon must have dropped the eye patch in storming so from the mansion. And why wouldn't he have? Surely it was the last thing he'd want to hold on to now that his sight had been restored, and his strength *more than* restored. And Cézette, ever needful of currying favor, no matter the means, had handed the eye patch over to . . .

"Who?" That was all I said, the one word: *Who?* And Cézette knew fully well what I meant.

"Poole," said she. And so: The eye patch had made its way from Cézette to Poole to Doctor Jekyll; and finally he, as Hyde, had used it to lure me further into this web of . . . weirdness. *Damn him!*

As for Cézette, well . . . Conniving though she'd been, her apology, now, was as true as her tears, and I accepted it. Too fast, perhaps; for suddenly she set in with myriad questions:

Had I made it up to Montmartre?

Had I found my brother?

Had I found Julien? whose name she now knew from the letter she'd posted. (And said she, meaning no harm yet causing my poor heart to seize: "Things being as they are, Odile, we might as well have mailed that letter to the moon.")

And finally: *Whyever was I back at the mansion?*

"Cézette," said I, stemming the flood, "thank you."

She nodded. She understood: *All in due time.* I'd answer her questions (those I *could* answer) *all in due time.* And then she settled me onto the kitchen bench by the fire and slid a bowl of broth and a heel of bread—bread!—before me.

I had countless questions of my own, of course; but one was predominant.

"Who is here, Cézette?"

"I . . . I hardly know anymore. I hear doors opening and closing at all hours, and commands come from behind the closed doors of the laboratory. 'Leave a tray!' 'Bring us tea!' It's . . . it's horrible, Odile! The only positive," she continued, her voice falling to a whisper, "if I may even call it that, is that Poole is positively beside himself!"

"Bring *us* tea," had she said? Indeed, there'd been two cups on the silver tray, for an unbroken one remained upon it. And so Doctor Jekyll and Mister Hyde had succeeded thus far in their ruse, convincing both Cézette and (presumably) Poole that they were two persons, physically so, and not a single man split, with his two selves alternately ascendant.

"Has the other—?" I ventured, only to be interrupted:

"Mister Hyde, do you mean?" She shivered in speaking the name.

"Has Mister Hyde . . ." I resumed, awkwardly, carefully, "shown himself since coming to the house?"

"Hardly, the brute! And the doctor has been in a right foul mood since that cousin of his has been here. I know it's his house, after all, but if you ask me, he ought to—"

"Cousin?" However had she learned that much?

Cézette nodded. "Come from London, he has. Son to the sister of the doctor's dead mother," said she, refilling my tea. "Me? I think he's a spy. . . . Or something like that."

"Did Doctor Jekyll tell you all this?"

"Well, no. I . . . I overheard him explaining things to Poole."
So she was still at the occasional keyhole, then. Good. I was
glad for it. I asked what else she'd *overheard*.

"Well, as for Mister Poole . . ." said she, leaning closer now
and smiling, smiling at having someone to take into her confidence, "Poole, well, he's fit to be tied, having to take his orders
from 'a two-bit Jekyll relation I 'aven't never 'eard of, neither
'ide nor 'air.'"

Her impression of Poole was so good, so uncannily good that
I nearly choked on my broth; for I'd laughed. Laughed! I'd not
have thought it possible. How I loved Cézette then, and regretted the long months we'd been at odds.

Poole, for his part, was rather less amused by the imitation.

He'd snuck into the kitchen unseen. "Get up, girl," said he
to Cézette in measured tones, for he was swallowing his anger,
"and see to them dishes. And you'll pay, you will, for that broken cup in the trash there. You think the Jekyll family crest
on that cup is easily come by?" His tones were changing now,
growing angrier; it was as if he had a Hyde of his own coming
on. Goodness, no: *Please* don't let the doctor have experimented
upon Poole!

I could see Cézette in profile as she stood at the sink, her
back turned to Poole. She was mouthing his words as he spoke
them. I might have laughed again, save for the fact that Poole
must have seen her mimicry reflected in the windows and was
reddening with rage. He took up a knife and tossed it, no *threw*

it into the standing dishwater, the same dishwater into which Cézette had sunk her hands, elbow-deep. The effort, or the anger behind the effort, set Poole's scabbing forearms to bleeding anew. Pure Poole, this; he'd no need of salts to unleash his crueler self.

Cézette stood frozen, suds falling from her fingers like wax from candles. It was with great relief that I saw that the dishwater was not red.

I wheeled on Poole; but before I could say a word—and what, I wonder, might I have said?—he commanded me:

"And you, you're wanted in the laboratory. *Go*, before I . . ."

I went.

Alas, by night's end I'd surrendered both the brewed salts and the books.

Why? Well . . .

I'd gone upstairs and straight to the laboratory door, lamp in hand, remarking along the way the effect Mister Hyde had had on the household. (It was unkempt, undusted, and nearly, well, *undone* by the mere presence of Doctor Jekyll's supposed cousin.) And the first thing I'd do upon entering the laboratory was raise that lamp to my summoner's eyes to see *precisely* who it was I had to deal with.

Others were befuddled by Jekyll and Hyde *physically*, but I could never have mistaken the two selves for separate beings, never, not when they were fully turned, with either one in the ascendant. For me, the greater difficulty lay in judging *the degree* to which one or the other personality prevailed; and that problem was readily solved if I could see his eyes.

I pushed open the door, and there I stood before him.

"Welcome home, Odile."

No ironic asides, no insults; so here then was Doctor Jekyll. And hearing his words, spoken in the smooth tones of old, well, dare I say I almost felt welcome and *at home*. Almost.

"Where is he?"

"He is . . . away at present, our Mister Hyde."

Pity, this: I'd have to wait to take up the business about the eye patch with him once again, as such deceit had Hyde rather than Jekyll written all over it. Perhaps it'd be best to not compromise Cézette further. As for the doctor? Well, do not assume he was allowed to slide into my good graces, not for an instant. In fact, I hated it, *hated it* when he referred to Hyde as *ours*, as if he were the fruit of some dark congress carried out between Doctor Jekyll and me, and now I told him as much in no uncertain terms. His response, however, was hard to argue with:

"Was Hyde not born of your salts, your spellwork and . . . witchery? Was it not you, Odile, who named him, even?"

"Well, yes, I suppose so; but . . ." and I sputtered out something about his own theft and misuse of the salts, about how he'd . . . But truth to tell, Mister Hyde was precisely that: *The fruit of our dark congress*. What's more: I no longer had the heart to accuse, to recriminate. Things were as they were. It was, simply put, high time to make the most of a bad, bad and very, *very* strange situation.

Which was precisely what Doctor Jekyll then proposed, and, with some debate, some back-and-forth, I agreed to all the terms he put forth. After all, it had been made abundantly clear, had it not, that Mister Hyde could track and find me at will? So it was I surrendered the salts, the books, and all . . . no, *nearly* all I knew.

⁓

The terms of our peace, such as it was, were these:

I would surrender the vial of brewed salts—that which had recently been stolen and *re*stolen, and which was, at present, in my pocket—as well as the waistlet and all its accoutrements, its charms and pendant pouches, et cetera, and together Doctor Jekyll and I would decipher my birthright. Together we would cull what sense we could from Mother's pages, the better part of which were yet a mystery to me; for, if I had that certain Cagot . . . *something*, Doctor Jekyll had the means: the money, the laboratory, the science . . .

I heard again Mister Hyde's odd counsel: *If you can't beat them, join them*. Was that what I was doing? And if so, was it surrender or strategy?

For his part, Doctor Jekyll's maxim of the moment might well have been this: *Give a man a fish and you feed him for a night; teach him to fish and you feed him forever.* For the doctor might well have stolen my . . . *fish*, if you will, the last of the salts; but what then? No, he needed me if he were to learn *how to fish* for a lifetime.

He wanted my salts, yes; but even more so, he sought my

secrets, my mother's secrets, regarding the source of the salts, how best to *safely* brew and use them, et cetera . . . all secrets I'd yet to learn myself.

So it was that Doctor Jekyll—speaking (so he said) for Mister Hyde as well—agreed to two points upon which I, surprising myself, *utterly* insisted.

One: He could experiment with the brewed salts and whatever else he alighted upon in my mother's books, but *only in my presence*; after which the books were to be returned to my possession.

Two: The final disposition, the fate of any and all Cagot secrets, *anything at all* that he, I, or we culled from the books was to be determined by me and me alone.

Upon this last point the doctor hesitated before putting forth a plethora of *what if's*. Indeed it seemed briefly that our negotiations might come to naught; for, when pressed, not to say threatened by all the doctor then implied of Hyde, I said, yes, he might work himself up into a Hyde state and follow me day and night, might even *steal* what it was he coveted so; but the chances were good that I'd get to the river first, there to drop the salts, the books, *all* my birthright into the blackness of the Seine, conferring those Cagot secrets to the sea.

Rather cheeky of me, that insistence, that threat; but I believe I would have carried it out, would have surrendered *all and everything* to the Seine if forced to; for hadn't those secrets—the salts, in particular—cost me both my brother and the boy I thought, *thought* I loved? And hadn't they ruined what (I thought) had been a friendship with Doctor Jekyll? And hadn't they indeed birthed the man-monster Hyde? And, and, *and* . . . I could have gone on.

Fortunately, Doctor Jekyll acceded to my demands, and so it was I began living the strangest days of my life, the strangest days of *any* life, I'll wager.

⁂

"Governments often begin in blood," was Doctor Jekyll's offhanded, too-casual observation regarding recent events. And indeed, the massacre in Montmartre would lead, yes, to civil war, but also, in the days, weeks, and months to come, to a brand-new, albeit short-lived government for Paris proper. It would be called the Commune, and just as it was born in blood, so would it be washed away on a blood tide.

That, alas, is a tale for historians to tell, while this, *this* is a tale only I can tell; but the two tales entwine, most improbably, in the person of my brother, Gréluchon Ricau, who, though he was a boy of a *particular* type, to say the least, was nonetheless a boy. Yet as Doctor Jekyll would put it, rather unpleasantly, after perusing a list of ruling Communards published in the newspaper, "Well, well. It seems that donning a red sash and singing *La Marseillaise* as loud as one's lungs allow earns one a post in this new government, no matter one's prior profession or even one's age." And there was truth to this:

Boys little older than my brother bore new and significant responsibilities now alongside those "politicians" who'd been cobblers, caners, carters, and whatnot a day before. So it was I scanned every newspaper and posted pronouncement for Gré-luchon's name. I never found it; nor did I truly expect to, suspecting (rightly) that Grel's contributions to the cause were of a more . . . *shadowy* sort.

Alors, the day after the insurgency in Montmartre, the regular forces of the French army, what had formerly been *our* army in the war against Prussia, had retreated to Versailles, yes. Paris was soon walled off from the world once again; but this time the enemy beyond those walls was not Prussia but rather France. Our brethren . . . Civil war, this was; and there is no war worse than that.

It was within those walls that the Commune struggled to its feet, coltishly, amid steady shelling. *More* shelling, rather; for still the Prussian shelling of the Siege echoed in our ears. Elections were held in defiance of the National Assembly, which had forbidden the establishment of a municipal government in Paris. But no matter, that: Politics was now as easy as papering the city with this or that decree. White broadsides appeared daily, hourly even; and thusly was this or that law overturned, this or that law enacted:

Three years grace was given to all debtors.

There would be no more mandatory night work in the bakeries.

Education was deemed a universal right; further, it was secularized, meaning priests and nuns were removed from their teaching posts. This renewed antipathy toward the religious would come to embroil my brother; for it was he who . . .

No, wait. Allow me, please, to put off the telling of that horrid tale.

. . . I marveled now at the rumors being carried back to the mansion by those who dared to leave it. By which I mean, yes, everyone but me: Within days of returning to the mansion, I'd fallen into a mood of the worst sort, sleeping through the morning shelling, caring not if the roof caved on my head, and rising only to nibble at a late luncheon at the prodding of Cézette, who then had to push me into the laboratory, where I worked, if *work* it can be called, in relative silence at the side of Doctor Jekyll. I was more melancholic than I'd ever been before, including when my parents had been murdered; for what I learned was this: It is easier by far to mourn the dead than the living; for now I no longer mourned my parents, but rather Gréluchon and Julien.

And further from home, I came to pity the priests and nuns their particular plight as well. I'd never paid the clergy much heed before, truth be known, but now, to see them set upon so . . . It was horrid.

In the churches, that oldest of sports—sacrilege—was once again being played, and how Mister Hyde loved to carry back the most sordid of the sporting news. At Saint-Germain-l'Auxerrois, a long-prized statue of the Virgin had had her mouth chipped at so it might accommodate a pipe; but *that* was mere statuary. As for the people of the Church, hated from the pope himself down to the least parish priest, plans, dreadful plans were afoot for their . . . disposition. At the trial of one nursing nun, accused of poisoning hospitalized Communards, it was proposed, proposed and debated, that she and all her order be sacked—literally put in sacks!—and drowned in the Seine! And Mister Hyde howled, *howled* at recounting another proposal he'd heard put forth at Saint-Nicolas-des-Champs: That the Commune should fortify the city walls against the Versaillais onslaught with gunnysacks containing the bodies of the multiple thousands of priests still in Paris. Horrid! So horrid, so hell-born I might have thought the plan had been put forth by Edward Hyde himself, had he French enough for it. At the time, of course, I'd never have believed that my brother would be the one to . . . Oh, but again I stall on the verge of telling the tale. Tears well, my skin crawls, and I find (*most* improbably) that I'd rather return to talk of Mister Hyde.

. . . Edward Hyde. A subject I must address, even though I cannot do so, even now, with even a modicum of pride; for just as Doctor Jekyll had used me—he had used me before, was using me presently, and would use me forthwith—so too was I using Mister Hyde; for yes, I had found in Hyde a most effective spy.

It was I who, by agreement, deemed when it was that Henry Jekyll might salt himself, Hyde-ing his better self and giving rise, rise and free rein, to his lesser. And though we had only the one vial of brewed salts remaining to us—for I refused to brew more with the few salts still in my possession, which, unknown to all, I'd secreted away, sewing them into the hem of a shift I'd brought from home—yes, I doled out what remained of the brewed salts to Doctor Jekyll with increasing regularity, dosing him so that Mister Hyde might rise just long enough to take to the streets for a few hours before reporting back to the laboratory. Thusly did I, did *we* finally learn to control the dosage, to control the coming of Mister Hyde. This was deemed a great success, of course, not least of all by Doctor Jekyll himself, who sought greater control over his hidden self. (His notes on the topic—kept in a book tabbed with "Effects on Mice," "Effects on Cats," and "Effects on Me"—were copious. I looked within that book once when he'd forgotten to lock it away in his desk . . . okay: Twice, thrice *at the most*, I riffled its pages. It was there that I discovered the reason why the doctor seemed so newly deferential toward me: *Foster her Talents/Find her Truths*, was what he'd written. A shorthand version thereof—*FT/FT*—was scribbled throughout its pages, here, there, everywhere, as though he were mimicking the marginalia Mother had added to her books.)

Yes, it was I who controlled the risen Mister Hyde; and only in so doing was I able to retain the slightest control over my life, such as it was. Yes: Both selves, Jekyll and Hyde, came to understand that their redemption, their existence, depended on me; and so—though neither self would ever have admitted as much—they saw to my contentment, such as it was. *FT/FT.*

Hyde was my spy, yes, my eyes upon those warring streets of which I was now very much afraid. So it was that the last hopes I dared harbor of . . . of my own redemption, of happiness, depended on none other than Edward Hyde himself.

And if Jekyll and Hyde were fostering my talents to find out my truths, well, my fostering the talents of Mister Hyde led only to more lies. Lying *was* his talent. But what other hope did I have for news of Gréluchon, of Julien . . . of the life I'd once led and had now lost?

Need I say those hopes grew ever more slim?

Whereas Doctor Jekyll would have preferred to salt himself for days on end, retaking to that *secret sinning* of his, I now was able to dole out to him precisely the portion of salts I wanted, Hyde-ing him, as it were, down to the hour. I would do so, and the doctor—begging, always begging for more of the salts—would then descend in a rush from the laboratory, from the mansion, and find some darkened street where he might suffer the changes unseen. Often, said he, he did so in the galleries of the Place des Vosges, mere steps from the mansion door. Afterward the city was his—rather, Mister Hyde's—for a few hours' time, and the salted hours I allotted him were his to pass as he pleased, as long as he returned with some news, some *truthful* news, useful to me.

Mister Hyde would return after those hours of who-knew-what to light a candle he kept secreted in a tin that he'd buried somewhere in the park in front of the house. Seeing this agreed-upon signal, I'd descend from the laboratory in my turn, bringing Doctor Jekyll—he was almost always fully Jekyll by now, at least nine-tenths so, for he often slept off the salts' effects in the park before lighting the candle—a clean change of clothes, whereupon I'd either hurry him into the house as a smuggler would or walk behind him, depending on the state of his self and whether, if espied by Poole or Cézette, he'd have been pegged for the master or his maniacal cousin.

I would then watch as the transformation, Hyde-to-Jekyll, ran its course, its most *unnatural* course. Typically, there'd be some residual Hyde to suffer up to the very last second: slights, insults, and the like, or boisterous, boyish bragging about what he'd gotten up to that night. And then, only when the lamplight showed that it was Doctor Jekyll before me, only then would I set in with my questions.

And I had but two each time, and they were always the same:

What had Hyde learned of Gréluchon? Of Julien?

And how I'd come to rue that constant questioning of Mister Hyde, for he did sometimes answer me true.

Alors, oui: I heartened one night in late March when Hyde returned to report that Julien was safe and living in the western suburbs; but it wasn't long before he told me, too, the tale about my brother's first murder.

CHAPTER TWELVE
Spellcaster

I did not want to let Hyde see the tears occasioned by my having news, *finally*, of Julien. Yes, tears came when I heard that he was all right, ensconced with his family out in Auteuil, secreted there, even. I was so greatly *relieved*; for rumors were rife that the Commune was readying a door-to-door search for any able-bodied men who hadn't yet signed up to fight the Versaillais forces. And knowing Julien to be safe (for now), and giving silent thanks that Mister Hyde had found him and knew where he was . . . well, only then had I dared to ask after Gréluchon. *What news?*

At first, the details of Gréluchon's misdeeds were just that: details; and they were only welcome in that they let me keep track of my brother's whereabouts. Too, of course, I never knew if these details were lies or truths. But now came mention of *murder?* Oh how I hoped then that these were lies, lies and more lies, coming from Hyde.

All this was some while into our agreement, understand; and Mister Hyde had already returned of a night to report on the ease with which he'd found Gréluchon. He was, said Hyde, always at the center of the Commune's more . . . *extreme* work; which, for better or worse, was precisely where Mister Hyde put himself on those nights when he was let to roam.

If Mister Hyde were to be believed, Gréluchon was making quite a name for himself among the Communards. Hyde had already reported that he'd been given the charge of a regiment of drunkards and idlers whom he'd fast whipped into shape. (*Literally so?* I wondered.) And it seemed he'd fallen into favor with the new prefect of police. No wonder; for my brother must've been quite the wartime weapon. Even Mister Hyde seemed enamored of him, in fact, owing to all he heard.

Indeed, one night, I made the doctor promise that he, as Hyde, would never make contact with Gréluchon without my express permission. I secured the same promise regarding Julien, telling Mister Hyde he could, indeed *he would* deliver a letter to Auteuil as soon as . . . as soon as I knew what to write in it! That I'd be writing to Julien from the Jekyll mansion, *still* . . . well, this posed a problem. In the meantime, Hyde was to watch the family—a task predatory in nature, and thus happily seen to by Mister Hyde—and keep me apprised of their movements. I'd *not* let Julien slip away a second time.

Meanwhile, I tasked myself with trying to justify *all and everything*—explain all the strangeness, if indeed it could be explained—in letters to Julien, letters more sensible than the one I'd posted with Cézette's help (and which now I hoped was indeed lost). Soon I had a slew of letters, all unsent. *In time*, I told myself . . . *in time*. And until such time, I would keep Mister Hyde on watch, as it were, holding him in check (so I hoped) with the promise of a steady stream of salts.

Enfin, the doctor consented to my terms regarding Julien, though of course that scarcely put my mind to rest regarding the matter, as I knew Mister Hyde would *so* love to meddle in my (dare I say it?) *amorous* affairs.

And the matter regarding Gréluchon was this: What if he, Grel, met Mister Hyde and thereby discovered that the salts would work on non-Cagot humans as well? Or that, with proper dosing, one could transform *at will*, control it, as Grel, evidently, could not? (Mister Hyde had yet to see the "captain"—as he sometimes referred to Gréluchon—in any *in*complete stage of transformation.) Or most ominous of all: What if my brother came in search of that birthright that was, truly, half his, wanting to salt into being a band of warriors, of Communards?

I kept this concern to myself of course, for I'd no confidant now, not with Julien so distant—distant in every way—and Doctor Jekyll rather less than trustworthy, unable to even trust . . . yes, *himselves*. And as for poor Cézette, well . . . Yes, yes indeed: Allow me to set all talk of murder aside some moments more and instead tell how it was I finally made a fast and lasting friend of Cézette.

I helped *la pauvre* Cézette whenever I could.

Not only had I come to like the girl, and she me—a pity: all those wasted months of animosity—I also came to feel somewhat responsible for the abuse she now suffered.

Previously, Poole had had my brother and me to bully as well. (And how part of me wished Gréluchon would return to the mansion in search of more salts, for wouldn't he teach Poole a lesson or two about abuse?) Now, however, Poole was being abused in his turn by the being(s) for whom he worked; and he had no one but Cézette upon whom to exercise his innate cruelty. As for me? Well, I can only assume I was spared Poole's pettiness and punishments because Doctor Jekyll, or perhaps even Mister Hyde, had simply told the manservant to leave me be; or Poole rightly supposed I played a role in the . . . *strangenesses* he'd been party to of late, from events at the primate house to those now unfolding in the mansion.

Perhaps it was both. I never knew; but neither did I care. All I wanted was for Poole to leave me alone.

And though I like to think I might have pitied Poole under different circumstances, well, I cannot imagine what those circumstances would be; for, then, I came to hate the man anew, not for what he'd done to Grel and me in the past, but for what he was doing to Cézette in the present.

Bref, one day in late March he backhandedly slapped, *slapped* Cézette for daring to bring the master a breakfast that he, not Doctor Jekyll, deemed "insufficient." Heaven forfend that his precious Hal go hungry! This, mind you, at a time of siege;

and although famine was not the issue it had been when we'd been besieged by the Prussians, still and all it was far, very far from a time of plenty.

And what's more: I knew that half of the breakfast meat that might have gone onto the doctor's plate that morning had gone onto mine instead, brought secretly to my attic door by Cézette herself. So: More guilt; such that I determined to do something about Poole having dared to lay a hand on the girl. That he'd done so once was his fault, but if he ever did so a second time, I'd hold myself to blame.

I rang for Cézette later that very day. This was after the common luncheon she'd brought up to the laboratory for Doctor Jekyll and myself, who'd spent the late morning trying to make sense of some pages in my mother's books, specifically *Flora*, for he then supposed the salts were derived from a plant of some sort. And though I'd been absorbed in my own work, I'd not been so absorbed that I'd not heard the slap, heard it where I sat at the laboratory table, a full two stories and many rooms removed, and heard, too, the accompanying crash of china. And when Cézette came carrying that luncheon tray some hours later, still I could see the impression Poole's hand had left upon her cheek, and the swelling of her right eye that had been occasioned, no doubt, by the bully's knuckles.

Cézette came cautiously into the laboratory, peeking around the door to ask:

"Who . . . ?"

She needed to speak but the one word, and I understood.

"Doctor Jekyll is napping," said I, for indeed he often would nap after a salted night out; and then, remembering the household ruse, I added: "And Mister Hyde is elsewhere at present. Come in, Cézette. Come in!"

Now the Cézette of old would have been too proud to have taken even so simple an order as *Come in!* from me; and she'd have been jealous, too, to find me in precincts that were now off-limits to her, as the laboratory most decidedly was. Indeed, the dust on the sills and every other surface, as well as the dirt upon the floor—tracked there nightly by Mister Hyde—testified to Cézette's long absence from the laboratory.

"What is it that you two do in here anyway, night and day?"

I smiled now to see Cézette return to her old inquisitive ways; and so it was I let her have a brief look about the laboratory, stopping her only when she alighted upon Mother's books, which, to judge by the sudden arching of her eyebrows, roused more interest than I could safely allow. For *Flora* was open to a page entitled "Slobberweed," and I'd been quite busy with certain weeds and seeds and such that I'd had Gréluchon harvest long ago out near the Bois de Boulogne.

"Did Poole strike you earlier, Cézette? I'm certain I heard—"

Not only did she forget about the books (blessedly), but Cézette then fell into my arms, crying. I consoled her as best I could, but time was of the essence.

"When do you bring Poole his afternoon tea?"

She answered plainly: "Three," said she. "On the dot."

I had but a half-hour then. "Go," said I, kissing Cézette on the forehead and patting that cheek that still tingled, surely. "And when his tea is prepared, bring it to me *first*, here, before serving it. Understand?"

Cézette's puzzled expression bloomed into a smile. She nodded, and she did not ask why. For that, I was glad.

And I returned to my work before she'd even closed the laboratory door, quietly, so as not to rouse Doctor Jekyll. That was wise, and fortuitous, too; for the doctor would never have allowed me to do what I did to Poole. Mister Hyde? He'd have allowed *that* and then some. But Doctor Jekyll, no.

With the clock about to strike three, I heard what sounded like . . . well, it sounded like a skeleton was dancing a jig on the far side of the laboratory door. I opened the door to disclose Cézette standing there with the tea tray in her trembling hands.

"Breathe, Cézette," I counseled. "Close your eyes and breathe." This had its effect: The teaspoon stopped chattering in the teacup, the teacup stopped its shivering upon the saucer, and the saucer fell still upon the silver tray. "Good," said I. And while Cézette's eyes were still closed, I plopped a few drops of distilled slobberweed into the teapot.

I was still stirring it and imprecating over it a bit—casting the spell I'd discovered in *Flora* and, yes, feeling quite the fool—when Cézette opened her eyes. This I'd asked her *not* to do.

Looking down at the tray, she asked, "What did you do?" And then, staring at me: "What is that you were whispering?"

I now formed my lips into a *shh*, complete with the accompanying index-finger-to-lip gesture, before saying, "Go. *Go*, before the water cools!"

A slyly smiling Cézette now puckered her own lips into a kiss that she smacked in my direction before pivoting on one heel and heading off, down to the parlor with tea such as Poole had never had before. Of that I was certain. I was, however, decidedly less certain regarding the *effect* of the bewitched brew.

After all, this much I knew: *Danger inheres in the dosage . . .* and, alas, I'd never brewed slobberweed tea before.

The tea worked, and it worked well.

I was in the laboratory alongside Doctor Jekyll that night. We were working on the pages of *Medicum* still, comparing this or that tincture or salve or balm mentioned in Mother's book to those known to the doctor, indeed to any medical man worth his salt . . . if you'll pardon the pun. Indeed, the hour of the doctor's salting was drawing near: midnight; and as it approached he grew ever more anxious.

I'd gotten Doctor Jekyll to summon Poole to the laboratory, opining that our work might progress better if we had an iron— yes, it was an iron I asked for—a plain old household iron for flattening some of the broader leaves of the specimens Mister Hyde had harvested the night before in the far western woodlands. (Hyde liked to dig in the dirt. *So be it*, thought I. *Let the beast be of some harvesting use.*) I didn't know what else he'd lately gotten up to, in the far west of Paris or elsewhere, but whatever it was, the doctor seemed *most* eager to return to it, post-haste: He badly wanted to be Hyde that night. As he counted the minutes to midnight, his clock-watching became contagious; thusly I can report that Poole came to the laboratory door at precisely half past nine.

"Poole," said the doctor, his back toward the door through which the manservant had just entered, "it seems we are in want of an iron, according to Mademoiselle Ricau." Doctor Jekyll sometimes used my formal name now, as if to accord me a status I'd not had previously. I knew it was mere flattery. In truth, I cared not a whit what he called me; though I *did* revel in Poole's reaction, which was a wince, as if the master had spat upon him. "I imagine we have such an instrument around here someplace, have we not?" Such was the privileged life of Henry Jekyll, M.D.: He'd never once worn a wrinkled *anything*, yet he wouldn't have known an iron from an aardvark.

"Indeed we do, sir," said Poole in reply, or rather attempted reply; in point of fact, his speech sounded like that of some sea monster risen from the depths. It was positively *aquatic* in tone, so slippery, so spittle-ridden, so . . . so very *wet*.

I kept busy at my work. However, had I a third hand, I'd have used it then to surreptitiously pat myself on the back. Or perhaps I'd have clamped it over my mouth to keep from laughing.

Doctor Jekyll was midway through his standard dismissal— "Thank you, Poole. That will be all"—when he paused over the pine bark piled before him, from which he was tweezering tiny beetles, and looked up at me, *me*, as if to ask *Did you hear that?* In reply, I simply stared at the doctor. I may have shrugged. In any case, I betrayed neither pride nor joy (though I felt both). And so Doctor Jekyll finally turned to his manservant and asked, "What*ever* is the matter, Poole?"

The response, when it came, was downright . . . salivary. And indistinguishable. Not to mention *disgusting*.

Poole was in the midst of switching kerchiefs, drawing out a fresh one to replace the sopping one he now wadded and pushed into a pocket of his pants. The fresh one he held up to his chin in an attempt to stop his slobber before it fell onto his shirtfront or the floor at his feet. And all the while, Poole kept glancing at me. Warily. Which was just how I wanted it.

Pleased with myself, I was also wary of what Doctor Jekyll would say when finally he put the pieces of that particular puzzle into place. After all, he too had seen the slobberweed spell in my mother's book that very morning.

"Do you . . ." began Doctor Jekyll now, seeming to want to go to Poole's aid yet visibly repulsed, and wanting to keep his distance; for Poole's spittle bubbled and bounced from that baggy lower lip of his and flew from the tip of his tongue. "Do you fancy you're in need of a dentist, man?"

Poole shook his head, sending saliva spraying east-west, as he said that no, he thought not. "No pain, sir; just—"

"Yes, yes, I see," said the doctor.

Not even a little pain? I wanted to ask. Alas, I could not content myself with the shame and embarrassment the man was suffering, for I so wished that Cézette was there to witness it as well. Further: It'd have been greater fun if I'd been able to find betel nut juice, which would have rendered the saliva blood red. Maybe next time; and there *would* be a next time if Poole didn't learn to keep his hands to himself.

Doctor Jekyll dismissed Poole then, instructing him to leave the iron at the foot of the locked laboratory door when he found it, and then to take himself off to bed. "I would suggest you sleep on your side . . ." said he, "and have a bucket on hand."

Poole bowed, loosing strings of saliva southward, and took his leave.

Doctor Jekyll shut the door behind his manservant, slipping on a puddle of Poole-born spittle as he did so. He then eyed the clock before retaking to his work. For my part, I was engrossed in plucking the stinging hairs from some cowhage (which, if Poole persisted in his ways, Cézette could sprinkle on his sheets). Or so I hoped I seemed: *engrossed.* But when Doctor Jekyll spoke, well . . . Said he, simply:

"How long?"

In the hope that he referred to his imminent self-salting, I consulted the clock, did a quick calculation, and said: "Two hours, twenty minutes."

"How long *will it last*, Odile? That sloppy business with Poole, I mean? All that infernal spittle he's spraying about?"

His tone was vaguely Hyde-like, and I hoped I'd not angered

him so as to bring on an . . . *unscheduled* visit from Edward Hyde. (It seemed that this could still happen, despite our ever more careful dosing.) But no: Here was Doctor Jekyll alone. And so it was that I quickly said, in my defense:

"He slapped Cézette! And—"

"I've asked a pointed and simple question, Odile: *How long before the spell wears off?* Slobberweed, was it? Into his tea, I presume?" I fancied I heard a measure of . . . amusement behind his words, and those angrier tones soon ceded to mere curiosity. Indeed, who'd have been more pleased than Henry Jekyll to learn that other spells culled from my mother's books were also efficacious? Wondering this, I left the doctor's question unanswered; and only when he prompted me a third time did I say:

"I don't know! A week?" And then, returning to my work, I mumbled, "Maybe more."

In truth, I'd no idea how long the spell would last. Nor did I care, really: I was simply happy, *very* happy that it had worked so well, rendering the despicable Poole a veritable font of spittle!

We worked on in silence—we may have been *cooperatives*, but the days of friendship were long past—as the minutes till midnight ticked slowly past; and then Poole returned, presumably to deliver the aforementioned iron.

"Leave it, Poole!" commanded Henry through the closed door; yet Poole persisted with his knocking and entered the laboratory anyway—having waited, as was *law*, for the master to unlock the door and grant permission to pass—and delivered, yes, the iron, but also a most distressing bit of news.

It was from the late-day newspaper he carried—and decidedly *not* from the man himself, whose every effort at speech the doctor preempted—that we learned that the Communards had "brazenly kidnapped" the archbishop of Paris.

"My word," muttered Henry. "Who next: The pope?"

It seemed they were demanding ransom in the person of certain Communards who'd been captured by the Versaillais. Further, if their demands were not met by the appointed hour, the Communards were threatening to . . .

"*Kill* the archbishop?" Doctor Jekyll had read the article aloud, and now repeated the Communard threat. "My word, indeed! Thank you, Poole. That will be all." And only as Poole departed, with a slobbery "G'night, sir," did Doctor Jekyll think to call after him, with as much reassurance as he could muster: "Oh, and Poole? I have it from certain reliable . . . *sources*, let me say, that such afflictions run their course, albeit sloppily, within a week . . . maybe more. It . . . it must've been something you ate, Old Socks. Or perhaps drank."

Thank you, sir, said Poole, though it sounded rather more like "Slank youth, slur."

Leaving, the door cracked just so, Poole dared look my way; yet for the first time since I'd met the man there was . . . *nothing there*, nothing polluting those pallid blue eyes of his. No hatred, no rancor, and certainly no promise of revenge. In return, I nodded, just so, and I may even have offered a smile of acknowledgment, as if to say, *Yes, it was me, Poole,* and *Yes, let this be both a lesson and a truce, then*. He'd think twice before raising a hand to a servant again! Indeed, he'd probably think twice before raising a cup of tea to his lips.

With Poole gone, Doctor Jekyll checked the clock. I did as well. Of course, Jekyll had his reasons for doing so (whatever they were . . . and how I pitied the person on the other end of *that* appointment!). As for me? Well, no newspaper could ever tell me more about the situation on the streets than Mister Hyde could gather in a night's time. And I didn't even have to give voice to my question about the archbishop, for the doctor's thoughts were twinned to mine. Said he, still bent over his piled bark, "Hyde will find out."

Whereupon we awaited the witching hour with impatience.

Hyde would find out, indeed. Find out if the "brazen kidnapping"—and worse—of the archbishop of Paris by the Communards involved my brother, as we both supposed it had.

Midnight was nearing now. I sat in the laboratory, thumbing the last pages of *Flora*. My heart wasn't in the work, though, despite the spellcasting success I'd had with Poole, for one nonspecific yet disturbing question kept coming back to me: *What*ever *had happened to my brother? What was happening to him now? Was he strengthening still, or weakening? Was he* . . .

Alors, so many questions; and so I decided I needed to speak

264

to him, face to face. No matter that he'd told me, in no uncertain terms, to leave him alone.

And so, as Doctor Jekyll sat drumming his fingers atop the laboratory table, eager, *quite* eager for me to administer the night's salts, I tore a page from the back of *Flora* and wrote upon it:

I must see you at once!

I carefully folded the note in quarters and handed it to Doctor Jekyll just as midnight struck, directing him to give the note to Gréluchon if indeed he, or rather Mister Hyde, found him that night.

"*If* he finds him? You doubt our Mister Hyde?"

"Fine: *When* he finds him. And be sure that you . . . that *Hyde* awaits a reply. Do you hear me?" I had but half his attention, as the clock had now ticked past the salting hour. Doctor Jekyll hated having to wait, but even he had agreed that to salt at too early an hour was risking discovery, here in the house as well as out in the streets.

"Yes, yes," was his impatient reply. "I shall see that Edward obeys your every order, *mistress*. Now can I please have my damnable drink?"

Damnable, indeed.

Strange as it may sound, I had every confidence in *our* Mister Hyde. Loving *to track*, reveling in the chase, as he most certainly did, I knew he'd find Gréluchon that night. Too, Hyde could apparently scent the salts on him, *in* him. *Like unto like*, et cetera.

And so it was that I eagerly awaited Mister Hyde's return that night, his return with news and (how I hoped it!) an answering note. If Grel were weakening, perhaps his heart would *un*harden and he'd . . . Alas, I held to my hopes. Still.

So hopeful, so eager was I, in fact, that I took to the galleries of the Place des Vosges just before dawn, to attend Mister Hyde there rather than at the laboratory window, watching, waiting for the candle signal. In truth, I'd another reason for descending: Watching from the window, I'd have sworn, *sworn* that a shadow I'd seen pacing in the gallery across the park had been Julien. I could discern no detail, of course; but somehow I knew it was he, simply *knew* it. And not for the first time, either: I'd fancied I'd seen that same shadow another day at dawn, there, across the park, and again on the boulevard Beaumarchais that day I'd stolen from the mansion under cover of Cézette's screams. But when I descended, hurriedly, to see if . . . Alas, nothing and no one. I ascribed the sight to my fevered mind, to all the strangeness I'd seen of late and, yes, to the thought, *the wish*, that it had been he, Julien.

I now paced that same shadowed gallery myself; and sure enough, with dawn about to break, he snuck up behind me. Not Julien, no. Decidedly not.

"Fancy finding you here." And, as ever it did when it came so unexpectedly, so suddenly, Edward Hyde's voice gave me gooseflesh.

Quickly I ducked out from under the heavy hands, redolent

now of turned earth and who-knew-what-else, that Mister Hyde had dared to set, clamplike, upon my shoulders. Turning, I was dumbstruck, dumbstruck and . . . scared.

I'd not seen *the other*—Hyde, fully ascendant—in some while. And I knew at once that it was a mistake to have met him before he'd begun to *re*transform, before he'd signaled up to me with candlelight that he was once again mostly, *mostly* Doctor Jekyll. A mistake, indeed; but might it have been a . . . *grave* mistake, and literally so? Despite his cynical greeting, Mister Hyde looked like he might strike me down at any moment. Still, somehow, I managed to ask, "What . . . what news?" Then, without waiting for an answer, I drew the eye patch from my pocket and presented it to Mister Hyde. "And please," said I, "spare me more of your lies."

Whereupon Hyde laughed aloud, handed me back the eye patch—implying, dare I say innocently, that he simply had no need of it now, *merci bien*—and sneered as he said, in perfect, albeit mincing imitation of me, "'What news? What news?' . . . Wouldn't *you* like to know, spellcaster?"

That was it? Now it may have been a mistake to have descended, yes, to have come outside (for the first time in ages!) to meet Mister Hyde, but so be it: I could forgive myself a mistake . . . perhaps. But I could *not* forgive such poor strategizing! I'd waited so long to use that eye patch to effect, and now . . . *rien*. Nothing. Indeed, I'd only put Hyde in a position of increased power, showing such desperation. And of course he used this, as always he would: He now sought to bargain;

and I'd little choice but to accede when he said through the wryest of smiles, his *sss* snakier than ever:

"Salt me . . . sorceress."

"Fine," said I after a bit of back-and-forth, "agreed: Double the dosage tomorrow in exchange for what you've learned."

"Oh, it was your brother all right," spurted Hyde, "and apparently it was a night the archbishop will not soon forget. The damned fool resisted!" Here Hyde loosed that hyena's laugh of his, and all around the square I saw shadow cats scattering. "As if . . . !"

As if we can be resisted, was what he was implying, of course. And so it was worse than I'd imagined: Mister Hyde put himself on a par with Gréluchon. Was Gréluchon as bestial as our benighted Mister Hyde? Brutish enough to beat down the archbishop of Paris? . . . I had to admit: It made perfect sense. After all, if a mere mouthful of the brewed salts was sufficient to give regular rise to Mister Hyde, imagine the changes that befell Gréluchon, who'd drunk off an entire test tube of the very strongest brew, that entire sixth vial.

Alas, this was not the time to cry over spilled . . . salts.

"Tell me more," said I to Hyde, as commandingly as I could. "Tell me everything or it's into the Seine with the lot of it—salts, books . . . *the lot of it*! I swear!" I forbore adding that I might cast myself into the river as well. In truth, it was a thought, an impulse, that dogged me daily, as death did sometimes seem preferable to the life I was leading.

Hyde set in with the details of the kidnapping, of the "brazen" act itself, as proudly, as cockily as if he were recounting some sporting hero's exploits on the cricket pitch. The beating, the blood . . . for the archbishop was but a hostage still, and things would not devolve to death, to murder, for some while. But already I'd heard enough details to wonder, sickly, if my brother, my Gréluchon, could really have done . . . *all that* to an old man whose only fault was his professed faith. "Tell me about my brother, damn it! What state is he in?"

"He is strong, I will say that. Nearly as strong as myself."

Oh dear: If Edward Hyde admitted as much as *that*, then surely Gréluchon was twice, thrice as strong as he. Which meant that he'd be twice, thrice as mean, too, did it not? It was a wonder that the archbishop was still alive!

"And from what I hear from those under his command, Captain Ricau and his band are the Communards' . . . strong arm, shall I say?"

I'd no need to ask what he meant by *strong arm*. I knew. "What else?"

"Well . . ." Hyde drew the telling out, teasingly.

"Hyde, *damn you*! Speak!"

"Your brother, well now . . . He isn't exactly much given to *talk* these days. No, he is most definitely a man of action now. What he wants is to *fight*, or . . . worse; and he's become quite the adept, is what I hear."

Killing? Was Gréluchon killing for the Communards?

"Oh, and by the way, Odile," said Mister Hyde, recalling me from a most unpleasant reverie, "I've been meaning to congratulate you on your success with the slobberweed tea. Even Doctor Jekyll was impressed."

I ignored this last.

"Did you give Gréluchon my note at least, Hyde? Say you did, or else . . ."

"Tsk, tsk, don't threaten me, witch! I'll snap your neck and *steal* all you own, and to hell with the rest of your precious secrets!"

"Edward," said I, persisting, "you promised."

He laughed again. "Tell you what: I'll promise in one hand and piss in the other, Odile, and then you tell me which hand is full. Ha! . . . Oh, but still and all, Doctor Jekyll *did* insist; and so, yes, I handed your note to Gréluchon myself, I did. And it was a pleasure to meet the man."

"And . . . and . . . ?" I pressed. "Where is his response?"

"Now . . . where . . . did I put . . . ?" He pleasured in pausing so. And it seemed he paused an *eternity*. By now the high, bare branches of the plane trees in the park were lit by sunlight. A milkmaid came by with her cart, steering it clear of Hyde, as one would steer clear of a bull in open pasture. High on the distant hills of Montmartre, the day's first gunfire could be heard. "Ah yes, here it is," and finally, *finally* Hyde produced from a pants pocket a crumpled sheet of paper.

"That is *my* note," said I, snatching it from Hyde.

Perhaps Gréluchon had scratched his reply on the note itself. Of course, he'd done just that. I smoothed it out and read my *I must see you at once* . . . and nothing more.

"I told you to attend a response!"

"I did," sneered a much satisfied Hyde. "That *is* his response." And with a rattling laugh and a long, filthy forefinger he pointed not so much at the note as the crumpling thereof.

⁓

I sat crying in the park as the sun slid down to light the trunks of the trees, to light the park entire. It was cold, but I didn't care.

I'd told Mister Hyde to sleep off the salts on a bench across the park. There was no option but to sleep, to wait out the salts' effects; for I say again that neither Doctor Jekyll nor I had discovered anything in Mother's books about an antidote, though that had been our central objective. No: Careful dosage would have to do. But it was high time I wake him, high time we return to the mansion. He'd be fully Doctor Jekyll when he woke, surely; and so, with a little cleaning up and a quick change of clothes, he'd have to lead the way home.

"Wake up, Henry." I stood there wondering if a Jekyll had ever spent the night in a public park. "Wake up!"

And indeed it was Henry Jekyll who awoke upon that park bench in a still-wintry, warring Paris, his head smarting from the salting of the night before. He struggled to make sense of his surrounds at first and, that done, he visibly, *visibly* tried to sort the prior night's events, and the memories Mister Hyde had made for them both. *That* must have been a most unpleasant task.

And so it was with a half-measure of pity and some patience that I brushed the dirt from his dark slacks, and dabbed the dirt from his hands, neck, and face with a cloth I'd dipped in the park's icy fountain. He rose, put on the doctor's cashmere overcoat that I'd carried down, and together we snuck into the house across the square, into the house and straight up to the laboratory, unseen.

We both wanted sleep, and badly so. But as I took my leave of the laboratory, not even bothering to bid the doctor adieu or what-have-you, he called to me.

"Odile, wait." He looked terrible, years older and much the worse from . . . it all. I wondered what toll the salting, this recurrent splitting of his very self, was taking on him. I knew all too well that Doctor Jekyll sought an eternal supply of salts, but even as I guarded the last of the brewed salts—in my pocket, for safekeeping, *my* safekeeping, was the sloshing, stoppered tube containing all that remained of vials four and five—I wondered how much more of the salts the doctor could survive. And that was just the salts! Never mind whatever worldly dangers Mister Hyde was exposing him to.

I stood at the laboratory door, awaiting what it was the doctor had to say. I supposed it'd be about the work plan we'd tackle later that day, for we were progressing through the pages of Mother's books one by one, with *Animalis* to come. And so it was I was surprised to hear Doctor Jekyll speak on behalf of Mister Hyde:

"He . . . he remembered one thing more from last night, Edward did."

How odd, these so purposeful pronouns. "Go on," said I.

"Gréluchon did say . . ." He wriggled first one foot and then the other into his slippers, staring down at the monogrammed silk as if wondering who *HJ* might be.

"Yes? *What* did he say?"

A shy Henry Jekyll? Awkward, monomaniacal, distant, and distrustful . . . ? Yes, all that and more; but not since that first day in the Jardin des Plantes had I seen a *shy* Henry Jekyll, so hesitant to say what he meant to say.

"Gréluchon did say that there was one way you could see him again."

"And that is . . . ?"

"That is . . . if you join the fight. That's what he said: 'If she fights alongside us.'"

Silence then.

"Is there anything more?" My patience was exhausted; as was I.

"Well, yes. Edward says . . . Edward *has suggested*, rather, that I remind you of something he said."

"Who? Gréluchon?"

"No, Edward himself . . . 'If you can't beat them, join them.'"

Now it was my turn to rattle the room with laughter. Absurd, this! Here I was at my wit's end and Doctor Jekyll was quoting to me some . . . some commonsensical claptrap spouted by his lesser self? What's more: If I hadn't known what Hyde had meant when first he'd uttered the maxim in Montmartre, after the massacre, I surely didn't know now!

273

It was then that I looked down to see I'd taken that vial containing the last of the brewed salts from my pocket. It seemed somehow . . . *alive* now. As a stick of dynamite is alive once its fuse has been lit.

I must have stood there staring down at it some while; for when I looked up again, Doctor Jekyll had slipped away and I was alone in the laboratory. Alone with the last of the transformative salts.

CHAPTER THIRTEEN
Marginalia

There I stood, salts in hand. I needed only to uncork the vial, tip it to my lips, and I . . .

I didn't dare. My better self had come to seem loathsome enough, so why would I want to summon my lesser and increase the chaos? *Non, non, non.*

After that morning that Mister Hyde had returned with my crumpled note and Doctor Jekyll made that strange suggestion regarding the salts, well, things somehow returned to normal. *Normal?* Hardly, but alas . . .

The doctor's suggestion—and still I wondered if he were in fact *suggesting* that I experiment with the brewed salts myself, something that seemed quite contradictory and out of character: He wanted the salts, *all* the salts for himself—his suggestion only strengthened my resolve to never, *ever* self-salt.

Yes: I *was* so resolved. Then.

I finally left the laboratory that morning, salts securely in hand, and retired to my room, as the doctor had to his. I'd not have thought I'd slept, save that Cézette woke me some hours later when she came to my door, knocked lightly, and then said, on behalf of the master, "Doctor Jekyll wonders if you are ready to resume your work."

I dared not open the door. Cézette might take that as license to ask some question I could not answer. And so I simply said, through the door, "Yes; you may tell the doctor yes. I'll be down presently." *Damn the doctor and his work!* was the more private response, left unspoken.

I sat up now. All was silent, save for the rat-a-tat-tat of rifle fire in the distance. I could see Cézette's shadow beneath the door, quite still.

"Odile?" She whispered now, speaking on her *own* behalf.

"Yes?" I half-rose from my cot. Oughtn't I to open the door to the poor girl?

I saw the shadow in motion now; and a moment later I knew she'd crouched low, low enough to whisper through the keyhole. "I just wanted to thank you, Odile. I . . . I don't know what you did to . . . You-know-who, but he has relieved me of all responsibilities regarding his afternoon tea, *thankfully*."

I smiled.

"In fact . . ." and how it did my heart a world of good to now hear the girl giggle ". . . in fact, he doesn't even *take* tea at present, as every swallow must be half spittle!"

I opened the door.

Cézette looked well; rather, as well as could be expected. It saddened me that she was not the beauty she'd been before.

She hugged me, and I hugged her in return.

"We girls . . ." she began.

". . . must stick together," said I; and so we would.

Cézette—who quickly took her leave, post-hug—had brought me the day's newspaper, *La Commune*, by which I would keep abreast of the war, this second siege, et cetera.

I would continue to get my news from the newspapers, yes, but moreover from Mister Hyde. Rather, it was he who brought me the news I most sought now; for, at my direction, he kept his jaundiced eye on the Deboos family out in Auteuil, though still I forbade him to make contact with Julien. "For now." (Was I not still resident with Doctor Jekyll? Indeed I was; and I dared not give Julien *that* reason to deny me again.) In addition to my reports from Mister Hyde, I would scan those papers for news of Gréluchon. And every time I did so—so very reluctant to even approach the page—I wondered what would be worse: Reading that my brother had *been* killed or *had killed*? (He never appeared by name: There was never a single mention of a Captain Ricau, for indeed Gréluchon had become, as Mister Hyde had put it, the Commune's *secret* weapon.)

A monstrous Mister Hyde and the propaganda of the new government, such were my eyes on a world I'd grown very much afraid of, from which I'd wholly withdrawn; for I never left the house now. Never.

And while secreting myself in the mansion through those first weeks of the war, there was but one room in which I felt secure, safe: the laboratory. It was illusory, that feeling; for it was born of the fact that still I had secrets to discover, but as I surrendered those secrets, one by one, I grew less secure, less safe. Until finally I found that I was, in a word, weak.

Our work? Well, Doctor Jekyll showed scant interest in the pages of Mother's *Flora*, nor in her *Animalis*, nor even her *Medicum*, for it seemed we'd traveled down those avenues without success; and so it was I worked—and *re*worked—those books alone, or largely so. Always the doctor seemed to overhang my work, watching. It was *Physicae* and, above all, *Humanitas* that interested Doctor Jekyll now, and not for the purposes of his long-planned redemption at the Royal Society. (He hardly ever spoke of the Royal Society anymore, whereas his London failures had earlier seemed to haunt him.) No, the doctor had long ago made it known what he sought in Mother's pages: The secret of making more salts, yes, of course; and hence more of the transformative brew. But still he sought that all-important corollary to the Cagot secret as well: *an antidote*, the merest mention of an antidote. Without an antidote, some means of *controlling* the salts' effects, he'd remain at their mercy. That was *our work*, and the doctor's stated goal—"Control!" he'd often rail as Hyde, hating that the salts were wearing off— though I very much doubted we'd ever succeed at it. (I was certain, now, that Mother had recorded no *anti*-salt secret, no antidote.) All the rest, I knew, Doctor Jekyll came to dismiss as mere witchery, and so I supposed it was.

For I learned how to curse cats and dogs (and, presumably, larger animals) into silence—useful, I suppose, if one finds oneself on a farm crowded with crowing cocks or whatnot, but the secret to suppressing meows, barking, moos, and braying was hardly a benison in a city, let alone a city at war.

More: I could soon tie knots no non-Cagot could ever untie. I could render fields uncommonly fertile with spells culled from *Flora*; and so it was that I conditioned certain seed beds in the courtyard for Cézette, who soon had Paris's most pleasant *potager*, or soup garden. I could also safely stifle a colicky newborn (supposedly); discern real coins from counterfeit; and, if I'd the means (not to mention the will, which I very much lacked at present), I'd have been able to outfit a weathervane with cockerel feathers so as to predict the coming half-day's weather with uncanny accuracy ("93/100," was the annual percentile, the rate of accuracy, my mother had proudly recorded for the year 1869).

Alas. The better part of the books? Witchery, yes, and it was all well and good, I suppose; but nowhere, *nowhere* did Mother mention how I might get my brother back, win Julien to my side, and escape the strangeness I was living alongside Doctor Jekyll and Mister Hyde. *That* would have been witchery worth pursuing.

It all came to seem rather pointless, and poring over the books made me sad, sadder than I already was. I missed Mother. How might she counsel me now? What might she have told me, if only she'd had the time? I'd never know. Instead, here I was having to decipher and make sense of her books on my own; worse, I was being urged to do so at speed by a self-serving Doctor Jekyll. And nothing made me miss my mother more than the seemingly casual doodles and such that she'd scribbled in the margins of all the books, *Physicae* in particular. *Very* unlike her, I remember thinking: Mother had been a purposeful woman, neither a doodler nor a scribbler. That marginalia made me sad, yes; for here were my mother's last words to me, and yet I could make no sense of them! It was as though she were whispering to me from . . . beyond, but too low for me to hear.

In time I would learn that there was nothing *purposeless* about that marginalia at all. It hid . . . keys, and it would be one such key that allowed me to finally unlock the greatest and darkest of all the Cagot secrets.

It happened on a mid-morning in very late March.

The news, well . . . the news had hardly been news at all. We were once again *waiting*. All the world was waiting:

The French forces, the *national* forces marshaled at Versailles, were waiting for the Communards to carry their fight out beyond the city walls, if they dared.

The Communards, in turn, were waiting for the Versaillais to invade, to bring the battle *to hand*. Meanwhile, they were trying to govern Paris with their edicts, decrees, and endless committees, all of which efforts were recounted in *La Commune*,

La Sociale, et cetera. (Yes, there were still newspapers, just no *opposing* papers: They'd been suppressed.) And all news of the "Committee," which is how Doctor Jekyll referred to the Commune, led him to opine, sourly, that a camel was naught but a horse built by committee. No, the doctor did not hold out much hope for the Communard cause; nor did he care overmuch. It was a matter for *les ouvriers*—the workers—which epithet he often used to deride the rebels and their cause. Hyde? Mister Hyde continued to enjoy his nights—every other night now, owing to the dwindling supply of salts—and from one such night, out in the fray, he returned to report that Julien was waiting as well.

The Deboos family had indeed shuttered both shops and was still waiting out the war in the western suburbs. Hyde teased that he'd been close enough to call to Julien one day on the avenue Beauséjour . . . but he hadn't. "Not to worry, witchling." I was not yet sure what to tell him. Hadn't he essentially made my leaving the Jekyll house a condition of our ever communicating again? I certainly hadn't done that, it was true. He'd presented me with a choice, and only in hindsight did I come to realize I'd actually chosen, that night I'd left him on the banks of the Seine and returned to the Jekyll mansion. And still this maddened me so: *What had he expected me to do?* And there were times when I told myself I didn't care if I ever saw Julien again . . . but I never believed myself for very long. Alas, scant consolation this, but at least I knew I had a capable messenger in Mister Hyde. Capable, yet cunning. And in time I'd know what message to send with my maniacal messenger; in the meantime, I'd simply have to suffer his, Hyde's, having the upper hand.

Indeed, Mister Hyde teased me meanly, mercilessly about my "butcher's boy," sometimes telling lies of long days' duration—that he'd seen Monsieur Deboos beating the boy (though this may have been all too true), or that the family had been kicked out by their relatives and had left the capital, or that a good-looking girl of my age ("*La Cousine*," Hyde called her) had suddenly appeared upon the scene—only *un*telling the lies when I'd worried myself sick and refused to work. This, of course, was owing to the influence of Doctor Jekyll, for whom *the work* was all and everything. He'd not let his Hyde delay it by distracting me so.

As for the doctor himself, when free of Mister Hyde, he mentioned Julien *not at all*; which, in its way, seemed as strange as Hyde's teasing and lying.

Gréluchon was waiting as well; for Mister Hyde reported that he was a very vocal part of that Communard contingent pushing for a sally on Versailles, wanting to take the fight to the traitorous troops gathered there. In the meantime, said Hyde, Gréluchon remained quite active ". . . behind the scenes, let me say." And when Mister Hyde persisted in telling me the gory details, which I somehow knew, *knew* to be true . . . well, I stormed from the laboratory on such occasions, leaving Doctor Jekyll to chastise Hyde when next the two confabulated as only they could.

Hyde (damn him!) did manage to convey to me one disturbing detail, and cagily so:

"Tell me, girl," said he, for he'd taken to calling me that, "tell me: Which of the boy's eyes was bad?"

I said nothing, at first; for I had just tried (and failed) to stop Mister Hyde from detailing my brother's behavior, witnessed as he, Gréluchon, stood atop a barricade at the Place d'Anvers. It seemed he had succeeded well in stirring up his soldiers, rallying them for a mission of some sort.

"Why? Why do you ask?" He was up to something; for, of course, Doctor Jekyll knew all too well which of my brother's eyes had been diseased.

"Because I want to know, girl!" Hyde slammed a filthy hand down upon the laboratory table. "And because *you* want to know, too. Trust me."

"Oh, do I now? Well . . ." I was stalling. Hyde had been back in the laboratory that morning for nearly a quarter-hour, and Doctor Jekyll was already ascending. The longer I waited, the more I spoke with the doctor rather than the evildoer; but I could not forbear. "The left," I said, finally. "Gréluchon was losing his left eye. Why?"

"Interesting," mused Mister Hyde, dramatically. "Most interesting . . . The left, you say?" He could never truly smile, Hyde. It was always a sneer, and now it was so extreme as to show his left canine.

"The left, yes! Now tell me why you ask, damn you!"

Suddenly Mister Hyde was upon me. He'd crossed the

room fast as a jungle cat. I had, most improbably, the impression that he'd *leaped* across the laboratory. And now he stood at my side, so very close, cradling the back of my head in his left hand while pressing the palm of his right over my eye, my left eye.

"Because," said Hyde now, so near I had to gag back the breath, the fetid breath that he blew into my open mouth, "he's taken, no, *re*taken to wearing an eye patch, *sister*. That's why!"

This, of course, was a point of great interest to all of us: Jekyll, Hyde, and myself, certainly.

"Why . . . ?" But I left off, knowing I'd get no answer from Mister Hyde.

Was I to be hopeful, then, that perhaps the salts were finally wearing off? That Gréluchon's transformation had *not* been permanent, as I'd come to suppose? Or was I to worry that my beloved brother was again going blind? And if he were weakening, what would happen to him out on those increasingly unsafe streets? Or what if he were to become both newly decrepit *and* salt-strong?

My questions were legion; but I refused to speak further with Hyde and waited for a fully ascendant Doctor Jekyll. Later that morning, the doctor and I assessed the situation, determining that there was little we could do. This was all too clear. And so, Mister Hyde would continue to keep watch over Gréluchon as best he could while Doctor Jekyll and I (said he) must redouble our efforts regarding Mother's books and speed through the last pages, for further word had come from London of his father's ever-worsening health: If earlier Jekyll Senior had been on death's doorstep, now that door was wide open. (Or so it was put by a most impassive Poole.)

I agreed, though I confess that I did not know what the doctor meant by a "redoubling" of our efforts, though I knew, of course, that said efforts would be for *his* benefit, not my brother's.

"Source," the doctor would say time and again, as if I needed reminding of what our "work" was. "Source and antidote, Odile." To me it had all come to seem rather pointless. As had life in general. And so it was strange, then, when I returned to *Physicae* and saw it as I never had before.

And what I saw in its pages made me sick, sick with supposition of the strangest sort.

For I began to *suppose* that Mother's marginalia, the doodles, the scribbles and such she'd set in the margins of the book, were hints, keys to the seemingly simple text. And to suppose, further, that the scribbles on the pages behind those mentioning the salts for the very last time were a message. A message for me.

I was shaking where I sat across from Doctor Jekyll, and I dared not look up lest he notice my state; but it was already too late.

"Odile," said he, "are you unwell?"

"No, *no*," I said at first, before beginning to nod that yes, yes I was; but so as to preclude the doctor's examining me—I did not want him to touch me—I held my clasped hands to my heart. *This is all too much, sir*, is what I meant to meekly imply. (As indeed it was!) And then I cried, perfectly on cue, and, ever the faux-supplicant, petitioned the doctor, "Might I please be . . . ?" and I pointed vaguely upward, toward my attic room.

"Yes, yes," said he, spurred by my sudden tears—men, it seems, are either spooked into silence or spurred to action by sudden tears—"Please, go to your room, Odile. Compose yourself. Take your time, just . . . just don't take *too* long, please; for we've much to do here."

Thinking fast, I presented him with a compromise of sorts: I'd retire to my room, there to "compose myself," as ordered, yet I'd take *Physicae* with me, studying it in private (for the umpteenth yet seemingly first time). That way "the work" would not be slowed at all. To this the doctor assented, showing not the least sign of suspicion.

Once in my room, I sank to the floor with my back against the door so that no one could barge in or spy upon me through the keyhole. I then opened the book to the pages in question and . . . and yes, there it was again, of course: That marginalia repeated in its many forms, scribbled there the way I sometimes (only sometimes) wrote, absently, childishly, yet with the hope of the lovelorn, *Odile Deboos, Odile Deboos*, in the margins of my own notebooks. But what did it mean?

Nossels

Notresel

Noussels

When first I'd seen it, or rather when first *we'd* seen it—for Doctor Jekyll had been hovering at the time—we'd both supposed that Mother had simply meant to record a name she had misremembered or did not know how to spell. Perhaps that of a fellow Cagot, or some daring townsmen who'd come to her for help; for the books, especially *Animalis*, did feature such everyday details of a farmer's wife: Who owed for eggs, which cows were due to calve, what horse had to be shoed . . . And there the matter had lain, till now.

As ready as I was to blame my hardheaded self for not seeing it earlier, well, I was more than twice as glad that I had not. Glad, too, that Doctor Jekyll, despite the great strides he'd made with his French (all thanks to me, of course), still neither thought nor read as a Frenchman. And gladdest of all that he'd not had me translate the seeming scribble for him, for I'd have done so, unthinkingly, as I had a hundred times before; and I'd have said:

Nossels must be *nos sels*, meaning "our salts."

While *notresel*, similarly, would be *notre sel*, or "our salt," in the singular.

Nothing revelatory there, no; but what of *noussels*? *Nous sels*? It was ungrammatical, and therefore very unlike Mother as well; for, when broken in two, like the other entries, it became, yes, *nous* and *sels*, or "we" and "salts." But what of that elision, what of her writing it again and again as one word on those final pages of *Physicae*? Wesalts? Odd.

We . . . make the salts?

We . . . possess the salts?

We . . . are *the salts?*

It was this last reading that had set me to shivering down in the laboratory, when first I'd supposed what that might mean, what Mother may have meant to convey. To me!

We are the salts!

I listened carefully at the door now, till I was certain that there was no one creeping about, innocently (Cézette) or otherwise (well . . .). And then I crawled across the plank floor to my low bureau. From the bottom of its two drawers I took out what I still thought of as my second shift, that second-best blouse I'd brought with me to Paris. Of course, I'd not had to wear it in a long while, owing to Doctor Jekyll's generosity (and I must credit the doctor for that, at the very least). And then, from the top drawer, I took the small sewing kit that had belonged to Cheffy, and which was given to me by Cézette when finally she admitted to herself that her aunt was gone for good and she'd divvied up what little the woman had left behind. And right she was to do it, too: Cheffy *was* gone. I'd long known it, but I'd not dared to tell Cézette of the incriminating discoveries I'd made in the cylinder. Had she not discovered the same? It seemed not. Doubtless she'd looked, but perhaps the English had stymied her, kept her from diving too deeply into the fetid depths of the Blackmail Sea. Regardless, I would never mention the cylinder to Cézette, ever. It seemed the wiser course, and seems so still: Hadn't I enough secrets and lies to tend on my own? . . . Apropos of which:

I'd long ago sewn that packet of the very last of the salts into the hem of the shift, yes, secreting them away. Here was all that remained of the *un*brewed Cagot salts I'd carried from home. Knowing what I knew now, I guessed that it was enough to brew two, maybe three vials more of medium strength, of a potency not even half that of that fateful sixth vial Gréluchon had downed.

Of course, I was not cutting free the packet of secret salts so as to brew them, no.

Rather, there I sat with the salts in my open left palm, feeling them, tentatively at first, with the fingers of my right hand, rubbing them between forefinger and thumb. *Could it be?*

My disgust had quickly ceded to wonder. *Could it be?* I thought so, yes; for the salts had never really seemed like *salts* at all.

Alas. Would this *strangeness* never cease?

When, some hours later, Cézette came to my room with luncheon and asked through the door if I were awake, and if I were feeling better, I said yes, I was well enough, and thank you. I asked her to set the tray down outside the door, if she wouldn't mind; and then—through the door, still; for the request would seem a strange one and I'd not want to see the look upon her face—I asked Cézette for one thing more:

Would she be so kind as to carry up to me here—"Here to my room, Cézette, *not* to the laboratory!"—a cup of ashes gathered from the kitchen hearth?

Poor Cézette. She'd surely given up on ever having answers to the myriad questions she already had, yet rather than ask another, she said, simply, *"D'accord."* Okay.

So it was that within the half hour I once again sat with my back against my bedroom door, comparing a handful of ash and a handful of the Cagot salts.

And one can hardly compare the two: common, household ash, composed of firewood, kitchen scraps, et cetera, and . . . and human remains.

No comparison at all.

I know that now.

CHAPTER FOURTEEN
Keeping the Secret

The secret, our Cagot secret, seemed less terrible once I knew it to be true.

We are *the salts*.

And I did come to believe it to be true; for now I recalled that eerie admonition of my mother's, addressed to me with her last breath: *Take us away with you!* I had never understood that simple command, rendered so very strange and sad by circumstance. They were a dying woman's last words. My *mother's* last words. But what had she meant? For Grel and I to carry her and my father from the site of the act? Bodily? To bury them? Of course, I hadn't had time to wonder, not then, chased as we were by those men who'd murdered my parents and, no doubt, would have done the same to us. I supposed now that she had meant for us to claim them, to take possession of their bodies, secret them until such time as they devolved to ashes . . . to salts. What became of my parents' bodies, I cannot know. Will never know.

Which begged the question, of course: *Whose remains had I brewed?* Who, precisely, comprised the salts I still had in store, secreted away? There were, of course, those Cagot grandparents whom I'd never known, who'd died when I was young, who'd devolved to salts as had, presumably, my own parents, there, in that crossroads, or wherever it was they came to rest. Alas, I let all such questions lie, and I was happy to do so. It was all rather sad-making and, yes . . . *dégoûtant.* Disgusting.

Oh, but the past is another place entirely. It was the present that concerned me. And that word from the past, *murder*, made my blood run cold now; for what mightn't Doctor Jekyll, let alone Mister Hyde, do if they knew this secret, *the* secret of the Cagot salts?

If lately I'd feared losing my mind, now I feared for my life; and Gréluchon's as well.

My most immediate concern was hiding the salts I now had in hand. So, having resewn the packet of . . . *ashes* into my shift with trembling hands, having refolded said shift, having returned it to the bureau, I then shut the drawer on both the salts *and* the secret, supposing (rightly) that I did so not for forever, but for now.

⁂

In keeping the secret of the source of the salts from Doctor Jekyll and Mister Hyde, I was aided and abetted by . . . events. Thankfully; for the doctor sensed something. I was sure of it. And if he sensed something, Mister Hyde would as well, for he seemed at times to have an animal's heightened senses.

Alors, mere days after I'd surmised the secret of the salts the Communards finally, *finally* (and quite fatefully) marched on Versailles. The date was April the third.

Gréluchon (reported Mister Hyde) had been in the vanguard. This I learned after the fact, of course (for Hyde was there at the sortie); and thusly was I spared an added measure of worry. "Yes, yes," said a wholly unsympathetic Hyde, "of course he survived!" Though I will admit this: The thought occurred to me—it was not a *hope*, merely a thought—that if Gréluchon *did* ever die in battle at least his body would be disposed of along with those of his fellows, his comrades.

Hyde, horrid Mister Hyde, also continued to speak of Gréluchon's eye patch—"He's like a pirate, he is, atop those barricades commanding his blokes!" said he, admiringly—and even went so far as to opine that it seemed to him, Hyde, that perhaps the boy *was* weakening, that perhaps (as he put it) the taste for blood had finally fallen from his tongue.

Alas, yes, the Communard sortie on Versailles failed, and miserably so; such that now here came the combined armies of France, united against the Communard-held capital. They'd had time enough to regroup, to strategize. Meanwhile, the Communards had busied themselves in committees! And so while they sought (admirably, it must be said) to *remake* the city, the Versaillais plotted to *retake* it.

In truth, we never stood a chance.

Starvation was not at issue as it had been during the Prussian siege, thankfully, for the Versaillais could not enclose the city: Prussia yet occupied outlying forts in the north and east, and through these forts they let food be brought in. For they, the Prussians, welcomed this fight, *les paysans* versus *les Parisiens*. Not only had they defeated us in the war, but now they needed only to wait, to watch as things worsened and France *entière* weakened herself further through civil war.

✦

Doctor Jekyll and I continued our work, of course. What else was I to do? Days of work—such as it was—were preferable to days of worry. He, of course, grew ever more insistent now, and I ever more distant, ever more . . . secretive. And with the war worsening, the actual work itself came to seem a charade.

Pouring from beaker to beaker, or engaging in some careful calculation, we had to do it all between blasts, so bad was the bombardment. Indeed, the cannonade—worse than anything I could recall from the first siege, though that may have been because these were Frenchmen firing on Frenchmen!—the cannonade began each day at dawn, coming at us from Mont Valérien, from Issy, from Neuilly, for the Versaillais had been allowed to move into the Prussian fortifications in the west. *Bâtards*, all!

Oh, it was horrible, that shelling; and it was not much better in the supposedly peaceable west, where Julien was. There, the whistle of the shells flying overhead into Paris, *at* Paris, must have been deafening; and, of course, the returned fire *from* Paris often fell short of its target, and landed in those western suburbs. Parisians were scurrying for cover, were quitting the city with all they could carry. It was Cézette, a strengthening Cézette, who told of seeing people passing on the boulevard Beaumarchais, heading toward the Gare de Lyon in the hopes of catching a train to . . . elsewhere, *anywhere.* And that exodus was worst of all in the west; and thusly did an ever so slightly chagrined Mister Hyde report that he'd lost track of his prey, of Julien. "Temporarily, *only*," said he.

This he told me one morning at dawn, quite casually—if Edward Hyde can be said to have ever done anything *casually*—for he knew that where Julien went so went my heart, and Mister Hyde was growing even crueler as our store of salts diminished. It was as though he thought he could hurry me in this way, hurry me in my search for the secret and thus secure more salts. And indeed, I feared I might have to access the secreted stash and brew more salts if I were to secure Hyde's help—strange to call it that: *help*—now, when I needed it most. (I could *not* lose track of Julien!)

Of course, Doctor Jekyll would deem it a betrayal if I suddenly produced those salts now, at such a late date. And so it was I suggested we ration what remained of the extant salts, planning Doctor Jekyll's transformations to coincide not with his own pursuit of pleasure, such as it was, but rather with . . . *events of worth*, events of interest to persons more important than Mister Hyde. (Namely: Me. For still I thought I'd be able *to use* Hyde in obtaining my own ends. What a fool I was!) No more mere carousing, causing who knew what sort of trouble. Mister Hyde, of course, hated us for this; but the doctor (surprisingly) had seen my reasoning and stood firm against his lesser self.

And a night of true worth—to me, if not to Mister Hyde—occurred some days later, on April the seventh.

White papers had been pasted up all over Paris, decreeing that every man between the ages of eighteen and fifty-five was now required to present himself *at once*, to join the fight against the Versaillais. The price for not doing so was imprisonment. Julien had only lately turned eighteen, and *damn it* that he had!

Poole, for his part, was clucking about his Hal like a mother hen; for, yes, this law could be applied to Doctor Jekyll as well. The Communards, in their desperation, were disinclined to consider any able-bodied man's excuses owing to cause. *Bref*, the doctor's Englishness would present no impediment at all to his being conscripted into the Communard camp. Poole—whose nerves had begun to weaken with the slobberweed incident a few weeks back—appealed to the master: Mightn't they please, *please* pull up stakes and quit Paris while it was still possible? (And lest they end up trapped there when the time came to secure the Jekyll legacy in London. For the houndlike Poole was ever on the scent of his precious Hal's inheritance, as it would bring the money that much nearer himself.) This Doctor Jekyll refused, squarely, saying (neither for the first time nor the last) that he'd come too far in his work not to see it through.

Of course, Poole knew nothing of the specifics of said work, nor why it had to be achieved in Paris of all places, *warring* Paris; but he knew, somehow, that I was central to it all. And so, in addition to inveighing against that unruly and rude Jekyll cousin, the much-hated Mister Hyde, Poole came to hate me anew. I might well prove to be the reason the inheritor would put off laying claim to the inheritance, and Poole would be dead and damned before he'd let *that* happen. That said, he was rather more careful about it this time; and indeed I stood with spells at the ready, should he see fit to *act* upon said hatred.

Enfin, Doctor Jekyll would not leave Paris, but Poole secured his permission to make it appear as though he had. The windows were papered over and the lights behind them kept low at night. Supplies were hoarded. We were told to keep off the streets—not a problem in my case, not at all—and in no way advertise our presence to the (no doubt spying) neighbors. And, as insurance against conscription, Jekyll allowed Poole to do what rich men have long done in such circumstances: stockpile cash, bundled and ready to be paid out in bribes.

Meanwhile, I had more pressing matters on my mind. One, in particular:

I finally wrote to Julien, offering Mister Hyde an additional dose if he would find him—Hyde, of course, preferred the verb *to track*, but I could not abide it—put my note in his hand, and, yes, attend a reply. (A note only, yes: My letters I yet hoped to hand over to Julien myself.) "Say nothing more than is strictly necessary, Hyde, or so help me . . . !" Hyde agreed, albeit rudely, *crudely*, and headed west shortly after midnight on the eighth of April. I could only hope that Julien's response would be more than my own note returned, crumpled.

Hyde somehow eluded me that night upon his return and when I entered the laboratory early the next morning, well, Doctor Jekyll was rather in a lather. Too, he looked like he'd been hit by the Hammers of Hell. Said he, in answer to my inquiries, yes, Mister Hyde had tracked and made contact with the boy. The doctor now produced a note, pulling it from the pocket of his black velvet waistcoat.

"Not so fast, Odile," said he as I reached, as I *lunged* for the note. "Perhaps you ought to have asked my permission before issuing such an invitation?"

"You've read it? You've read the note?" How dare he!

"No," said the doctor, cagily, "of course not . . . Mister Hyde did. I merely have the memory of it."

I was livid, and surely it showed; but really, I ought not to have been surprised.

"You know, Odile," said Doctor Jekyll, "that you can have no secrets here, no secrets at all."

Was this a warning? A threat? A simple statement of fact?

No matter now. *The note!*

I snatched it from Doctor Jekyll and retired, no *ran* up to my room to read it in what little privacy I was allowed in that huge house (and I'd long ago checked every square inch of that space for a spy hole).

It had been an invitation, yes, and perhaps I should have sought the doctor's permission before I'd written to Julien asking him to . . .

He'd accepted! Julien had written back, accepting the invitation!

. . . Albeit conditionally.

❧

I'd invited Julien to come into the city to hide with me from conscription, and he'd replied that yes, he'd come, but not *to hide*; rather, *to fight.*

To fight? I set those words aside, literally so: I tucked the note in my drawer, beneath the secreted shirt with its sewn-in salts; and then I counted down the hours till sunset, for that was when he'd said he'd come.

I was more pleased than surprised at Julien's response, and I was *hugely* surprised! I'd deemed it a long shot, indeed, that Julien would ever deign to enter the doctor's door, let alone take shelter under his roof. *Never!* But as it turned out, his parents had left Paris the week prior, bound for Bordeaux, and Julien, in the company of some cousins, was due to follow behind that very day. I'd written him at the last possible hour! And in so doing, I'd spurred him to a decision. The *right* decision. And fortunately, Mister Hyde ("Who *was* that man?"

would be among Julien's first questions when he came) had been able to find him. *Track* him, yes.

My invitation, though far from perfect in its particulars, as far as Julien was concerned, had presented him with a plan when no other availed itself. In accepting, he'd both be breaking with his parents and (very much against their will) reuniting with me. But Monsieur Deboos's temper had worsened as the war came on and "those damned rebels" had cost him both shops. Not only had his father continued to abuse Julien, he'd begun to abuse his mother as well. Julien had stayed in Auteuil only to protect her. She'd pled with the boy to do so, all the while confiscating those letters Julien had written to me explaining the situation and—said he, now—apologizing for his long silence, as I now apologized for mine when handing over my own passel of letters. Julien's letters? His crying mother had turned toward the fireplace when finally confronted, such that Julien knew she'd sent his heart up in smoke. So, too, had she burned all remaining filial bonds. Not to mention *words of love* that were mine by right. And I couldn't help it: I hated her for that.

Enfin, we put the past behind us as fast and as best we could. For his part, Julien was all too happy to be done with both that particular butcher, Monsieur Deboos, and butchery itself. As for his scheming mother, she'd made secret plans to slip from her husband in Bordeaux. I said I wished her well; in truth, I simply sought to console Julien on the dissolution of his family. (*Good riddance*, was what I really thought.)

Regarding our reunion, however . . . Well, how I heart-ened to hear from Julien that he'd long sought it himself, as I so desperately had. Of course, I was rather more sly than that in speaking of my own long-standing desperation, even though I knew my letters were about to betray me. And (damn Hyde!) there had never been *une belle cousine* out in Auteuil. I'd had to ask. As for those *im*perfect particulars of my invitation . . .

Julien came into the house as himself—albeit the "butcher boy"—which was a relief; for maintaining the one fiction about Mister Hyde's identity had been hard enough. Predictably, Poole was displeased (and sometimes even dared to show it) while Cézette flirted, at first (and simply couldn't help herself). As for Doctor Jekyll and Mister Hyde?

Suffice to say that I did not let Julien wonder for very long who Edward Hyde was.

The very night of his arrival I took him into a corner of the courtyard and sat him down with a bowl of some Cézette-brewed broth in his hands. I knew I had to, indeed *wanted* to tell him everything. I would be happy to unburden myself so. Yet, even though Julien knew a great deal about . . . *me and mine*, still he'd have to take in some hard truths this night. And so I'd tell him in the courtyard, despite the coldness of it, the strangeness of it, so as to ensure that I'd not be overheard, for I now had secrets I was keeping from every member of the household.

The telling took a long while. It was quite late, nearly

midnight, before I was done; and that was precisely as I'd planned it, for words could take my tale only so far. Some things Julien would simply have to see for himself.

On some pretext, some pseudo-scientific errand I can no longer recall, I'd gotten a most displeased Doctor Jekyll—who'd not offered a word of welcome to Julien—to leave the laboratory for a few moments, to search out something in his consultation room. It was time enough. Quickly, I took down the periodic table that the doctor had guiltily hung over his peephole; and though I was in the habit of making sure it hung there each and every time I entered the laboratory, Doctor Jekyll had developed no such habit. Luckily; for I'd positioned Julien in the doctor's darkened bedchamber, told him to keep his eye fixed to that very same espial portal, which I'd reopened.

Who was *that man?*

Alors, Julien would know soon enough.

With the deed done, as it were—Mister Hyde had spouted a few choice words at me regarding our, no *his* diminishing store of salts and then bolted downstairs and out onto the streets—I went next door to Julien, *le pauvre.*

His pale face shone like a moon in the darkness of the room; and when I lit the lamp, well, his appearance did not improve. He had fallen into the doctor's armchair. There he sat, deathly still. I saw that he'd emptied a vase of silk flowers onto the floor, no doubt thinking he might need to empty his stomach into the vase itself.

"Are you all right?"

He shook his head. *No, I am* not *all right.* And then he tilted his head up to look at me, balefully, and ask, "Were *you* all right, the first time you witnessed . . . that?" It was all he could do to nod toward the wall, toward the peephole.

And of course he had a point: I'd been far from all right then. Time and silence was what I'd needed to take it all in, and time and silence would be what I'd give Julien now.

"Come," said I.

He rose, unsteadily; and so I went to him in a rush, took him by the arm, and said, again, "Come. Follow me, Julien."

We made our way upstairs.

Shells whistled overhead, sounding like the literal winds of war. Shouting could be heard in the streets below, followed by footsteps, running footsteps. There came, too, the muffled *pop* that could only be the report of a pistol, fired somewhere in the square itself.

Before I knew what had happened, we lay together atop my cot. I cannot say who was holding whom. I suppose we held each other. There were no kisses, no questions, indeed no talk at all as together we simply bore the moment as best we could.

In time, we slept; and on the morrow I returned to the warring world.

☙

I'd not left the Jekyll mansion in a long, long while, so mired had I become in my own mind. And now here I was back on the streets. I could never have done it without Julien at my side.

But the streets, they were different now. They were . . . streets of war. As it turned out—and here was one of the countless truths Doctor Jekyll and Mister Hyde had conveniently "misremembered," to use the doctor's word, though *lied about* would be mine—Julien knew those streets well, for he'd been coming into the city to fight alongside the Communards since the failed sortie to Versailles. And yes, he'd watched the mansion from far across the square on occasion, hoping to catch sight of me yet too prideful to approach the doctor's door. ("Fine," said he, when I'd pressed him on the point, "on *every* occasion I could.")

"Ah, so it *was* you!" I said, remembering the shadowy figure I'd seen that night I'd watched from the laboratory window, waiting for Mister Hyde to light his signifying candle, to return with his nightly report. And that day upon the boulevard, too. "I knew it!" And I kissed his forehead, so happy to know he'd never abandoned me. Of course, I didn't tell him *how* I'd known him that night, how I'd recognized the shadow of that beautiful body I'd recalled so often to memory. The broadness of his shoulders, their tapering to his waist, his gait as he'd paced in that shadowed gallery far across the park, pausing now and again to peer across from behind a pillar . . . No, I thought, smiling still, best to keep all that to myself.

And while Julien had heard tell of *a* Gréluchon, he'd never once supposed it could be *the* Gréluchon. That is, not until he'd seen the transformation of the night before, of Jekyll into Hyde. Now he could all too easily believe that my half-blind runt of a baby brother had become . . . was *indeed* the bestial boy he'd seen in the shadows behind the butcher's shop, was the boy they spoke of as the Beast of Belleville.

. . . *Alors*, we had two objectives that first day:

One: Find Gréluchon, see if perhaps I could reason him into . . . what? Safety? Seclusion? I didn't know. I only knew—and what a fool I was!—that, ever the big sister, I still sought to protect, *to save* him. And worse: I was convinced I could! For if the eye patch Mister Hyde spoke of was any indication, the effects of that *singerie*-strong dosage of salts Grel had swallowed might finally be on the wane.

Two: We had to make ourselves useful to the cause if we were to stay upon the streets, Julien *to fight* and I to continue my search.

Regarding our first objective, well, no one would speak of Gréluchon. Each time I spoke his name—or that nickname I so hated—even the most upright (which is to say sober, still sane) Communard would turn on a heel and walk off, sometimes *run off* as if the name itself were a bomb about to burst. As for our second objective, a guardsman in the Place de la Bastille presented us with two options, pulling from his pocket two sets of papers for us to sign, depending on our choice.

Said he, "You can earn one franc *per body* for undressing the dead." Uniforms, apparently, were in short supply. "Or it's three francs per day if you help build barricades in either the first or the twentieth arrondissement. What'll it be, then?" he asked, proffering the papers and his pen. "Hurry now."

Julien and I looked at each other. There was but one question to answer, of course. "The first," said Julien.

The guardsman's eyebrows arched and he said, "Well, well . . ."

"The first *arrondissement*," I added, quick to clear *that* business up. I'd not be undressing the dead, *merci bien*.

The guardsman gave us a name, someone to report to at the Hôtel de Ville, and soon we were hurrying back to the dead center of the city . . . what would soon be the *literal* dead center of the city.

By day we pried paving stones from the rue de Rivoli, alongside the Louvre, packing them onto carts that were then trundled to key cross streets nearby. From the Louvre itself we witnessed an endless parade of pieces being shuttled elsewhere for safekeeping. (It was rumored that the Venus de Milo had been hidden in the filing room of the Prefecture of Police and that the Mona Lisa had been smuggled outside the city in an empty fish wagon returning to Calais.) And as things worsened, our confreres grew even less inclined to speak of Gréluchon. If Mister Hyde knew where we might find him, well, he wasn't saying; and no manner of bribe or would-be bullying could get him to do so. He'd just stand before me, smiling that nonsmile of his.

By night I sought to maintain some semblance of sanity chez Jekyll. This was not easy. Not easy at all. For, since Julien's arrival and my subsequent choice of the streets over the laboratory, Doctor Jekyll spoke to me only as needed and spoke to Julien not at all. Still he pored over Mother's books, ever more frustrated at failing to find any mention of an antidote or anything regarding the source of the salts. Without the first, he'd never be able to control the saltings; without the second, soon there'd be no more saltings at all.

As for Cézette, well, it was she who worried me the most; for all too easily I could imagine her—a Francophone, after all, with serviceable English—pressed into service in my absence as a translator for a desperate Doctor Jekyll and innocently deciphering *noussels*. I slept through the shelling now, but fear of *that* would wake me in the night! And so it was that I did wrong by the girl. I had to! (But believe me when I say I would later make it up to her.)

I stained some insignificant pages of *Physicae* with a big blot of ink and casually, oh so casually let the doctor know that Cézette had bumped my copying arm while delivering luncheon to the laboratory, to which she and her feather duster had only lately been allowed to return (the bombardment causing an insupportable amount of dust to rain down regularly over *all and everything* and foul the simplest of experiments). Doctor Jekyll, whose nerves grew ever more frayed with each passing day, *re*banned the girl from the laboratory, indeed from everywhere he was likely to even *see* her. Henceforth she had to move through the mansion as a phantom.

Poole? Poole was the machinating mass of meanness he'd always been; but still he kept clear of me. (I had only to say the word *tea* in his presence to see him trail away like vapor.) In time I'd learn what he was plotting: Word had somehow come to Doctor Jekyll from London, word that his father was, finally, dying. While this news was met *un*emotionally by both the master and his manservant—who'd evidently decided to share said news rather than secrete it within his armored accomplice—*alors*, there were no emotions, as far as I could tell, yet still the situation presented certain . . . *matters*, matters needing to be seen to.

Indeed, Henry Jekyll, Junior, would soon have to go to London to present himself, sporting a sad mask, at his father's deathbed; or, at the very least, attend the later reading of a will that would render him heir to the Jekyll fortune. *Finally.* Poole had waited decades for that day, when his Hal would hold the purse strings, but now, yes, he found his monomaniacal master disinclined to leave Paris even for this! No, Jekyll Junior *still* would not leave Paris without that long-sought something that had enslaved him to both his laboratory and me. War hadn't made him go, now neither would his father's waiting millions. . . . *Alors*, there was Poole, omnipresent and plotting.

As for Mister Hyde, well, he alone sought out Julien; and it was unpleasant, indeed ugly, on those few occasions (not few enough!) when he found him. Jekyll would begin with verbal taunts of the schoolyard sort (". . . butcher's boy, witchling's toy," was a favored refrain) and when these found no effect he progressed to physically taunting Julien, poking at and finally, lightly, slapping at his face. It was light, yes, but it was a slap nonetheless and Julien would not stand for it. He sprang at Hyde. Or rather, would have, had I not interceded at the last second, leaping between the two as they were about to tangle upon the second-floor landing, just outside the laboratory. Hyde would never have harmed me now, not grievously so; for he needed me more than ever and knew it. But Julien? I feared for his safety. Jealousy personified—and literally so, though I could not have said if the more jealous self were Jekyll or Hyde—Mister Hyde would have happily torn Julien to shreds.

On the night in question, Doctor Jekyll had only just self-salted, and very lightly at that. (Owing to that paucity of blue brew, Hyde rose now but for an hour, maybe two.) Indeed, Mister Hyde's irises, I saw, were yet wholly brown when he went for Julien; and so Doctor Jekyll had been very much present. Peculiar, this; for Doctor Jekyll would normally have had Hyde back down from such a confrontation; and in the mansion, no less! Not this night. And though they—Jekyll and Hyde and Julien—did not resort to fisticuffs (or worse), it fell to me to ensure that they never would, for the hatred and jealousy they shared showed no signs of dissipating. And so, henceforth, after each midnight salting, I stood upon that landing outside the laboratory, directing the devilish traffic: Having already sent Julien *up*stairs, I would ensure that Mister Hyde went *down*, down and out of the house, ". . . or else."

The happiest of households? Hardly.

April passed; May came; and as the weather bettered, the worse worsened.

Once again, Paris was in a stranglehold. The national forces were closing in on the city, and one met each day with the same question: *Is today the day?*

We kept from the house as best we could, returning there only to sleep, really; and for me to do just enough to remain in Doctor Jekyll's (relatively) good graces. He labored on, despite my telling him we'd culled all we could from the books, that there was no antidote, that the closest we'd ever come would be to carefully control the dosage. I told him, too, that there was no secret, *period*. I will not say that he *dis*believed me, but regardless, he worked on, focusing his efforts on *Humanitas*, thankfully; for I'd had to leave all the books in his possession, including *Physicae*, so as not to rouse his suspicion.

As for me, I was no longer suspicious: I was *certain* regarding the source of the salts. Julien, while no less horrified than I, agreed: They were ashes, not salts at all. Cagot ashes.

At midnight on the agreed-upon days, I'd return to the laboratory and oversee Doctor Jekyll's salting. This posed no problem at all, of course: We had *no* inclination to share the nighttime streets with Edward Hyde. Neither would I meet him in the morning, as previously I had. But just as I was chary with my presence in the laboratory, so too was Doctor Jekyll disinclined to share what, if anything, he (as Hyde) may have learned of Gréluchon. Now I saw the petulant, nearly pouty

Hal that Poole must've known all too well: The spoiled son of a man of means, accustomed to getting his way. And so Julien and I were alone in our search for my brother, the much-bruited Beast of Belleville.

Finally, on the sixteenth of May, we found him in the Place Vendôme. Along with what seemed a million others.

The Communards had decided to pull down the Column of the Grande Armée standing at the center of the square, its sculpted sides commemorating victory in the Battle of Auster-litz. The column's forty-odd meters had been forged from those cannon confiscated from the defeated Austro-Russian forces, and Napoleon the victor stood atop it all dressed as Caesar. How could it remain standing there, vaunting the victories of a France we now fought? That was the question the Communards had answered in the negative: *It could* not *remain*. Down it must come.

A huge contraption, seeming like a reversed catapult of sorts, was now in place; via its winches, pulleys, and whatnot, the column would be brought down. And all the city (so it seemed) had come to see this.

It was Julien who'd supposed that Gréluchon might be pres-ent for the toppling, and it was he who now muscled us as near to the column as he could. When the column landed with a great thud—so great it would later be said that on a nearby statue Joan of Arc now rode sidesaddle—*alors*, it was when the dust quite literally settled that I spied Gréluchon.

He stood not fifty paces distant, still holding to the rope by

311

which he and his fellows had felled France (metaphorically, at least). While the other red-capped Communards fraternized, flush with success, Gréluchon stood apart. No one spoke to him. None dared even congratulate him. No huzzahs, no back-slapping for the boy who'd become a beast, *the* Beast.

Despite having spied him in the alleyway, despite what he'd seen through Doctor Jekyll's peephole, Julien could not believe that the person I pointed out to him in the center of the Place Vendôme could actually be my brother. No matter. I knew it was he. But if we didn't get closer, I'd not be able to see if Gréluchon wore the eye patch of which Hyde had spoken . . .

And then we lost him. Like *that*, he was gone.

Everyone else was leaving the Place Vendôme, of course, while we struggled to get nearer its center, where last we'd seen Gréluchon. We now transformed ourselves into a beast of four elbows, doing all we could so as not to lose him to the crowd.

"There!" I found him, for I saw the crowd parting to let him pass—as one would "let" a charging bull pass—from the square and onto the rue Saint-Honoré. "Come on!" And we were off without any apologies offered to those we so rudely displaced en route.

We followed in his wake. People were still remonstrating, calling after the coward who'd pushed past them so brusquely—taking care to do so, of course, only *after* said coward had passed from within earshot—when we pushed past them similarly.

We, too, were harangued, harassed; but I didn't care. I'd keep sight of Gréluchon *at all cost*.

Down the rue Saint-Honoré we ran, all the way to the Palais Royale. It was there that I lost Gréluchon to the crush of carousers crowding the galleries: celebrating Communards—could they not *sense* the end was near?—shopkeepers, window-shoppers, idlers, and soldier-rich whores.

It was Julien who spotted him next, up near the northern end of the park enclosed by the galleries, by the palace itself.

We ran, *ran*; and just as we lost him again and were about to despair . . . he found us.

He had suddenly appeared, as surely as if he'd dropped from the sky; and he now stopped Julien with an outstretched arm, one that caused all the breath to burst from his pursuer's lungs. As Julien struggled for breath, Gréluchon spoke in a voice I'd never heard before—lower in timbre since last I'd heard it in that blood garden in Montmartre—asking, so pointedly as to puzzle me:

"What do you want? Why are you following me?"

"Grel," said I, "it's me: Odile!" And I realize now that I'd identified myself because, well, I was unsure who *he* was. For he'd changed so! If before he'd been brutish, now he appeared positively . . . *feral*, for want of a kinder word. Filthy, and at once skittish and scary, both.

Of course, he recognized *me*—his flat and (yes) one-eyed, patched stare said so—and I felt a total fool. The more so when he repeated his questions verbatim: *What do you want? Why are you following me?*

As I had no ready answer, he turned to take his leave.

"Wait!" It was a plea I uttered as I ran to him, and a plea I dared to accompany with a hand set atop his shoulder. "Grel, please . . ."

Wincing as if my hand had pained him, he then threw it from his shoulder with a force I felt high in the socket of my own shoulder. Had it not been attached to my person, my hand would have landed in the faraway gardens! I'd not touch him a second time; and likewise I motioned behind me to Julien to stay where he was. "Gréluchon, please! Why won't you speak to me?"

" 'Speak'? Speak of what?"

"Of . . . of this!" said I in response; and I made a gesture with my hand, one meant to take in . . . *him*, him and everything that had happened since he'd swallowed the salts.

I looked him over where he stood. If previously, post-salting, his muscled flesh can be said to have rippled, like water coursing over stones in a brook, well, that water was now stagnant, still. He was weakening, yes. I saw it.

Yet here he still was, strong and *quite* formidable. Still the Beast he'd become.

"Speak? No. I'm afraid, sister mine, that I've grown less fond of speech. Action . . . *action* is more my thing nowadays." Whereupon he flipped up his patch to disclose . . . Alas, I can hardly call it an eye.

The black patch had kept the surrounding area clean, such that now it shone white upon his filthy face, framing that ruined . . . *void*, the sightless socket where once an eye had been. It was as though an acid had eaten away the lid and had begun to ingest the eye itself. The pupil was covered with a caul seemingly ten times thicker than the one that had blinded him before, and it had spread now like a web over the iris, over the whole of the eyeball. And what first I took for tears was but pus, seeping from just the one eye, and trailing down over a face that had once been pink but was now dirt-darkened. Yes, I remembered all too well that pink-complexioned baby brother of mine. *Wherever had he gone? However had I . . . ?*

"Grel . . ." I stammered, "I . . . I didn't know."

"And I," said he, "no longer care." It was not accusatory, but rather a simple statement of fact. He sought no apology. And indeed it was all too clear: *He didn't care.* Neither about the eye . . . nor the salts . . . nor me. *None of it.* He cared only for the fight, the Communard cause; and when it seemed he was on the verge of turning away, limping away, leaving, I sought to hold him with a rather unfortunate question:

"Have you seen a doctor?" It was, I knew, a silly-sounding substitute for *You are sick, and growing sicker.*

Gréluchon sniggered; and a like-minded Julien said, from where he stood behind me, "This all *started* with a doctor."

"Yes," I ventured, "but perhaps if we went back to Doctor . . ." I dared not even say the name Jekyll.

"No," said Gréluchon. "It is too late. Too late in every way."

"*No!* It is not! I . . . I have more, Grel!" I surprised myself in saying so; and Julien, for his part, stared aghast as I drew forth the last of the pure salts, which I'd *un*sewn from the shift and brought for . . . for just this very purpose. "Here! Take them."

"Odile," said Julien, "what are you doing? When did you . . . ?"

"It makes sense!" I said, trying to convince myself as much as Julien. "More of the salts might strengthen him again." I spoke as though my brother were not even present . . . and perhaps he wasn't. Too, I spoke with a conviction that was not true. I had no clue as to what more of the salts might do. I had only hope, hope that . . . "They might stop the rot of his eye, undo the damage! Might even—"

"Stop!" This from Gréluchon, who continued, commandingly. "Tell me, Odile: Do you suppose that more of the salts will undo the deeds I've done as well? . . . Yes? . . . No? *Answer me!*" I saw now that his other, *good* eye was as black as Mister Hyde's. "Undo what I've done with these!" And he held out his hands, his Cagot hands, webbed as mine were. The gloves I'd sewn him were long gone, and his hands were filthy, the nails long and cracked, clawlike. I took a step back as slowly his hands unformed their fists, fell slackly to his sides. "No," said Gréluchon, finally. "I thought not."

Now he reached deep into a pocket, pulling from it his red Communards' skullcap. He tossed the hat to me and . . .

And then he was gone.

Strangers turned to stare as I called out, *cried* out his name.

The echo of it snaking down the stony galleries seemed to mock me.

"Leave me!" said I to a blameless Julien then, denying him as he moved to embrace me. I felt unworthy of him, of his sympathy. Unworthy of *all* sympathy.

Alone, all alone, I fell crying against the cold stone of a centuries-old wall.

CHAPTER FIFTEEN
Bloody Week

After that ill-fated meeting with Gréluchon, after his latest denial of me, I once again took to my attic room. I would not rise for days, and I lay abed not sleeping but rather holding tight to that red cap and wanting somehow to punish myself. *What had I done?* How had my best intentions gone so horribly wrong? And what, precisely, *had* Gréluchon done? Too easily I imagined that the capture, the *brutalizing* of the archbishop was not the worst of it.

And then one day at dawn there came a harried knocking at our door. A crying Cézette carried the news: The Versaillais had done it, had finally breached our defenses and entered Paris via the Porte de Saint-Cloud. No more waiting. Now there'd be only war, outright and open.

We—Julien, Cézette, and I—climbed up through the attic to the mansion's belvedere, thus affording ourselves a view of the city. *Could it be true?* Yes; for already we could see a string of *engagements*—a too-polite word, perhaps, for what these really were—extending from the Jardin des Plantes up to Montmartre, and we could hear musket and machine gun fire in the Marais as well.

Julien thought he could see the national tricolor already flying over Montmartre but he could not be sure, given the distance, the insufficient strength of the spyglass we had, and the fact that Cézette and I had begun *begging* him to descend along with us, for the shells were now passing uncomfortably close overhead.

Cézette insisted that they sounded like the meowing of kittens, or perhaps the ripping of silk; while to Julien the sound recalled that of a sharp knife moving through sinew, severing meat from bone. Me? To me it simply sounded like war, a terrible, taunting sound seeming to say that, yes, I'd seen the last of my brother; for surely, *surely* Gréluchon was at the very center of it all now.

Julien took to the streets that day. I did not. I *could* not.

A sorely shaken Julien finally gave up these excursions, withdrawing to the relative safety of our room on the day a shell burst near where he'd been huddled behind a barricade before the new opera house, loosing a balcony that fell like a scythe to sever the leg of the soldier beside him. This was later in that most ignominious week. Bloody Week, it would come to be called. Already thousands, *thousands* lay dead in the streets, and the Seine was reputed to run red.

Julien had not seen Gréluchon while out on the streets, but Mister Hyde hinted one day at dawn that he *had* seen Gréluchon. Oh, the gore of it all had Hyde in his glory then, and the midnight hour could not come fast enough. He'd quaff what he could of the remaining salts—in truth, a sip was all the doctor dared at this point—and head off like a belle to a ball. *Alors*, as Hyde's eyes were fast returning to that more believable brown, I supposed he spoke true when he reported that the Communards had been pushed back and were now cornered in the east of the city, indeed in the Père-Lachaise cemetery.

This, then, would be the Communards' last stand, surely; for they'd been outnumbered, outgunned, and, yes, nearly undone all that week long. And Gréluchon would be no man's prisoner. No, my brother would sooner die, would *indeed* die unless I . . . Yes, I still believed I could save him. Rather, I had to try. I simply *had* to.

Alors, all week I'd been making the most dire threats about what I'd do if I lost Julien *and* Gréluchon, both. I suppose I meant it, yes; but it was also a strategy intended to keep Julien close, off the streets, at my side and safe. And so imagine his surprise at waking one morning very late in that infernal week to find that *I* was gone . . . that I'd snuck off to the war all alone.

Doctor Jekyll had salted at midnight; and so Mister Hyde had already gone. I went up to our room, climbed into the cot, and feigned sleep. It was all I could do to let the small hours of the morning pass; then, finally, while all the house slept, I rose, dressed in that second-best shift, donned Julien's overcoat, kissed him where he lay, and went off to war with no weapon but the one: The last of the Cagot salts, once again sewn into the hem of my shift.

I would find my brother, the legendary Beast of Belleville, and—whether he wanted it or not!—somehow salt him back to that strength which had earned him that hated sobriquet. Strengthened, he might stand a chance; weakening, going blind, he would not. He'd soon be but another martyr to the lost Communard cause.

Alas, such was my plan.

❦

As first light came on, the sunlight sparkled on the exposed stonework strewn about the streets, soon to be but the ruins of war. I kept to the last of the shadows, as if taking my cues from the cats slinking about.

I hurried east, up and into Belleville and its cemetery, drawn there by the report of rifle fire. It was yet inconstant, that sound, but when the sun rose the battle would be well and truly joined. And the bloody, the *very* bloody end of the war, of Bloody Week, would begin.

As had been the case in the Place Vendôme when the column had come down, I now had to make my way into Belleville against a stream of people: soldiers, prisoners . . . Yes, already the Versaillais were rounding up the last of the rebels.

A black-bearded man on horseback, his saber drawn, led a

string of Communard soldiers and suspected sympathizers—prisoners—roped to one another at the hip, their hands tied behind their backs. The lot of them had been stripped of their makeshift uniforms of Communard red, such that some of the men were made to parade in shame, without their trousers.

One of the more fortunate women had been allowed to turn her red smock inside out, such that now she showed only its gray lining, save that one of the red-lined pockets was turned out upon her breast, looking as though her very heart hung there, broken and unbeating. They all seemed so very . . . vulnerable. Fearing I might see them slain on the spot, I hurried on.

Finally I arrived at the high stone walls of Père-Lachaise. From the reconnaissance I'd done—if I can call it that, for it amounted to my having pounded on the chest of a laughing Hyde, seething, *screaming*, "Tell me more!"—I knew that the very last of the rebels had been pushed back into the cemetery's northeast corner. ("It'll be like shooting rats in a barrel!" said a nearly gleeful Edward Hyde, who shared *le snobisme* of his other self where the Communards were concerned.) When finally I arrived there, skirting first the surrounding Versaillais soldiers and then bands of retreating rebels as well, I saw Communards in exodus, some hurrying out through the gates while others clambered down ropes thrown over the walls.

"It's over!" cried one man wildly, limping on a shot leg. "Run, girl! There'll be nothing for you here but blood and a square home of stone if you stay!"

I let the man pass. And when finally I found a rope of knotted, bloody sheets hanging untended, I slipped from the shadows and started to climb up and into the cemetery as fast as I could.

Inside the cemetery, I fell to my stomach as if by instinct. Bullets were biting into the trees and sparking off the stones of the graves and cobbled alleys. They sounded nothing like kittens or ripping silk or knifed sinew, no: *They sounded like bullets!* And it seemed each one sought me twice, thrice, as it ricocheted around the cemetery, stone to stone.

The cemetery is hilly, its hundreds of winding *ruelles* set about with tombs both upright and flat. I snuck into one of the former, for its iron door had lately been kicked from its hinge; and in so doing I roused a cat and her kittens. The cat hissed at me but led her brood back onto the battleground, where they broke like billiards, scattering this way and that. And there, in that stony booth stinking of . . . *time*, I sat shivering both from cold and fear. An urn of ashes sat upon the tomb's single, altar-like shelf, and I supposed the ashes of the ancestors of the tomb's inhabitant had been poured behind said shelf when he or she had come, as is the practice. . . . *Ancestors. Ashes.* I realized I was gripping the hem of my shift in my fist.

It may have been an hour or more before I dare moved from that tomb; but I could see nothing peering through its panes of stained glass, its broken door, and so move I must, and did.

In a crouch, like a stone skimming over a stream, I went from tomb to tomb. Finally I found one from which I could see.

Through its grilled door I could peer down into that northeast corner where the cemetery's bordering wall of stone separated it from the city beyond.

Alas, it was from that vantage point that I watched as now the Versaillais closed in from the south and west.

The last of the Communards fought back, futilely, firing from behind this tree, that tomb. The gunfire slowed, which set me shivering anew. It had been better when the firing was more constant. I'd had more hope, then; now I had none.

I saw bullets bite into red-clothed flesh, causing one Communard—he seemed but a boy—first to jitter and then dance that jig which cannot be mistaken for anything but the fast dance of death. Bodies lay strewn over tombstones, spilling blood that ran the maze of carved names and dates. The living shouted desperate strategy, but too often the response was a scream. And all the while I watched for some sign, *any* sign, of my brother; but none came.

Hours passed. Midday unto dusk. In my stolen tomb I cried till I could cry no more, and I listened as that gunfire slowed, slowed and finally stopped; and the ensuing silence was the worst war sound I ever heard, for I knew what it meant:

It was over.

I was about to surrender my hiding place, trade it for another from which I might see more, but now here they came. I could hear them: Men on the march.

I had seen and, yes, *heard* the Prussians when they'd marched into Paris, but these marching men made a different sound; for this was a forced march, one not of conquerors but the conquered. And then I saw them, Communards all.

Good! thought I at first, foolishly. Here came a parade of sorts, one that would have Gréluchon passing by me if only I waited and watched. My search for him would end. I'd have only to wait a while longer, then retake to the shadows and follow the line of prisoners to whatever depot they'd go to, and maybe then I could . . .

Foolish indeed, and so naïve.

I was a long while watching, wondering why they were lining the Communards up against the cemetery wall. And I didn't come to understand why, *fully* understand why, until a facing line of Versaillais soldiers raised high their rifles and the first of the bullets flew. And the first of the red-clad men fell.

As they fell, blood and brains spattering on that stone wall behind them, a corps of Versaillais soldiers—*French* soldiers!—dug the ditch into which the slain would be dumped. Like so much refuse.

With each successive lineup of Communards, I held my breath. My heart seemed to skip every second beat. And I watched, *I had to watch*—some men cried, others spewed every epithet they knew while their neighbor stood stoically by—until the call, "Fire!" From that I turned my crying face away . . . again and again and again.

And then finally I came to hope, *to believe* that Gréluchon . . . that the Beast of Belleville had somehow escaped the cemetery. Of course he had! Not once did I consider that he'd not

325

come in the first place, no. He'd have been at the battle all right, that much I knew in my bones. But he'd not been captured! He'd escaped!

Those hopes all died when I saw my brother alive for the last time.

I could not have said how many of his comrades had fallen—tens certainly, more likely hundreds—but when finally they had all fallen, fallen from life and into a long pit lined with quicklime, where their bodies were sprinkled with more lime so as to speed their decease, their devolution . . . only then was the last of the Communards hauled before the wall.

He stood alone. He was hooded, as no others had been; but this was only for show, for when the hood was torn from his head a cry rose among the assembled riflemen. *Hurrah!* He'd also been bound at both hand *and* foot, as the others had not been. Even so, he fought off two soldiers before two more came to their aid. Four men! It took four men to secure Gréluchon against that red wall.

Oh yes, it was he. And I knew it long before they unhooded him and tore from him, too, his eye patch, disclosing a dark target for each of the thirteen riflemen.

I whistled. With those rifles raised, I somehow stilled my trembling lips and whistled as we had as children, rousting bats from the caves of our youth, falling to our bellies and laughing, covering our heads lest they tangle in our hair, and yes, laughing as they winged us by. And Grel heard me, I know: He lifted high his head at the last minute, his one eye casting about,

Where? Where? And I saw his lips slowly curl into a last smile before . . .

"Fire!" came the call.

One of the executioners beat the others to the draw, and it was he, I saw, who was first to stake his lowly claim to that dark target, that now blackened eye socket; and thusly did he claim my brother's life with a bullet through his brain.

It must have been hours before I came to, that tear-soaked red skullcap clutched in my hands.

The moon was full and high—it must have been past midnight—and by its light I saw soldiers standing guard at the gates of the cemetery. They passed cigarettes, sharing; one even dared laugh.

The pit, it seemed, was unguarded; and without thinking, with no thought at all, somehow I knew what I had to do. Had I stopped to think about it, I'd have never found the strength to act, as now I did.

I crept from the tomb, stole tree by tree to the pit's edge. It was indeed unguarded, yet still I stifled my sobbing. Indeed, I dared not even *breathe* lest I be heard. And there—center-all atop the pile, for he'd been the last to fall—lay Gréluchon.

I shooed a cat from atop the tattered corpse—the thirteen riflemen had had but one target at the end, and the body had been riddled with their bullets—and, mindless of what, of *who* I braced against for balance, I took my brother by the arms and pulled with all my might, pulled him from that pile and away, away into another nearby tomb.

Closing the tomb, replacing the door as imperfectly as I'd found it, I saw that its present . . . occupant had come to Paris from elsewhere. I could hardly read the sculpted script through my tears, but I felt the three carved letters for surety: Yes, Pau. He'd come from Pau, that city in the southwest so near where we'd been born, Gréluchon and I.

It was then I truly started to cry, to loose great wracking sobs that surely would have discovered me to the Versaillais soldiers had I not then left the cemetery as I'd come hours earlier, long before entombing my beloved brother, the last of my blood.

❦

I wandered, floating like a ghost through the eerily still streets; and I can account for neither the time that passed nor the distance I covered. Somehow, at some point, I found myself beside the Seine, as always I did, and soon I'd followed its flow to the Hôtel de Ville, drawn by the flames rising there.

Paris's city hall had stood for how many decades, how many centuries, before being burned by the retreating Communards? It seemed as though they'd sought to take the city with them into defeat, forgetting it was *their* city, for they'd burned a swath eastward from the Tuileries—where before there'd been a palace, now there was nothing—to Châtelet—where the theater had been burned; I saw sequined costumes glittering upon the dark sidewalk like distant constellations—and all the way to and *through* the Hôtel de Ville. I recall being surprised to see that a distant Notre-Dame was still standing, and free of flames.

And if I have to identify the thoughts then coursing through my head, my heart, and my soul, I would say *the waste of war.* Not just the buildings, no; far from it. And not just my brother either. All too soon it would be said that ten, fifteen, perhaps twenty *thousand* people had perished during Bloody Week. (Including, yes, the archbishop of Paris.) The numbers would numb both heart and mind. *The waste of war,* indeed. And I was certainly numb that night, when a too-familiar figure suddenly appeared at my side as I stood staring into the flames rising from the Hôtel de Ville, wanting to be one with all the destruction, with those consuming flames.

"The household fears for you, Odile," said Mister Hyde, sounding more reasoned than I'd ever heard him before; and a *reasoning* Hyde was cause for concern, surely. Was he near to transforming back into Doctor Jekyll—quite possible, that, given the late hour—or had the master imbibed only a bit of the blue brew this night in an attempt to stretch the last of the salts? Regardless, Hyde was undoubtedly Hyde that night; though, yes, he would manifest some Jekyll as well. And the two, working as one, would once again prove a most formidable foe.

"Are you coming home?" he asked. "I was told to track you, to bring you back."

Told by whom? By his Doctor Jekyll, surely; for Julien would never have appealed to Hyde for help of any kind. Or would he? Surely I'd rendered him heartsick, disappearing so. "I'll return in time," said I. "Now leave me. Go!"

I returned to the great show of flames, for that petrol-powered fire was mesmerizing, drawing from the stone all the colors of a peacock's fanned tail. Oh, how I wanted to lose myself in those flames now. "Leave me," I said again.

Hyde did not go, as commanded. Of course not; for he was Mister Edward Hyde. "You don't tell me what to do, witchling . . . or whatever you are. No one tells me what to do!"

"Save for that half of yourself that belongs to another," said I, as coldly, as cruelly as I could.

"Jekyll answers to Hyde, not Hyde to Jekyll!"

"Indeed?"

"Indeed!"

"Well, let me tell you both again: *Go!* Leave me! I'll return home . . . rather, I'll come back to that house when I'm good and ready." And then I made a mistake: I showed weakness in asking, "Is . . . Is Julien all right?" Surely it was known that he was the sole reason I'd return.

Hyde struck, for he fed on weakness as jackals feed on meat. "What's the matter, then? Need a bit more time . . . *to mourn?*" The meanness of it verily lit the man, and darkness danced at the center of his black eyes, flickering amid the real flames reflected there.

He *knew*, the devil! And still he dared to tease me.

But what did it matter now? Let him taunt, let him tease.

To hell with him, with *them*! With Gréluchon gone, I was done with Doctor Jekyll once and for all. I would leave the capital with Julien. Oh, but first I'd tell that pseudo-scientist Jekyll and this damnable doppelgänger of his a thing or two, indeed I would! "You can search all your lives long for the secret of the salts," said I, "but you'll never learn it from me. No indeed, I'll never tell!"

All this and more I (quite mistakenly) said to Mister Hyde, adding, again, as cruelly as *I* could, "And why aren't *you* mourning? Surely you, too, are about to die, Hyde; or at least lie dormant a long, long while. The doctor cannot have but a thimbleful of the brewed salts remaining now, eh?"

Mister Hyde fell silent, and I thought for a moment that I'd gained the upper hand; but then he came closer, taking me by the collar of my shift and saying, "There *is* a secret then, Cagot, and you know it!"

He stood too near to even strike me, but still I jutted forth my chin as if to say, *Go ahead, do your best, devil!* But then suddenly Hyde unhanded me and . . . and the strangest look came over his face.

"What . . ." he began, as if speaking to himself, perhaps to Jekyll, his black eyes rolling skyward, "What is that smell?"

"It's fire, fool! Paris is burning, or haven't you . . . ?"

Now he did slap me into silence, *le bâtard*! And well I might have fought back, but for . . .

Alas, I'd never have thought that Hyde would scent it upon my person, especially not among the commingled odors of tombs,

331

dirt, blood, petrol, flame, and ash that now clung to me as well; but catch it he did, such that now he closed on me again, this time sniffing at me, *sniffing*! His eyes were wide, and what he did—that doggish sniffing—felt so very . . . indecent. But he could not be stopped. Said he, excitedly, "You have some upon you. Now. *You do!*"

As indeed I did, sewn into the shift he'd lately had in hand.

There was no point in denying it, this I knew. Hyde had caught the scent of the salts—I'd not known they *had* a scent—through his every heightened, animal-like sense. I would not have had time to deny it even if I'd tried, for the next words between us came quickly and they were Mister Hyde's. It was both a command and a threat, and it chilled me like nothing he'd ever said before.

"Give. Them. To. Me. *Now.*" And he held out his hand, palm up, his fingers curling, pulsing inward as if he were plucking the strings of some invisible harp. "Now," he repeated, too calmly, "or I shall search for, find, and seize them by main force." Those fingers were a fist now. "I will, and you know it."

He would, and I knew it. And no matter who might witness it.

Slowly, imperceptibly, he'd backed me nearer the burning building. I felt the heat of the flames now on my back, saw them lighting the murderous intent upon the man-monster's face.

"All right, all right!" I said. I only appeared (so I hoped) to be fearful, to be trembling; for in fact I was stalling. Hyde was taking me in, tip to toe, with his every heightened sense—never had I seen him more animal-like—but I saw that he'd not alighted on my hem as the hiding place of the salts. "Please," said I, willing tears to well in my eyes, "it's been a hard, very hard night and—"

"Yes, yes," said Hyde, "but the news from Père-Lachaise is already old, Odile. Old and as cold as your brother's body. Those who wage war run the risk of losing it, and then, well, the winners *will* have their way." He sneered, baring his teeth in the process.

"How," I began, "how can you be . . . ?" And I lifted my shift to my face then, baring my body, yes, but hoping, *hoping* that Hyde would believe I meant only to wipe at my tears, perhaps even blow my nose. ". . . so cold . . ." I sobbed, "so cruel and unfeeling? How does your blood beat, Hyde, without a heart to pump it?"

The question had the intended effect; and as Hyde tilted back his head to loose that horrid laugh of his, as I knew he would at so sentimental a question, his eyes were off me just long enough for me to tear the packet of salts free with my teeth and scatter them onto a strip of dirt, a long untended garden running alongside the burning building.

I ducked the long arm, the long and *fisted* arm of Edward Hyde as it swung toward my face, then I scurried from him and stopped some feet away. And turning back, I saw him leap a low fence and go down on his hands and knees in that disused garden till he looked for all the world like a hungry hog at its trough.

I stared in disbelief.

The salts, the ashes, had taken fast to that warmed earth and now weeds, weeds and wildflowers—bloodred poppies—were sprouting in profusion! Moss and lichen, too, bloomed upon the rocks and wrought-iron railing. It seemed the salts were speeding every possible process. And none more alarmingly—dare I say more beautifully?—than that which followed from certain of the salts finding a trellis that supported a great climbing vine, arms of which yet clung to the burning building; whereupon, beginning low, at the ground, roses began to bloom where nothing but the tiniest buds had been a moment before, and extant roses that had withered from the so proximate heat of the fire now flowered anew. The white and yellow roses bloomed and burned like sudden suns, while the red and orange roses seemed to siphon off the fire itself. And then, fast as they'd bloomed, the weeds and wildflowers and fire roses and whatnot began to wither and rot in seeming mockery of the salts' transformative effects on humans.

Meanwhile, there was Hyde upon his hands and knees picking at, *pinching* at the soil in an effort to salvage the salts one by one. In so doing, he ate dirt and dead flowers, horribly sucking at the hot petals. His hands, his face, even his lips and tongue blistered and went bloody soon after he set upon those roses still on the vine.

It was then I began to laugh. *To laugh*, yes, though the sight of Edward Hyde had never been more disconcerting. He was—dare I say it?—not himself. And hearing my laughter, Hyde looked up. He'd forgotten me, then he'd forgotten himself; but now here he was again, and more savage than I'd ever seen him.

In truth, I thought he'd abandon that garden, leap the iron rail, come to me, *at* me . . . and kill me. I did; for such was the look of hatred upon his face. I looked around: To whom might I appeal? No one; for those present either fought the fire or stared into it, fire-struck, and none seemed to have noticed Hyde's strange behavior. And of course there'd be no escape from him. To run would be to incite him to action. Tracking, torturing action. And so I simply stood there. *Come. Do what you will.*

I saw it too clearly then: I saw Hyde's eyes fall from my eyes to my hand; and only then did I realize that still I held to the packet that had contained the salts, that *still*, tucked in an untorn corner, contained some of the salts. Not much, no; but they were pure salts, unbrewed and very, *very* strong.

I made the decision in a split-second. Hyde was twitching with intent, and I saw that he was about to leap the railing and take the salts from me, *come what may*. And I'd be damned if on this of all days . . .

As prisoners are said to do with smuggled notes, I stuffed all that remained in my hand—packet *and* salts—into my mouth and, with Hyde watching, seeming actually to smile, as if cheering me on, I swallowed it down as quickly as I could.

"Brava!" said Mister Hyde. *"Finally!"* He still stood in that garden, backlit by fire, screaming now over the roaring flames. Rose petals fell from his hands as his fists unfurled: a confetti born of all the carnage. "Won't Henry be happy to now number *you*, Odile, among the self-salting? Indeed, he will. And I am thrilled as well."

Only now did he come to me. To take me by the shoulders,

not to beat or shake me senseless but to . . . *thank me.* "Thank you, Cagot!" said he. "For now you'll know. Now, *finally*, you've joined us!"

Behind him the ceiling of the city hall caved, and sparks rushed up, scattering on the wind. I saw, too, that the garden was yet . . . *alive* from the scattered salts. All that was strangeness enough, yes; but now what was Edward Hyde saying? *Thanking* me?

Only then did I come to understand what Doctor Jekyll and Mister Hyde had long been hoping for, waiting for. *If you can't beat them, join them.* They'd been hoping that I'd succumb to temptation, that I'd self-salt, yes; and when, as they had, I grew addicted, I'd of course commit myself to discerning the Cagot secret *at all costs* and we'd all have salts forevermore. Had I set and just sprung my own trap? I had, but I hardly had time to consider the consequences of all that; for . . .

Already I'd begun to turn.

My bones were breaking, breaking only to reset themselves beneath my skin. I could hear this happening, even over the sounds of the fire before me; and of course the accompanying pain, the wracking pain that succeeded, was the worst I'd ever known and cannot be exceeded, *cannot*, neither at the hour of birth nor death.

The bonds of obligation dissolved, and I was conscious of a heady recklessness. I felt nausea, too, but it fast subsided to something . . . sweet. *Bref*, I felt wondrously . . . wicked. Wicked and free.

And though at first I ascribed it to the flames, I soon learned the truth of the adage *seeing red*; for as I stood there, *transforming*, with the burning Hôtel de Ville before me and Edward Hyde beside, laughing, *laughing*, it was as though a red-dyed scrim, a see-through stage drape, descended over all and everything.

Just then, my long-pent-up anger broke upon me in waves until finally I screamed and fell upon Hyde, kicking, scratching, yes, even biting him, till finally, no longer laughing, he threw me off, threw me nearer the fire. I landed catlike in my turn, skidding onto the hot cobbles before I upped and ran . . . and ran . . . and ran, knowing not if Hyde came behind, tracking me.

I ran from fire to fire along the riverside till finally I took the fire up, literally so. For if Gréluchon had been the last Communard . . . alas, I was to become the last of those infamous *pétroleuses*, those women who'd stolen through Paris of late with their petrol bombs, tossing them into cellars and causing centuries-old buildings to crumble.

I tore off the gloves I'd worn all my life, caring not who saw my deformity—what did *that* matter, now?—caring only that the fire I threw not catch hold of the fabric and burn me rather than *the world* I sought to burn. And that is the last I can recall of thought—that very deliberate removal of my gloves—for instinct, some horrid, salted instinct took hold of me then. I remember running, too, but I don't remember where, so overwhelmed was I by the effect of pure, unbrewed salts. Where did I go? What did I do? Well . . .

On the morrow it'd be said that late fires had been set and (blessedly) fought at the Palais Royale, the Palais de Justice, and the Louvre, all of which would later be ascribed to me by . . .

Alas, the sun had begun to rise, the salts had worn off and I, *I* returned. Ascended.

I must have slept off the salts in the lee of the church of Saint-Louis, on the rue Saint-Antoine; for it was there that I woke—with a head full of a hundred drums!—to the slow realization of what I'd done. *What I'd done!* Good God! Could these memories really be mine! I'd not looked in a mirror or reflective surface during the night—at least, I'd no memory of having done so—but now I did, and quickly. *Was I me?* Yes, yes I was. But who . . . ? No: *What* had I been the night before? And what had I looked like? Had I become, physically, *other*, as Doctor Jekyll did when he salted himself into Mister Hyde? I will never know for certain . . . and now I no longer care.

All I wanted, then, was Julien. Would he, *could* he, ever forgive me for what I'd done? Stealing out into the warring night like that without a word?

I ran to him, ran though my body was sore from all I'd done the night before.

And rounding the corner onto the Place des Vosges, running down the western gallery toward the Jekyll mansion, I saw him! *There*, standing before the door, in the shadows that were fast ceding to the dawn, waiting for me.

Yet as I neared, I saw that it was not Julien at all standing there.

It was a soldier of Versailles. And then suddenly two more soldiers were beside me, each taking an elbow. Rather forceful escorts, they were, their grips viselike. I asked what was the matter. *What was happening?* But neither soldier said a word as they led me to the first soldier, who proceeded to knock upon the doctor's door.

Strangely, it was Henry Jekyll himself who answered.

"Is this her, sir?" asked the soldier.

Doctor Jekyll . . . There was something strange about him, though all the world would have known him as Doctor Jekyll just then. Then I saw what it was: He sported spectacles of colored glass. He turned to me now, pulling the spectacles low on his nose, low enough to peer over them with the as-yet-unturned, black-pupiled eyes of Edward Hyde. "Oh yes," said he, "that is she . . . the *pétroleuse*."

Before he could receive the thanks of the arresting soldiers, before he could shut the door, and while still flashing what only I knew to be the nonsmile of Edward Hyde, Doctor Jekyll excused himself and hurried up to the laboratory, there to let the last of the transformation run its course in private. I now saw past the foyer into the salon beyond, where I'd introduced Gréluchon to Doctor Jekyll so long ago; and there, seconds before the door was shut, I saw an assemblage of Versaillais soldiers surrounding both a stunned Julien and a crying Cézette, while off to the side stood Poole, seeming rather more puzzled than pleased.

I was then led away. Arrested.

And though I did manage to turn back once to see him, *them*, Doctor Jekyll and Mister Hyde, peering down from the laboratory window, it was, oddly, Poole's puzzled look that lingered.

Perhaps Poole was wondering, as was I, what the leveled charges would be? Or perhaps he was wondering why, after all this time, the master had betrayed and abandoned me now, as indeed it seemed he had. *That* question I could not have answered, not then. As for the former question? Alas, the official charge would be treason, punishable by deportation or death.

CHAPTER SIXTEEN
I Create My Fate

After a forced march of twenty-odd miles, through the city and off to Versailles, I was put into one of the camps for Communard captives on the property of the palace itself. Upon arrival—bone-tired, both soaked through and sunburned, owing to weather as fickle as France herself now seemed—I was asked several questions. Rather, I faced several accusations, none of which I had the strength to refute; and, in fact, they may have been true for all I knew, for all I could recall of my salted night in the city. And at this summary trial—for such it was: my trial, on charges of treason—my silence was taken as an admission of guilt. I was convicted—based largely on that incriminating silence, yes, but time and again I heard reference made to the "quality" of my oh-so-upstanding accuser—but in the end I was sentenced not to death but to deportation.

Pity, that.

I would await transportation to New Caledonia—a desert island in the faraway South Seas—at Versailles, in the open-air camps, rather than on one of the boats then abob off the Breton coast, converted now to the most pestilential of prisons. For this I might have counted myself lucky, had I cared about luck . . . had I cared about life.

My allotted space was a sliver upon the parterre, that garden in the very shadows of the gilded palace itself, out past the first reflecting pool, down the broad steps and on the western side of a great fountain. There I had a lice-ridden bedroll and (supposedly) a place to sleep beneath a canvas roof riddled with holes, its edges ragged from the whipping spring storms.

Alas, I was soon crowded from beneath that slight shelter by others of the palace's ten thousand prisoners and soon lay claim, as best I could, to an edge of the fountain itself. There, by night, I curled my back against the cold, carved marble of its base, while by day I sat in stony contemplation of the sculpture at the fountain's center. I stared, *stared* at that sculpture through the three long days of my captivity, through cold rain and blistering sun. The staring was, I suppose now, a penance of sorts: Until France could punish me more, I would punish myself.

For all I knew was self-loathing. I did not *miss* Julien, nor *mourn* Gréluchon, nor *revile* Doctor Jekyll and Mister Hyde, no. I had been laid too low for any such emotions. Oh, but I could hate myself still, and I did, seeing my tale told again and again, there, in the sculpted stone of the Fountain of Latona.

She was a goddess, Latona, who'd meddled with man's very

nature, appealing to Jupiter to transform some spying peasants into lizards and frogs. The spitting sculptures showed half-turned amphibians mid-leap, while humans with frogged features were shown in supplication, begging to be spared. And there stood a smug Latona at Jupiter's side. How I begrudged her that self-satisfaction, for I was she; excepting, of course, that I was far, *far* from self-satisfied (and hardly a goddess).

Thusly did I await a most deserved punishment, deserved not for treason but rather for *hubris*: for daring to do a god's work . . . not a witch's.

And then finally it seemed my punishment would begin, for I heard my name being called beneath that canvas covering that third midday.

I rose. I looked about. I think I raised high my hand, even. *Here. Here! Punish me.* I was ready to be deported, ready to be sailed to the far side of the world, ready to die at sea or toiling beneath a broiling sun on some South Seas island. The crowd parted as best it could, making way for two figures—I could not see them within the shadowed tent, but surely they were soldiers—the first of whom called, "Odile? Odile Ricau?" But there was something too insistent, perhaps even panicked, in that voice. Something . . . *Could it be?* Certainly not. Impossible! Yet soon I saw that first shadowed figure transformed, if you will, by sunlight: Julien. It *was* he.

And what did I do?

I hid; such was my shame, and the lingering shock of all I'd been through.

Blessedly, he found me.

It had begun to rain; and as I stood there—ragged, stinking—in Julien's embrace, my arms slack at my sides, I saw over his shoulder. There, standing not five feet distant, was the second figure I'd seen. No soldier, this. It was Poole.

I suppose it was the presence of Poole within that palatial prison yard that roused me; for seconds later I took Julien's embrace, took it and returned it in kind. Had I thought the boy a dream before? I may have. But Poole? He had no role in any daydream of mine, and so this must all be real, *too* real.

"What is *he* doing here?" Such were my first words to Julien, my love, whom I'd thought I'd never see again.

I cannot recall his response, if he made one. I cannot recall any talk at all. And the next thing I knew, I was leaving the park at Versailles by a guarded back gate. Poole, of all people, was bribing me free, no doubt with the doctor's money.

A coach and four took us quickly back to Paris proper.

En route, I could only cry as my senses, as my reason, indeed as my *sanity* returned. Now I did *miss, mourn, revile,* and *hate,* all that and more. Julien knew it, and so he held me close, held me tightly, as I sat staring daggers across the carriage at Poole, who stared out the window in his turn, refusing to even see me. And Julien whispered, repeatedly, "Just listen to him, Odile. *Please.*"

Of course, he was referring not to Poole but to Doctor Jekyll.

Listen to him? I nodded that I would; but I was not at all sure I could listen to anything said by Doctor Henry Jekyll, no. What's more: I wondered how it was that Julien was now in league with Jekyll, with Poole. Why were we even going back to that mansion in the Marais, and not the train station? I must have asked this with my eyes; for Julien, tacit in his turn, simply held me tighter: *All in due time*, were his unspoken words.

⁂

And in due time, indeed, we three found ourselves standing in the foyer of the Marais mansion.

Still, words were few. Even Cézette, who came to help me bathe (blessedly!) and dress, did so in (relative) silence, saying, rather *crying* that she was well enough and so very, *very* relieved to see me again. And once I was presentable, she kissed me and led me to the laboratory, as she'd been instructed to do.

There—shocked I was, anew, to see the scene, the locus of all those late horrors!—there, in the laboratory, I found Julien and . . . Doctor Jekyll.

And before I knew what I was doing, I'd grabbed a glass beaker full of who-knew-what and hurled it, *hard*, at Doctor Jekyll. He ducked, and luckily so for him: The beaker broke against the wall behind him, against that very same periodic table, and soon it showed a smoking, acid-eaten hole, one that disclosed the peephole of old.

"How dare you!" were my first words to Doctor Jekyll, standing there now with his hands raised high, in a pose somewhere between self-preservation and surrender. And when I wound up again, this time with a fistful of empty test tubes, my pitch was stayed by Julien, who rushed me to say, to *remind* me that I'd promised him I'd listen to Doctor Jekyll. And so I had, I supposed. And I now would. Oh, but it wasn't easy, what with so much at hand to be hurled, and with all the material of my craft still there in the laboratory. A bit of datura distillate dropped onto his tongue would set his hard heart to hammering and Doctor Henry Jekyll, "lately of London," might find himself very late indeed.

Alas, his words were two parts apology and one part proposal.

As for the apology, suffice to say that he and Hyde, both, had feared I'd run away, now that both Gréluchon and the last of the salts were gone. Nothing but Julien would tether me, said he. (The means by which they held to Julien? *Kidnapping* seems as apt a description as any.) And they needed me near, now more than ever; for Jekyll Senior had finally passed and his millions must be claimed in London, but not, *not* before the secret of the Cagot salts was claimed by his son and heir. Money was money, true; but the ability to meddle with mankind, his very nature and makeup . . . *Alors*, as Doctor Jekyll had long said, he'd come too far toward the inexplicable to turn back.

Now I'd all but told Mister Hyde that there was indeed a secret, albeit one only lately learned by myself; and of course, Doctor Jekyll knew this as well. And so, yes, said he, with what may have been remorse but was certainly *not* regret, Doctor Jekyll and Mister Hyde, both, had quickly conspired to have me arrested as *une pétroleuse*. I'd thusly be detained in ways they could not have arranged—damned right he was about that, too!—until such time as, "Julien here," said he, strikingly, "could be won over by reason."

Reason? No doubt Julien was finally swayed toward reason by the knowledge that Doctor Jekyll's cash, as applied by Poole, had secured, in order, my arrest, my conviction, and a stay of sentence. (I was *not* to be deported without the doctor's consent.) And so his money would secure my freedom as well, if only Julien could deliver what the doctor desired, what he *would have*, presented to Julien, apparently, in the form of a proposal.

"About this 'proposal' . . ." said I now.

"It's . . . complicated," said Julien, though I'd expected Doctor Jekyll to speak. "And of course I could not promise Henry that you would agree to it. That I could *get you* to agree to it."

"And now you *have* promised on my behalf? Promised *Henry*, as you call him now? How dare you? How dare both of you . . . *all of you?*" Again I cast about the laboratory for things both breakable and light, and likely to fly true. I even wished for the sudden ascendancy of Mister Hyde, so that I might have a go at him as well!

"Odile, listen," pled Julien, while still I steamed.

"Fine," said I, finally. "Someone speak and I will listen, but as for promises, I make no—"

"Please, Odile." Julien came nearer and I let him take my hand while, in a whisper, he said, "There may still be a way out of this." *May* be? Whatever did that mean? A way out of what? Had I not lately left my prison behind? Was I not finally free?

Doctor Jekyll now took on the role of host, so oily, so unctuous, saying:

"Shall we?" He gestured now to three stools ranged around that same table at which I'd worked my craft to such ill effect.

"We shall *not*." I'd stand where I was, thank you very much, with my back to the door. "Now speak!"

"Very well," said the doctor, taking his seat. And then he cut right to it:

"Have you discovered the secret of the salts, Odile?" His eyes were wide, and they widened even more when I replied:

"Yes."

There followed a sudden and quite audible inhalation on the doctor's part. "Such that we . . . such that *I*, rather, might make more of the brew?"

"Yes . . . I suppose so."

He looked at me, hard. "And just what *supposition* do you refer to, Odile?"

"The supposition, *doctor*," said I, snidely, "that I will ever tell you the secret."

Julien sighed, for he knew things I did not. Yet.

Doctor Jekyll now let his face fall into his hands, but what I first took for exasperation, despair, was not that at all. Rather, he was disinclined—by nature, if you will—*to threaten*, and he was summoning the strength to do so.

He needn't have bothered; for Julien now did the doctor's bidding.

His hand still holding mine, Julien led me to the window-sill, the very same on which I'd sat all those long hours, wait-ing, watching for Mister Hyde's candle sign. And there, now, in the streets below, stood a half-dozen Versaillais soldiers. I was still taking in the threat they represented when Doctor Jekyll spoke, almost painfully so, in tones implying, *You leave me no choice.* Said he:

"Poole is putting them off at present; but if you and he"—the doctor dared a glance at Julien, who looked fit to kill—"are caught, recaptured, this time as escapee and accomplice, your sentence will be commuted from deportation to—"

"*Quel bâtard tu es*, Henry Jekyll!" said I.

"In point of fact, I am not a bastard at all but rather newly orphaned; and time, Odile, is of the essence. For both of us: I must return to London post-haste, and you, well, I imagine you'd very much like to see those soldiers sent off."

I looked at Julien. Did he know, truly, what was at stake in my telling the secret of the salts, what they *were* . . . and what must, perforce, follow, if Doctor Jekyll knew as much? Did he know what the doctor would *do*? He did. I saw as much. And for his part, he reminded me, with a nod toward the streets beyond, of what was at stake if I did *not* tell.

"You would see me dead, Henry, taking the secret with me, rather than—"

"I would see you, Odile, thusly pressured, *share the secret.*

But yes, if you refuse . . ." And now it was his turn to cast a sly glance toward the sill, toward the soldiers waiting in the street.

"And if I tell?"

"*When* you tell," corrected Doctor Jekyll, "you and Julien will walk from this house free, and you need never see me again."

"Mister Hyde?"

"Nor Mister Hyde. You . . . you have my word."

At which I could only laugh; but my levity, such as it was, was short-lived.

"Have Poole send them away. I'll not say a word with them down there." I was commanding this even as I tugged that tasseled cord that would summon Poole to the laboratory.

Doctor Jekyll did as he was directed, and meanwhile I turned to Julien. "Tell me," said I, blinking back tears, "*convince* me, please, that it is no longer he, that . . ."

He understood, for Julien, my Julien, always understands. "It is but a body now, Odile. And Gréluchon . . . I'm so sorry, Chérie, but Grel is gone from it." He, too, was teary-eyed. "But, Odile: Do you even know where they . . . ?"

I nodded: Of course I knew.

With the soldiers sent away, and with both Poole and Cézette waiting out on the landing beyond the unlocked laboratory door, just as I'd directed, I told Doctor Jekyll to sit, to open his notebook and ink his pen; and then I told him everything I knew.

I would brook no questions, nor repeat a single word; and the last thing I gave him were directions to the doubly tenanted tomb in Père-Lachaise of two men who'd come to Paris from Pau.

Doctor Jekyll stared at me, dumbstruck, when I was done, till finally:

"And this is not a ruse, right? Not some goose chase to—"

"If it weren't redundant," said I, addressing Doctor Henry Jekyll for the very last time, ". . . if it weren't redundant, I'd tell you to go to hell."

I turned then to quickly consult with Julien; but it was too quick a consultation: He misunderstood my meaning entirely, saying in reply, "But, Odile, you know I've saved enough money for us to—" and I didn't have time to explain. Instead:

"Poole!" I cried. "Poole, get in here!"

I set a hand upon Julien's arm. *Trust me.* And Poole came into the laboratory more quickly than he ever did when summoned by his master, and how I reveled in the fear manifest upon his face!

Only lately had I noticed that all Jekyll's books had been packed away, and the rest of the laboratory sat in disarray. He was indeed readying to leave for London (although what he'd just heard was sure to slow him down some . . . but I'd not think about *that*, no). And I presumed other packing, other planning had been seen to as well; and so, said I:

"Poole, I want you to bring to me here, in the laboratory, packed in a carrying case, two if need be, every last hoarded bill of his," and I nodded toward his master, "and yours as well. *All of it*, Poole. The money set aside for bribes and the store set to sail for London. Is that clear?" Whereupon the old man looked to his master, dumb as a dog. "Don't look at him, Poole! Pack the bigger bills at the bottom. And if you hold back a single sou, I'll bewitch—yes, *bewitch*—more than your tea, you old bully!"

While waiting for Poole, I made plain my plan to Julien; and he heartily approved, so much so that I fell back and let him actuate it.

Taking the two canvas bags from Poole, Julien snapped their clasps and inspected their contents, whereupon he winked at me. *Plenty*, said he. *Enough for a new life.*

Only then did he call Cézette into the laboratory.

"Take this," said Julien, and she did though it was almost more than she could carry. "Take this, guard it, and go to the Gare de Lyon straightaway. Board the first train headed out of Paris, whichever way you please. Understand?"

She nodded. She understood to do as directed, even if the *Why?* of it, the wealth of it, would be a long time sinking in.

"And good luck, Cézette," I concluded, hugging the girl to me. "Have you someplace to go?"

"Yes," said she, "I . . . I have family in—"

But I stilled her speech with my fingers—ungloved now, and never again to be gloved—and said, with a nod toward master and manservant, "*Shh.* Just go." And she did.

Within the hour, Julien and I would be at the *gare* as well, eager, more than eager to set the city at our backs. Where would *we* go? What would *we* do?

I cared not. "Somewhere new," was all I said to Julien as he headed toward the ticket window, but then suddenly I called him back to add, to ask, "You'll be my home, won't you?"

He said he would. No: He took to a knee and *swore* he would.

As for the rest of it all, the witchery and whatnot? Alas . . .

I will miss my baby brother till the very day I die, and till then I'll hold to the memory of who he was before all this began, before I made mistakes I could not unmake. And I have come to believe that Gréluchon knew me to be true in my intentions and therefore forgave me, and forgives me still.

Doctor Jekyll? I like to believe that he will come to realize that not all strangeness is science, and that some secrets are best kept. Forever. But I haven't much hope . . . not for him.

Author's Note

One of the pleasures of writing novels like *The Strange Case of Doctor Jekyll and Mademoiselle Odile* is slipping in and out among the shadows of history, just as these characters do. Of course, many readers come to wonder exactly what is fiction and what is truth, or nonfiction, in the novel. To those readers I like to say, "It's all true! . . . Well, *most* all of it is true." And it is.

In writing, I take my cues from the history; history, however, does not always cooperate with the very particular needs of a novel. And so sometimes I find I must "amend" history a bit. I do this as infrequently as possible, trying very hard to keep the authorial meddling to a minimum. In *The Strange Case* I can hardly identify a single, significant instance when I veered from the historical truth. In other words:

Yes, the Commune was a very real period in Parisian history, following upon France's loss in the Franco-Prussian War. A punishing "peace" led the Parisians to revolt, and the alternate government they established in Paris is depicted here as accurately as possible.

Yes, the people of Paris grew desperate during the famine that resulted from the Prussian siege of the city; and yes, unfortunately, they did resort to eating the animals in the zoo in the Jardin des Plantes, including the elephants, Castor and Pollux, whose blood brings the *purely fictional* characters of Henry Jekyll, Poole, and Odile together on New Year's Day, 1871. That, by the way, was the actual day of the elephants' demise. I've even retained the name of the butcher, Deboos, who bought the elephants' meat (though I took the liberty of giving the butcher a second shop in Les Halles, in addition to the actual, historical shop in the avenue Friedland . . . and that's about as far as I ever stray from the historical truth).

Yes, the Commune ended in one of the bloodiest periods of French history, *la semaine sanglante*, or Bloody Week. Major monuments were burned to the ground. Some, such as the beautiful city hall—or Hôtel de Ville—were rebuilt; others, like the Tuileries palace adjoining the Louvre, were not. And though no one really knows how many people perished that week in May 1871, estimates, on both sides of the battle, range into the tens of thousands. Our fictional Gréluchon has been added to the toll here. As for Odile, her sentence of deportation is in keeping with historical fact: Many convicted Communards—including *les pétroleuses*—were sent to French colonies in the South Seas, where they lived (and many died) under extremely harsh conditions. They were not able to return to mainland France until a general amnesty was declared in 1880.

And yes, the Cagot are a historical people, traceable to the French southwest, though they harbored no such secrets as the transformative salts . . . as far as anyone knows.

Finally, the younger Henry Jekyll has been brought to these pages from those of the great Robert Louis Stevenson, who created an older Doctor Jekyll (and his horrible other half, Mister Hyde) in 1886. I like to think that he, Stevenson, wouldn't mind the new lease on life I've afforded his characters here.

If you have any other questions about the "truths" of the novel, or anything else bearing on *The Strange Case* or my other work, please visit my website at www.jamesreesebooks.com.